"I LOVED THIS BOOK—the subtle magicks, the sweep of landscape, the particulars of time and place. R. García y Robertson's is a new and very special voice, blending the fantastic with the actual and letting us read history with a new and brilliant lens."
JANE YOLEN, author of *Sister Light, Sister Dark*

"FASCINATING ... INTENSE ... A STRONG, WELL-WRITTEN WORK ... Exceptionally well-researched, detailed and very accurate"
Amazing

"THOROUGHLY ENTERTAINING AND EN-GROSSING ... A skillful, seamless weaving of folklore, fantasy and history ... Full of interesting, exciting, believable characters ... By turns earthy and elegant—but always precise, witty and enjoyable."
TOM DEITZ, author of *Soulsmith*

"A HIGHLY LITERATE, METICULOUSLY RESEARCHED HISTORICAL FANTASY"
Science Fiction Chronicle

"A RICHLY DRAWN, HAIR-RAISING TALE ... A stirring combination of Scottish ballad lore, border magic, and swashbuckling shape-shifting adventure."
ELIZABETH ANN SCARBOROUGH, author of *The Healer's War*

The Spiral Dance

R. GARCÍA y ROBERTSON

AVON BOOKS • NEW YORK

Portions of this work have appeared in somewhat different form as novelettes in *The Magazine of Fantasy and Science Fiction*: "The Auld Religion" (January 1990) and "The Spiral Dance" (May 1990).

AVON BOOKS
A division of
The Hearst Corporation
1350 Avenue of the Americas
New York, New York 10019

Copyright © 1991 by Rodrigo García y Robertson
Cover illustration by Daniel Horne
Published by arrangement with the author
Library of Congress Catalog Card Number: 91-2342
ISBN: 0-380-76518-7

Published in hardcover by William Morrow and Company, Inc.; for information address Avon Books.

First AvoNova Printing: February 1993

AVONOVA TRADEMARK REG. U.S. PAT. OFF. AND IN OTHER COUNTRIES, MARCA REGISTRADA, HECHO EN U.S.A.

Printed in the U.S.A.

RA   10   9   8   7   6   5   4   3   2   1

Contents

And ever, by the winter hearth,
Old tales I heard of woe or mirth,
Of lovers' sleights, or ladies' charms
Of witches' spells, of warriors' arms.
—SIR WALTER SCOTT

THE FOOL'S SEASON

(Halloween to Twelfth Night)

The Fool's Season—A burlesque festival presided over by a boy (or whore) dressed as King, Queen, or High Prelate. Celebrated at various times, usually between Halloween and Twelfth Night, but sometimes as late as May Day. Lower clergy and minor officials join in the fool's revels, parodying court ritual and church rites. Fools are free to play tricks on their betters, satirize religion, and speak the truth—crimes that would normally be punished by torture, burning, or dismemberment.

Hark, hark,
The dogs do bark,
The beggars have come to town;
Some in rags,
And some in jags,
And one in a velvet gown.

—MOTHER GOOSE

Durham Cathedral

Riding west of Durham, Countess Anne of Northumberland heard there was a madwoman on the Brancepeth Road using her name. Lunacy did not surprise her. These abbreviated days between All Hallow's Eve and Twelfth Night were the Fool's Season—with Elizabeth Tudor playing both Queen of Clowns and Whore's Pope. She turned in the saddle, saying to her husband, Tom, "Madness is very much in fashion. Any sensitive North Country woman of lively imagination *aught* to give insanity serious consideration."

Tom sat on a fidgeting charger, peacock proud in his polished armor. He and Anne were a good match; by far the most famous couple in the North Country. Anne was near as tall as he, with that great mane of pale yellow Plantagenet hair that crops up in old Anglo-Norman families—a fit daughter for King Edward Longshanks himself. By birth she was a Somerset, descended from King Edward's grandson, through a boy born on the wrong side of the royal blanket. On the whole she felt she had a better claim to the throne than Queen Elizabeth, but half the nobility in England could say that much.

What really astonished Anne was that some woman on the road wanted to be her. She shook her head. "Shows shocking poor taste even in a lunatic. The mad may be whomever they please—why not be Queen Mary of Scotland, or an empress of Moscovwy? Why risk prison or whipping to pose as a paltry countess, with all of my problems?" In her mother's day wandering maniacs had more initiative. A Yorkshire lass went about then, claiming to be Princess Mary. (When asked what a princess was doing wandering the roads, the girl had a pat answer; her aunt *"la reine blanche,"* the Queen of France, read her fortune

3

one day in their bath—"You will go a-begging once in
your life, either in youth or in old age." Being a sensible
mad princess, she chose to beg in her youth, rather than
take to the road in old age.) Since then the North Country
had seen pauper princes, and Lord knows how many Lady
Jane Greys.

To Anne's annoyance, Tom did not answer—he had
been distracted of late by the Duke of Norfolk's marriage,
and threats to his own life. Now he was deep in plot with
Lord Darce and the Earl of Westmorland. Anne decided to
ride ahead of the men to have a look at this impostor. For
tuppence and a smile she might even trade places.

So she rode off to meet herself. Galloping over the November mud and slush, in velvet dress and satin jacket,
gave a thrilling illusion of freedom. Frost flushed her
face. The hoofbeat of her retainers turned every beggar's
head. Nobility commanded attention, and Anne loved having the eye of the world on her—it was a chief joy of being a countess. Crazed women never imagined themselves
to be shepherd lasses or subtenants' wives. Or if they did,
no one noticed. Gaunt trees flashed past. In the steep pastures standing stones looked bare and hungry, like the teeth
of some archaic monster. The hills above Brancepeth were
intolerably old, built on ancient millstone, mixed with grit
and coal measures laid down before Britain was an island,
when dragons walked the earth. Cottagers—living closest
to the land—swore the hills were alive, haunted by rock
imps, trolls, and earthen giants.

Behind her rode her sergeant at arms, a pair of brawny
huntsmen, and a sturdy lady in waiting—the demented
might wander the roads alone, but not Anne of Northumberland. She used to rely on high spirits and warmhearted
good humor to inspire loyalty in her people and confound
her enemies, but Anne had seen all the good humor go out
of the North Country. Each year she saw more vagabonds
on the road: day laborers, cripples, masons, quack herbal-
ists, whores, hedge priests—families of destitute cottagers.
No matter how many the justices whipped and hanged,
new homeless came to replace them. In winter they sank
to a trickle, in spring they became a stream, in summer a
flood. Now it was late in the fall, and the whole of the

North Country had taken to the roads. Most were honest tenants in arms, marching on Durham with bow and bill, but beside them sturdy beggars carried quarterstaffs, with murder in their eyes, determined to be fed.

North of the Borders, in Scotland, malicious vagabonds were nailed to trees by their ears—much more humane than hanging, and one of the few sensible things Anne had heard about Scotland. What was the use of seeing beggars swung, with Westminster so set on making more? Anne did not share Parliament's opinion that cruel punishments would cure poverty. It hurt to see her people feeding on grass and fighting for kitchen slops. The homeless shivered in linen shirts and deerskin coats, looking unbearably skinny, spoiling the appetites of those who ate.

Anne thought she was numb to it all, able to pass even hollow-eyed children without a backward glance. Then she saw someone who made her rein in.

Sitting among the beggars was a tall blond woman in a velvet gown. She was clean. Her gown was well mended, without a rip or tear. In her blond hair was a wreath of dried flowers—heather, forget-me-not, and thistle—which she wore like a crown. She stared straight at Anne, a half-smile on her lips. Instinctively Anne slowed her horse, sensing some monstrous mistake. The good gown and insolent look were wildly out of place. Somehow a woman of quality had got in among the beggars, or somehow a quality dress had got on a vagabond.

Then she realized who the woman was. This had to be the madwoman. Stopping in the middle of the road, Anne asked, "What is your name and station?"

The woman rose. "I am Anne Percy." Her only touch of commonness was a tartan shawl wrapped around her shoulders, hinting she had spent time in Scotland—enough to drive any feeling woman insane.

Anne felt saddened, seeing much of herself in the stranger. They were nearly the same height (hard to judge from horseback), with eerily similar features, though the vagabond was thinner and older. Anne was past thirty, but this woman looked closer to forty, skin cracked and darkened, blond hair bleached white in places, but the resemblance was compelling; perhaps it had triggered her mania. "Which Anne Percy?" Anne fished for a sensible answer.

"The Anne Percy that is Countess of Northumberland, daughter to the Earl of Worcester. All the North Country knows me." She sounded as proud as if it were true.

Anne saw how melancholy madness was—how terrible and implacable—how touched with witchcraft. Impersonation was akin to stealing souls. Old King Harry had hung Perkin Warbeck for imagining himself one of the Princes of the Tower; though not before Perkin had convinced the Scots and an army of Cornish bumpkins to back his claim. When a London lad named Ralph Wilford claimed to be the Earl of Warwick, Old Harry proved he was an even-handed tyrant by beheading the real Earl of Warwick. No good ever came of someone using your name, especially if you lacked friends in court. Right now Anne had strong and determined enemies at Westminster.

She tried to jog the woman into sanity. "What would Countess Anne of Northumberland be doing standing by the roadside?"

"I am here to point your way." The woman gave each word special weight.

"And where am I going today?"

"You are going to Durham, to commit sacrilege and high treason. After that you will go to Yorkshire, then Scotland, and to the Ends of the Earth."

Anne shied back. She heard her sergeant mutter, touching the three feet of forged steel that hung in his saddle scabbard. Here was the horrible danger of lunacy. This woman had slandered the Countess of Northumberland, calmly accusing Anne of treason to her face. *Treason* was one word Tudor justice never took lightly, not on anyone's lips. Walsingham, the Queen's minister for espionage, had ears everywhere. No one was high enough to be safe. The Queen's mother, her stepmother, several favorites, her father's trusted advisers, and a brace of cousins had all been beheaded for treason.

Anne turned her horse and trotted off, motioning for her retainers to follow. Only a dozen ears had heard the charge; only six tongues could report it. Far better for her and this poor woman if things stayed that way.

Worst of all, half what the woman said was true. Anne was going to Durham, doing what Queen Elizabeth was bound to call high treason; though *no one was supposed to know that yet.* At least Anne hoped beggars and lunatics were not debating her private plans all the way to Durham. As for sacrilege, she had no more desire to commit *real* sacrilege than to visit Scotland, or the Ends of the Earth.

She passed more tenants in arms, tramping toward Durham in grim array, pikes resting on their shoulders. The commons had been told to assemble for a weaponshow, where Tom Percy, her Simple Tom, Earl of Northumberland, would make a speech to carry the crowd into revolt. *How had the woman known that?* Tom had decided to defy the Queen's summons at Topcliff, and they had ridden at once to join Westmorland at Brancepeth—*there was no time for news of their treason to have spread north.*

The woman's tartan wrap conjured up the wild, dark Highlands, full of sibyls, witchwives, and roadside Cassandras. Anne was cousin to the Kings of Scotland; her ancestral aunt, Joan Beaufort, had married King James I. Joan and her royal husband had been followed all the way to Perth by a Highland woman raving that the King would never recross the Forth alive. King James was joking with Joan about the warnings, when his royal cousins let in a Graham that he had wronged. Frantic to escape, James wrenched up the floorboards and tried to crawl down a drain, forgetting that the drain had just been blocked to keep his tennis balls from rolling away. The Graham pulled him out, stabbing him twenty-eight times, twenty-eight being a lucky number fit for dispatching a king.

Joan was wounded, but survived to see the conspirators soundly tortured before turning them over to the executioner. (Somerset women had a streak of steel in them, and were unsafe to trifle with—at least to the extent of killing their spouses.) Anne wished her own prophetess had been a Highland hag, ranting in Gaelic. Instead her beggar had been cool-as-you-please and so believable.

Twice Anne turned about, but thought better of it. Then, unable to stand the mystery, she turned for the third time and cantered back, trailing her small retinue, patting her horse and saying, "You must think me the madwoman, turning circles on the Brancepeth road."

Telling her lady to wait with the sergeant, Anne gave shillings to the huntsmen. "Pay the beggars, then shoo them off." While they obeyed, she studied her mad pretender. Though not a cripple, the woman favored her left foot. Otherwise she had the calm, enduring sureness that saints and lunatics show the world. Anne imagined her delusions would have broken a weaker woman. With everyone properly out of earshot Anne spoke simply and tersely. "I am Anne Percy, Countess of Northumberland."

The impudent female gave her an amused look. "Did I ever deny it?" She even had Anne's mannerisms, which was irritating, like talking into a flawed glass.

"How can there be two Anne Percys of Northumberland?"

"We plainly have two bodies, but we share a single soul."

The lunatic was hopeless. "Impersonation is a dangerous illness," Anne warned, "as deadly as the pox. Women who knew right well who they were have been burned alive, merely for hearing false voices."

"Men might call them false, but when Mother Mary speaks, all women know her voice."

"Even the mad must mind their tongues," replied Anne. "Chat with Virgin Mary if you must, but do not talk treason to a countess."

Mad Anne laughed, cocking her head, "If a mad fool cannot talk treason by the wayside, then there is indeed no liberty in the land. Surely times are not so bad."

Times were that bad. Anne leaned on her saddlebow wondering if the woman were being secretly clever, trying to trap her into saying something treasonous. Elizabeth was well served by her spies, but planting lunatics on the road was oversubtle even for Walsingham.

"You think I mean to trap you."

Anne straightened up, startled at having her mind read.

"I do mean to trap you, and I will. You stand at the start of a long journey, facing danger and despair. Be prepared to pay a heavy price, for an even greater prize." Addled or not, she had the sure and easy delivery that makes true prophecy chilling.

Anne laughed. "Shall I meet a handsome stranger too?"

Mad Anne took a wistful look up the road. The north breeze blew blond hair across her face, softening her hard edges. "That you will, Anne, that you will."

Anne looked north as well and saw the men coming— first the lances and banners, then the horses and riders beneath them. In the lead came *cuirassiers,* household gentlemen in half-armor. Behind them cantered ruffians on border hobbies—Fenwicks, Robsons, Dodds, and Milburns—Tynedale and Redesdale riders wearing raffish whiskers, steel bonnets, and studded leather coats. Such blunt-faced horsemen were the unblessed hands of the Border lords, ready to work both sides of the law. At their head rode the greatest lords in the North Country— Crookback Darce looking more than ever like a hangman's helper, and next to him, Charles Neville, the ne'er-do-well Earl of Westmorland. Before them all, beneath his blue-and-gold lion rampant banner, rode "Simple Tom" Percy, Seventh Earl of Northumberland.

The vagabond looked to Anne. "Now is the time for us to travel together. I would be your fool, for as far as York-shire." She spoke flatly, not begging for the position, merely saying what would be. In Wales Anne's mother had employed a female fool, "Michelle La Folle" from France—skilled at acrobatics and pantomimes—a dark and pretty waif, suspected of whoring on the side. Accustomed to a manor full of servants, Anne had never needed some-one just to amuse her. "'I do not want a fool."

"But you need the truth. We share the same heart, and I shall never lie to you." Before Anne could answer, the men were upon her.

Tom drew rein, asking peevishly, "Where have you been all morning?" He was tall, darkly handsome, and ath-letic, a Hotspur in battle and a lion in bed, but prone to funk and vacillation at other times. Anne could see him anxiously losing his wits. She would have to stick at his side for the rest of the day. From the beginning their mar-riage had been a partnership, a wedding of Worcester and Northumberland, Somerset and Percy. And as a bride she had been in awe of him—he was older, and the Percy heir. But respect and devotion were tempered by the discovery that Simple Tom's bluff honesty and sixteen stone of noble bearing were no match for the wiles of the world. She could no longer wait for him to make up his mind, or watch patiently while he changed it a dozen times. To stop him from fretting, she made her morning excursion sound like a lark; "I rode ahead to meet a woman with omens for me."

The men studied the grandly dressed vagrant. Darce's glance was calculating, Tom's wide-eyed. Westmorland affected disinterest. Confronted by the greatest men in the North, the wayside countess lost none of her breezy manner. Her gaze lingered on Tom, then turned sharply away, seeming to see beyond the men.

"What omens did she give?" Tom sounded ready to change plans again if her predictions weren't first-rate.

"She said I will go to Durham and beyond."

"Safe enough," noted Westmorland. "You are mounted. The road leads to Durham. Only cheap roadside oracles work without cards or palmistry. All the best prophetesses have curtained booths and crystal balls."

The beggar smiled up at the Earl, blond hair blowing wild in the wind. "Charlie Neville, 'tis a bad bargain to know everything and believe in nothing."

Westmorland lifted an eyebrow. Lord Darce laughed. "She read your name without a glass ball."

"She read nothing but the Neville cross." Westmorland tapped the Saint Andrew's cross on his red surcoat—the arms of the House of Neville. "Roads are infested with cunning tarts. Smiths and cobblers must pay triple to tumble her, pretending she's a lady."

Neville's pettiness disgusted Anne. "Whore or not, I mean to have her for my fool. It's the Fool's Season, and we need some mad luck if we mean to win." The woman was wild as Lucifer's aunt, bound to raise all hell, but Anne would not part with anyone who could take Charles Neville down a notch.

Westmorland rolled his eyes. "She has the airs of a French whore, and we have clowns aplenty in this enterprise already."

"But our clowns all wear arms and surcoat"—Tom ordered up a horse so his wife's madwoman could ride—"a fool in skirts will be damned diverting." Tom was transparently smitten with the handsome beggar woman. Anne marked his interest as a compliment of sorts, since they were similar as sisters. To remind Tom which Anne he had married, she settled in between the two of them. Her ensign trotted up, unfurling Anne's personal banner of the three Marys: the Mary who lived, the Mary who was dead, and the Mary who was Mother of God.

Riding down from the paleolithic uplands, Anne saw the Wear Valley scarred with coal diggings—pits cut through thin soil into the carboniferous rock to unearth the remains of ancient forests pressed solid by the weight of ages. Miner adventurers no longer contracted freely with lord and tenant, but owed their livings to Crown monopolists who bought and sold the right to work. Anne mentioned to her fool they could expect to see more pits, smelting works, and similar eyesores.

The fool wrinkled her pert nose in agreement. "Nearer to Durham the air itself is cancerous."

Anne nodded. "Coal smoke, alum plants, leadworks—all annoying if you mean to breathe—but no bad air can compare with London's." The road beneath them was rutted by thousands of coal carts. Some of the coal went to Durham, or to saltworks built on the ruins of coastal monasteries, but most went to London, that monster sprawling along the Thames devouring mountains of coal and multitudes of people.

Her fool smiled. "You can smell the London air from St. Albans."

Anne looked her insane twin over. "So you have been to London, or at least St. Albans."

"I have been wherever you have been."

Anne tilted her head. "Only in your mad imagination, I hope. I am a married woman."

Past Neville's Cross, Anne saw Durham's pall of coal smoke, a brown blanket hanging over Maiden Hill. In pagan times "Deer Home" had been the site of a Deer Park and a place of pilgrimage. Now Durham Cathedral and

Castle filled the loop of the Wear—stately islands in the
sky, topped by square towers of stone.

A river of people swelled the road behind them, sweeping up peddlers, tramps, and cutpurses. Tom ordered
woodcutters to cut fagots for a fire, then he led them up
the steep stone steps to the Cathedral Square. Here he addressed the crowd, using words cribbed from the stage, the
stock funeral orations, and speeches of kings before battles. "Friends, tenants, Northumbrians . . ."

("Knaves, villains, bumpkins . . ." echoed Westmorland
in sotto voce.)

In blunt terms Tom listed what the North had suffered at
the hands of Westminster: their faith made mock of, ab-
beys and convents torn down, offices given to strangers,
taxes raised, and land taken. No one was safe when the
heir to the throne, Queen Mary of Scotland, was imprisoned for the crime of being Elizabeth's closest kin. Tom
would force no one to go with him. "Let him go home
who holds his manhood cheap, and has no love of Heaven.
I would not go forth in that man's company, that fears to
go with God."

No fainthearted idiot took Simple Tom's offer. There
were more private times to drop by the wayside. Percy retainers spread among the crowd began the chant, "To
York, to York . . ." Priests and laity joined in, the sea surge
swelling through the multitude. Master and servant, lord
and tenant, plowhand and shepherd, sang in a single voice:

> *"To York to York,*
> *The Lord has led us forth."*

The whole psalm-singing parade stormed up the cathedral steps, inspired by Tom's pirated speech. Anne dismounted, lifting the hem of her velvet dress to climb the
steps, Tom and Westmorland at her side. She thought the
cathedral was a most beautiful example of the old Norman
type, laid out like a cross, and containing the bones of the
Venerable Bede. Here their ancestors had knelt in thanks
after the bloody vespers at Neville's Cross; having
smashed a terrible host of Scots—capturing King David II,
along with Saint Margaret's Holy Black Rood and the
Lion Standard of Scotland. No one greeted them. Inside

the cool, dim cathedral, giant Romanesque columns—cut with Celtic checks and chevrons—ran the length of the three-story nave. Soaring gothic arches and groin-vaulted ribs held aloft a curving ceiling of saillike stone surfaces illuminated by recessed windows.

Anne strode into the immense hollow space, walking the entire four hundred feet of the nave, and through the transept. Unearthly light streamed down through enclosed air. She smelled that acid church odor—mildewed stone and old incense.

People poured in behind her.

Reaching the choir, Anne curtsied toward where God's altar had stood, then lifted up the massive cathedral Bible, saying over her shoulder, "Bring out the prayer books."

Country folk tumbled over the pews to obey, grabbing every printed book. Not one in two could read, and they spoke a broad Northumberland that never saw print. Written English, the language of law courts and tax rolls, had done little to earn their love.

As Anne emerged into the sunlight, the cheering started. She was a stirring sight, standing on the wide stone steps, framed by twin bell towers, the ponderous big Bible in her hands, golden hair spilling over her stiff collar. Crisply she ordered the fagots piled before the broad cathedral steps, telling her priest to bless the pile. She meant this to be a sacred burning. A hush came over the crowd as her chaplain sprinkled holy water and spouted Latin.

Tom kindled the torch that set the prayer books ablaze. A clear November wind whipped the flames, tearing burning leaves from the books, scattering them over the happy throng. Country folk clapped and capered, singing that the Heavenly Kingdom had come.

Anne stood so close to the blazing pyre that firelight gleamed red-gold in her hair. Deliberately she opened the huge Bible as though she meant to choose a text and read a sermon to the flames. Instead she tore pages out one by one, casting them onto the fire, letting London know how the North Country felt about Bibles in English, pressed out by machines.

London had done no less to them. The Reformers had destroyed not just prayer books, but "all missals, manuals, journals, processionals, and primers in Latin or English," leaving the North Country nothing but printed Bibles and government-approved prayers. Add to that the destruction of icons, altars, altar cloths, religious statues, and paintings; and churches were reduced to four bare walls and a pulpit where some pimp of a preacher could recite the Crown's sermons. Queen Mary, showing typical Tudor patience, had burned the prayer book's authors. The best Anne would do was burn the book. This paper offering was her sacrificial stone, flung at everything Anne hated, her blow at the ghastly machine age rolling on iron wheels from stone-faced cities, smelling of sulfur and smothering her land. Burn the books, cast the cannon into bells, melt the money back to candlesticks. First Durham, then York, and if need be she would march to London and throttle the New Britain in its stinking bed.

Flames singed her hair. She continued to feed the Bible page by page into the fire, until the red-tongued monster reared over her like the all-devouring dragon in a pagan funeral pyre. Its black serpentine body coiled past the cathedral and the Prince-Bishop's castle, into the blue above.

In the heat and roar of the fire, Anne had her miracle.

A living image formed in the very heart of the flames—the grave-faced Maiden cloaked in smoke. It was not a trick of the wavering air, but a real, breathing woman, her features knowing and gentle, unmarred by the flames. The Maiden reached out to her: *"Come to me, Anne. You are the kindling, and I am the flame."*

Anne stood awestruck. Her hands stopped tearing the pages, holding fast to the book. Before her was the Holy Virgin on her banner. Anger washed away; Anne felt only longing and wonder, frozen at the entryway to eternal mystery.

"Come, Anne, you are the tinder. I am the flame."

The fire beat at her, and she dropped the Bible. Sweat poured in rivulets down Anne's face; sparks landed in her gown, setting it alight. Mary waited scant steps away, cool as a salamander amid the scorching heat, beckoning—but what did God's Mother want of her? Suddenly Tom was at her side, pulling her back from the fire, beating at her dress to put out the flames. Mother Mary vanished in a twist of smoke. Anne turned to her husband, hollow and shaken. "Tom, did you see? Did you hear?"

Tom gave her an uneasy look, telling her to come away, kicking the remains of the Bible into the fire. Anne stared about, blinking like a sleeper at daybreak, realizing that Mary had come only to her. Even her chaplain was blind to the miracle, holding up his silver cross and bawling out the *Te Deum*, when he should have been listening for the Virgin's voice.

The bonfire burned down to embers, and the crowd surged into the cathedral to sing a Latin mass in the old way. While they knelt in prayer, bells overhead rang backward, the ancient announcement of revolt. Emerging after the service, Anne saw her fool left standing on the cathedral steps. "Did you see her?" Anne asked. "Did you hear her too?"

Mad Anne gave her a crooked sideways smile, like the face Anne saw in the morning mirror after drinking and dancing until dawn. "Of course I saw her. We share the same heart."

Anne knew madness was the most contagious of diseases, but did not for a moment think her miracle was false or insane. Shyly she took her fool's hand, happy to share her vision with someone, if only the lunatic she had met that morning. The hand was rougher than hers, but comforting, surprisingly strong. "What does Mary want of us? What did she mean by the tinder and the flame?" Anne did not think to get answers, but she could not hold back her questions.

They stood hand in hand on the same dressed stone step, the fool's blue-gray eyes looking straight into Anne's. "Anne, you may think it is a fine thing to know the future. Well, it is not. It is maddening to see the same mistakes made over and again. What Mary means is it is a shame to be burning books, when it is hearts and souls we must set afire."

> *Your sheep are very fat,*
> *And we must thank you for that;*
> *We have left their skins,*
> *To pay your wife's pins,*
> *And you must thank us for that.*

—NOTE PINNED TO THE CARCASS OF A SHEEP
DURING KET'S REBELLION IN NORFOLK, 1549

Maiden Hill

Anne was ecstatic. Seldom did plain, solid upcountry folk sack a great cathedral. The fire lit in Durham burned far into the night, and she made love to Tom between silk sheets in the upper apartments of a gabled town house. Decorated with exuberant *quatrefoil* panels, the stone-and-timber manse—with mews, stables, and kitchen attached—was kept fully staffed by the Percys for family members calling on the Prince-Bishop of Durham; now besieged in his castle and not receiving.

Afterward Anne lay listening to Tom (snoring like a choir organ) and thinking of the miracle she had seen in flame and smoke. Firelight streamed through slits in the shutters from bonfires burning on Maiden Hill. There were not near enough town houses and feather beds for everyone, and country folk lit fires to celebrate and keep warm—Tom had bought up granaries and tavern ale stocks to keep the monstrous assembly fed and happy. Anne considered her high-gabled house and canopied bed adequate, and the sex excellent. She always found town houses cramped and shabby compared to a palace or castle—but making love had not been so special since her marriage night. She and Tom had been wed at Warkworth, in the old Norman Church of St. Laurence, whose tall bell tower pointed straight into heaven. She came to her wedding a cloistered virgin, fresh from Catholic girlhood, physically terrified at the thought of leaving her home in South Wales to be intimate with this male stranger in his strange land; though Tom was honest, handsome, and an easy man to love.

Mary had been Queen then, and Anne's family was free to offer her up in the old style, with full Latin nuptial mass—appealing to Heaven in God's own tongue. (Her

16

royal forebear, Edward Longshanks, had read French and Latin, but known only enough English to curse.) Butts of ale stood open on the street corners; happily drunk crowds had lined Dial Place and Castle Street to watch her parade past attended by two score bridesmaids in identical gowns of blue satin and cloth-of-gold. Tom and fifty men at arms—dressed as Moors in yellow cloaks with blackened armor—escorted the bevy of maidens. Behind came barons, knights, esquires, the mayor of Warkworth, and lesser worthies without number, a wave of people that carried her to Warkworth Castle, the towering Norman stronghold dominating the town.

Like Durham, Warkworth is set in the loop of a river, a large meander where the Coquet cuts through carboniferous griststone between the Cheviots and the sea. The motte-and-bailey castle rose higher than the church tower, nearly cutting off the narrow landward approach to the town. Her wedding procession wound along three sides of the big bailey before climbing to the main gatehouse—a castle in miniature, its great gate opening away from the town onto open fields and woodlands. Crossing the bailey—past stables, buttery, and brew-house—the wedding party filed into the keep through the Lion Tower, named for the Percy lion carved on the central boss of the vault. Percys had turned the square beveled keep into a lofty palace—with polygonal turrets, tapestried interiors, carpeted floors, and carved hardwood ceilings—all standing on an artificial hill overlooking the broad Amble estuary and a grand panorama of Percy orchards, fisheries, and sheep walks. It was the family home, their second-best castle.

The wedding banquet had twenty double courses of flesh and fish—all different—delicacies such as gilded peacock with sturgeon or heron with lamprey, as well as more mundane pairings like veal with eel, and venison with carp. (Commoners lined up for the leftovers.) Gifts came with each course: paintings by Brueghel, arctic falcons, a billiards table, capes trimmed with ermine, and a clockwork man that bowed and doffed his hat. Then, with a final hallelujah, the tables were pushed back for the most wild and pagan part of the wedding, the drinking, dancing, and piping until dawn.

This lavish scene had a single purpose, and culminated with Tom leading her half-sober to their dark, curtained bed, stuffed with goose down, piled with feather pillows, smelling of myrrh and spices. Beneath burning tapers he slowly undressed her. Hundreds, even thousands, of people had worked, sweated, gathered, cheered, drunk, and gorged themselves, just so she could be taken to that big white and soft bed in the dark, perfumed bedchamber, where this man—handsome, experienced, ten years her senior and nearly a prince—could lift her up and lay her down, covering her with his kisses and pushing up her nightdress, spreading her legs, wetting and caressing her, entering her, his every fiber straining with passion, while music played beneath them and couples danced round in the Great Hall. The mysteries of sex and marriage had not been perfect— nothing under Heaven is—but Lord knows they had not been disappointing either.

Making love in their Durham town house was fun, though not so memorable. Even in Tom's arms she felt more thrilled by the burning, seeing fiery pages ripped from the prayer books by tongues of flame, hearing Mary speaking to her. After so many years of marriage there was no such fire and mystery left between her and Tom. She knew Tom as thoroughly as any woman may know a man, and she was no longer the timid West Country girl who had stood on the walls of Warkworth Castle, awed by her husband's mastery and possessions. She had borne him two children, and both had died in infancy, twin tragedies that had drawn them together spiritually, but separated them physically. Making love to Tom was a familiar but infrequent act, tinged with sadness. With another man it might be different, but Anne had never made love to another man.

Tom understood. As Sir Thomas Percy, Lord of the North, he did not live a monk's life, nor did he have to whore about. A belted earl had few problems finding riding partners. Anne understood that, being herself descended from "natural children," royal and noble bastards.

By chilly morning light she and Tom left their apartments, arms linked, still feeling warm and intimate. Darce and Neville were camped in the paneled dining room, feet propped on the table, sending servants scurrying after wine and meat; generally acting like dangerous rebels with no respect for anything.

Together they had cold venison, fried kidney, and battle plans for breakfast. Tempers were testy. There had been one botched beginning already—the Rising had been intended for the end of summer, to catch the better weather and cooperate with the Duke of Norfolk. Norfolk was a Howard—coddled by the Queen and sharing her Reformed religion—but pining to wed Queen Mary of Scotland. Being plain and barren herself, Elizabeth felt immensely threatened by her pretty cousin and kept Mary locked away. Any man who mentioned marrying her prisoner was like to leave the interview a head shorter. Duke Norfolk, however, was hugely popular, the first peer in the realm, the wealthiest man in England. Most of the nation thought him a fine match for Mary—a better king than Scots deserved, and a fitting monarch for England too, if Elizabeth left no heirs of her body.

Anne, however, thought Norfolk was a high and mighty idiot, chicken-lipped and beady-eyed, so vacillating that on his best days he made Tom look decisive. That summer the Northerners had called up their riders, a virtual act of rebellion signaling their plans to Elizabeth, only to have Norfolk tell them they shan't be needed and should all go home. They disbanded, much against Anne's will, since she would sooner serve brandied pork to the Grand Turk than provoke Elizabeth to no purpose. Then at Topcliffe, the Queen's order came for Tom to come to London. Things had got a deal worse. Norfolk was in the Tower for plotting to marry without permission. Tom agonized, and Anne offered to turn herself over to Elizabeth in his stead—but James Neville, Norfolk's sister and Westmorland's wife, had goaded the men into action. This second rising was late out the gate, ill prepared, ill organized, planned in fear and anger. They were in Durham, 20,000 to 30,000 strong—no one kept accurate count. Most were armed. Alnwick and Warkworth were in Percy hands. Elizabeth's forces were far weaker, and news of their rebellion could not have reached London yet. Westmorland, reckless to a fault, was for pushing south at once. But Tom had a

feverish number of reasons to do nothing—clearly he
would never be ready, not with the Golden Horde of
Tamerlane at his back. Queen's troops held Berwick,
Bamburgh, and Durham Castle, and Tom claimed, "It is
not fit strategy to let the enemy hold fortified places in
your rear."

· "Nor is it fit strategy to sit on your rear," replied the
tactful Neville. "I want to be in York Minster for Christ's
Mass. If we must reduce every castle and locked cupboard
from Berwick to Knaresborough, we'll be lucky to see
Yorkshire by Easter."

"Old John Forster opposes us," declared Tom.

"With nothing but his march riders and the garrisons of
Berwick and Bamburgh."

"West of the Pennines is Lord Scrope."

"Cowering in Carlisle," sneered Neville, "afraid
Hetheringtons will murder him, or Scots will come over
the border demanding their Queen back."

"Sussex and Hunsdon will raise a real army."

"And will no doubt have a rough go of it." Westmorland scoffed at the sort of lackwits and cannon fodder
foolish enough to hunt the Percy Lion in his lair. He
shoved breakfast meat across the table, saying Tom could
use more kidney.

Darce managed to disagree with everyone, beginning
with a jab at Anne and Jane Neville. "I thought it better to
leave my wife at home. Now it seems I should take my
riders back as well, to deal with Scrope. I can raise the
West March, and call down the Border Scots. There are
Maxwells, Johnstones, and Armstrongs ready to ride south
when we give word."

Westmorland snorted that Scots sheep thieves were not
worth the mischief they would make. Tom demanded
Darce stay with them—where he could be watched.

Unfamiliar with military terms and unused to strategic
discussions, Anne assumed that histrionics, backbiting, and
hysterical appeals to Heaven were a normal part of staff
conferences. With Tom more irresolute than usual, she was
forced to exercise real command over the largest field
army in the British Isles. Most of the people camped
around Maiden Hill were loyal only to her and Tom. Any

plowhand able to tell left from right knew Westmorland for a hopeless plunger, and considered Darce too shifty to trust. She drew Tom aside, her arm around his waist. "We must push on into Yorkshire. Only movement keeps us afloat. Otherwise winter will do Elizabeth's work for her. We cannot wait for castles to fall while our host starves in the snow and rain."

Tom admitted that perhaps inaction was riskier than action. Norfolk had played a waiting game, and ended up in the Tower.

"And let Darce go," she added. "We cannot hold him anyway. If we win, he will stand by us. If we lose, it hardly matters that he will betray us." It bothered her to take the other men's side against Tom. Being right did not make Darce any less treacherous, or Neville any less an ass.

Tom told the two disgruntled lords they could both have their way. Darce could take his men to the West March; the loss of his unreliable cutthroats would not much diminish the main body, which would head south for York. Anne warned Westmorland, "First we must have Hartlepool."

"Hartlepool?" The port was less than thirty miles off, but the Neville acted like he had never heard of the place.

"Yes, Hartlepool. I want a harbor where we can get help from Flanders."

"Woman, we have more troops than we can feed."

"And not one man in ten has a gun," Anne noted. Most of her tenants had come in sallets and quilted jacks, armed with brown bills, pikes, or scythes. "I fear that trained hackbutteers would mow them down like summer hay." Anne remembered how the commons of Cornwall and Devon had risen, refusing the new prayer books, but the Reformers paid Italian papists to shoot their fellow Catholics. The Italians went at their work with a will, proving a mercenary's true religion is money. Westmorland tartly reminded her that their castles had cannon.

"So I have seen. They are not the sort of monstrosities I would gladly drag over muddy roads in mid-November."

Across the sea in Flanders the Duke of Alva had hectored and browbeat the Netherlanders into voting him a standing army of ten thousand troops, with a core of disciplined Spanish infantry and two thousand musketeers. As Anne saw it, Alva should be elated to send troops. The Spanish had been grossly patient with Elizabeth's insane pretension to speak for God, and with her seizing Spanish treasure ships in Southampton. "We have written to Alva and received friendly replies. Last year twenty-four hundred infantry came to the Low Countries by sea. If the next shipment of Spaniards lands at Hartlepool instead of Dunkirk, it might make all the difference."

"Friendly replies never stopped a hackbutt ball," responded Westmorland. "And Dagos are less trustworthy than Scots."

She admitted foreign help was chancy. The Pope still wanted to win some small toleration for the Old Religion in England, and Philip of Spain wanted his ships back. Anne only hoped patience had its limit. Hartlepool must be held open in case Alva's infantry dropped in unannounced. With ill grace Westmorland gave in, saying Hartlepool was there for asking. "We can take the place with a blunt pike and a whore's protector—and at least we'll be bloody doing *something.*"

The meeting broke up without the three men pointing pistols at one another, which Anne considered a vast improvement. She suggested a trot to Maiden Hill, to see how their people were faring.

Westmorland shrugged. "We can smell them well enough from here." Tom buried himself in details of supply, so it was Darce and Anne who got mounts from the stables—an odd combination. Crookback Darce was a cousin, but Anne knew he cared next to nothing for family, nor would he worry if Mary of Scotland died unwed. Darce was in arms because last May a nephew had fallen off a vaulting horse, breaking his neck. Elizabeth had given this late nephew's lands and title to her pets the Howards; reason enough to rebel if you were as touchy and treacherous as Leonard Darce. Riding through narrow, garbage-strewn streets to the town gate, Anne tried to make conversation, asking if her support for him in council had made Darce think better of bringing wives along. He gave her a cool look. "Not at all. *My* darling wife is

still an empty-headed fool." Anne had long ago marked
Leonard Darce as a bitter and dangerous man. Her only
difficulty was deciding if he was more unnerving at her
side or out of sight.

Maiden Hill seethed with people, as if a dozen hanging
days and market fairs were folded into one. Westmorland
was right about the stink, an overpowering mixture of
woodsmoke, vomited wine, and privy odors—not that
privies were dug; the bushes along the Wear bank served
that purpose, doubling as dressing rooms, wash lines, and
places for private assignations. A fastidious few were
bathing in the river, women wearing shifts, men buck naked in the cold, dirty water.

Thrilled by the fleshy carnival, Anne saw all manner of
people mixing freely: from upright peasant families in sad
greens and gray homespun to professional killers in black
leather. Vendors hawked food and wine. Montebanks and
all manner of mummers entertained, turning Maiden Hill
into a curious mixture of pilgrims' rest, May Day gathering, beer holiday, and armed camp—all knit together in ru-
ral good humor. Blackmailers and rustlers broke bread
with their victims. Border feuds were forgotten; Storeys
drank with Darces, and Herons ate with Carnabys around
the small breakfast fires. She even saw Scots in the crowd.
Black Dick Nixon, a heavyset, swarthy Liddesdale felon,
sat bold as a codpiece among the Carletons. Tom had
vowed to swing Nixon from the first available pole if the
man so much as stumbled over the border—but this was
hardly the time to make good on the promise. They were
all outlaws now.

People pressed close, and she heard her name go
through the throng. Such attention was both tender and
frightening, since there were weapons everywhere, and
Darce did not seem to care how many commoners plucked
at her dress. He was all business, finding his riders, passing the word that they were leaving. Terrified that a child
would be pushed under her mount and trampled, Anne
stopped her horse, trapped by the sea of faces. Then the
sea parted. Mad Anne, her fool, appeared—fit and
scrubbed—the beggar in velvet politely took Anne's reins,

asking with easy insolence if Darce would accompany them. Perhaps to address the crowd.

Darce had no desire to speak to the louts and ladies. He bid Anne a gruff good day, adding beneath his breath, "When we are done with Elizabeth, we must suppress this too. There is a spirit here as dangerous to us as to the Queen." Anne watched him ride off through the press, wondering how treachery had got so ingrained. The man could not so much as see something without thinking of reasons to betray it.

Her fool echoed her thoughts. "That man has a heart as black as Satan's knickers—and will betray you."

"Oh, doubtless he will." Anne made light of the warning. It was not a beggar's business to pass judgment on the nobility.

"Not once, but twice."

Having given her offhand prophecy, the fool led Anne up the hill, through a gap in a circular bank that marked the remains of an ancient ring fort. Sitting on horseback, where some pagan chieftain had once held court, Anne saw the crowd stretching off on all sides—a heaving mass broken by cook fires, patches of muddy earth, and clumps of makeshift tents. Music throbbed—a lute and pipes—and a gaunt young man was standing before a rude cross, speaking to the multitude. He had the earnest, useless look of a defrocked cleric or perhaps a daft grammar-school teacher.

". . . no secret conclaves," the youth bawled out. "Do not let the gentry plot policy apart from the rest of us. Make them come here to Maiden Hill and debate in the open. Make them swear by the holy mass that they will take no more in rents than is usual or customary."

Fresh from her breakfast conclave, Anne felt angered. The morning's meeting had not been *secret*—not with servants bustling about pouring wine and clearing dishes—but there was no thought of inviting anyone from Maiden Hill to the town house. What was the need for that? There had been enough ignorant opinions around the table without hearing some square-headed oaf saying, "Yor ladschip, let's hang the lawyers, put an end ta kings, un' pass the fried kidney."

Northumberland tenants doffed their hats; others copied the gesture, sending a ripple spreading through the crowd. Border ruffians and blackmailers did not bother to bare their heads. The impassioned young man probably did not own a hat, but he stood tall beneath the cross, determined not to bend for a countess. He ended his speech with a vulgar couplet:

> *"When Adam delved and Eve span,*
> *Who was then the gentleman?"*

Anne recognized the obscene and inflammatory rhyme from John Ball's sermon to the insurgent commons at Blackheath; passed down among peasants by word of mouth for almost two centuries. The Blackheath rebels had managed to behead the Archbishop of Canterbury and the Lord Treasurer of England—the nation's two chief tax collectors—showing King's service can be a chancy business. Instinctively she stayed mounted, keeping the advantage of being on horseback. She had not come to speak, but there was no stopping it now. The stammering scholar was talking treason against the whole nobility; people must be shown how that diminished their cause.

Staring about like a lost ewe, Anne hadn't the least idea where to start. (Oh, Mary, pity me. Tell me what to say.) Without even Darce at her side she was perilously alone.

Her fool reached up and took Anne's hand.

Mary's voice rang in Anne's head, a clear bell pealing in the blackness, as strong and gentle as in Cathedral Square: *Give them the truth, Anne. Give them the truth.* The Mother of God was speaking through Mad Anne, just as she had spoken through the flames—perhaps madness was another form of divine fire. Whatever the reason, her fool had the Holy Virgin in her touch.

Fortified by Mary's presence, Anne addressed the up-turned faces. "God blesses you all. . . ." Men farther back turned to shout her words to the rest of the crowd, creating a curious disconcerting echo; gruff male voices repeating her message, garbling it in broad Northumberland (ye all . . . ye all . . .). "You have come out for our cause, which is just and holy" (. . . jest holy . . . jest holy). She heard men amending her speech, adding wrongs she did not mention—land taken, new taxes, fines added. For these people the chief horror of the last twenty years was not the new prayer book and reformed mass, instead it was woods cut down, commons fenced off, fines raised.

Flustered by the mistranslations, and the gap between them, Anne tried to be more personal. She told the crowd how she had been twice a mother, and how twice her babies had died, just as many of theirs did. "I must turn my mother's love toward *you,* my children. Your suffering shall be my suffering."

People cheered the promise. Mad Anne's hand tightened on hers, and Mary's voice grew louder, more insistent. *"Let them speak, Anne. Do not fear the fire."* Anne did fear what they would say, but she had to be true to Mary. "If you suffer, bring your problems to me. I will hear them." Heaven only knew what she could *do* about them.

North Country folk are never shy about presenting complaints. A score of villeins stepped forward—not reedy young scholars either, but plain-faced peasants and brawny alewives—all eager to speak against their betters. They said that since London had begun putting lead in the money, and selling the rights to make a living, the cost of everything had gone up, profiting those who raised their prices—the town monopolists and the most predatory landlords. Coal for heating, soap for washing, dyes for clothing, fish for eating, ale for drinking, and salt for seasoning were all Crown monopolies—and people who produced for themselves and their neighbors were called thieves by the law. Rack rents and intolerable fines drove families off the land. "Lawland landlords tear doon cottages ta make sheep crofts, turnin' land ower to luggish hired hands. Famines once came fram God, boot now are made by men."

Anne heard the new rhyme going round:

> *"Law locks up the man or woman*
> *Who steals the goose from off the common,*
> *But lets the greater robber loose*
> *Who steals the common from the goose."*

All the Jacks and Janes wanted was bread and ale, and grass to feed their flocks. Anne heard more about Ket's

Rebellion in Norfolk, twenty years back, than about the Duke of Norfolk they had gathered to free. (Not that she cared overmuch for Norfolk—that Reformed Church prig with royal airs—but it showed the insolent temper of the crowd.) They thought their problems were at least as important as the Duke's.

Feeling like God's own idiot for coming alone, Anne held tight to her horse, answering that the New Religion was at the root of it all: "When Mother Church is plundered, can her children hope to be safe? Do you think that men who rob nunneries would scruple at stealing from the poor? It was Percy custom to grant leases for life at customary rents. Your increases came when Percy lands were in ward to the Crown, and after the Pilgrimage of Grace, when the Earldom was given to the Reformers. Fail now, and such hard times will come again."

Her people replied with heated respect that they were already in hard times. Not cowed to argue with a countess, they said the Percy's had their Earldom back; now it was only fit that rents be what they were. They knew Reformers were at fault, but they did not trust their old lords overmuch. ("Acceptin' of course yor ladyschip.") Westmorland was an infamous encloser.

Her ladyship was heartsick. Yes, Tom had his Earldom, but how long could he keep it if he must fight Elizabeth while throwing away rents? This horde on Maiden Hill had supped last night and breakfasted this morning out of the Percy war chests. They had not eaten venison and kidney—more likely breakfast had been biscuits and beer—but did the fools think Percy chests were bottomless? At home Tom headed a court in miniature with constables, stewards, porters, and receivers—four out of five shillings went to feed retainers or feast tenants. Anne and Tom had pawned and leased to raise eight thousand crowns. Neville had contributed nothing.

Mary spoke again, so loud that Anne thought everyone must hear her. *Anne, do not make the easy hard. Speak from the heart.*

Anne stared at the hushed crowd, knowing that only one answer would do. "I am pleased that you are not radicals, but sworn protectors of tradition, wanting only what has been." That was for the troublesome scholar, afflicted with too much learning. She rose higher in her stirrups, speaking deliberately: "I can only swear by the Holy Mother of God, Percy tenants who march south with me need never pay more than their grandfathers did, even if we have to roll back rents and fines to the Old Harry's time."

It was said, and she felt better for it. The hush dissolved in waves of cheering as her words were repeated through the throng. Heaven knows what the fringes heard—free crumpets and raspberry ale, no doubt—but the promise to roll back rents must have come through clear. It was what they wanted to hear. And it properly shut up that young idiot savant who had been so busy stirring the crowd.

Singing broke out, then piping and wild, impromptu dance.

Anne descended Maiden Hill in a glorious haze, her people clinging to her stirrups, subjecting their Countess to more than normal adulation. Crying mothers held up their infants, saying these children were hers now. "Do nowt mourn ower yor lost babes. These are yor bairns, for ye are feeding them." Anne too was in tears by the time she reached the stables, trembling so much her fool had to help her dismount. She stood on straw manure, between a hayrick and a dovecote, shaking, holding her fool for support, surprised a few dirty infants could affect her so much. Mad Anne took the opportunity to be pertly familiar. "We did well this day. They will never take that away."

Anne shook her head. "Oh, it was easy enough to say. The hard part will be making good." She had real responsibilities, more than the most inventive lunatic could imagine.

"No, it was hard to say." The fool gave her a solicitous smile, gradually broadening into an idiot grin. "Don't fret over your promise. You will never make good on it—but that will not change today."

Anne stepped back, putting distance and dignity between them. Mad Anne's face was like a demented mirror. One moment her fool seemed incredibly prescient; then she would say the most appalling things with a witless smile, as if nothing in the world mattered. Of course Anne meant to make good on her promise. These were her people, the most loyal and willing, the ones who had come out for her against the Queen.

Tossing the mare's reins to a gaping stable boy, she steered Mad Anne into the white-walled kitchen, seating her beside a brick oven. Drying tears on a napkin cloth, she told an officer of the pantry to feed her fool, then she went into the manse to find Tom. He was in their private apartments, seated on a plush window seat. The tapestry curtains were drawn back, revealing the roofs and chimneys of Durham. Anne told him everything, only holding back her conversations with Mary, not wanting to sound as wild as the woman in her kitchen.

Tom tried to seem indulgent, sipping wine from cut Venetian crystal, but her story could not hold him. Captains interrupted, coming to consult and track mud on the costly carpets. Westmorland came in leading a grizzled, squint-eyed sergeant major. The pair stood shifting from foot to foot, studying the carved ceiling. Every horse, pike, and pistol ball in Durham was being bought up for the march south, since the huge army was not half-equipped. Tom nodded absently, spending the Queen's shillings like a drunk sailor.

"Spare no expense," advised Westmorland. "If we lose, I for one will mount the scaffold all the more cheerfully, knowing I am in debt to the merchants of Durham."

"And if they will not sell?" asked a veteran cutthroat with black whiskers and a gruff manner.

"Be polite, but put a noose around their necks." Tom turned back to Anne. "Town merchants feel more comfortable bargaining with a hemp collar. Saves them a lot of explaining if Elizabeth ever asks why they sold us arms and oats." He treated her story as a morning adventure she was relating for lack of better to do. When Anne came to her promise to roll back rents and fines, Westmorland grimaced. Tom laughed outright. "Yes, and we'll give them Sunday games all week. You are a smart woman, Anne, but you have no head for sums."

He cocked an eye toward the sergeant major. "What are we paying for remounts?"

"Too bloody much, your lairdship." The sergeant major

presumably knew his stock, having the face of a horse thief.

"Right." Tom sat back, resting booted feet on a cushion. "You see Anne, horseflesh has gone up, so has the price of everything from pickled herring to the French pox. It follows that rents and fines must rise as well."

"I swore to them," insisted Anne. "I cannot go back now and tell them no."

"So you won't," Westmorland yawned. "Cottagers will march all the better, believing what you have said."

"I know it pains you." Tom stared out over the sooty town. "The commons love you, Anne, and you love them—yet love may lead a lady astray."

"Thank goodness that's so." Westmorland winked to the horse sergeant, who smirked behind his stiff whiskers and probably much preferred boys. Tom took that chance to remind the cavalry man to round up every nag and plow horse with more than three legs. "Those that won't make cavalry horses will mount hobblers."

The cavalry sergeant snorted at the notion of mounting shire infantry. "A brigade of Berkshire hams on horseback would be more military."

Westmorland laughed. "Just so long as they move fast. Got to give Elizabeth no time to get her garters up."

Anne felt foolish and dismissed. Neither her husband nor her fool took her seriously. But Mary stood behind her, and tens of thousands on Maiden Hill believed her. She vowed to herself, and to the Virgin Mother of God: No tenant who went with her to York would ever suffer for it.

The noble Duke of York,
He had ten thousand men,
He marched them up a hill,
And he marched them down again.
And when you're up, you're up,
And when you're down, you're down,
And when you're only halfway up,
You're neither up nor down.

—MOTHER GOOSE

Yorkshire

Anne wondered if every army went to war so painstakingly unprepared. They had people aplenty, but not much else. The shortage of powder and shot was offset only by the lack of muskets and hackbutts; nor had Durham been able to supply much in the way of pistols, helmets, and armor. (As it was, they were leaving the town swinging empty on its hinges—almighty glad to see them go.) Tom purchased food for the march, but not near enough. No general provision had been made for shelter. Tents were for nobility, butlers, maids, and household troops; the rest of the moving city had no roof. Not caring to see her people sleeping in the ditches, Anne bought up every bit of blanketing and stout cloth she could lay hands on, stripping her town house as well. She saw one tenant family huddled under an embroidered tapestry with cloth-of-gold tassels, waiting for the march to start.

On a willing horse Anne could gallop the distance from Durham to York in a day and a half of hard riding, but she expected their heavy-footed army would find the road south longer and steeper—loaded down with carts, tents, cracknels, weapons, babies, and whatnot; her people would be lucky to reach York in a fortnight. And it was well into the Fool's Season, with winter coming on fast.

Frost hardened the roads, bringing a whisper of snow to see them off. Trotting in the lead were the household cavalry and gentlemen adventurers. These were demi-lances, *cuirassiers* in back-and-breasts and crested morions, the best-armed and most reliable men, with swords, lances,

31

half-armor, helmets, and huge horse pistols. They were also the fewest in number.

Behind them came Tom and Westmorland's march riders in leather and mail, hard men ready for mischief; all of them thoroughly bad characters—handy in war and a terror to the neighbors in peacetime.

Marching with the guns were the shire levies in deerskin jacks and iron hats, completely untrained and doubtfully disciplined. She knew some had come out of love of the Percys, but others were just restless and landless—poachers, debtors, and vagrants, reliable only because they had no home to run to. Enclosures and sheep runs had turned out an army of idle, desperate men.

Behind the gun-train came the carts, with their victuallers and wagoneers. And last of all the great struggling mass from Maiden Hill, making up more than half the march. Here there was no attempt at order. Families of cottagers and knots of laborers strode off together, raising pilgrims' flags and rude crosses, singing psalms as they tramped—many completely unarmed. For them the Rising was not a campaign, it was a new pilgrimage to put right a world that had gone so wrong. Seeing them come on, wave after wave, feet wrapped in rags against the cold, Anne felt proud and humbled. These were her people, who had set aside loom and plow to risk what little they had for what they believed; for what she had promised.

Darce had taken his mounted hooligans over to the West March, and most of the hawkers and whores had gone home. Some few ravaged souls remained in the muddy wreck on Maiden Hill, squatting amid the bonfire ashes, too dazed or weak-willed to take the road south. Such subtractions did not amount to a loss. If numbers alone counted, Anne estimated they had enough people to take York and London, then go on and free Jerusalem from the Turk.

On that first day the great struggling mass got no farther than Bishop Auckland, a brisk gallop from Durham. There Anne heard Hartlepool had opened its gates, securing the sea road to Flanders and Spain. On the following day they made even less progress. Westmorland insisted on stopping at his stronghold of Raby—after prodding and pushing to depart half-prepared, jeering at every delay, the Neville could not pass up a night at his own hall. While he dined on partridge and slept in a feather bed, the army huddled in bitter cold beneath the castle's long, crenelated walls.

At Anne's insistence they were up and away before the Neville could down a proper breakfast, hurrying along the Roman road through Bath Wood, straight past Barnard Castle, perched on its steep bank above the Tees. Tom fidgeted, hating to cross the Tees without taking a whack at the castle. But Anne would brook no delay. Her fool warned they would have rain before the new moon, and Anne did not need a weatherwitch to know a November gale was like to come ripping over the Pennines. Tom complained, acted petulant, then compromised. "Send north for siege guns, and push into Yorkshire." He was never happier than when he could do both at once.

The Valleys of the Ure and Swale, and the Vale of York beyond, comprise a great intrusion of lowland sediments thrust into the stony flank of the Pennines. The land is so low and wet, it sometimes resembles a swamp. Here Anne saw two Britains, two ways of life running together. The Ure and Swale rose in the Highlands, Old Britain, Arthur's Britain, her pagan roots anchored in ancient sediments— millstone, cavernous limestone, and igneous rock—forged in fire, compressed, faulted and folded, then ground down by glaciers, and weathered by gales blowing off the Western Sea. Upland soils are thin and acid; growing seasons short. The dales and fells were better fit for pasture than for planting. Upland families went their own way, working as they saw fit, but bonds were tight between lord and servant. Law was what people made it. To "ride" and "raid" was a single verb, and tenants were bound by manor rolls to "be ready to muster with horse and armor, in person or in proxy." A holding did not mean so much meadowland, or pasture, or so much money paid in rent; it meant a man on horseback with lance and steel bonnet.

But the rivers flowed into a different Britain, a New Britain, with shorter roots in softer sediments eroded from the older landmass—clays, chalks, and sandstone, gently folded and lightly drained. Sheltered by the uplands, the

Lowlands retained rich, deep soils, marked by fences and
enclosures, each field noted in a landlord's copybook; producing so much wool, grain, and timber. In this New Britain a written order from Westminster meant more than
faith or family. Money measured everything. Anne saw
cottagers driven out to prosper or starve, and ancient
houses of God—Eggleston, Jervaulx, Fountains—stood
empty, or were mined for building stone.

They reached Ripon by the middle of November. Tom
and Westmorland issued a proclamation calling on Yorkshire to join their crusade. The men would allow no mention of Queen Mary of Scotland, though it was plain as a
pikestaff they were marching south to wed her to Norfolk.
They merely promised to restore "the ancient liberties of
this land and God's Church." Like proper British rebels,
they said nothing against Elizabeth, blaming everything on
"diverse evil-disposed advisers" who had "abused the
Queen" and "disordered the realm."

("Three cheers for the Queen of Tarts," snorted Westmorland.)

A generation before, the North Country had risen up as
a whole in the Pilgrimage of Grace, streaming south into
the Vale of York to present its grievances, carrying the
Banner of Christ's Five Wounds. Young Harry found the
Pilgrimage of Grace too powerful to stop—so he offered
its leaders free pardon to come south and treat with him.
The North sent its leaders south, where they were dispatched to the block and scaffold for the novel crime of
trusting their King. Anne and Tom had wed in the shadow
of that betrayal. Only Mary Tudor had kept faith, restoring
the Earldom to Tom, but now Young Harry's bastard
daughter was warming the throne. She too had called them
to London, but this time no one was going meekly south
to set his head on the block.

The proclamation cast a wide net, claiming support
from the Duke of Norfolk, and the earls of Arundel and
Pembroke. However, Norfolk was in the Tower, and the
two earls under house arrest. The people who came out
were Yorkshire gentry—Gascoignes and Markenfields,
Nortons from Ripon, Ingelbys from Ripley. Though people
joined the march, each town and village was happiest to

see the hungry army move on. Anne saw how well Yorkshire had been tamed since the Pilgrimage of Grace. The
Tudor Council of the North had pruned the Vale, cutting
down the overmighty or the just plain uppity—abolishing
the old shire levies. Most of the North Riding sat on the
sidelines, ready to throw up their hats for whoever won.

After Ripon came the rains, slashing at their backs,
drowning the fords, turning roads to gummy mire. Every
rivulet swelled into a torrent. Mad Anne predicted rain until the last week in November, and Anne found her fool's
forecast true to the letter. Each morning the sodden mass
of people rose to tramp southward. Towns became a blur
of rain, a market street crosshatched by little lanes and alleys, glazed windows staring down on steaming midden
heaps. One damp morning Tom had to order a man
hanged, for raping and mauling a Yorkshire lass. Anne
was sickened by the wretch's pleading, but they were determined to lead God's army—not the Devil's. The constant drizzle made him appear to weep while dangling
from the gibbet, though it would have been a dismal business even on a sunny day.

Insanity defies rank and station—Anne found she could
sit with her fool and have the most normal conversations,
as long as they did not question each other's identity. In
these private talks Anne admitted that winter campaigning
was worse than she ever imagined. "It needs more than
psalm-singing and blankets. I expected grand battles, with
God deciding the right—but what we really need are magazines and food stocks organized in advance. Movement
has taken the place of planning. Towns and villages are
our magazines, but how long can that last?"

"It will last as long as it lasts," was Mad Anne's cryptic
half-answer, brimful of foreboding.

Anne came to rely on her fool's more sensible prophecies and oracles. Her mad twin seemed to know beforehand who would rally to them, and where the bridges
would be out or the fords underwater. Ignorant cottagers
took them for sisters. Side by side, hair drenched by the
downpour, dresses spattered with mud, there was not much
to choose between them. Anne herself could no longer say
offhand which of them was the great lady, and which the

mad fool—neither seemed to have the mother wit to keep out of the rain. They rose together, worked together, even menstruated on the same days—which Anne found completely eerie.

Local gentry protested that Anne treated her fool too well. "She is not nobility, you know."

"She thinks she is," Anne replied. Being a countess meant she could shrug off meddling advice—no upcountry squire complained half so much as the man Tom had hanged. Still, many thought the resemblance between them was less than canny. A beak-nosed Dalesman took Anne aside, warning her that Mad Anne "wor a witch ar sorceress far sure."

The gaffer did not mean it badly. He was merely being helpful—Northerners of all ranks relied on white witches and midwives' cures. But Anne knew that to the South things were not so free and easy; Elizabeth's mean-spirited Parliament had passed a General Witch Law. Already Reformers found the law too lenient—it only hanged witches who committed actual harm. They preached a return to the law of Moses, which executed all witches, burning the innocent alongside the guilty. Anne thought Elizabeth's law offered little enough protection—murder by witchcraft had always been a crime, like murder done with poison or a dagger, but "harm" was broad enough to hang a woman for sick swine, or fainting spells. In speaking to her fool, Anne edged around the question; trying to sound sympathetic, saying the new witch law was "part of that attack upon women that began when the Virgin was dethroned. Reformers will not be happy until all worship of Mary is abolished, and England has a holocaust like in Germany, sending whole villages of women to the stake." Anne doubted that Elizabeth would stomach that—the Queen was a woman of sorts.

Mad Anne returned her concern with amusement. "You are worried that we are witches?"

"No, I worry that *you* are." Anne knew right well that *she* was not a witch.

Her fool's eyes sparkled. "Anne, we share a single soul; we must be witches together or not at all."

So far, not a pike was lifted to oppose them. And best

of all, the rains stopped. The sun shone in splendor when they reached York, the ancient capital of the North sitting on its moraine ridge above the clay and silt of the flood-plain. Here the parade halted. York would not open its gates. Word slipped out that Crown officers were in complete charge, preparing to withstand a siege. They rode around the city as far as Selby Abbey, then turned back for another fractious conference.

Westmorland sat in Anne's tent, teeth on edge, sour as a Muslim at mass. "York is held against us, and the Queen of Scots is out of our reach." Elizabeth had been clever enough to move Mary of Scotland farther south, to Coventry. Anne stared at the Neville, not knowing what to do. York had opened its gates to the Pilgrimage of Grace, and she had counted on the city doing the same for them. York had meant food and shelter and warmth; the holy grail she had held out to her people. And Elizabeth still held both Mary and Norfolk, making it an awfully empty wedding. If needed, the Queen would not hesitate to order up a double beheading for bride and groom—as her sister had done for Guilford Dudley and Lady Jane. That was the Tudor way with pushy relatives and inconvenient heirs.

Tom alone had a plan. "We must turn about—go back and besiege Barnard Castle."

"Barnard Castle?" Anne remembered the dark pile of stone brooding on its bank above the Tees. She saw no reason to revisit it, much less try to take the place—they might just as profitably march to a cliff and all leap into the sea. "We said no sieges."

"Woman, have you been listening?" Westmorland had lost his reckless air, but not his acid tongue. "York is held against us, the strongest city in the North. Would you lay siege to it? We shall have sieges whichever way we go."

She felt the noose tighten. Going back sacrificed momentum, giving Elizabeth time to assemble an army, but they could not simply stagger south, knocking on doors that would not open.

"Barnard Castle we can take," Tom argued, "but a failure in front of York would be fatal to our cause." She felt any turning back would be fatal, and told them so. Tom looked hurt and badgered. Westmorland adopted a tone of

surly authority—she recognized the bitter anger of the
forestalled man of action—"our siege guns are near to
Barnard, and Barnard is near to Raby."

Right, she thought, let's all return to Raby Castle and
warm beds, where Lord Charles Neville can nurse his
funk. Westmorland would have profited from a kick in his
lordly rear, if only Jane Neville were there to administer it;
as it was, Anne had nothing to put against the men's hurt
feelings and remorseless logic. Commoners and gentry had
joined the Rising, but no great nobles had rallied to them,
not even Anne's own family. And Hartlepool was empty—
Alva had not come. The Pope, the Spanish, the Somersets,
were leaving her to face Elizabeth alone. Of course it fell
to Anne to tell her people. Tom planned to issue a flat order, and Westmorland could give a rat's rear how the mass
of pilgrims took the news.

When the men were gone, she railed at Mad Anne,
"You might have warned me. York closing its gates to us
is worse than a cloudburst, or a bit of mud on the roads."

For once her fool looked dead serious. "Anne, suppose
I had told you—and you had believed me—would it have
made a bean's worth of difference? This whole grand rising would not turn about, just because a woman says,
'Wait folks, it won't work. Time to go back to our milk-
ing.' It was hard for me to come south, knowing all was
for naught. Why inflict that on you? Believe me, there are
worse days than this ahead. Do you want to hear about
them now?"

Anne snapped back, "No, one disaster is enough for any
day." Instead she turned to Mary, praying before her banner, begging for guidance. The men were going back.
Should she lead her people on alone? That sounded pre-
posterous. Her only answer came in the Vespers bells from
a nearby village. *"Be strong, Anne. Be strong."* The words
were faint, seeming to beat back and forth, fading in the
distance. *"Be strong. Be strong."*

After Vespers the pilgrims gathered at the base of the
great cross, by the Banner of Christ's Five Wounds. There
Anne told how the earls meant to take Barnard. She tried
to make it sound like a call to arms, and not retreat, but
her people took it as badly as she had. Those who always

spoke for her were silent. Naturally the young scholar from Maiden Hill popped up to denounce the decision. "This is what comes of secret conclaves—betrayals made behind our backs."

Weary and angry, Anne replied, "I am here before you, ready to listen to a better plan."

The smug boy announced, "We should take the road south, down to Derbyshire. Last summer the peasants of Bakewell broke down enclosures and fences, taking up clubs and staves to defy the Queen's officers." Bakewell was in a wild country of splendid gorges in the lower Pennines, south of the Peak.

It sickened Anne to hear talk of Derbyshire and last summer. Summer was when they had planned the Rising. Summer was when they should have marched, with the sun overhead and hay in the fields. She had even hoped the Earl of Derby might support them—his countess was one of that cabal of noblewomen loyal to the Old Religion. Instead they had waited on the grand and gutless Duke of Norfolk—who was no doubt begging to get back in Elizabeth's good graces. Anne hoped the Queen had him hung and quartered.

Patiently she explained how it was too late for a descent into Derbyshire. "That would have made sense when they were keeping Mary of Scotland in Sheffield, but now they have moved her to Coventry."

"First Derbyshire, then Coventry," the upstart scholar shot back. "The road south leads through both. From Sheffield to Chester, folk have heard prophecies that the Old Times will come again."

"More rains are coming too," Anne reminded him. "How will we haul the cannon all that way?" By now she hated these brass-and-iron monsters. Without forage, the gun-horses were weak as hares, straining to pull the heavy metal.

"Abandon the guns," he replied, as easy as if they were his to throw away.

"Shall we take Coventry with clubs and staves? A castle is not some landlord's sheep pen."

"Trust in God," intoned an ancient hedge priest. He stood up, a gray ghost from Old Harry's time, a worn mass book and battered chalice hanging from his belt. His parishioners took up that call. "Abandon yon cannon and trust in God." Anne was torn, hating the guns but not believing that prayer and prophecy would bring down the walls of York, or even Coventry—if they ever got so far. Falling silent, she listened on out of duty. One impossible idea after another paraded past her. Plainly nothing was going to be decided. It began to pour, but people kept arguing as the rain sizzled in their fires. Tomorrow Tom would lead his men north, then people would decide with their feet. Those who wanted could follow Tom, those who didn't could push south, without guns, supplies, and household troops.

Of course they all went north. Next morning even the complaining scholar and the old "Trust in God" cleric trailed after the earls. Anne had the grim satisfaction of seeing one huge culverin left behind, too heavy to be hauled home, buried to its wheel hubs in the mud, its muzzle pointed in empty defiance down the road toward York.

They retreated up the Roman road, past green undulating hills, and belts of trees hiding Stanwick Camp, the ring fort where North Britons had made a final stand against the legions of Rome. Going south, Anne had barely noticed the place, now it seemed sinister, full of foreboding. Barnard Castle was a low, sprawling fortress on the far bank of the Tees. Outer walls were lime and brick, but the heart of the castle was the stone Inner Ward overlooking the river, far from any practical point of attack. The curtain towers had guns served by marksmen, fowlers, and soldiers of the garrison, so as soon as the army arrived, a lively exchange of small shot and sixty-pound mortar rounds got under way.

Seeing what the siege did to her people, Anne found it hard to care whether the castle stood or fell. Marching had been bad, but sitting over a week in one place was infinitely worse. Food was quickly consumed and converted to human excrement, overwhelming any feeble attempts at sanitation. Hunger, exposure, and filth sent fevers raging through the camps. People deserted in droves. Anne had no heart to stop them, considering it criminal to drag them back to die in disease and squalor. Tom was totally ab-

sorbed in the minutiae of the siege: plotting lines of attack,
moving the mud about with trenches, sighting his guns as
if they were a brace of pistols. Periodically he would form
up storming parties, men in armor followed by masses of
Percy tenants with pikes and bills. Anne discovered night
assaults had a ghastly sort of beauty: Cannons blazed and
roared; shouting masses of men surged forward; firelight
winked on steel; grenades flew overhead in flaming arcs.
Dawn revealed the cost, bodies sprawled in the breech like
so many swatted flies, and another inner wall to be battered and assaulted.

In Yorkshire Anne had agonized over hanging a single
rapist. Now she tended brave, blameless boys shot screaming in the stomach, or smashed to rags by round shot. After each assault she and Mad Anne assisted with the
surgery, helping doctor wounded men with strong drink
and crude stitches. Mad Anne was especially tender with
the hopeless cases, seeming to know which would die, and
when. She talked and took their hands for as long as was
needed—becoming mother, sister, and sweetheart. Men
called her the Angel of Death.

One by one Barnard's walls came crashing down.
Ditches in between were filled with fascines, rubble, and
bodies. A final assault was made through a curtain of
snow falling so steadily out of the sky that Anne wondered
where so many flakes could be coming from. Masked by
the storm, Tom and Westmorland led a furious charge with
petards and scaling ladders that breached the innermost
bailey.

Eleven days after the opening bombardment George
Bowes, Elizabeth's steward, ran up a white flag on the
Balliol Tower. Entering the shattered castle, Anne found
everything covered over with a white blanket, softening
the rubble, making even the corpses seem peacefully
asleep. They whispered up at her, "Step lightly, you might
have been me."

In the frozen dawn Westmorland ordered the entire garrison to strip naked on the snow, while troops looted the
town ward and castle. Anne protested at seeing women
nude and shivering, fingers and toes turning blue, but the
Neville informed her curtly that it was a military necessity.

"Stripping down is mild punishment for holding out so long. By the laws of siege warfare, these women have no defense from rape, or even massacre. If resisting garrisons are not punished, the next one will have no reason to give in."

Anne lost patience with Westmorland. "I am not eagerly awaiting the next siege, and the next. And I greatly doubt that serving girls and scullery maids were given much say in Sir George's defense plans." Once the vicious ritual was done, she demanded the women be dressed and cared for, not locked up with the male prisoners in Brackenbury's Tower.

The victorious army was in as great a shambles as the castle. Pilgrims and shire levies had been decimated by casualties and desertion. The old cleric had defecated himself to death with dysentery, and the complaining scholar had his mouth stopped with earth. A few thousand infantry and half that many horsemen were in fit condition to fight. That night they banqueted on the castle's stores. (Anne discovered that salt pork in lentils can be a feast, when you have been living on saddle leather and horse stew.) The Great Hall stood snug against the west curtain, at the farthest point from the attacking batteries. Several sixty-pound rounds had come through the roof, but otherwise Sir George's quarters were comfortably intact. Rosy with wine, Tom hinted that he and Anne needed to celebrate the way they had done in Durham.

Anne replied that she had seen sickness, privation, gangrened wounds, and severed limbs—none of which put her in the mood to make love. Tom was taken aback. "With men it is different. Dodging death puts a fellow very much in need of a woman. This is the first victory we have had to fight for."

"If this is victory, what must defeat be like?" The dead were stacked outside like winter cordwood, covered with clotted blood, waiting for graves to be hacked from the frozen ground—only the cold kept them from stinking clear to Scotland.

"Anne, you must accustom yourself to war. I have known women that would couple like coneys after a good fight."

"Then find an eager cottontail among the camp follow-ers. I will never accustom myself to such disasters." She stomped off to pray in the castle chapel. The little church was deserted, in part because a mortar round had split the pews into kindling, splattering the walls with shrapnel. Since it was a Reformed chapel there was not much to break; no proper altar, no paintings, no images of Mary and the saints. Anne sent for her banner, and knelt before it, praying to the Mother of God—who had not spoken to her since that awful Vespers in Yorkshire. The floor was gritty with stone chips and dust brought down by the bom-bardment. Splinters dug at her knees. Anne lit candles and poured out her soul, asking for some sign, some ray of guidance in this most ungodly hour.

Nothing. Mary did not answer. Heaven seemed as dead and vacant as the new astronomers insisted. After an hour or so on her knees, Anne saw prayer was pointless. What a weakling she had been to turn back from Yorkshire. Mary had told her "Be strong." But she had trusted to cul-verins and battle plans instead of her people's hearts. She saw plain enough what came of that. Why should Mary waste words on such a simpleton? Staggering onto numb limbs, she took a candle and went to find Tom. Clearly it was not too late to rekindle the spirit of pilgrimage. She was more sure than ever the Old Religion would not be re-stored by blood and mortar fire.

Entering the keep through the dining hall, she bolted the big door behind her, crossing to a presence chamber be-neath their apartments, avoiding the main staircase and guardroom. A privy staircase in the back of the presence chamber led straight up to a small curtained alcove off the master bedroom. Mounting the stairs, she heard move-ment. Glad to have Tom awake, she pulled aside the heavy dressing curtain.

She was struck speechless.

The bedchamber was lit by tall tapers, and Tom was ly-ing half on the bed, head lolling back, stark naked, obvi-ously the worse for drink. Kneeling between his bare thighs was an equally naked woman with a wild mane of white-blonde hair. She was hard at work, Tom's shaft be-tween her lips, sucking with puffed cheeks, while Anne's husband writhed and moaned on the bed. Tom was spec-tacularly endowed, and there was room for both her hands as well. The woman's eyes were closed. Her face was Anne's face, and that of her fool.

Stunned, Anne stood watching, then slipped back down the stairs. Halfway down she stopped, wanting to look again, to be sure this was actually happening—but she heard the bed begin to creak, and descended the full dis-tance.

A massive carved oak chair sat in one corner of the presence chamber; she settled down and waited, having nowhere else to go. Sitting in semidarkness, her votive candle burning down, she could still hear them thumping as though they meant to break the bed. Looking up, she saw only a coat of arms carved into the wooden ceiling. The central device was a small shield with its center cut out, the escutcheon voided, the hollow shield of the disin-herited House of Balliol. Barnard had been a Balliol castle.

She sat there, betrayed and abandoned. Betrayed by Tom, and by her fool. Abandoned by Mary. She cried for herself and for her lost crusade, and for Tom in his fool-ishness, and for that smug young scholar who had so often angered her. He was now lying facedown in a frozen ditch, his fine thoughtful head laid open by a halberd. She cried for her two babies, who had died knowing so little of life. There were no end of things to cry over.

Her family abandoning her was almost a blessing. Why involve them in her downfall? Having her father beheaded and her mother widowed would be thin comfort. The hol-low shield on the ceiling seemed to mock her. The Balliols were pathetic play-kings of Scotland, betrayed by both Scots and English; a lost cause if ever there was one. Her royal ancestor Edward Longshanks, the Hammer of the Scots, had torn John Balliol's insignia from his tunic, turn-ing him into Toom Tabard, the Empty Coat. Anne could even spare a tear for the House of Balliol.

The galloping bed stopped. She waited, gripping the heavy arms of the chair, hearing the light steps of bare feet on the privy stairs.

Her fool descended the stairs, entering the presence chamber. Flushed and naked, she seemed not the least surprised to find Anne. Her disheveled hair cast wild shadows in the candlelight; her thighs gleamed, smelling of Tom. The tattered plaid hung about her shoulders, the green-blue tartan of who-knows-which Highland clan.

"Anne, I have come to bid good-bye."

"After betraying me with my husband, in my own bed." Actually it was Sir George Bowes's bed. Anne was never likely to use it now.

Her fool would not give one mad inch. "He is my husband too, and I have been a long time without him. I needed to give him a good-bye, and that is the one he wanted."

"Shut up!" Anne was shaking with anger. "No more of your mad foolishness. I saved you from hanging, or dying on the winter road. Is this appreciation?"

The woman wrapped the ragged tartan round her bare shoulders. "Half my life I have been married to him. I missed him much. Neither you nor I will be able to stay faithful to him, so love him now, for the time you have left together."

"Good—leave. Be gone." For better or worse, everyone was deserting.

Mad Anne backed toward the dining hall. "We will meet again—in Scotland."

"I hope never to see you this side of hell."

The fool stopped, framed in the doorway like some lewd Italian painter's notion of a Highland nymph. "No, Anne, not in hell, but in Scotland and at the Ends of the Earth. By then you will understand, though it means giving up all the foolish lies we come to love."

Anne let go the chair, aiming to shoo her out. But before she could reach her, Mad Anne disappeared—not out the door, but directly into the night air. Her naked body vanished like smoke up a flue.

Thinking it must be some trick of the half-light, Anne strode to the doorway, but the long, moonlit hall was empty. There were no retreating footsteps. The far door was bolted with the bar she herself had dropped in place. She looked over her shoulder into the empty presence chamber. There was nowhere her fool could have gone.

The bloody lunatic really was a witch.

Retreating to the presence chamber, Anne crumpled into the great carved chair. All these weeks she had been harboring a sorceress, and this was what came of it—Elizabeth's Witch Law seemed excessively lenient. Wind whistled through high windows shattered by the bombardment.

Tom took that minute to totter down the privy stairs in his nightshirt, shamefaced, still woefully drunk. "Anne, I thought she was you at first. . . ."

"Thought she was me?" The question came mechanically; it took her a moment to understand he was making pointless excuses.

"Well, you denied me," he started a surly drunken defense. "You denied me, and actually suggested . . ."

She rose wearily from the chair, shaking her head. "Tom, I do not much mind the deed—it is the timing that is too marvelous. Things are truly desperate. Our pilgrimage is dead. I can no longer hear Mary. . . ."

He stared at her, dumb, drunk, and bemused. As though he had never heard of God's Mother before. Anne realized that she had not shared her miracle with him; she had shared it with no one but the witch.

There was a pounding on the huge hall door, and a nervous sentry descended the main stair to draw the bolt. Half the castle must have heard her shouting. Clanking spurs marched across the dark flagstones in the dining hall.

Without a by-your-leave, Westmorland strode into the presence chamber, fresh off his horse, unsealed dispatches under his arm. He had obviously ridden down from Raby. Wife and husband must have been a fine sight, because the Neville made a short, mocking bow, flourishing the dispatch papers. "Good to find you up. Perfectly hideous news here."

He pitched the papers onto the chair. "Old John Forster has brought down his Border riders and a force of hackbutteers from the Berwick garrison. He has taken Warkworth and Alnwick, and holds the passes against us."

Anne stood blinking like an idiot, horrified by what had happened. She pictured Warkworth where they were married, and Alnwick—the great seat of Percy military power, with lofty walls, huge towers and multiple baileys. Losing both castles at a stroke was like hearing Northumberland had slid into the sea.

Westmorland seemed compelled to revel in the details. "The game is in. There will be no reinforcements, no food for the troops on hand. Forster is harrying the roads. My messenger had to come through the hills at night, lying by day in the hedges."

"What about the Scots?" Tom looked utterly relieved to be discussing military disaster, not defending adultery.

"Hiding in their hovels and caves. Forster and the Earl of Moray have gone about the Borders burning all the usual places."

Tom straightened his nightshirt, to look more warlike. "We still hold Durham and a dozen lesser places. We can retreat and retake the castles." Retreats and sieges had become his all-purpose solutions.

"With Warkworth and Alnwick held against us?" Westmorland cocked an eye. Anyone could see the impossibility of mounting another siege, particularly against those two magnificent Percy castles.

"Well, then it's over the Pennines to the West March," decided Tom. "We can combine with Darce. He is our only haven between here and Scotland."

Westmorland gave a hollow laugh. "If Darce stays true. What a pretty hope to hang your neck on."

Now Liddesdale has ridden a ride,
But I ken they had better have stayed at home,
For Micheal of Winfield he is dead,
And a prisoner taken is Jock o' the Syde.

—"THE BALLAD OF
JOCK ARMSTRONG OF THE SYDE"

Liddesdale

Anne knew they were nearing Scotland when she saw a wolf herding sheep. They were English sheep, no error— Anne had followed the flock through the thorn and heather of Bewcastle Waste. But who would be driving sheep in the dead of winter? She expected to see Border reivers, Liddesdale riders in blackened armor, but instead she saw a grinning Scots wolf with yellow eyes. He had to be a Scots wolf; the last English wolf had been killed in the Old Harry's time. Back and forth he ran behind the flock, growling warnings and nipping at the strays as if he were born to the task. Anne shivered. Scotland must be bleak indeed, if even the wolves came into England to steal.

Her mare shied, snorting and trying to back off. Anne leaned forward, patting the mare's neck, saying silly things to calm the tired animal. "You shall sleep in hay tonight instead of straw. You shall eat oats off a silver plate, and share my feather bed."

A month earlier Anne had owned a hundred feather beds in two dozen manors. She had owned linen to fit the hundred beds, and table service for two hundred. Now she had nothing. After the debacle at Barnard Castle, it had been back to Brancepeth and Durham, their numbers steadily dwindling. They had dithered about in Durham almost till Christmas, then decided to take a few hundred riders over the Pennines to join Darce in the West March. All the while Forster, Scrope, and Sussex gathered strength.

Darce, of course, had betrayed them. The man could no more keep faith than breathe underwater. The night before they had arrived at Naworth Castle to find Darce readying to ride out and help Lord Scrope hunt for them. That awkward scene ended with Darce showing them the door. His brother Edward offered them a guide across Bewcastle to the Scots border. Tom glared, fumed, and accepted. When the guide arrived, Anne saw the lumpish face of Black Dick Nixon grinning from beneath a bonnet.

Betrayal no longer surprised Anne—she was familiar with all its forms. She knew why the poor tenant deserted the march, and why the great lord turned his coat. Darce had rebelled for gain, and since he was manifestly not gaining by their cause, he had made his peace with Elizabeth. Anne told herself that she had rebelled on principle, and those who rose on principle got no peace offers from the Queen. Anne knew Elizabeth rather well, though no one would count them close. Like her sister and father before her, Elizabeth Tudor had only two remedies for principled heads: the rope and the ax.

Now Anne was riding north on a horse as weary as she was, guided by a ruffian overdue for hanging. The thousands who had gone with her into Yorkshire had shrunk to forty faithful riders in dented armor, trotting after her and Tom. She was exhausted of riding, mortally sick of being on a horse. Riding in retreat was more tiring than riding in an advance, and there was no end to retreat; the roads just got worse. They had left the high roads long ago, fleeing over black frozen tracks. And here nearly to Scotland, Anne could see no road at all; just moor, heath grass, and bare sod, cut by steep gullies and sprinkled with snow. To the north the tangled mass of the Cheviot Hills blocked their flight, forcing the fugitives westward toward the Scots border.

Nixon drew rein amid the sheep. Anne saw the flock stop and stand bleating on the bank of a stream, until the wolf forced them in. Sheep slid down the bank, splashing through the thin ice, scrambling up the far bank and milling about, shaking themselves dry.

A devilish-looking horseman in black leather and Scots bonnet appeared amid the shadows on the far shore. Anne thought, This man is deliberately showing himself, silhouetting himself and his horse against the setting sun. The wolf drove the flock straight by him, sheep parting to pass on either side of the horse. The rider was a big, bearded Scot, who did not seem surprised to see forty desperate riders on the tails of the stolen flock. A long lance hung

across his back, a short-barreled hackbutt swung from his
saddle, two heavy pistols were thrust into his boot tops,
and he wore a wicked-looking dirk in his belt—the man
clearly expected to meet more enemies than friends. The
thin rapier slung over his shoulder seemed redundant, but
Anne supposed it was to show he was a gentleman. She
was learning where not to place her trust, and she dis-
trusted this Scot even from a distance.

Leaving Black Dick Nixon under guard, Tom and Westmorland rode down into the stream and up the far bank.
Two armed and armored Englishmen should match a single Scot. Anne prodded her horse right to the icy bank,
where she could hear without crossing over.

The dark stranger spoke with a trotting Scots cadence;
Anne had to strain to catch his words. "I am Laird
Wormistoun, come ta welcome yer lairdships ta Scot-
land."

"You know us?" Tom took time adjusting to the unex-
pected.

"There be no much that does not come ta me. I heard
that two Inglis earls, o' Noorthumberland an' Westmoor-
land, were coming wi' two score riders. If ye be not them,
then who else would ye be?"

"What do you want with these earls?" Tom was still
pretending to be someone else.

"I am here to receive ye into Scotland, offering plain
food and a poor roof."

"Out of love for English earls?" Westmorland was even
less trusting than Tom.

"Out o' respeket for fellow outlaws."

"I can easily believe you are an outlaw, but what was
your crime?" Neville wanted to know.

A gap-toothed grin appeared above the man's bushy
beard. "Regicide was the charge, but it was no fouled."

"What was that last?" Tom whispered to Westmorland.

"He is claiming innocence, not too convincingly."

They turned back across the stream to talk things over
on the English side. Westmorland was first with an opinion. "There was a Teviotdale outlaw, Lord Ormiston,
among Bothwell's men. The King he is accused of killing

must be Lord Darnley; merely Mary's husband and not much of a king."

Anne could see Tom torn between the fear of pursuit and the expectation of treachery. Both had become as common as bread and breathing. His own brother Henry had betrayed them; Anne imagined Elizabeth had offered Henry the Earldom.

Tom shook his head. "I do not care how many kings or small dogs he killed in Scotland. Has he slit any English throats of late?"

"Most likely he has"—Westmorland shrugged—"but we dare not deal with honest men. It is him or lay our heads under a hedge."

Tom turned to Anne in bewildered anguish—as usual seeing all sides of the question.

"I do not like him either," she declared, "but I am learning of late that I cannot always have what I like. Last night we were turned away by a traitor. Tonight I am willing to sleep under a murderer's roof if it keeps me tolerably dry."

"Right now we are forty to this man's one," Westmorland reminded Tom. "If he betrays us, we can take some consolation in killing him."

In the end they agreed, as Anne knew they must. Where else were they to go?

Ormiston waved with his lance. "Follow the sheep."

Crossing onto foreign soil, Anne did not feel she was leaving home. Home was long gone. Alnwick and Warkworth were gone, along with her stately houses, her acres of plowland and pasture, her woods, her gowns and gloves; all were lost for good. She did not think that borders would protect her. Scots soil was not magic. Elizabeth's vengeance would make the border merely a small stream.

She found Ormiston as friendly and personable as the French pox. The villain talked on to her in his lilting Scots accent; mostly about his own exploits, which consisted of riding, stealing, and taking keen revenge for slight cause. The Scot assured her that he abhorred unnecessary homicide, but he found a multitude of occasions for necessary murder, and could not carry on a quarter hour's conversation without convicting himself of a dozen offenses against man or God. Listening to the scoundrel was like witnessing some ghastly accident; the decent thing was to turn away, but the details had a horrid fascination. Anne was provoked to ask if he had really killed Lord Darnley, Mary's consort and Ormiston's nominal liege.

"Darnley was vain an' vicious." Ormiston gave his head a sorry shake. "He braked in on the Queen at Holyrood and murdered her musical master merely for spite. Poor Mary, young and wi' child, was made ta watch."

Anne had already heard some of the horror of Queen Mary's few years in Scotland. She had offered Mary of Scotland sanctuary when the young woman fled south, but Elizabeth had snatched her cousin up and imprisoned her. Anne knew Elizabeth could hardly help herself—the Queen had been declared a bastard by her own father, who had beheaded her mother and stepmother. Mary would have found more family feeling in a pit viper.

Ormiston finished his show of concern for Mary. "While Darnley lay sick abed in Kirk o' Field, someone filled the cellars wi' black powder, not wanting ta dirty their hands wi' killing. Anly Darnley was a demon. Kirk o' Field blew itself halfway to heaven, but Darnley was not scratched an' still in need o' strangling. He had been a petulant fool, suffering from a plague of enemies, an' was never a well man besides. His death was as natural as old age. Still people accused me o' lending a hand, as any man might."

"Oh." Anne rode on in silence.

"Lending a hand?" asked Tom.

"Wi' the strangling," Ormiston explained. "It was not my feud, but it be a custom as auld as the pines to throttle a poor king when the queen's bed needs new blood. Earl Bothwell had his bonnet set on Mary, and took a dislike to Darnley—which was not hard. Everyone knows how ready I am to help out an earl in need." He smiled at the Earl of Westmorland, as though the murder charge were a sign of his good faith to them.

Remembering how James Stewart was stabbed twenty-eight times by a Graham, Anne asked if it was truly common for Kings of Scots to be murdered.

Ormiston laughed. "In olden times it was practically a

requirement o' office. Kings were regularly drowned or hanged, so their bodies could be quartered an' spread on the fields, ta improve the crops. But these days rulerschip is more Christian, an' scientific. Scots have struggled ta devise the perfect Commonwealth, balancing Kirk, Parliament, an' King—an' we have settled on a system of government that suits our character."

"What system is that?" Westmorland asked.

"Absolutist monarchy, tempered by assassination."

"What a perfectly appalling country," Westmorland shuddered.

"England is no better now, or else why are we leaving?" Anne took a long breath, feeling raw December air in her throat. In three nights it would be Christmas. She must enjoy each breath, each free heartbeat. *Let me have Christmas at least.* She did not know how long it would be before she sat in a stone cell, or how long her neck would be working.

The sheep bleated louder; the wolf was driving them into a fold. Ormiston sang out to beware of the stone pen, and Anne edged her tired mount toward his voice. Ahead she could see the solid blackness of a low hovel, its mud-and-stick chimney looming against the sky like a giant swallow's nest. She wondered why they were riding through some poor crofter's barnyard, until Ormiston called a halt, and she realized this was the night's lodging.

"Sleep here?" Westmorland gasped. "No Englishman would kennel dogs in this."

"Perhaps an Inglisman would not, but we Scots are keen lovers o' canines. We would no let even an Inglis dog sleep in the snow."

Anne dismounted, not worried that Westmorland would see her smiling in the darkness. She was happy to be off her horse, happy to have a place to lie. A heavy door swung open, spilling firelight out the threshold, and she was greeted by a woman, gray and old as death, who might have been Ormiston's mother, grandmother, or aged tenant. Beneath the woman's wool shawl Anne saw a face as wrinkled as a bud in winter. Fine skull bones showed she must have been beautiful when young. She motioned for Anne to enter, giving no more than a look and a sniff to the two English earls.

The hut was small, thick with woodsmoke and animal smells. The old woman kept talking in a kindly way, with an accent so strong and ancient that Anne could not understand a word. Ormiston had to translate. Through him the crone offered her the only bed, a straw mattress wedged between a rounded log and mud-daubed walls.

Exhausted, Anne strove to sleep, lying down fully clothed with a log for a pillow. Men went in and out. Ormiston left to tally the stolen sheep, then Tom went to see to his retainers. Every time the door opened, she could hear bleating sheep, restless horses, and boots tramping about.

Ormiston returned, saying the wolf had done well. "A fine night's profit is in the pen."

"Do not let the beast in here," Westmorland groused. "The place smells badly of dog already."

"Why not? This wolf be family here, earnin' his keep better than half my relations."

Anne opened her eyes, but in place of the wolf Ormiston brought a stranger, a dark, slender man of middle height, with a dagger-sharp beard and a swing in his step, legs slightly bowed like a horseman. A handsome fur-trimmed jacket hung from one shoulder. Another villain to be wary of. His deepset eyes looked her over, as frankly as she studied him. How long did it take him to see that she was a woman, clearly indisposed? By way of introduction, Ormiston sang out to Westmorland:

> "He's well kenned, Jock o' the Syde,
> A better robber ne'er did ride."

The man did not blink at being called a thief. He wore a blue-and-white ribbon in his bonnet, Armstrong colors, the worst riding family among the Liddesdale Scots. Anne closed her eyes. Let the men deal with him. Her husband and forty armed horsemen were within Westmorland's call. What more safety could she expect?

Anne awoke in the Hour of the Wolf, well toward dawn. Gray light came through the chinks in the door, and the fire had sunk to embers. Breastplates, backplates, and crested morions lay piled by the door. Tom was hovering over her, his hand on her shoulder. Ormiston was gone again. The remaining men seemed to stare at her.

"Anne," Tom whispered, "we need your help."

She nodded, too sleepy to speak or question.

"This old granny"—Tom indicated the crone of the cottage—"claims to be a seeress. She is willing to cast our fortunes, if a woman will turn the cards."

Shock roused her. That final scene in the presence chamber of Barnard Castle had cured her of any curiosity about witchcraft. "Tom, ours is a holy cause." (Or had been a holy cause.) "I will do nothing that is against God."

He took tight hold of her hands. "Anne, it is so hard to know what to do, or whom to trust. I do not ask for any unholy help. I only want some white magic, a dip into the future as far as this crone can see; but she wants a woman, a woman of our party. You are the only one."

Anne smoothed the wrinkles from her gown. Now it had come. Marching south, she had put herself in God's hands, asking Mary to guide her steps. She threw aside safety and security, knowing that Christ could overcome impossible odds. During the whole horrible retreat from Yorkshire she had felt God's hand lifting, heard Mary's voice receding, leaving her to wander aimlessly. "Thomas, to be by your side I have given up my home, my estates, my standing in the world; lending my hand to *more* witchcraft will be the last I can do."

"Just this, I would not ask more."

Anne wondered how the man could ask less. Sitting down at the plank table she thought of her fool and winced. Jock o' the Syde sat uncomfortably close to her elbow, like Lucifer's poor relation. The crone reached out and took her hands, cooing in that weird tongue. Anne could feel frail bones through parchment skin. The hands had once been shapely, but now they were a web of veins and wrinkles. Here was a living mirror. If Anne lived, it would only be to become as old and wrinkled, and as close to death as this woman. She did not feel sad; defeat had pressed the sadness out of her. She was just desperate to face death with a clear heart. When the end came, she must say she had done no evil. Could Elizabeth claim the same?

Jock o' the Syde spoke to her, sounding rough and low as he looked. "This granny is a Lady in her own right, an' she calls on the fates wi' cards."

"But will they answer?" Westmorland was standing by the burned-over fire, looking down his long nose at them. Anne was weary of the man's cynicism. If the Neville thought this was nothing, let him turn the cards.

"O' course the Norns will answer," Jock grinned. "They are three auld women, too ugly for fornication, wi' only one eye between 'em. They got no better to do but answer." He spoke fast words to the old woman. The crone gave a slight nod, not taking her gaze off Anne, as though the men were of no concern. I am in her hands, thought Anne, and my soul is all she wants.

Jock leaned back. "To show there is no chicanery, we will start wi' yer past; which is plain ta everyone."

Wrinkled hands drew Anne's over the cards, spread in three long facedown rows. The old woman indicated that Anne should choose a card from the first row. Anne felt over the line of blank paper rectangles, edges and backs worn from many readings. A card tugged at her fingers. She turned it over and revealed:

A tall tower blasted by lightning, afire and breaking in two, toppling two people and a crown toward distant ground.

She watched Tom flinch and even Westmorland wince at the painted image. The crone's hands held her steady.

"La Maison de Dieu; overthrow, defeat, an' disaster," Jock chuckled. "There is yer past all right, but it is not all bad. Ground must be cleared for new planting."

"Spare us the philosophy," muttered Westmorland. "I doubt you have ever planted anything more fertile than a dagger."

"True, I am no plowman," Jock replied. "My holdings are in sheep an' kine."

"Yours or your neighbor's?"

"We would no be neighbors if ye Inglis did not keep coming north."

The old woman gave Jock a stern sass-me-and-see-what-happens look, directing Anne's hands to the next line of cards.

"Here is what is," whispered Jock o' the Syde.

This time it was harder. Several cards pulled at her. One pulled more than the others, so she turned it over:

A man borne down by a bundle of ten staves, walking toward a house, woods, and field.

This image was not as obvious. She looked at Jock o' the Syde, who spoke low and directly to her. "Ten o' Wands means yew carry a burden—problems to be met— with yer goal still a ways off."

He looked up at the two earls. "The card also hides a traitor or deceiver."

"We need no cards to know that," Westmorland snorted. "Traitors are shopping themselves cheap this Christmas season."

Jock eyed them evenly. "Are ye ready for yer future?"

The men nodded. Anne ran her hands over the final row of cards. She could see Tom leaning forward, watching as she touched each card in turn. They all felt cold. Why was she doing this? Anne did not think the witchcraft would work, and wanted no part of it if it did. Feeling only frustration, she flipped over a final card.

A farmer leaned on a hoe, beside a bush with six coins blossoming on its branches. A seventh coin lay at the farmer's feet.

"A rich card," was Westmorland's verdict. Tom too seemed relieved not to see more death and disaster.

"Yes." Jock o' the Syde looked sharply at Anne. "There is success in the Seven o' Coins, but anly for those willing to work hard an' ta grow. Naught will come o' impatience except imprudent actions."

Anne felt drained. Again she had soiled herself and her faith. She saw no success in her future, and wanted nothing except to sleep.

Shots, yells, and the pounding of hooves jerked her alert. Her husband drew his rapier and flung open the door. Westmorland whipped a pistol out of his doublet, cocking the wheelock and covering Jock o' the Syde with the muzzle. The Scotsman made no move for the dirk in his belt. He seemed neither surprised nor disturbed by the noise and confusion. Through the open threshold Anne saw her husband's retainers running about beneath black trees, gaunt limbs, and gray sky. Ormiston came to the door, shaking his head, saying without entering, "Liddesdale lads have run off wi' yer mounts."

"Who would dare?" asked Westmorland.

Ormiston cocked his head toward Jock. "Ask the Armstrang. Him an' his kin run the stock in West Liddesdale. I am a Teviotdale thief myself."

Jock drew his dirk slowly, leaned back, and began cleaning under his nails with the blade. Anne noticed for the first time that his fingers were long like the crone's, his nails unnaturally sharp. "How were yer horses tethered?"

"Picketed to a rope stretched between pins," answered Tom. "I put a double guard on the ends, with a sentry pacing the length of the rope."

Jock shook his head. "In Liddesdale such careless picketing is like lettin' a horse run loose. Go see how our mounts are tethered. Each beast is tied to an iron stake as thick as yer thumb, driven deep in the ground. Then the horse is hobbled crossways, right foreleg to left hindleg. That is how to picket a horse in these parts, unless yer plan to sleep in the saddle; an' I have heard o' mounts stolen from under heavy sleepers."

A shamefaced young captain came to report that the picket line had been cut and the horses stampeded.

"'Tis a sorry thing to have happen to guests." Jock slid his dirk into the top of his boot. "An' I admit it were more likely Armstrangs; if it were not Nixons or Elliots. On the morrow I will speak wi' my kin, to see if yer mounts can be found. Lifting stock is in our blood. Half the horses in the Dale would no recognize their legal owners."

Hearing the name "Nixon," Tom ordered his captain to find their guide. The lad replied that Black Dick was gone with the horses. Anne thought of the promises she had made to her poor tired mare, and lay back on the mattress. She fell asleep feeling forgotten because she was not a missing horse.

Her second waking was in full daylight. Horses stamped and snorted outside. Thinking Jock had been astonishingly good to his word, she stumbled to the door, brushing straw off her dress, anxious to see to her mare.

Instead of their horses, she was surprised to find a hundred Scots outside, mounted on the quick little Border horses called hobbies. They were Liddesdale riders, wearing crested morions or plain bowl helmets, loose quilted jacks, and large leather boots—each with a lance, supplemented by whatever weapons the man could muster; ugly dirks, long swords, calivers, and huge horse pistols. In the cold morning sun they looked exceedingly cruel. Only one was familiar. The face of Black Dick Nixon stood out like a brass penny.

Her husband's men formed a ragged ring around their earls, all afoot and badly outnumbered. Ormiston and Jock lounged to one side.

The man next to Nixon introduced himself as Martin Elliot of Braidley. Speaking to Ormiston instead of the earls, Braidley announced that the Privy Council of Scotland was denying refuge to English rebels. "I do no want ta enter feud wi' ye, Wormistoun, but these Inglis lairds must be gone from Scotland before dusk on the morrow, and no more Inglis may cross the border. I have both Scots an' Inglis law behind me."

Jock Armstrong laughed. "That must feel passin' strange fer an Elliot."

Martin of Braidley flashed him back a smile. "It almost makes me itch."

Jock turned to the earls. "This man is a cousin of mine, an' I would just as well not kill him. Most days he kens his manners as well as any Elliot may, but he is under pledge to Regent Moray."

"It is useless ta fight," agreed Ormiston, telling the Elliots they accepted the terms.

Martin of Braidley tipped his morion to Jock, then he and his riders turned and rode back up the dale, lifting their lances like men proud of a brisk morning's work. Black Dick went with them. No word was said about the horses.

As the Elliot pennants fluttered out of sight, Ormiston began to amend his agreement with them. "It would be better to get yew inta the 'Bateable Land before sun-down."

"The Debatable Land is still Scotland." Tom eyed the vanishing lance points.

"Aye," Ormiston agreed, "Scots in name, but Moray himself must come for ye there. The Elliots will make a morning trot down the Dale for Moray, but they will not risk a lang ride among soo many Armstrangs an' Gra-hams."

"And Regent Moray hates us?" asked Anne. In Scotland for only a night, Anne was not surprised to hear she al-ready had important enemies here.

"Earl Moray hates yew because yer for Mary," ex-plained Jock. "The bastard is Mary's half brother, an' can no forget that the thickness o' a blanket bars him from the throne. Nor is Moray like to forgive Mary for chasing him out o' Scotland wi' steel on her head an' a pistol on her hip."

"And when Moray comes down to the Debatable Land, what then?" asked Westmorland.

Ormiston laughed. "Lad, it be plain that yew do no ken what a sore trouble it be governing over Scots. Moray has visited these Borders twice this year, burning, hanging, and getting pledges o' good behavior from Martin o' Braidley and such like. Now, less than two months after his last ride through, new problems appear in the shape o' yer lairdschips. He cannot keep runnin' back here, Scot-land has other hot corners to worry Earl Moray. The Re-gent is no a well man, not fit to spend perhaps his last Christmas shooing off Inglis earls."

"Moray is ill?" Westmorland's eager tone did not wish the invalid well.

Ormiston winked. "The Earl o' Moray suffers from Darnley's disease—a vain disposition and a suffet o' enemies. It may yet proove fatal. We can pass a snug Christmas with Hector Armstrang o' Harlaw."

Anne's heart sank, seeing Tom turn to her with excite-ment. "I know this Hector of Harlaw. I saved him from hanging when he was caught in a hot trod." Tom was grasping at his new destination like a drowning man grab-bing at flotsam.

"No." She shook her head. "I will not go another league."

Tom looked shocked and puzzled, Jock and Ormiston amused. Westmorland put on the patient scowl he saved for when someone said something unexpectedly insane.

She took her husband's hands. "We are fleeing to nowhere. Without our Maker's Grace we have nothing even if we win free." She was not going to spend her last free days running from one false sanctuary to the next.

"I know we are nothing without Him"—Tom shifted from foot to foot—"but I hoped to save a little something."

"It is hope that hangs a man who would otherwise die fighting." She compressed his hand as hard as she could. "We put ourselves in God's hands, then slipped through His fingers. I do not know why, but He let our cause fail. We cannot run from that, even if we flee as far as Baghdad."

He gave her his most stubborn look. "I must take this chance. The Ferniehurst Kerrs, the Johnstones, and Maxwell of Herries, all fought for Mary at Langside. I might bring together Mary's men on both sides of the border."

Ormiston came to Tom's elbow. "The West March will rise fer Maxwell. The Kerr o' Cessford, Moray's Warden in the Middle March, is at feud wi' his Ferniehurst cousins. Ferniehurst is ready for any ride that will do Cessford ill."

Anne assumed half the ruffians on the borders were always ready to ride against the other half, out of greed or boredom. She did not need to know the names. "You can go," she told Tom, "but I cannot run anymore. I want to find out what God has waiting for me." What use was running more if Mary had abandoned her?

Tom looked pained. She pulled him toward Jock of the Syde. "We can ask this Armstrong if I may stay a day or so." She did not expect it would take longer than that for pursuit to find her.

Jock of the Syde was telling Westmorland that he could not go into the Debatable Land wearing silk hose and a black Spanish doublet. The Earl looked down at his fashionable puffed and slashed sleeves. "I would not think a Scot could criticize my dress."

"Wi' all that silk, an' a gold-mounted sword, yew might better be dressed in a placard saying 'fugitive Inglis laird,' considering how few o' us Armstrangs ken letters."

Westmorland looked suspicious. "I would think that most of your relations in the Debatable Land are wanted by English wardens themselves."

"That they are, and there's not a rat's respeket for Inglis law among the lot o'em—but when the reward is high enough, the best o'em will turn honest wi'out warning. Some villains have no pride when a silver shilling is put in their palm."

Westmorland began to strip off his hose and doublet, while Jock did the same. Anne realized the stock thief had planned this trade in advance, since he was wearing a rough sheepskin coat instead of his fine jacket trimmed with wolf fur. Anne turned her back on the disrobing.

Tom asked, "Would you swear it was safe if I left my wife here, until I could send for her? Would the Elliots harm her?"

Jock swore straight and sideways, "The Elliots would na touch her. They live up the Dale, close by the Hermitage, an' ken what a lady is. We are the wild ones, living down here so near to the Inglis. She'd be as safe as a hundred stone statue o' Saint Bernard."

She inclined her head to thank the Scot. His invitation would have been more courtly if he had not been half bare-assed and half in Westmorland's hose. "Send for me when you can," she told Tom. "I have silver to pay for my stay." She spoke as warmly as she was able, expecting these might be the last words between them.

He kissed her and told her he would send for her. "I will find us a safe hole for the winter, where we can celebrate Christ's Mass in a real church."

Anne did not want a hole for the winter, but knew it was useless to say so. She watched the small parade march off; only Ormiston was mounted, and many of Tom's retainers had discarded their armor and trailed their lances. Tom himself looked strong, striding ahead, still fearless in retreat.

When he disappeared, the cord was cut. Through sleepy eyes she took her first long look at Liddesdale. A light powdering of snow topped the rumpled hills. By day the Dale did not seem the bleak and brutal place the ballads sang about. She thought that Scotland might be beautiful, were it not for the cold, the accommodations, and the natives.

Her host was seated on a stump, still struggling with Westmorland's Spanish doublet, which was small on him. He offered her the pick of the sheep in the pen for breakfast, with the happy generosity of a bandit giving away another man's mutton. She hesitated.

Jock added, "If ye will na eat stolen stock in the Dale, then ye should be prepared to fast."

Anne declined, not because the sheep were stolen, but because she was in no mood to butcher a lamb. Two days short of Christmas was a fine day for purging her body and reclaiming her soul.

Jock continued to admire his new hose and doublet, preening himself like a male bird in spring. The man seemed marvelously vain. Noting his sure movements and how his thighs bulged under the tight silk, she saw a man who might be impossible to handle, with only an ancient crone for chaperon. Considering how neatly he had stripped Westmorland, Anne decided to set a proper tone by asking, "Is there a church nearby?"

"A kirk?" Jock made it sound as if she wanted fresh peaches for her Christmas pie.

"Yes, for the Christians hereabouts."

"Christians? Na, we be mainly Armstrangs and Elliots here. There is no kirk nearby." He waved at the white hills. "In the *sheilings* there is a small shrine of the Virgin Mary that the shepherds use in summer."

"Where are these *sheilings?*" she asked.

"There"—Jock pointed—"just over that bare crest that catches the light."

The winter sun made the air sparkle, and Anne saw the spot where sunlight spilled along the ridge, bright against the frowning mass of the Cheviots. "I want to walk there."

"It is no walk for a lady, even in summer, and this were winter, as yer ladyschip may have noticed."

She looked down at her travel-worn gown. "Then I will not walk as a lady. Can your granny find suitable outfit for me to walk in?"

Jock said something incomprehensible to the crone, and Anne followed her into the cottage, where the old woman produced a homespun cloak and smock, along with rough leather boots. The homespun had a hair-shirt roughness against her skin, and Anne welcomed that part-penance. The boots felt strong and sturdy. She emerged to find Jock leaning on a bow, wearing his jacket trimmed with wolf fur.

She shook her head. "I am going alone."

"Yer will na find the shrine alone."

"It is Mary's shrine. If she wants me, she shall lead me there." Having not bent for Queen or husband, she would not bow for any Border ruffian.

The Border ruffian sat back on his stump, the bow across his knees. "I am no the worst thing ye might meet among the hills and bracken."

"I will risk the worst. Between the Queen of England and Regent Moray of Scotland, there is no more safety for me here than in the hills."

Anne turned and set off, using the bare crest and patch of sunlight for a compass. After so much riding in retreat, it was a wonder just to take long, stretching steps, to walk free and choose her own direction. She counted out a hundred paces, then another hundred, her boots crunching through thin layers of snow. If there was a stone cell waiting for her, she wanted to remember every free step.

At the edge of Jock's pasture a footpath wound upward, cutting under the bare ridges. When she was level with the ridge, she plunged into the bracken. Heather came up past her waist, roots tripping at her feet. The slopes were slick with frost and cut by deep gullies. Soon she could no longer see the sunlit crest, just stunted pines and jutting crags overgrown with lichen. She had lost her compass. Somewhere above her was the shrine, but when she tried to go uphill, huge rocks blocked her path. She lost the sun.

Not wanting to go back, Anne sat by a patch of bog, pulling thorns and burrs from her wool smock, hearing only her own labored breathing. Her fingers were white

with cold, their tips torn by frozen stones. In this stillness
was a peace of sorts. She no longer felt like a countess,
nor even like a married woman, but like a shamed girl
who had run off to hide.

Far off, under some pines, she saw a flickering where
lanes of sunlight slanted down into an open space. Anne
got to her feet and pushed through the tangle, hoping to
find her bearings. At the edge of the clearing she stopped.
Something was moving, making the branches sway and
the sunlight dance. Only fear was holding her back, so she
cast it aside and stepped into the light.

The movement came from a half-grown deer struggling
in a snare. She was a doe fawn, hanging from a noose
fixed to a springy sapling. One hind leg had got twisted
in the rope, keeping the deer from strangling quickly.
The other hind leg hung straight down, straining to reach
the ground. Anne could see where the rope had torn the
deer's delicate skin. Neck and noose were speckled with
blood.

Seeing Anne, the fawn froze suspended for a moment,
ribs heaving, head twisted sideways, watching her through
a big brown eye. Then in a flurry of limbs the deer struggled again, free legs kicking at the noose. Her hooves
could not cut the rope, and only opened more gashes in
her neck. As she fluttered and pulled, the sapling bobbed
above her, making a hole in the pine canopy and splashing
light across the clearing.

Anne ran to catch the deer while she was still struggling. She stood swaying under the young animal's weight,
feeling a heart beating faster than hers. How to free her?
Anne had no knife, and she was holding a strong, frightened creature in her arms. Her hands could not both hold
the deer and undo the noose, nor could she keep supporting the weight. She bowed her head and tore at the
bloody knot with her teeth. The fawn stopped struggling
and lay heaving in her arms, head next to hers. Anne could
feel wet panting on her cheek.

The knot gave and Anne knelt, laying the deer down on
the moss and needles. The animal relaxed, stretching out
its neck, doing nothing but breathing. Anne huddled over
the hurt creature, feeling useless, wishing she had water to

give. No knife. No water. But perhaps she could carry the
deer back to the hovel on her shoulders. Anne stood up
and looked along the slanting lines of light. The wane sun
was already sinking down the dale; she could follow it
back.

Anne glanced down at the deer, to gauge its weight. The
doe looked bigger than before; her white outlines ex-
panded and altered. Anne froze, frightened but unable to
look away from the transformation. While she watched,
the doe fawn turned human . . . becoming a half-grown
girl, with big soft eyes, long, strong limbs, and child's
breasts. Wearing only a fawn skin about her waist, the deer
child lay on the brown needles, breathing hard, looking up
at Anne. A red ring of torn skin circled her neck.

The child did not move any more than the deer had, but
Anne backed away, awed and terrified. Fear of the unknown and unnatural welled up inside her. What she had
done instinctively for a snared animal was not so easy to
do for a witch girl. Anne wanted to help, but was horribly
afraid.

With soft-padding steps a third body entered the clearing. It was the sheep-herding wolf. Compared to the half-
naked girl, the beast looked coal black—bigger and more
menacing than in the night, when Anne had been mounted
and among armed men. A strong staff would keep off the
boldest wolf, but she had not even brought a staff.

Too terrified to move, she let the beast trot past her, going straight for the girl. Ears pulled back, tail down, the
wolf sniffed the blood on the girl's neck, thrusting his
muzzle against her jaw. The strange child rose silently on
all fours, keeping her chin level with the animal's muzzle,
pushing against his snout. She seemed no longer the
frightened fawn, but instead a bitch cub greeting her litter
mate.

The wolf backed down, tucking his tail. The girl leaped
up onto two legs; in an instant she was at the edge of the
clearing, where she turned and stared at Anne. At that moment the child seemed most human, dropping her animal
guises. Anne saw in her only the wildness of a child, the
wildness of an imagination not knowing the confines of
adulthood.

"Wait," Anne pleaded, but the girl turned and ran, flicking off between the pines with the giant black wolf at her heels.

> But word is gane to the laird Scroope,
> In Bew Castle where that he lay—
> "The deer that yew hae hunted sae lang
> Is seen into the Waste this day."

BORDER FOLK BALLAD

Mother's Night

Anne knelt in the silence of the clearing, praying for God's Grace and Mary's guidance. The fawn girl's inhuman beauty made Anne fear for her soul as much as when she touched the crone's cards. Slowly sunlight crept away, and shadows rose out of the pines, but she did not leave the darkening woods until snow began to sift through the black boughs, wetting her cheek. Then she rose and walked down the dale, weary and hungry, hands torn by rocks and thorns.

By the sheepfold she saw a black knot of people huddled with their backs to the stones. They were most likely English, since Scots rode everywhere, counting walking a worse crime than horse theft. Drawing closer, Anne recognized the frightened faces of her people, Percy tenants fleeing the West March, following in her footsteps.

A cooking pot bubbled over a small fire. The better dressed ate bread and meat, while others watched. No one had touched the sheep. Jock o' the Syde sat on his stump, wearing Westmorland's gold-mounted sword and toying with his bow, tossing it from hand to hand.

Anne saw a white-haired woman tending the fire, working with quiet unconcern, ladling soup into small bowls for children. She had a long, formidable face, and a brisk, even manner. A heavy rosary hung about the woman's waist, and Anne guessed she had been a nun before they closed the convents. In the kettle Anne could see lumps of lard and dried nettle stalks floating in a barley broth too thin to be called soup. The thought of infants eating such swill sickened her.

She turned to Jock. "This morning you offered me a sheep. I want it now."

Jock shrugged.

Anne went over to the nun, telling her to pick out a sheep from the pen for the stew. The woman gave a grave nod, and several men leaped over the stones. Anne listened to them argue over which was the fattest, then she heard the bleating from the frightened victim, louder and more insistent, until it was cut short by a knife.

She did not want to think about killing or about eating. Instead she thought about a deer transformed into a girl; not a gaunt, terrified girl like these, desperate for barley broth, but a supernatural child with strong limbs and a wild, proud face. Anne sat down on a stone for some time, letting nothing intrude on her awe and foreboding.

Without warning, a sure hand placed a steaming bowl and crust of bread in her lap. Anne savored the smell of boiled meat. With her mouth watering, she tried to push the bowl away.

"No, my lady, we all must eat."

She felt the firm grip of the nun on her shoulder, bringing back her childhood, the smell of incense, processions of priests, white-robed children, the huge and bloody crucifix carried before the image of the Virgin. Anne remembered her own mother bending down to wash the feet of old beggar women. Anne's mother was a queenly woman, who wore gowns lined with marten's fur, with sleeves so wide that they trailed on the ground; but on Holy Thursday she poured perfumed water over old women's lame and withered feet. She would rub herbs into the open sores, dry each foot with cloth-of-gold, and kiss it tenderly. Then she would shuffle to the next pair of feet, without ever rising from her knees, while Anne trailed after her, carrying the heavy silver ewer of warm scented water. "How did you know me?"

"I saw you several times on the road to York, riding at the head of the march beside your husband and the banners."

So Anne ate, finding the meat hot and good. The bread was English. She studied the starved faces of her people, their mouths moving mechanically. Jock sat back, a sardonic look on his face. The crone was nowhere about.

Silence was broken by the beat of hooves on the sod, a clatter of stones, someone crying out. A small troop of Elliots cantered into the yard, carrying lances and bows, riding with careless agility into the crowd. People scattered, clinging to their soup bowls. Anne was surrounded by border hobbies, high-topped boots, and leather stirrups. Brutal faces shone above her in the firelight. Their leader, a crisp young felon with a hackbutt and a curled lip, called out to Jock, "Yew were told ta entertain no more Inglis."

Anne looked to Jock for some support, but the Scot only strummed his bow, saying, "These are no my guests."

The Elliot glanced at the blood on the stone where the sheep had been butchered. "They are eating yer sheep."

"These are no my sheep."

Elliots laughed. One younger one rode over and tipped the soup kettle with his lance, spilling the mess of meat and nettles over the stones. "Yer all ta be gone," announced the leader. "Back ta Ingland. Yer no wanted in Scotland."

The nun strode over to stand in front of his horse. "Young man, do you call yourself a Christian?"

"I call myself an Elliot."

"Well, these people are Christians, who only want to worship God as they will. For that crime nooses await them in England."

"That is no my problem," replied the Elliot. "My problem is ta get yew out o' Scotland."

Anne stood up. He seemed like a wanton boy, made godlike by a gun and a horse. "It is two days until Christmas. Surely you cannot turn us out now."

"Lady Anne." The Elliot tipped his lance. "I do no

mean to discomfort ye. Yew are free to go or remain. Unless some o' them are ladies an' lairds in clever disguise, they must go. As ye said, tomorrow is Christmas Eve. I aim to be drunk by tomorrow night, an' in kirk Christmas morning, so I must see my work done now."

The wretched people stared wide-eyed at Anne, seeing for the first time a countess in homespun. A woman flung herself at Anne's feet, dragging the boy beside her down to his knees. "Our lady, let us stay. Lord knows we are ancient tenants to your husband, holding in copy hold from his father and his father's father, but now we are utterly beggared. They hanged my oldest for wearing your husband's colors. He was a strong and handsome lad, good at Sunday games and at his letters; everyone loved him." She pulled her living son forward. "Don't let them take this one. Tell them one is enough from each family. There are so many others they could hang." The woman started sobbing and choking, and stopped making sense, but kept clinging to Anne's dress. The boy looked scared, but also stubbornly resentful. Anne guessed he had spent half his life being compared to his handsome, brainy older brother.

"Lady Anne." Even the Elliot looked touched. "Tell them to go. I am a man that abhors unnecessary murder, but the laws must be satisfied. If they do no leave Scotland, I will start hangin' them here."

The white-haired nun walked over to the kneeling lad, taking his hand, helping him to his feet. Then she did the same for his mother, prying her fingers off Anne's dress. Her voice came calm and soothing. "We know the way, and it is not a long walk. They cannot hang everyone, and those they do will sup with God." She started to sing the *"Adeste Fideles"* of Saint Bonaventura.

Anne stood rooted, watching the Elliots prod the others to their feet, pricking with their lance points, pushing with the butt ends.

The nun sang louder:

> *"O come, all ye faithful,*
> *joyful and triumphant;*
> *O come ye, O come ye to Bethlehem."*

Elliots escorted the people and their bundles back toward the border with the nun leading the frightened lad, still singing. Anne thought of the deer-child struggling in the snare.

> *"O come let us adore him,*
> *O come let us adore him,*
> *O come let us adore him . . ."*

"She's the bell sheep that leads the others." Jock sighed.

Anne sat down on his stump. "A bell sheep likely to be slaughtered."

"Da ye no ken the sacrifice?" asked Jock. "It has always been this way in hard times. Them that's called, goes. An' like she said, law cannot hang them all—though strict-minded judges ha'e been known ta try."

Anne put her head between her hands and cried, letting her whole body shake with racking sobs. Jock's arms circled her, but she did not care. She no longer cared about her honor or his touch. All she wanted was to cry until she had vomited up the stew in her stomach and could lie empty in the snow.

Jock led her into the hovel and set her down at the plank table. He poured her a mug of pale gold liquid from a small oak cask. "Here, drink." He forced the wooden mug between her fingers. " 'Tis the water o' life."

Anne lifted her shaking hands and sipped. It tasted like brandy, but with more bite. "I did want to go with them, but I did not dare."

Jock poured more into her cup. "Drink up, drink up, that's all there is to do for it. They will come for ye soon enough. Many's the time I thought of throwing my life away on a point o' honor, but were saved from such arrant stupidity by the wisdom o' Jock Barley Corn."

"Jock Barley Corn?" Anne was unfamiliar with the philosopher.

"In the cup," Jock tapped the mug. "We brew water o' life from malted barley. We cut him, flail him, mash him up, an' Jock Barley Corn gives his blood to warm and comfort us."

She stared at the heathen across the table. "It is not the

same with me. When we mounted up and rode south, I
promised my life to Christ. I was willing to die for the Old
Religion."

"The Auld Religion." Jock laughed.

"It may not matter to you, but it matters to many. We
wanted to keep the faith we were born and baptized in,
and not have to bow down to a queen in London town."

"Ye do no see me bowing to the Regent in Edinburgh,
and that is far nearer here than London. Would ye have
people getting their religion from Rome?"

She glared at him over her cup. "The Bishop of Rome
remembers us in his prayers, but as Pope he will not ex-
communicate Elizabeth." Rome preferred to deal directly
with London. "What were we to do?" she asked, drinking
more of Jock Barley's Blood. "London stripped silver off
the altars and the lead off the abbey roofs. They took the
nuns' gardens of herbs and flowers, the monks' hostels for
homeless travelers, the bells that break the night at Prime
and Matins. When Mary of Scotland was made prisoner,
and Tom was summoned to London to take a cell in the
Tower, we all rose up and marched south. People put
down plow, loom, and chisel to carry the Cross. It was a
grand thing to see; commons and gentry singing as one,
lords and cobblers marching together—springtime in November." She drank more from her mug, watching the firelight dance in the corners. Images flickered before her;
empty villages, ruined churches turned to sheepfolds, old
forests cut down for charcoal, coal mines and alum plants,
armies of beggars on the roads.

Jock shook his head. "Now ye ken what comes o' fool-
ishness. Half of them marching behind yew expected a
new age wi' no lairds, rents, and fines, and everyone being
brothers. I ken the way farmers think. But lairds and commons are no alike, else the Elliots would have sent yew
packin' too."

"I would have gone with them, but I was afraid." She
let him refill her cup.

"O' course ye were afraid. I have come uncommon
close ta dyin' myself, and wished ta heaven some other
poor sod was in my place."

"No, it is not that way. Ever since Yorkshire I have not

felt God's hand nor heard Mary's voice. I was afraid to die without Grace, with only my sins before me."

"Ye do na seem an overly sinful lass. Did ye no confess at the shrine?"

"I prayed today, but not at the shrine." She said no more about sinning. Barley blood was making her dizzy, and she did not mean to bang tails with some handsome bandit just because she was alone, and sad, and drunk. She was sure this pagan knew all about the demon child in the wood.

Instead of finding the shrine, she had saved a wood demon from a snare. Now she was the one snared. Anne was sure that saving the girl had pushed her soul onto the knife's edge. Good impulses could lead to evil ends. She and Tom had rebelled for the best of reasons and brought ruin on themselves and on anyone faithful to them. She drank more of Jock Barley Corn's blood, thinking of the Earl of Sussex hanging Christians for Christmas. "I will go to the shrine on the morrow." It was not a promise to Jock, but a vow to the Virgin who awaited her on the ridge.

Anne awoke late in the morning with a miserable conscience and a worse headache, hoping that Jock Barley Corn and his cousin of the Syde had not got the better of her in the night. She wanted only grief to contend with, and not shame as well.

The old granny was back, spooning coarse breakfast porridge from an iron pot hanging over the heath. Anne remembered Ormiston's promise of plain food and a poor roof. That one promise the Scots seemed keen to keep—breakfast was barley porridge, with prunes and a pinch of salt. As she ate, Anne watched the old woman hang mistletoe and holly over the hearth, and among the herbs in the rafters. Had she not known her as a witch, Anne would have thought the crone was getting ready for Christmas. She had always supposed that witches spent their spare hours stealing corpses or suckling weasels and bats, but this witch seemed to have no duties except to please herself—it was Jock who tended the sheep, cut peat, and kept the fire. The old woman left as soon as her Christmas trimming was done.

Not until well into the short afternoon did Anne decide

to tackle the ridge again, whittling an oak staff before setting out. As she walked, she noticed the wolf behind her; the beast that herded sheep and ran with demon girls in the woods. She was glad to have her staff. Anne did not expect an attack, but did not want to be at the animal's mercy either.

She followed the footpath up to the base of the ridge, and was once more waist-deep in bracken, blocked by gullies choked with broken rocks. The deep woods and bleak crags would have been eerie even in summer sunlight; on a wet winter day they were a damned landscape, even though the morrow was Christmas morning. She advanced and retreated, looking for a trail that led to the top, but always being turned about. Several times she took long rests, then began again, determined to reach the one bit of holy ground in this wilderness.

At dusk she was standing in a small meadow, studying the ridge, trying to see by fading light where the bare expanse came closest to her. Behind her came the clop of hooves, and a familiar voice: "Lady Anne, it be surprising an' pleasing to find ye alone."

She whirled about. Ormiston was there on horseback, looking dirty and tired; every bit the border ruffian, his beard unkept, lance at rest, raffish boots thrust through rough stirrups.

"Why are you here?" asked Anne. "You were with my husband and Hector Armstrong of Harlaw."

"Hector o' Harlaw prooved ta be a greedy traitor, grasping an' thieving even for an Armstrang. He means to shop yew husband to the Earl o' Moray, giving me not a groat's worth o' profit."

"May God have mercy," Anne gasped. Expecting treason did not lessen the shock.

"Aye, he may"—Ormiston rolled his eyes—"but I hope not on Hector o' Harlaw. Ye may be sure I will not direct any more valuable fugitives to his door."

Anne stood still, feeling the cold and coming dark, thinking of her husband. Tom was captive, Henry a traitor; her family had disowned her. One by one, everyone dear to her would be hunted out, forced to abjure her or die. She could barely stand such savage sorrow.

Ormiston ran on, though Anne hardly heard him. "The treachery does not stop there. The Elliots are going to sit tight in thar holes, telling Scrope they will no oppose a Christmas trod. Inglis riders are expected in the Dale by nightfall, looking for me an' ye."

"And you came to warn me?" She was startled, even touched by the unnecessary gesture.

"After a fashion." Ormiston brightened. "In my deepest despair I remembered the money yew mentioned to yer husband. If I am to have an ounce of profit fer my labors, it has to come from the purse yer carrying."

Anne realized she was being robbed by this smooth-talking, over-armed brigand. Never having been robbed before, she felt outraged, also stupid and inept in this novel social situation. Her staff was a thin stick to put against his lance, sword, and brace of pistols, so she said something silly and graceless about him not harming a woman.

"Perhaps I would, and perhaps I would not," Ormiston observed, "but neither o' us wants to know for sure. Do we? So for both our goods, give me the silver, an I'll be off. We need not stand here arguing till Lord Scorpe's riders arrive."

In pique and anger she threw the purse on the ground, watching the Lord of Ormiston spear it with his lance. What did silver matter? Elizabeth's warden was coming tonight. Not even giving her Christmas.

"An' now yer rings."

"Rings?"

"The ones shining on yer fingers." He pointed helpfully with his lance.

Standing there, hardly believing the command, she saw the black wolf glide out of the pines. The beast's jaws opened in a carnivorous grin, showing a fleshy pink tongue and sharp white fangs. Panting in short white puffs, he approached, displaying no special excitement.

Ormiston followed her gaze, cursing when he saw the wolf. He kicked his horse about, to position himself for a charge, speaking calmly and clearly to the oncoming animal. "Jock, I would have yew keep yer pointed nose out o' my affairs. I did not bring any silver bullets today, but

I have the fixings for 'em." He rattled her purse in his belt, lowering his lance.

The wolf snarled and danced sideways, making Ormiston's hobby shy. Ducking under the waving lance, the black beast snapped at the horse's heels, driving the hobby like a frightened lamb, letting the horseman know he was at the mercy of his bucking mount. Ormiston clawed helplessly at the pistol in his left boot top.

"Stop!" screamed Anne. Sick with rage, she damned the heartless, graceless, witless, thieving Scots. Finding they paid no attention, she ripped at the metal circling her fingers, flinging the rings one at a time at the horseman. "There!" she yelled at Ormiston. "You took my husband, my mare, my money; why should you men leave me anything?"

Hands bare, she stalked off down the Dale.

Before reaching the hovel, she heard the wolf padding after her, but did not bother to look back. When she had crossed into Scotland, Anne thought she had nothing. In a pair of days the thrifty Scots had neatly shown her that was not the case; stripping her of every valuable she had brought over the border, all with hardly even a harsh word. She had nothing left but the linen shift beneath her borrowed homespun smock; all she had got in return was barley porridge, barley blood, and English mutton.

Finding the shrine would have been victory enough. Kneeling on sacred ground, she might have made the only peace that mattered. Even that had been denied her. If Ormiston could be believed, Border riders were coming for her that night.

It was dark when she reached the croft. Anne could not see the wolf. The crone had not come back, and the cottage lay frigid and empty. She sat shivering at the plank table—gaps in the gray wood looked like crevices into an icy northern hell.

The door opened behind her. Jock of the Syde swaggered in, wearing Westmorland's clothes, his fur-trimmed jacket, and a thin smile. She shrank back, remembering how Ormiston had called the wolf "Jock." Now she was certain that the man was a warlock, a shapechanger or *loupgarou*. His handsome, animal attraction reeked of sorcery. If the old woman was a witch, here was her devil: the black-clothed horseman, booted and spurred, with sword at his side.

"No need to shy from me." He laid his fist on the table. "I have something for yew." He opened his hand. Lying in his palm was her gold wedding ring. "It was no easy task to get this back."

"It must have been hard, running with the ring in your teeth." She made no move to take it from his palm.

Jock laughed. "That was no the worst of it." Turning his hand over, he spun the ring on the table. Anne watched it whirl about in a golden circle and then lie still.

Picking it up, she slipped it on her finger. Familiar metal made her feel more married, even though Scots had taken Tom away.

Jock lit a fire, fixing her porridge and fresh oat crackers. Anne ate, no longer denying her hunger. It was easy to see why the Scots got on so famously on this abominable diet. Tramping about in the cold and muck made the blandest food unbearably attractive. She fed her body until the bowl was empty. Now there was naught to do but wait for Lord Scrope.

Her host poured three mugs of barley blood. "Ye have heard Ormiston, the Inglis are coming tonight. Hector Armstrang o' Harlaw has betrayed us, an' the Elliots plan to stay drunk in their holds. I can hardly blame 'em." He lifted his mug. "If drink alone could save us, I would dedicate the night to serious study o' the bottom o' a cup. But drink be a deceiver. We must put our faith in Mother's Night." Anne did not touch her mug. She knew that heathens celebrated Christmas Eve as Mother's Night, but she had never seen the ritual.

At midnight the crone returned, and Anne retreated to the straw mattress. The old woman lit candles and a bundle of oak roots. Light danced about the room. Anne saw Jock kneel before his granny. She watched the crone take salt from a mouse skull around her neck and place it on Jock's long tongue. The witch's words were still impenetrable, so Anne only understood the rituals Jock repeated, but these were wild lays, pagan enough to damn a hundred souls:

> *"Turn the wheel,*
> *winter ta summer;*
> *Turn the wheel,*
> *darkness ta light.*
> *Old Black King ta be*
> *the Bright Child,*
> *Sun be born fram the Womb o' Night."*

There was more of it, horribly heretical, making Anne
feel all the more lost. It was near the longest night of the
year, and she spent it listening for Lucifer's footsteps. By
midnight she was exhausted from waiting for night riders
to come, or for Satan to arrive dressed as a stinking goat
or giant toad. She fell into a fitful sleep.

Again Anne awoke in the Hour of the Wolf, but this
time it was Jock who shook her shoulder. "Listen to the
howling in the hills; my cousins say the Inglis are coming."

Anne could hear the long, keen wailing, but the language of the wolves meant nothing to her. She assumed
Jock o' the Syde found it more familiar than English. He
helped her off the bed, then shoved the mattress aside. The
crone came over and began to brush furiously at the floor
beneath with a broom. It seemed a damned odd time to
clean under the mattress, even with English lords expected.

A clatter of hooves came from outside. Anne's fear
made it sound like a hundred horses. She heard the yips
and yelps of a dog pack as well. Dogs spoke to her plainer
than wolves—whoever was coming had come to hunt.

She saw Jock lean down, find a ring hidden in the dirt,
and pull back a trap, revealing a raw hole as cozy as an
open grave. By the light of the crone's candle Anne could
see it was not just a pit or root cellar, but a timber-braced
tunnel, showing more care in its construction than the
whole rest of the hovel.

"Neat, is it no?" Jock grinned. "This croft has been
burned down more times than Armstrangs can count up ta,
but we always had this tunnel ta build anew on."

Heavy fists beat at the barred door.

"Now ye must decide. Either yew come with us, or ye

wait for Scrope's riders to break down the door. There be
no third choices."

No one gave her a choice that mattered. The men outside would drag her back to England and bury her behind
walls, but Jock was asking her to enter the earth at once.
The hammering grew louder. She tried to tell her shaking
self that this was the body—what they did to it was not
important, all that mattered was her spirit. But she found
the fear of what they would do too terribly real.

Jock eyed her by quivering candlelight. "Ye may think
that martyrdom will be holy and wonderful; well, it will be
plain dirty an' boring. They will keep yew in coarse
clothes an' a clammy cell, livin' on poor food an' worse
water. When it pleases, some well-fed fellow in fine
breeches will come, askin' ye to recant. If yew will no say
what they want to hear, they can keep ye behind walls till
ye die o' cold an' loneliness. Or one fine day a priest not
to your likin' will lead ye out into the sunlight, an' march
ye up ta a scaffold, askin' ye politely to put yer head on
a block, so some big villain can chop at your neck. All fer
the edification of a crowd o' churls that yew would not
normally care to be so familiar wi'."

Anne knew he was right. Elizabeth would grant her no
victories, not even small ones. Staying would prove nothing to anyone but herself, and she no longer had faith in
herself. She had listened to Mad Anne, sheltered with pa-
gans, saved a witch girl in the woods, but never made her
peace with Mary.

Jock held out his hand, like the Lord of the Dance offering her his arm. Anne took it, and descended into the
timbered pit; rough walls rose around her, cool, damp,
reeking of earth. She heard Jock prop the mattress atop the
trap, then pull the door closed.

Clammy skin sweated beneath her smock. There was
nothing to follow but the crone's candle doing a drunken
dance down the passage. Light bounced off the dirt and
wood, turning the old woman into a thin silhouette. Jock
hurried her on from behind.

The shaft was mercifully short—its far end part blocked
by black branches. As Anne emerged, dead twigs plucked
at her, clinging to her dress, raking her cheek. She pushed,

squirmed, and stumbled into the open, finding herself in a gully beyond the sheepfold beside a toppled oak. Waiting in the blackness was the old woman, her candle set on the fallen oak. Lord Scrope's men, horses, and dogs were ungodly close.

Jock pushed past her. " 'Tis no time to tarry; they are burning the croft." Anne looked and saw flames leaping up beyond the lip of the gully, flickering red in the oak's dead branches, reflected from a fire above and behind them. Dogs howled. Sheep stampeded down the gully.

In terror mixed with amazement she watched the old woman toss aside shawl, dress, and smock. It was an incredible time to disrobe, but the old woman did it, as calmly as if this were her New Year's bath. Anne stared at the absolute image of a naked witch, a white-haired skeleton with sagging, flopping breasts, wearing only a mouse skull hanging from a thread about her withered neck.

The man at her side thrust something soft into Anne's hands. "Hurry, put this on afore the dogs sniff us oot." Anne saw she was holding a dress made out of light tanned leather that felt like doeskin. She looked at Jock, shocked to see him pulling off his own hose and doublet, stripping down, keeping only the jacket trimmed with wolf fur.

"Do as we do," Jock insisted. "Take off yer clothes and put this on. It's yer only escape."

The world was going mad—becoming a black place, filled with leaping flames and naked bodies. Rigid with fear, she let Jock cut away her smock and shift. Then, flushed by shame and exertion, she struggled into the soft doeskin. Paying no heed to her nakedness and distress, Jock dropped to all fours before the crone.

The witch started to coo over him, her voice rising into a high, weird keening. While Anne watched wide-eyed, Jock became the wolf. His curved nails turned to claws; hair sprouted to cover him, with the wolfskin jacket blending into the ruff on his back and shoulders. His triangular face turned pointed. Fangs grew down from his jaw.

Anne wanted to cry out, but the transformation gripped her throat. She could no longer speak. Her neck got longer and her legs wobbled, unable to support her. Forgetting

Jock, she fell forward. The arms she threw out to catch herself hit the ground with hooves instead of hands. Fear surged anew through her heart and body, but it was a deer's fear and a doe's body, built for running. The pack's baying terrified her more than hell ever had, and her hoofed feet wanted to dash off.

From the croftyard came a hunter's view halloo and the clamor of dogs let off the leash. She could no longer hold her new body; with a crash and a leap she was off, sailing over the bracken. Anne managed one frightened look over her shoulder, down her long tawny back. The crone had disappeared. In her place a small gray mouse scampered up the oak log, vanishing among the branches.

Terrified by the barking hounds and the animal body that bore her, Anne could not think fast enough. Four sprinting legs and cloven feet fled in pure white panic, leaping hedges, dodging pines, going up the one path she knew, running for the bare ridge and the shrine. Heather brushed past her shoulders. Her flanks felt the wet snow and earth thrown up by her forelegs. In an instant she was into the black belt of trees and gullies that had turned her back in human form.

The deep clefts and slick streambeds no longer stopped her. She soared from bank to boulder, skipping over fallen trees, going up rocky slopes at a run. A few fast heart-beats, and she was through the great mass of black pines and broken ground, bursting onto the open ridge.

Anne took a dizzying look back. The burning croft was a spark of fire far below. The ridge and upper reaches of the dale were lit by the first gray light of Christmas morn-ing. Darkness filled the hollows. A black shadow glided at her heels, brining on another burst of panic before she rec-ognized the wolf.

Dogs bounded out of the tree line. With the stark clarity of fear she could see huge, misshapen heads, excited grins, and white teeth. Her deer's heart imagined their hot breath and raking claws. Redoubling her speed, she ran on to the crest of the ridge, blind to anything but the dogs behind her.

At the top she stopped, checking her frightened hooves in horror. The ridge dropped off into a deep chasm, bottomless in the gray light. She could only turn and run along the narrowing ridge toward the mud and timber shrine, where the ground thinned, then fell away.

She heard another hunter's view halloo. Behind the dogs emerged men mounted on Border horses. Reaching the shrine, she dashed about the enclosure, looking for a way down. Anne had to restrain her legs or they would have flung her into space and down into the defile, anything to escape the dogs. Stricken, she cowered behind the shrine, watching Jock turn to face the pack. The dogs scrambled up and stood barking in a ragged half-circle, held at bay by the wolf's bare fangs. They could only come one at a time up the narrow path, and Jock was a hundredweight of wolf, half again as big as the best of them.

Men and horses mounted the slope, catching up to the dogs. Huntsmen let fly with a fusillade from the saddle, firing their horse pistols at the wolf. Bullets kicked up dirt around and behind the black beast, but he paid no heed, still snapping at the dogs.

A captain wearing a breastplate and steel cap pushed his way through the press.

Anne thought, I know this man, recognizing cousin Crookback Darce, fellow conspirator and betrayer, who had turned her away three days before. His cunning eyes examined the shrine. Men were reloading, a hard feat on horseback. Mastering her fear, she forced her cloven feet to move, stepping into clear view.

Darce stared her over, eyes narrowing. Then he yelled at his men, calling them fools, whoresons, and worse. "We are here on Queen's business, not to flush deer and bang at wolves. Get those dogs turned around. Get them on the right scent." Shamefaced men leaped off their mounts and started slashing at the pack with dog whips, sending them yelping back toward the belt of trees.

Anne crouched by the shrine, heart pounding with joy and fright, watching them disappear down the hill, follow-ing the progress of the hunt by the points of torchlight moving up the dale. She stayed crouched until the Christ-mas sun rose over the Cheviots, breaking through the gray day, splashing the ridge with light.

As the light fell on her, Anne felt her body changing.

Her deer's hair receded, leaving only bare limbs and the doeskin dress covering her torso and hips. She looked down and saw hands gripping the rock. Long blond hair fell in her face. She rose, shivering, to her feet, chilled by morning, shaken by the night.

Downslope from her, Jock sat on his haunches. All that remained of the wolf was a fur-trimmed jacket that did not even cover his naked buttocks. He fingered fresh bullet holes in the leather, poking a finger through them and wagging it on the other side. Then he called over his shoulder to her. "My lady, how are yew wi' a needle? My coat is in sore need o' mending."

Anne ignored him, feeling the cold Christmas wind cut through her thin skin dress, stabbing into her intestines, closing round her heart. Choosing magic over martyrdom cut her off from the Christmas miracle dawning around her. She edged over to the front of the shrine. The ridge fell right away on either side, and she was not so sure-footed as the deer body had been.

The shrine was a simple hollow space with three walls, a roof, and an earthen floor. A crucifix over the entrance and a painted image of the Virgin at the altar symbolized the comfort Anne had cast aside. She took a cautious step up to the threshold, knowing the damned were unable to enter sacred ground, held back by the invisible arm of un-alterable law. Cold wind whipped at her, chilling her bare feet.

She stepped again; nothing stopped her. The walls of the shrine blocked the bitter wind. Overwhelmed with relief, she fell to her knees before the altar, praying for forgive-ness, pleading to the Virgin to please take her back. With eyes closed she knelt, smelling the damp dirt, oily wood, and the wax from hundreds of burned candles.

No sign came to her. Doves cooed in the low eaves, and morning sun moved through the entrance. Her knees ached. Cold stiffened her joints, numbing her legs, but she accepted the pain, repeating over and again:

> "Hail Mary! Full of grace,
> The Lord is with thee;
> Blessed art thou among women,

And blessed is the fruit of thy womb, Jesus.
Holy Mary, Mother of God,
Pray for us sinners,
Now, and at the hour of our death. Amen."

Dove wings fluttered over her, but she did not open her eyes until she heard the soft voice of the Virgin. For the first time since Yorkshire, Mary spoke to her. Anne looked up, seeing first a pair of dirty bare feet. The Virgin herself stood between Anne and the altar, surrounded by light and doves. She wore a fawn skin around her waist, and looked down with young girl's eyes, the marks of a braided rope still on her slender neck. She said in a small, solemn voice, "Anne, ye never left the Auld Religion."

FEAST OF LIGHT

(Twelfth Night to May Eve)

Feast of Light—From Winter Solstice through Spring Equinox the ritual centerpiece is the return of the sun's light from the long winter night. Hanukkah, Yule, and Christmas secretly or openly celebrate the rebirth of the sun; New Year's, Twelfth Night, Brigid, Candlemas, Eostar, and Easter all glory in the waxing of the reborn light.

MARY   *Peace, you rogue, no more o' that. Here*
       comes my lady; make excuses wisely . . .

FOOL   *Wit . . . put me into good fooling! Those*
       wits that think they have thee do very oft
       prove fools; and I that am sure I lack thee
       may pass for a wise man. For . . . "Bet-
       ter a witty fool than a foolish wit"

                          —SHAKESPEARE, *Twelfth Night*
                          Act I, scene v

Twelfth Night

Of all the transformations and revelations Anne had en-
dured, this last was the most wrenching. Losing lands and
title, fleeing to Scotland, forced to live on oatmeal—being
turned into a wild doe—were all trivial incidents compared
to Mary appearing as an urchin huntress. Only in Scotland
could God's Mother have filthy feet. But Anne could not
doubt Mary. The Mother of God is all women in one. To
say she could not be young, wild, and untamed was as
false as saying she could not be old or with child.

Above all, Anne firmly rejected reason, letting faith and
senses rule. The Goddess before her was real, no matter
how unreasonable she seemed. Reason snared the Reformers into denying God even had a mother, claiming the only
rational Deity was faceless, eternal, remote, and
absolute—a God whose only fixed human attribute was a
penis. They defended these conclusions so logically that
Anne was mortally sick of hearing the arguments.

"Anne, I'm Mother of all, or I'm Mother a none." The
girl spoke gracefully, like a serious Scots child who has
learned her lessons by heart. But her grimy feet began to
fidget.

Kneeling before the young girl—knees pressed in the
dirt, with the cold Christmas wind howling around the tiny
shrine—Anne understood how trivial human affairs were
to Mary. What did Our Lady care about Pagan or Christian? Reformer or Catholic? She was as much the Mother
of Elizabeth as she was the Mother of Anne. In this hour
of triumph—with Mary speaking to her in the flesh—Anne
felt very much humbled. She no less than the Reformers

had tried to limit Mary, saying, "Our Divine Lady must be noble, chaste and married, Catholic and Christian." She must, in short, be like me.

Awed by Mary's tangible presence—and her own shortcomings—Anne could only ask, "Why have you come to me?"

Mary amused herself by doing a child's dance, not in the least awed by speaking to Anne. *"Yew must have prayed to me near a million times."*

"So have millions of others."

"An' how many of them see me, an' answer my call?" She touched the red line around her neck.

Anne bowed her head. "But what would you have me do?"

Mary gave her a look of mischievous amazement. *"Why all I ever ask is fer yew to find me in yer heart."*

Anne's heart was full—it was her stomach that felt empty. She stammered out thanks, assuring Mary of her love, but . . .

Rapture had not blinded Anne to the real world. Not yet anyway. It was all very well for the Mother of God to play at being a hill lass in doeskins, with lecherous wolves for company. Anne had no training for such a life. She could not live on bracken and field mice. "What am I to do?"

"Yew should be true ta me." The wild girl's attention wavered, showing a child's unconcern for future problems or weighty plans. She whistled her doves to her.

Of course, but . . .

"An', yew should no fear the riders." Birds settled on her bare shoulders, hopping and cooing with excitement, anticipating flight.

"Which riders?" Anne thought at once of Scrope and Darce.

"The ones outside." Cloaked in doves, the holy child smiled like a girl who has caught an adult in yet another absurdity.

Anne heard horses snort and stamp. Glancing over her shoulder, she saw mounted hobbies crowding the entrance to the shrine—their breath misting in the morning cold. A dozen riders waited outside, armed and booted, with lance butts resting in their left stirrups.

There was a flutter of wings behind her. Shocked and frightened, she turned back to Mary, seeing only a hollow shrine. The Virgin and her doves were gone.

Anne had to give herself to the horsemen. She murmured a short prayer, crossing herself with shaking hands; then she stepped out of the shrine into the womb of morning, holding the tattered doeskin dress tight about her. *"An', yew should no fear the riders—the ones outside."* Well enough for Mary to say. Anne might as easily not fear the pox. They were men who went to some length to be fearful—carrying horse pistols and wicked-edged metal. Their leader was a lanky, hard-bitten ruffian with a nasty, drooping mustache. His beard was salted with gray, and he wore a blue plaid cloak over his armor, pinned by a sunburst badge.

A smart young ensign bore a laird's banner—*gules with chevron argent, charged with three molets gules*—a red field with a white chevron carrying three red stars. These were Kerrs, blood enemies of the Percys. The sunburst was a Kerr badge, and they carried their laces on the left, Kerr-handed.

Jock was standing uselessly to one side, legs bare, shifting from foot to foot, wearing the sheepish grin of a beggar caught with a lamb in his jacket.

The tall Scot on horseback looked down at her. "Lass, yon Armstrang absolutely swears yew are an Inglis countess. I hope yew do no mean ta disappoint us."

Mary had said not to fear them, and the outlaws already knew her name. "Yes, I am Anne Somerset Percy, Countess of Northumberland." The title sounded strange on her lips. Shivering in her deerhide, she felt like plain Anne of the Lost.

A satisfied grin broke across the Scot's craggy face. "A merry Christmas morning, yer ladyschip. I am Laird Thomas Karr o' Ferniehurst, come ta take ya ta Christmas dinner." There were smirks all around. Riders began to chaff Jock. "Armstrang, what was the lady repenting in yon shrine? . . . We thought an Armstrang's pike was shaped specially for sheep. . . . Tell us at least how an Inglis countess tastes."

"Like a Karr lass, anly sweeter." The wolfman was not overly worried by so many armed men.

Lord Thomas of Ferniehurst glared about, red-faced. "Enough shameless yapping—stop or I'll stop yer filthy mouths for ye." He pulled the cloak of blue plaid off his back, using his sunburst badge to pin it around Anne's shoulders. "Yer ladyschip will find we Karrs ken our manners—anly a witless Armstrang would strip a countess doon ta her doeskin. I swear ta host you like a Scots knight hosts a lady."

They brought up a small, mean border hobby for her to ride. Laird Kerr's Christmas dinner could not be refused. She was already wearing the bandit laird's plaid, and had no more say about it than a stolen mare gets. Despite all the knight-and-lady nonsense, these were Northumberland's ancient enemies—Tom had hung his share of Kerrs—and the Ferniehurst Kerrs were the worst of a sad lot, outlawed by their own relation, Walter Kerr of Cessford, Scots warden of the Middle March.

She wished at least to give Jock a good-bye, but the riders closed around her, herding her downslope. Twisting in her saddle, she saw the lone Armstrong standing on the windswept ridge alongside Mary's shrine—hands thrust inside his wolfskin coat. He did not shiver, or seem to feel the cold. Keen animal eyes met hers, like a wolf looking into the fold, eyeing what he could not have.

Her heartless horse nipped at her leg. Laird Thomas of Ferniehurst reached over and took her reins, guiding her away from the hill. "Have yew a fondness for that light-fingered Armstrang?"

Anne straightened in her saddle, determined to play the countess and not appear the least bit common to these Kerrs—no mean role to act, costumed in a man's cloak and tattered deerhide.

"He was of help to me." From her tone Jock might have been a boy who'd held her stirrup.

"We ken that. Armstrangs help themselves to whatever comes up the Dale. Great pests they are, as bad as Turnbulls." Personally Anne could not imagine worse pests than the Kerrs. She did not look forward to being passed about among outlaw nobility for as long as she lasted, like a plundered bit of lace.

They rode single file deeper into the dale. Liddesdale was one of Scotland's truly terrible places, stark, forbidding country, untouched by the wheel. Anne had not seen so much as a wagon rut since leaving England. Such primitive isolation allowed brigands like Armstrongs, Elliots, and Nixons to live in immunity less than a day's ride from English law. There was no hope of finding them in these barren hills and bracken—not if they meant to be lost. Even these Kerr cutthroats looked nervous. It was easy to imagine Elliots among the high rocks, licking their lips and counting the Kerr lances; unless like the young Elliot had claimed yesterday, they were sitting hung over in kirk listening to Christmas sermon.

After an hour or two of bleak plodding, they came on a small glen. Through a screen of skeletal limbs Anne saw square stone walls crowning a bluff above water. It was an angular border keep of heavy brown sandstone topped by wooden galleries.

"The Hermitage." Ferniehurst nodded. "Queen Mary herself came ta this *torr* ta tend the Earl o' Bothwell, when he was stabbed three times by an Elliot he'd foolishly taken fer dead."

Anne knew Bothwell had repaid Mary's kindness with rape, carrying her off to Dunbar Castle and forcing himself on her—Ferniehurst tactfully did not mention that. The Hermitage had been a black Douglas keep; its dungeons still had a terrible reputation, and the thick, gloomy fortress seemed half-sunken in its earthworks, weighted down with menace. A furlong off lay the ruins of the abbey that gave the keep its name. Even the Kerr commented on the coldness of the place. "This is near the worst corner of Liddesdale, godless country crawling wi' Elliots, an' haunted by the ghosts o' its victims."

Above the Hermitage the hills were steep, trackless folds, cut by deep gorges, studded with standing stones. A land unblessed since Creation—not the place Anne would have picked to spend the Lord's birthday. Ferniehurst, however, found the country increasingly to his liking. "Now we leave the worst o' the Elliots behind. These are

Douglas lands. I have no special feud wi' Douglas, though
he holds fer the King, an' I fer the Queen." The villain
was full of such infectious patter, pointing out stark
landmarks—Queen's Mire, Swire Knowe, Tinlee Stones,
Dod Rig. By stages Anne accepted things for what they
were. Exhaustion dulled her apprehension. She was alive.
It was Christmas Day. If she must be some man's prisoner,
then why not this Kerr's? She dreaded being dragged to
his lair, but even a bear pit was better than being perpet-
ually in the saddle.

The day warmed. The brook they were following ran
into the Teviot. Ferniehurst pointed with his lance: "The
far bank belongs ta the Scotts—cousins who we were long
at feud wi', but now think better of." Scotland was not so
much a nation as a collection of quarreling neighbors and
relations.

Beyond the Teviot loomed another grim border keep, a
fortified manor with a round blackened tower attached to
one corner—walls and roof were stuffed with turf to make
them fireproof. For good or ill, here was her destination,
where she would find out how much she was a guest, and
how much a captive. "Branxholm"—Lord Ferniehurst
gave a negligent wave—"home ta Laird Walter Scott o'
Buccleuch."

Anne had reason to know the names. In the Young Harry's time Percy horsemen had burned Branxholm to the
ground, paying back the Scotts and renegade Kerrs for
raids into England. If these Border reivers wanted revenge
on her, there was nothing to stop them from indulging.

A particularly bold felon met them at the gate, wearing
sheepskin jacket, lumpy hose, a long rapier, and a tartan
cloak pinned at the shoulder with a crescent broach. His
black bonnet was pulled down to nearly cover his eyes,
but something in the fellow's gait was familiar. He made
a mocking bow, addressing Anne in exaggerated brogue,
"Wal-come ta Branxholm, m'lady."

Anne jerked her reins back, gasping as she saw his face.
It was Westmorland.

Lord Charles Neville was nearly the last man she would
have expected to greet her at the entrance to this outlaw's
hold. He swept the feathered bonnet off his brow, stepping

back to show off his Scouts outfit. "What do you think? A complete costume—all it lacks is the itch."

"What of Tom?" If Westmorland had not been taken, Tom too might be safe.

The Neville grimaced, as though the question spoilt his entrance. "Betrayed by those thieving Armstrongs. Harlaw separated us and took your husband. I am trying a rescue, rallying our own Forsters and whatever Scots are willing to cut their cousins' throats."

Anne slipped from the saddle, shaking after the long ride, overwhelmed to find someone here she could half trust. Westmorland helped her down. "Gawd, woman, do you know you're wearing a deerskin? Your costume makes mine seem half-civilized."

He led her through a gate of oak baulks, bound and studded with iron, introducing her to the laird, Sir Walter Scott of Buccleuch, and his small army of retainers and kinsmen. The men's faces were all a blur of beards and bonnets. Buccleuch, an amiable ogre, took pity on her, turning her over to his lady, Janet of Branxholm. Lady Janet was friendly and formidable, many years older than Anne, with the queenly beauty of a worldly-wise courtesan. She hustled Anne upstairs to dress. Half-frozen and exhausted, Anne wanted only to collapse, but everyone expected her to endure Christmas dinner first.

Lady Janet treated Anne like a familiar and expected guest—loading her with gifts, speaking intimately in French—making Anne imagine she had somehow visited the lady of Branxholm before. A strange absurdity. She immediately presented Anne with a serving girl. "This is Alison Scott, a poor but dear relation I have been saving just for you. She is a girl of great potential. Keep her for as long as you have need, and you will never regret it."

The girl grinned and curtsied. She was a slim redhead who spoke no French but seemed to understand that she was being given to Anne. Lady Janet ran on about Alison's "special" qualities, and Anne did her best to follow. "This girl speaks some English and a smattering of Gaelic. You'll find her head stuffed with old stories, but not a particle of formal education—I have been hoping she would

get that from you. You are really the only woman I would
trust her with."

Young Alison got Anne through dinner. The girl was
just fifteen, full of exuberant spirits, with a child's enthusiasm for pomp and dressing up. She decked out her limp
countess doll in Spanish silk, Flemish brocade, and stolen
English woolens—all the time encouraging her with excited patter. "Aye, yer lookin' passin' beautiful, m'lady.
Queen Mary herself would be green." Having to be held
up and dressed by a pretty young girl made Anne feel very
old and plain.

The feast was a mad parody of a genteel Christmas dinner. No plum pudding. No Christmas loaf. Instead they
had oat cracknels and hearth cakes, and ale so thick you
ate it with a spoon. Anne sat on Westmorland's right, near
to a platter of corn-fed goose and prunes, stewed in wine
too thin to be called a sauce. This plain fare was served up
by a great army of servants wearing blue caps and their
lord's livery, *azur* and *or*, with gold stars and crescent
moons. As soon as the meat was brought in, the servants
sat right down to eat their own pease porridge swimming
with greasy lumps of fat. The hall was hung with indifferent tapestries and carpeted with dogs and straw. Only the
crescent moons on men's badges reminded her of a real
Percy Christmas.

Westmorland, marvelously at home in this robbers'
roost, spent most of the meal plotting with Buccleuch and
Ferniehurst, and a captain named Trotter—a fugitive felon
even under the loose Scots statutes. As long as Tom was
won free, Anne did not much care who did it. Westmorland had plans for her as well: "Best place for you is Edinburgh, or maybe Linlithgow."

Anne replied that she had not the least desire to go
deeper into the maw of Scotland. She had not even hinted
to Westmorland about all that had happened to her. Being
turned into a startled doe was not a tale for Christmas dinner among excitable strangers. Nor was Westmorland in
the least curious about her adventures. She whispered
firmly in French, "I would rather ride into the Debatable
Land looking for Tom with a hackbutt on my hip than endure a day more of genteel Scots society."

"Nonsense." He answered her in very audible English. "I hear Linlithgow is civilized, and Edinburgh no worse than London. With Mary of Scotland in captivity, we need you to ornament the Queen's party—most young lairds in the Lowlands will go to war for a pretty woman."

"An half the auld ones too," Laird Walter assured her, "when the lass is as bonny as yew."

Gentlemen politely ignored her protests, and that night Anne was bedded down in a closed cupboard—with Alison sleeping on the floor outside, to be handy during the night. Feeling like a doll in a box, Anne prayed to Mary, but Mary did not answer. Perhaps there were others in greater need—Anne was as safe and comfortable as the Borders would allow.

In the morning Lady Janet loaded Anne with traveling clothes, and advice on Scots society. The Lady of Branxholm was intimate with all the best families, having buried a handful of husbands, and spread her favors liberally among the finest noblemen in the land—even counting Bothwell, the Queen's rapist and consort, among her conquests. She gave Anne quite personal advice on whom to avoid, and whom to cultivate. Lady Janet enjoyed showing an uncanny knowledge of other people's affairs. "As you know, Anne, I will continue to watch over you, even while you are away."

Anne insisted on asking Alison if all this was agreeable with her—going off as a lady's maid, leaving her home and dale. The peasant lass looked shocked. "M'lady ta see Edinburgh, an' ta dine on sugarcake an' spice wine with the court at Linlithgow? That would be passin' agreeable ta any girl wi' a mustard seed o' sense."

They bid their good-byes to Lady Janet at a sleepy hour. The Lady of Branxholm gave Alison a kiss, and a stern talking-to, telling her to mind Anne and guard her maidenhead. "Do as I say, not as I've done. There will be plenty o' time fer men when yew ken what beasts they can be. Pretty beasts, mind yew—but eternally in need of watchin'. Learn from Lady Anne."

She added to Anne in French, "Please watch over the girl. Now we must part again—I'm sure we shall meet yet again."

Anne leaned forward to take the woman's parting kiss. Lady Janet's skin was white and dry as parchment, smelling of herbs and woodsmoke. As the woman's lips brushed her cheek, she saw there was a string about Lady Janet's neck—from it hung a mouse's skull.

Anne pulled sharply back, looking straight into the Lady of Branxholm's eyes. They were bright and ageless.

"Well, now you know." Lady Janet gave her a wicked smile. "I have been watching over you almost since you set foot in the Borders. Thanks for returning the deerskin, and give my love to Jock, if you should see him." No wonder the old witch at Jock's hovel had taken her tasks so lightly—having Branxholm to fly back to. Before Anne could think of what to say, they were on their way.

Their guide was a young laird, Hamilton of Bothwellhaugh—fairfaced and curly-haired, with trim tufts of beard—going to Linlithgow on business of his own. Intense eyes gave him a fey look that Alison said was common among Hamiltons.

"Fer yer ladyschip's protection" Bothwellhaugh carried an extra long hackbutt, a fowling piece he kept loaded with two lead balls and a handful of buckshot. Anne assumed the young gentleman could be trusted, for she would be entirely at his mercy. At least he was not some great huge Scot with a mustache reeking of leeks.

There were no inns in the land, and they made themselves the guests of bonnet lairds or simple farmers—Scott and Kerr country extended almost unbroken to within a day's ride of Edinburgh. Seeing only wintry moors and naked hills, Anne asked Alison where the farmland was.

"Why all around yew, yer ladyschip. Sleepin' under the frost." She looked worried, as if her mistress might be addled, or secretly nearsighted.

"But I've seen no fences, hedges, or ditches." Mills, weirs, and fish ponds were also notably absent. In dead of winter Scotland bore a stark similarity to the dark side of the moon.

Alison shrugged. "The land is the laird's, an' we farm her. Few folks have the time to go diggin' an' fencin' up the countryside."

At the end of the Pentlands, where hills met the sea,

Anne saw Edinburgh itself—a stunning sight, smaller and not such an eyesore as London, ringed with the walls and turrets, crowned by Edinburgh Castle high on its rock. The lofty city was surrounded by gray skeletal orchards, fields that looked like fields, and the country houses of the nobility.

Up close the faerie city dissolved into another cramped walled town: gritty, filthy, smelling of decayed fish. The main market street had tall houses of unpolished stone, with ugly wooden galleries projecting over the wide avenue. Behind them was a warren of tiny side alleys, tunnel-dark *wynds,* shabby and dirty, inhabited by the poor and wretched. Soap seemed rare as spice in the capital of Scotland.

Alison led Anne through the streets at a fevered pace, gay as a child who finds the landscape of Faerie is real. She pointed out the church of St. Giles, and High Street where Kerrs and Humes had stabbed her old laird Walter to death. As Lady Janet had hinted, Alison's education was strange indeed. She had no French and pitifully few numbers—but a vast stock of family myths and history.

Anne marveled as the washerwomen plied their trade in the middle of High Street. Half of Edinburgh's wash was done there, with no place for the filth to go, insuring that your napkins and undergarments were "cleaned" at the dirtiest spot in town. No wonder cities were such cess-pits. They stayed only one night, at Hamilton House in Kirk o' Field. Across the quadrangle was the gap where Black Ormiston and his fellows had blown the old Provost's Lodge to high Heaven, hoping to kill Queen Mary's husband. Anne thought much of Edinburgh might profit from similar remodeling, with suitable quantities of gunpowder.

Linlithgow was more to her liking. The place did not pretend to be anything but a palace town, sited beside a beautiful lock bordered with rushes. People were not packed together—the town was dominated by palaces and country homes, with enough commons to see to everyone's needs. The Laird of Bothwellhaugh, having brought them safely through the Borders, and at night in Edinburgh, pronounced Linlithgow "safe enuff," since it was ringed by Hamilton and Livingston land. Safe or not, the young laird carried his loaded hackbutt right through the streets of Linlithgow, up to Archbishop Hamilton's gate.

To Anne, the entire Lowlands seemed an insane patchwork poised just short of war. She saw no peace in Scotland, just an armed truce—time taken out to bind wounds and sharpen dirks. Edinburgh town had been solidly for the infant King James, but Edinburgh Castle was held for Queen Mary, by a man who had helped depose her. When Regent Moray was in Linlithgow, he stayed a few doors down from his enemies the Hamiltons. A Scots Parliament had dissolved the Church and declared the Holy Mass a crime; but Archbishop Hamilton, backed by his clan, still laid claim to all his hereditary lands and titles. "From archbishop to parish priest," Bothwellhaugh assured her, "a Scot would rather live outside the law than starve within it."

Alison admired the Archbishop's town house, saying, "If the Stewarts were not monarchs o' Scotland, the Hamiltons would be." She claimed the Hamiltons descended from Norse-Celtic Kings of the Isles, and said that southwest of Linlithgow, there was a whole town named Hamilton, with a palace and castle. "Where the Archbishop keeps the Sacred White Cattle o' the Sun." The girl did not think it in least strange that a Christian archbishop should keep sacrificial cattle. "But fer all their luck an' power, there is something not canny about the Hamilton line. They say the true laird o' Hamilton is a madman—wanderin' wi' the faeries—an' kept locked away from sight."

They found the town house in an uproar, preparing for a magnificent Twelfth Night fete—a masque and pageant, done in flagrant pagan defiance of the new Kirk's bans on dancing and playacting. Anne asked Bothwellhaugh, "Won't that provoke the Kirk and the King's party?"

"Provoke them?" Bothwellhaugh laughed. "I hope it bluddy chokes them."

Normally the young Hamilton acted as if there were nothing funny in God's creation, except perhaps the sight of a Douglas trying to swim the Forth with hands tied and a millstone about the ankles. " 'Tis the end o' the Fool's

Season, an' we are obligated to make the occasion an insult ta any decent-minded minister."

"Why?" Linlithgow looked about as peaceful as Kirk o' Field before the gunpowder was lit.

"People will no allow the Kirk ta stop the dance. Not on an ancient holiday. Even in dull an' dirty Edinburgh they broke open the Tolbooth when the Kirk arrested Robin o' the May."

What saints there were in Linlithgow turned their backs as the Hamiltons gave a midwinter feast and procession, featuring fools playing gray-coated preachers, presided over by a young woman dressed as Mary, with an evil-eyed bastard brother that any simpleton knew was Regent Moray.

Anne joined in, gowned like a faerie queen in borrowed finery. This was a real feast with real food—pike, salmon, beef, venison, swan, and peacock, even baked gingerbread and spiced apples—as well as wine, claret, brandy, and aqua vitae.

Revelers spilled out of the hot, shining hall into the torchlit winter garden, snaking between gaunt trees and onto the frosty street, dressed as harlequins, fools, and faeries.

Alison laughed at masked blades from the King's party, sampling delights their kirk forbid. "Look at 'em, wearin' the Stewart tartan, but hidin' their clan badges." Anne recognized the blue tartan—it was the same one Ferniehurst had put around her shoulders. Each party claimed the plaid, since imprisoned Queen Mary and infant King James were both Stewart clan chiefs.

Weaving in and out, the mad dance went on by moonlight. A well built stranger wiggled his way in between Anne and Alison. He had a handsome frame, but his face was hidden by a red bull's mask. The minotaur stumbled through his steps, fuddled with drink, but Alison took pains to instruct him, while Anne hung on his other arm. From time to time the young man would stagger off to piss in a corner, but he always came back to the dance.

Stars faded as false dawn put an end to Twelfth Night. Anne collapsed in a heap, waving to Alison. "No more. We must get to bed by morning."

Her handmaid helped her up. At the Archbishop's gate she took a last look back. Their young dancing partner staggered up to an open butt of ale. Pulling off his bull mask, he plunged his head in. His face came up dripping with beer.

He was Edward Darce, Crookback's brother. Anne had last seen him at Naworth, ordering Black Dick Nixon to guide her and Tom over Bewcastle Waste. The red bull was a Darce badge.

What was a Darce doing in Linlithgow? She did not know whether to count him as a friend or enemy—but either way it was damned strange. An English Borderer dancing in the streets of Linlithgow was a bit of Twelfth Night fantasy turned alarmingly real.

That wild night jarred Anne's whirlwind to a stop. From Naworth to Liddesdale, to Branxholm, to Edinburgh and Linlithgow, she had supposedly been looking for a safety. Actually she had been letting others make decisions for her—Tom, Jock, Westmorland, Lady Janet, the Kerrs and Hamiltons, even Alison, her handmaid. Seduced by the ease of living off the Hamiltons, she had done nothing to solve her problems, nothing to free Northumberland from Elizabeth's hangmen, nothing to get Tom back. It was pleasant to have the best dressmakers, seamstresses, and lacemakers in Linlithgow fawning on her at the Hamiltons' expense; and her canopied bed, taffeta coverlet, Turkish carpets and cushions, all seemed as natural as the attention of servants. But none of this was natural, or even hers.

She felt anxious and frustrated all the next day. That night Bothwellhaugh broke more bad news. The Hamilton went down on one knee in ardent courtesy—a young Scotsman likes to impress a lady, even with evil tidings.

"Word has come up from the Borders. Buccleuch an' the Earl o' Westmorland failed to break free your husband. He is in Moray's hands now. Kept in Lochleven Castle, a prisoner o' the Douglas an' beyond our reach."

"What word, from whom?" The messenger almost had to be Darce. Edward's sudden advent could not be mere coincidence. There were many doings in this house that she was not privy to—secret links between sometimes-loyal subjects of Elizabeth and very rebellious Scots.

"I cannot say from whom, but 'tis a man we trust."

Trust seemed a chancy word to apply to a turncoat's brother—but the news was bad enough to be true. Lockleven was north of the Firth, on an island in a loch, deep in Douglas country; about as far as Tom could get from Northumberland and still be in the Lowlands. Lochleven was where Earl Moray had put Queen Mary for safekeeping—yet Mary had managed to escape. There was hope, if not much.

What should she do to affect her fate? She put the question straight to Mary in a private prayer session, but got no answer. Mary had been silent throughout the Twelve Days of Christmas, and now the darkest days of winter were indeed closing in.

Next morning Anne saw the man who held Tom prisoner. James Stewart, Earl of Moray and Regent of Scotland, rode down the market street, through the muddy slush and vomit left over from Twelfth Night. He was neatly bearded, with a proud Stewart profile and deep-set intelligent eyes. Anne could read ambition on his features. Bothwellhaugh pointed him out the first time, but the Regent became a familiar sight; Moray was in residence down the street and often rode about on business.

What would Mary do? The answer was obvious, but it took Anne several days to work up the nerve. Mary would confront the man. Mary had appealed to Anne; why couldn't Anne appeal to Moray? She would tell him Tom had broken no laws in Scotland. Kidnapped in the Debatable Land, and hauled in chains to Lochleven, Tom had hardly *been* in Scotland. Tom's real crime had been wanting to free the Queen of Scots from an English prison—men with much worse on their conscience walked the streets of Linlithgow every day.

Mind you, Moray offered no great prospect of granting Tom's parole—the man had locked up his pregnant half sister in Lochleven. Anne knew she had as much chance of moving him as she had of proposing marriage to the Pope. But Mary would give the man a chance, so how could Anne prejudge him? Besides, a lady appealing to her

husband's enemy, especially on the market street of Linlithgow, fit that fine Scots sense of drama.

She took time, having the proper outfit made, not a faerie queen's gown but black silk and lace with a cap of
pearls; simple, dignified, and striking. The dress and pearls
fairly shouted that she was a lady worth stopping for.

Then she sat down and waited on a bench just inside the
garden wall, listening for riders, while Alison watched lest
Moray came afoot. In her mind Anne went over what she
would say—not wanting to cry, or look the fool—while
half of her hoped Moray would not show, so she would
not be put to the test.

Hoofbeats. She looked through the gate. Three riders returning to Hamilton house: Bothwellhaugh, Edward Darce,
and Black Dick Nixon—another Borderer who had no
business being here. She watched them stable their horses
in happy moods. Perhaps they had been hunting;
Bothwellhaugh had his long fowling piece. Nixon and
Darce carried hackbutts.

Presently Bothwellhaugh called for Alison to come hang
his wash. Anne had no way of knowing when Moray
might come, and could not keep Alison from her chores.
She sent the girl off, telling her to be quick.

Trying to remain calm, she watched the street through
the open gate. Tradespeople lugged carts and baskets. Day
laborers trudged by. Linlithgow was charmingly free of
drunks. Bothwellhaugh's window faced the road, and by
looking up, Anne could see the progress of the wash being
hung out. Silently she urged Alison to hurry, wanting the
girl at her side when she put herself in front of the Regent's horse.

Another horseman coming. Anne looked and saw Earl
Moray, headed home, aiming to ride right past Hamilton
House. This was the moment. She heard feet skipping
down the stairs. In a blink Alison was crouching beside
her, panting apologies. "Yer ladyschip, I rushed, an' now
the wash is hung."

Anne tried to put her handmaid at ease, gathering her
own wits. So much depended on what she said. The words
had to be right, and with Alison here there was no excuse

for waiting. Regent Moray drew even with them, and Anne stood up. *(Mary, make him believe me, and aid me.)*

There was a great solemn bang—smoke and flame burst from Hamilton House. Laundry leaped outward. Anne started and looked up, seeing a long fowling piece being whipped from Bothwellhaugh's window.

The Regent was flung sideways, hurtled off his terrified horse into a heap on the muddy ground. The wild-eyed beast bolted down the market street. Twisting in pain, the man picked himself up, clutching his silk doublet, which had a huge hole torn in the waist. He tottered and staggered toward his lodgings. Anne had tended belly wounds like that at Barnard Castle. A man could walk, talk, and even smile with a ball in his gut, but in a short time he would surely be dead.

Booted feet came trapping down the stairs. Bothwellhaugh burst out of the town house, carrying his fowling piece, dashing into the stables. Heartbeats later he emerged, urging a fresh horse into a gallop. A servant was there to open the rear garden gate, and the curly-haired Hamilton disappeared.

Earl Moray stumbled up to his own door, which opened to admit the dying man. It happened so terribly quickly, before Anne could say a word or take a step.

Monarchs ought to put to death the authors of war, as their sworn enemies and as dangers to their states.

—ELIZABETH TUDOR, 1533–1603

Candlemas

Anne knelt over an open fire in a churchyard, cooking eggs and mutton tripe. The ravenously delicious smell of frying meat made her mouth water. She was still wearing her black silk and lace, now badly travel-stained. Her pearl cap was back in Linlithgow; head and shoulders were now covered by a horse blanket from the Hamilton stables.

Alison hunched next to her, feeding the fire. The two women were at Hawick, in the potter's field behind a tall Norman kirk, dedicated to Mary in one of her saintly guises—Anne no longer paid as much attention to names, since they mattered not a whit to Mary. Gravestones and unmarked mounds were scattered over the heath, but the Holy Mother's silent stone presence comforted Anne, giving her hope after a fashion. Otherwise things were at a terrible ebb. In a day and a half they had fled over a hundred miles, without stopping or alighting—a hellish ride over cold, damp, roadless moors, with owls hooting about them.

It had taken her no more than a minute to decide she could no longer stay in Linlithgow. The man who pronounced the palace town "safe enuff" had proceeded to shoot down the Regent of Scotland in the middle of the market street. King's lairds would descend on the Hamiltons, howling for revenge, and the only place Anne knew to fell was back to the Borders—even if there were no safe havens, the Borders had plenty of hiding places. Edward Darce had escorted her, and Black Dick Nixon had caught them at Ettrick Water, with the news that Moray was truly and thoroughly dead.

Silently she ladled out eggs and hash, purchased from a cottager in Hawick. Two months ago, if someone had told Anne she would be serving eggs in Scotland to the likes of Black Dick Nixon, she would have thought it a lunatic insult. Now she was too famished to care what criminals shared her meals.

Crookback's brother paced back and forth before the fire, sniffing the keen Border Country air. (After a hundred miles on horseback not a single member of the party felt the need to sit.) Tall and square-chinned, Edward was a near opposite to his bent, shifty brother. During the horrendous ride Anne had found him a source of courage. He had been comforting, hearty, and selfless—the perfect man to have when you are fleeing in blind panic. His only fault was an irritating tendency to make light of their troubles. Clapping his hands like a satisfied seal, he announced, "With a bit more riding we may be in Branxholm before dark."

No one leaped into the saddle. Anne's rear was so sore she never wanted to see another horse, but Edward Darce was the sort of hearty bully who saw opportunity in every hardship. For sure Moray was murdered. Naturally they had been driven from Linlithgow. But, with Moray dead (Edward never said how much *he* had to do with the murder), the King's lairds were leaderless. "The Borders are wide open. We can be in Branxholm in an hour, and over the Borders into Cumberland by tomorrow's eve."

Over the Borders? Edward did not say it directly, but it seemed both Darces were planning to change sides again. Crookback had proven false to Elizabeth, then to the northern rebels—now it was Elizabeth's turn again. Lord Darce was a shark who could not keep still.

Anne ate her eggs and tripe standing, to ease her saddle sores, then mounted up for five more miles of torture. They were in Branxholm by dusk.

Edward and Nixon reported to Buccleuch in private, showing that in the Teviotdale Laird Walter counted for more than the Earl-in-exile Westmorland. Buccleuch broke the news to everyone in raucous good humor: "The Regent is as cold as m' bridle bit."

Men raised a hooray. Speechless with excitement, Westmorland tore off the Scots bonnet he'd affected and flung it into the fire. Border reivers were on their feet, ready to ride—with Twelfth Night behind them, the best raiding season had arrived. The long nights and listless days of midwinter were made for slipping over frozen tracks, herding your neighbor's sheep.

With half the household up and plotting, bedrooms went for the asking. Anne no longer had to crawl into a cupboard. She collapsed in Lady Janet's bed, sleeping through supper and into the early hours of morning. At dawn she rose from the witch's room and found Branxholm emptying out.

She caught Westmorland getting ready to ride west. He was the happy gambler again, going over the hills to meet with Lord Herries and the Maxwells. "Hume is with us for sure, along with Buccleuch, Ferniehurst, the Darces. . . ."

"Both Darces?"

"Yes, Darce is about to change partners again, like a hunchback whore at a dance."

She remembered Mad Anne's offhand prediction that Darce would betray them not once, but twice. "How much help will we get from a liar and traitor?"

"Darce is a bitter, twisted, and greedy back-stabber," admitted Westmorland. "By Gawd, 'tis a marvel the man's not a bishop by now. But he swears he'll have three thousand horse ready at Naworth."

"And then?" On their last visit to Naworth Lord Darce had turned them out onto Bewcastle Waste with Scrope's sleuthhounds at their heels.

"Why, with these Scots, our own Forsters, and Darce's moss-troopers, we can crush Scrope between us an' take Carlisle. We'll shake loose the Borders. Moray's gone. Scotland can be drawn into open war with Elizabeth. Which is bound to help your husband, maybe even Mary of Scotland."

Anne pointed out that Mary Queen of Scots was still far off in Coventry. "Last November not even half the North Country could free her. How can a few thousand Border riders hope to do better?"

Westmorland stood for a moment with an astounded scowl on his face, then stalked hatless out the door into the winter drizzle, saying over his shoulder, " 'Tis useless to argue strategy with women, who have neither the head nor balls for hard action."

Branxholm hummed like a broken hive. Buccleuch went off over the hills with Westmorland, taking most of his hard cases with him. Gallopers dashed about, letting other brigands know that a huge foray was afoot, promising loot like none of them had seen. Lady Janet of Branxholm was on one of her mysterious absences. Anne wondered if Sir Walter of Buccleuch rode into battle with a mouse in his saddlebag—just for luck.

For the better part of two days Edward Darce beseeched Anne to come with him into England. First she refused outright. But the more she thought it over, the more it made horrid sense. Moray's murder soured what little love she had for Scotland. Over the border she would at least be with her people. Going with Edward would be "doing something," and she felt a morbid compulsion to know just how bad things were in England.

Anne tried asking Mary for advice, but Mary was as uncommunicative as she had been in Linlithgow. The new silence was disturbing, though Anne was beginning to understand Mary's ways. Mary would not come running every time Anne had a crisis of indecision. Anne had to commit herself, and stop expecting heaven to guide her every step.

She decided to go with Edward. The strong-minded brute always had good arguments, and Anne could not justify sitting in Branxholm sipping Scots broth, while people across the border died in her behalf. If she must be hunted wherever she went—better to be hunted for rebellion in England than for murder in Scotland.

Alison went with her, acting as cheerful as when they set out for Linlithgow. "Lady Janet made me yer handmaid, an' I have never yet seen Ingland." Carlisle was a mere forty miles off, but she talked of it with a curious wonder, as though it were Venice or America.

Edward timed his ride to cross the border at night, making the first part leisurely, allowing Anne to get accustomed to her escort, mostly Hetheringtons and broken men from the West March clans—rogues with names like Ill-Drowned Geordie, Lang Rowry, Sweet-Milk Milburne, and Sally's Jock. Not the usual companions for a countess, but all accomplished rustlers, knowing every byway and lurking hole along their stretch of the border.

The route cut back and forth, following intricate windings to avoid Turnbull country, and the Elliots at Stobs—

shunning a beaten path like the plague. Anne was impressed by the way they found each crooked turning riding at night through country sliced with sudden gorges and deep precipices. It was a men's magic, as miraculous in its own way as turning women into mice and deer. At the border they went straight over the tops, avoiding the better-known passages like Hell Cauldron, Keilder Edge, and Murders Rack. When at last Edward said, "This is England," Anne was so turned around in the mist and darkness they might as easily have been entering Switzerland.

Alison whispered, "This is it, my first glimpse o' Ingland."

Anne could not see the hobby she sat on, much less the land around her. All she felt was the night coldness in her gut, coming home knowing every hand might be against her. The law proscribed horrible deaths for anyone who aided her—simple hanging for those who saw her pass but did not report her. Lord Scrope and Old John Forster were seasoned border wardens, familiar with every hill, ford, and valley heading into England. Flying patrols would be groping through the darkness, guided by bloodhounds. But none of the men, from Edward Darce down to Sweet-Milk Milburne and Sally's Jock, voiced the least concern.

After an interminable twisting about they left hills behind, breaking out onto Bewcastle Waste. Avoiding Bewcastle and Askerton, they kept to the broad expanses of trackless fell and open moor, until coming to a pasture cut by a low line of stones stretching off into the gray foggy morning. Anne was back at Hadrian's Wall.

Seeing this ghost of the Caesars, she knew she was home, not in Northumberland, but in country where she had owned manors and people had worn her colors. Near the wall they picked up more Milburnes, and at the first crossroads Anne saw evidence of Sussex's occupation, a blackened body hanging from a gallows pole. The corpse was gaunt and leathery, mummified by weeks of twisting in the freezing dry winter wind.

Sweet-Milk Milburne rode up and cut down the corpse, working carefully with his dirk. Sally's Jock supported the body so it would not drop.

"Ye can no take him wi' yew," cautioned Lang Rowry, a long-faced, solemn-voiced reiver.

"He was my brother, Will." The Milburne's voice mixed love and hate. "Thet bluddy vulture, Sir George Bowes, hung him here. Fer the first day Will looked so natural, yew might think he'd take the rope from his neck an' be home fer supper. But over the weeks we have had to watch him mortify, being pecked at by birds. Bowes swore that if we cut him down, he'd hang another Milburne in his place."

And now Sir George would have reason to hang more. Anne remembered how when Bowes had been in her hands—after the fall of Barnard Castle—hanging him had been the last thing on her mind. She had stoutly protested seeing his garrison stripped in the snow. This was how justice repaid mercy. No matter how many times she did the right thing, she got equally grim results.

Sweet-Milk laid his brother by the road for Milburne women to find, then they rode on into Naworth.

Naworth was a superb stone fortress overlooking the River Irthing, with the ground falling steeply away on three sides. The vulnerable fourth side was guarded by a moat, gatehouse, and huge flanking towers. Both the castle and Naworth town were filled with the frantic sense of freedom that comes with being utterly damned. There could be no truce with the Crown, but for the moment no force in the West March could touch them—this small plot of England was free of Tudor control. Inside the fortress Anne saw men sharpening weapons and talking rebellion, while women cooked and washed for them, working with nervous smiles. Punishment for the Rising had been savage. In Durham, where Anne had burned prayer books, Sussex had hung sixty-three constables for obeying Tom's orders. She heard how Sir George Bowes followed her footsteps from Weatherby to New Castle, hanging rebels from every town and hamlet for hundreds of miles about. During the service she had seen the woman who begged her aid in Liddesdale, and her son, but not the nun who led them back to England. Anne hadn't the heart to ask what had happened.

Nothing was more abhorred these days than liberty and

toleration. Mary of Scotland had shown admirable lack of bigotry, remaining a strict Catholic but honoring and rewarding Reformers. She let Reformed ministers preach at her, and she struck down the Catholic Gordons when the Earl of Huntly grew too overweening. Her reward was to be hounded from the throne, reviled by the ministers she tolerated, imprisoned by men she promoted.

Anne found Lord Darce was cool as ever, acting as if they had just met from parting on Maiden Hill. He treated Anne's last visit to Naworth as a social slip, as embarrassing to Anne as to him. Better not brought up. She did not sully her new sense of freedom by arguing with Leonard Darce. The man was as he was. And for once he seemed fully committed. Many of Mad Anne's predictions had come to pass, but Anne had to give Darce his due, she could not believe he meant to betray them a second time. This was Crookback's rebellion, called by him, commanded by him. He had no one left to betray, no deal to offer Elizabeth. Desperation had made Leonard Darce constant, though not an inch more likable.

He had brought out his entire strength—squires and tenants, Threlkelds and Salkelds, Bells and Blennerhassets from Gilsland, and lesser men—Applebies, Porters, Huttons, as well as all the reivers and march riders he could muster, Ridleys, Hetheringtons, and Armstrongs from Bewcastle and Liddesdale. There were hundreds of Armstrongs camped at Naworth, but not Jock of the Syde. His cousins said he was in Liddesdale minding business, not mixing with the English.

The new liberty at Naworth allowed them to celebrate the Virgin's Feast of the purification in a blaze of light. In one of their most petty acts, the Reformers had banned the burning of candles at Candlemas. Ever since she was small, Anne had been thrilled to see chapel and castle lit by points of light. To her it seemed a promise of summer in the very depths of winter—a promise that penny-conscious Reformers were pleased to snuff out.

Not in Naworth, not this winter. Tenants and townspeople brought their candles for the coming year to be blessed by the priest—though no one knew whether the freedom to burn them would last out the month.

Alison knew the festival, but insisted on calling it Brigid's Fest or Oimelc, having never seen it celebrated in strictly Christian fashion. "It is the Washin' o' the World's Face. When Caileach, the Old Woman o' Winter, drinks from the Well o' Life an' is transformed to the virgin Brigid." Brigid was the wise young goddess of fire and handicrafts.

Anne made no attempt to curb her handmaid's heathen notions. No attempt to explain that Brigid the Wise was really the Virgin Mary, and that the Old Woman o' Winter was a pagan witch. Once she would have seen the devil hiding behind this girl's simple faith; now she believed Mary could be Brigid or even the Woman of Winter.

That night Anne walked alone onto the battlements of Naworth, wishing Mary would speak to her again, in whatever guise she wished. It was the first night of February, crisp and cold. Bright stars shone down, mirroring the candles in church. And all around Naworth balefires burned on the dark hilltops, like stars fallen to earth, calling in the Border clans. Perhaps neither Mary nor Brigid needed to say more.

Earthly news came in from all quarters—Mary of Scotland was still in Coventry, being moved from castle to inn to a house in town. Some though the moves were a scheme to confuse rescuers, but Anne guessed Elizabeth was the one confused. The Tudors had long ago closed down Coventry Castle, turning out the servants and retainers. After decades of neglect Elizabeth had ordered the castle reopened to hold Mary—only to discover the place was uninhabitable, with no furniture, servants, or working locks. A castle was more than standing stone, it was a living thing, an extended family; take away its people, and the dead shell crumbles. Even Elizabeth's excellent spy system could not keep track of the havoc wrought by Tudor greed.

Then one of Darce's patrols brought in a galloper, a poor frightened lad carrying dispatches for Scrope. Anne never discovered what had been done to him to make him talk, but talk he did. Darce gleefully reported the results of the interrogation, rubbing hands as he spoke. "Scrope is still hiding in Carlisle, sending out messengers in threes, hoping to get through to Hunsdon and Old John Forster at Hexham. Fearing that Maxwells and Irvines will descend on him at any moment." The Scots had been hard at work, giving Lord Scrope fits. Ferniehurst, Hume, and Buccleuch, along with Westmorland, were headed south, planing to swing through the Debatable Land in route to burn out Hector of Harlow for betraying Tom.

Darce waved the parchment taken from the dispatch rider. "He is squealing for Hunsdon to bring hackbutteers from the Berwick garrison. Scrope even suggests that Lord Hunsdon might stop in at Naworth on his way, to serve a warrant on me."

That got a grim gloat all around. Hunsdon would be outnumbered a good two to one, and had no gun bigger than a hackbutt with which to reduce Naworth's defenses. Elizabeth hated the expense of war. Anne guessed the Queen was hoping her wardens would put down Darce, and hold back the Scots, with whatever they had on hand.

"So we have them." Darce unfurled a map, bending down to plot distances with cheerful ferocity. "Hunsdon and Forster are at Hexham, hoping to unite with Scrope. But we lie in their path, twice their numbers and closer to Carlisle than they are."

"Thar double-teamed wi' us between them an' the goal." Anne turned to discover Black Dick Nixon putting the enemy's dilemma into football terms.

"And the Scots?" Edward Darce stood facing his brother across the map. "The plan was to fall on Carlisle together." Edward was the one who had spent the winter tramping between Branxholm and Linlithgow, collecting Scots promises.

"Aye, tegather," Crookback answered in a broad, sarcastic brogue. "We might as well make pacts with Will-o'-the-Wisp as expect the Scots to appear on cue."

Edward would not be pushed aside, and Anne listened to the brothers tear at each other over the map. Both came from a family violently jealous of its rights and prerogatives—Crookback was the elder and the heir, and Edward was the younger one who knew he was the better man.

Crookback would not be moved. He bullied Edward,

just as he meant to bully Hunsdon and Forster. He had the troops and the guns—"And I mean to strike my blow now. Once we smash Hunsdon, we may turn on Carlisle at our leisure, crushing Scrope between us and the Scots."

Anne elected to stay at Naworth, and miss the whole bloody show. But Lord Darce did not allow it. In a stormy private session he explained, "I want all my pieces with me."

"I am never your *piece*," Anne answered.

Darce laughed outright. "Yes you are, so long as I have three thousand lances at my back. All you command is a silly Scots handmaid with dung between her toes." To prove the point, he added, "Edward will no longer be escorting you. The boy suffers from a tender heart, especially with the ladies." Putting her in the none-too-clean hands of Black Dick Nixon, Darce seemed smugly pleased with how far she had fallen since Durham.

When it was time to ride, Nixon stood in her doorway, his blunt assassin's face swarthy and semishaven, his black bonnet pulled down over his brows. "I haf my orders." He looked more than willing to tie "her ladyschip" to a horse.

So Anne rode south behind Darce's Red Bull banner, with Alison at her side. At least the scenery was splendid. The small army rode through the Vale of Eden, a basin of Triassic rock, part of the Midland Plain rising from the ocean and poking into the midst of Highland Britain. Even in winter it was worth seeing. Stark woodlands lined sharp gorges of old red sandstone, cut by the Hell Beck and the Gelt. To the south lay the English Lake District, to the north the wilds of Eskdale and the Debatable Land.

Riders brought word that Hunsdon was only four miles off, hurrying toward Carlisle; now he would not get there without a fight. Darce deployed his guns and horsemen on a patch of heath covering the Gelt crossing below Brampton.

Anne saw it all from the slight safety of a wooded knoll. Gaunt tree limbs clutched at the gray sky. Black Dick Nixon hovered at her elbow. She had always marked him as a most soulless man, a felon who would as soon slit a throat as stir his porridge—with no passions but drink and fornication. But Anne was wrong. Nixon had a passion,

and Alison's cheerful chatter brought it out. The man was
not a drinker, and he seemed indifferent to having two
pretty women in his power, *but Nixon lived and breathed
football.* Once Alison had him talking ball-playing, there
was no shutting him up. He had memorized games played
on Hermitage green for fifteen years and more. Nixon
could describe with relish how in his father's day the
Crosers had got their comeuppance in a crucial tussle. " 'E
backheeled it, but right ta an Armstrang wi' the goal as
wide open as a whore on Tuesday. Bluddy ball did na stop
rollin' till it was in Ingland." He would have traded his
slim chance of life everlasting for a goal against the
Elliots.

After laughing at games gone by, Nixon analyzed the
coming battle in football terms. "Laird Darce is a charger,
wi' a big team at his back, an' guns ta goalie fer him. But
Hunsdon's hackbutteers will nae break easy, not unless a
few free kicks from the cannon loosen 'em up." He
glanced over his shoulders toward Scotland. "I'd feel happier if we saw black bonnets toppin' yon hills."

The opposing team ambled onto the field. Hunsdon's little army had slogged all the way from Hexham. He had
half as many horse and no cannon, but he was bringing
lines of hackbutteers stripped from the Berwick garrison.

Anne saw puffs blossom from the batteries along
Darce's line, followed by the bang of cannon. Hunsdon
formed his troopers into line, holding half his cavalry in
reserve, out of gun range, sending the rest forward. Pack-
ets of hackbutteers knelt between the forward blocks of
cavalry, in formations the French called *enfants perdus.*

Darce's shots were flying overhead, or plowing up the
heath in front of Hunsdon's men, who were spread rather
thinly, not making themselves much of a target. Such ineffective fire galled Lord Darce more than Hunsdon, and
Anne saw Crookback canter impatiently forward, accompanied by an ensign with the Red Bull banner.

On her mount amid the trees, smelling pine scent and
horse leather, breath misting in the frigid air, Anne
thought, My God, the lunatic means to charge. A shiver
went down the line as Darce's Gilsland spearmen lowered
their pikes.

Hunsdon had to get to Carlisle, which meant fighting his way through a superior enemy line, studded with cannon. But Darce was not going to wait. It was a bully's blow, bludgeoning his opponent with superior numbers before the battle even got started. Darce's horsemen lurched forward, masking their own guns, going from trot to canter to gallop much too fast.

"Tear inta 'em," shouted Nixon, rising in his stirrups, cheering on his team.

The hurtling formation began to break up even before it reached Hunsdon's line. Darce and a few rash fellows got far ahead, the weak or cautious lagged behind. Footmen could not keep up with the horses.

At point-blank distance there was a great blast of smoke and flame—the *enfants perdus* stationed between Hunsdon's blocks of horse poured fire into the oncoming moss-troopers. At such range not a shot could miss. Volleys tore through Darce's formation, emptying saddles, sending horses plunging sideways in panic. The line reeled, and the charge wavered.

At that crucial instant Hunsdon countercharged, a headlong gallop, going hell-for-leather at Darce. Hunsdon's cavalry burst through Darce's shaken moss-troopers. The Gilsland spearmen grounded their pikes to keep off the cavalry, but took volley after volley from the hackbutteers. The fight dissolved into frantic scrimmages between small groups. Up and down the Gelt Anne saw lances waving, and men hacking at each other. The end was obvious, even to her. Darce's momentum was gone. His guns were useless in such close fighting. He had no chance of reforming in the face of the furious attack, and the steady flanking fire of the hackbutteers. And Hunsdon still had his rear guard in hand, ready to push the pursuit.

Border riders were raising their weapons and surrendering. Small good it would do them. Tudor judges would not hesitate to hang a man just because he had yielded honestly in battle. Anne saw the Red Bull banner go down.

If only Darce had waited for the Scots. If only he had held out some reserve, not staking everything on a single charge. It was too late now for all those ifs. Crookback's overbearing instincts had betrayed them all—he had seen a weaker opponent, and pounced. Now there was no one to pick up the pieces.

Black Dick Nixon did not wait for orders. Darce would either be dead or flying for Scotland. "Well, the match's lost, an' we best be goin' hame."

She followed the brigand into the wood, with Alison behind her. Boughs screened the sound of shots and clash of battle. Winter woods seemed unnaturally quiet, without even birdcalls. Silent shadows lay on patches of snow in the clearings.

They bypassed Naworth, making straight for the wall, and the Borders beyond. With Darce's army scattering in flight, nothing could save Naworth; the brief freedom there was at an end. The fortress was bound to be looted by fugitives, then left to Hunsdon.

Nixon would not let up until Askerton and Bewcastle were behind them, then he had them dismount and walk their horses across the frozen waste north of Bewcastle. "It's back ta Branxholm. No hole in Ingland will be safe." The man had a Borderer's brutal, lizardlike pragmatism. Unmoved by the massacre at Brampton, he saw nothing beyond the next bolt hole.

Anne walked in the rear with Alison, whispering, "I do not want to go to Branxholm."

"Why, m'lady?" Alison whispered back. "Branxholm's bound to be the safest hold in the Borders."

"I cannot stand to be in the hands of these men for a minute longer." She said it with such force that she surprised herself.

Watching the battle, she had been hypnotized by the conflict, but now she was free to think and feel. Her Rising in Northumberland had been a tragedy, but Brampton had been a bloody farce. Whatever was good or noble in the rebellion had died before Barnard Castle. Whatever was merely naive and hopeful had marched off to prison with Tom. Now the very dregs of the movement were in command—harebrained adventurers like Westmorland, genial robbers like Buccleuch, bumbling villains like Darce. She pictured herself being dragged from one botched disaster to the next with Black Dick Nixon as her bear-leader, waved before her followers like a faded banner of days gone by.

"M'lady, where will we go?"

Anne was touched and amazed by her handmaid's loyalty. Alison acted as if she had no fears or needs of her own, wanting nothing except to find a safe and suitable place for Anne. Once she would have deserved such service, but not anymore. Alison did not need to go through this. "You must have a home, a family you could go to?"

The red-haired girl looked shocked. "My mother has a bothy in the Teviotdale, no place fer a lady like yew."

Until Alison put it that way, Anne had not considered going with the girl. She had merely wanted to assure herself that Alison was looked after.

Plodding along, staring at Black Dick Nixon's broad back, a fierce determination welled up within her. By all that was holy, she would not be used again. She would escape. She would flee overseas, become a nun in France, or even a Scots goat girl. Anything would be better than being dragged through mud and blood by men with loose principles and light fingers.

"Yes," she hissed, "take me to your mother's home. Or at least help me get away from him." She tilted her head to indicate Nixon, nonchalantly picking his path over the icy heath ahead of them.

But how to get away? By now Anne knew Nixon was no dullard. He had a primitive shrewdness, and a keen head for plots. The man had read Darce as easily as he might read a trio of Elliot defenders, with the score tied and the crowd howling at his back. He was heavily armed—lance, rapier, dirk, and a brace of pistols—and he had the strongest horse. Anne had only her bare hands.

And Mary. She prayed not to ask for advice of guidance, but for aid. Mary came to her most often when Anne was making her own decisions. *And Anne knew right well what she wanted*—to be out of this man's hands. All she hoped for from Mary was a little help in making things happen.

Skirting the flanks of the Cheviots, they entered Scotland, and Anne could see Nixon visibly relax. They stopped at a family croft, exchanging news from England

for easy hospitality. The story of Brampton amused every
listener. Nixon's cousins could imagine no better news
than to hear that Elizabeth's lairds and wardens were hacking each other apart. There was some sympathy for the
Darces, who had winked at forays out of the Dale against
the Musgraves at Bewcasle. But the Darces had severed
their stints as march wardens, and Nixon felt every English laird was in need of a hard lesson in manners.

Refreshed, they rode on. Near to dusk Alison approached Nixon in her usual whimsical way, getting him
to talk football. Which was easy. When Nixon muttered it
was time to pick up the pace, Alison demurred, saying she
had relatives nearby, at Saughtree. "No need ta tax the
hobbies. We can surely spend the night there."

"What sort o' relatives?" Black Dick was plainly
tempted. Saughtree was at the extreme east end of
Liddesdale, very nearly on the way to Branxholm. An un-
like place to face English pursuit.

"Oh, anly an auld, lame widower wi' three strapping
daughters. We're cousins, an' were playmates growin' up."

Nixon might be obsessed with football, but few Border
men could resist the notion of a night on a lonely farmstead with four lasses and an old, lame chaperon.

"The auld man goes ta bed early wi' his bowl o' milk,"
Alison assured him, "an' we always have jolly times afterward."

Nixon tersely accepted, and Alison led them to a well-
kept farmstead. A night wind whipped off the bare tops,
stirring the smoke rising from the stone bothy. Alison dismounted and shouted a cheery hallow. As Nixon got
down, the girl glanced at Anne, mouthing the words, "Be
ready."

Anne prepared to ride, praying to Mary that her handmaid knew what she was about.

The door was flung open by a glowering old man with
an ax in his hand. The gaffer was followed by a half-dozen
alert lads with bills and pikes. There was no sign of Alison's trio of nubile cousins.

Nixon stood rooted, astonished by Alison's betrayal.
The girl leaped back on her mount, giving Black Dick's
horse a hard slap on the rump, and yelling to Anne, "Let's

be gane, m'lady." The two women took off, with Black
Dick's frightened horse, leaving the Nixon to face the
alarmed farm family.

Anne caught Alison as they tore over the tops, saying
she was a most resourceful and excellent handmaid. The
girl laughed madly. "They're no my cousins. They are not
even Scots, but Crosers. We can be lost lang before they
sort out the confusion."

As they slowed, Anne realized she was really free—also
unprotected, almost alone, in one of the worst corners of
Scotland. The ridges around her looked empty and drear,
locked in winter. She let Alison lead, hoping the girl knew
her way. From far off over the waste came the low, quavering howl of a wolf. Hardly the sound two women
wanted to hear. Her handmaid stopped laughing and urged
the tired horses into a trot.

"How far?" Anne asked.

The girl glanced back, "Miles ta go m'lady. Miles ta
go."

Wedged between Liddesdale and the Cheviots, the country was totally desolate, a series of windswept ridges and
deep, tangled glens. A sharp violent rain swept over them.
Anne felt tired and chilled. Alison stopped her horse, looking back, breathing hard. The wolf call came again,
shriller and closer. "M'lady, 'tis a pack."

"After us?" Anne could hear several different beasts
giving tongue to the night.

"After somethin'." Alison started off again. Anne stuck
tight behind her. All three horses were tired, having come
the long way from Brampton, and Anne had heard of
Scots wolves running down red deer by working in relays;
a pack would not have near so much trouble with them.
What a horror, to escape an English army and Scots brigands, only to be eaten alive by some ravenous beast.

Without warning, a dark shape reared up in front of
them. Her handmaid screamed and reined in her horse.

"Yew gawdawful, bluddy bitches . . ." It was Black
Dick Nixon, mounted on a Croser horse and cursing them
furiously. He shouldered Alison aside and seized Anne's
reins.

Alison tried to push bravely between them, but Nixon

jerked a pistol from his boot top, cocking the wheel lock aiming at Alison's breast.

Anne screamed, "No!"

All three of them froze. Nixon let fly with a string of oaths. "I hae never kilt a woman, but I am anly a minute away from shootin' one of yew, ta get the other ta behave." The weird call of the wolves punctuated his threat.

Nixon glanced over his shoulder, then smiled grimly at Alison. "Give me no more bother, or I'll pistol yer horse, an' leave yew fer the pack."

"Just take me to Branxholm,' Anne gave in, "and leave the girl be."

Their hobbies climbed the next ridge line, stumbling and lurching over the slick dead grass and frosty stones. Nixon's mount was freshest, but none of their horses had wind enough to run. Anne was last, and as they reached the ridge top, she saw the wolves, swarming over the slope behind them, disappearing into the bracken below. Nixon pulled on her reins. "M'lady, get yer arse in motion. Do no stop ta see the sights o' Scotland."

Their horses made better speed downslope, but the silent, loping shapes came over the crest, still gaining. Anne could see their sharp, triangular heads and lean, terrible bodies. They would be up with her before she topped the next rise. Bracken closed about her. Heart hammering, she wondered what was the use in running. If Nixon had not been tugging at her reins, urging her on, she would have given up.

The pack caught them emerging from the glen, as their terrified horses struggled up the far slope. Slavering gray shapes with fiery eyes surged around them, closing in from both sides and behind. Anne's horse reared. Nixon cursed, dropped her reins, and drew his pistols. He banged away at the pack leader, a supernaturally black beast. Two shots and he was left with only cold steel.

Anne tried to control her plunging mount. Two wolves struck her hobby sideways, spilling her from the saddle. Cold, rocky slope slammed into her. Rolling over, she saw Nixon charging toward her, his rapier making a great figure eight in the moonlight, slashing at wolves on either side.

The man reined in nearly on top of her, reaching down with his free hand to lift her up behind him. The huge, cunning pack leader had circled upslope; now he sprang right at Nixon's throat. Nixon's horse toppled, and the man was thrown from his mount, flung down, a few feet from the horrified Anne.

She saw the pack leader spring onto the man's chest. Nixon gave a squeal of fear. The huge wolf looked him straight in the eye, opened his gaping jaws, but did not bite.

A very human voice said, "Woof."

Slowly the beast seemed to grow atop the terrified bandit, its body expanding, becoming man-sized. The fur on the wolf's face and body disappeared, except for a fringe lining his jacket.

"Gawd in hell, Jock," yelled Nixon, "yew scared the life out o' me, yew damned hairy devil."

Jock was sitting placidly on the big man's chest, naked except for his jacket. He got up laughing, reached over and plucked Nixon's rapier from where it had fallen. "It'll teach yew no to threaten a lass, nor bully a lady."

Nixon lay on the ground, surrounded by the gleaming eyes of the pack. Alison was still hanging on to the back of her hobby, her chest heaving, looking openmouthed at the Armstrong.

Collecting their hysterical horses, Jock made a neat, short bow to Anne. No French courtier could have shown a leg more handsomely. "Madame, we meet again." He helped her back on her mount. "An' where were yew headed this time?"

"Ta my mother's house." Alison sounded shy but thrilled—meeting a man-wolf on the moor was special even for a Scots lass.

Jock turned back to the pack. The lead bitch trotted up to him. He knelt and nuzzled her, rubbing his face against her snout. Scratching her ears and rump, he gave her a very intimate good-bye.

Then the Armstrong stood up, waving his hand. The wolves loped off, having had their fun at human expense. He swung into Nixon's saddle, saying to Alison, "Let's not keep yer good mother waiting. Lay on, ladies."

They set off over the tops, leaving Black Dick Nixon standing stolidly alone, facing a long walk back to Liddesdale.

> *Spring, sweet spring, the year's pleasant king;*
> *Then blooms each thing, then maids dance in a ring*

THOMAS NASHE, 1567-1601

The Kirk on the Green

Anne stood at the brink of the dance. Swaying to the ill-tuned fiddles. Smelling Jock Barley's Blood simmering in the still-pot. The Sabbath dance of these Border Scots seemed infectious, almost a mania—a madness strong enough to carry away the most sober heads. She felt tempted. The whirling Scots, the skirling pipes, the bubbling barley spirits, nearly swept her away.

Piping ceased, cut off in midmeasure. Anne rose to look past the crowd. Women in wide skirts parted from men in leather breeches, making a path for horsemen. Anne reached out for Alison, feeling responsible for the girl.

A party of riders in half-armor and pot helms came clattering up on Border hobbies; bearing bows, pistols, and two-handed swords. Blue-and-white pennants fluttered below their lance points. The lead rider was a bull-sized Scot, wild and grim-looking, wearing a blue Stewart tartan pinned with a gold sunburst.

"Kerrs, m'lady." Alison looked more excited than alarmed. By now Anne was overfamiliar with the Border tribes, and it mattered much to her what kind of Kerrs these were. She was on tolerably good terms with the

Ferniehurst Kerrs—who had only ridden off with her once. But beyond the Kerrs she saw the red Cross of Saint George, borne by an English ensign; behind him were men on foot in white coats carrying hackbutts, and farther back a hedge of pikes showed above the hackbutteers. An English captain lounged on horseback among the Kerrs, wearing the Earl of Sussex's badge.

Seeing her own people put real fear in Anne. She could only imagine that they had come for her. Holding tight to Alison, she backed into the crowd. Anne was dressed like a Scot, but half the North Country might know her by sight.

Alongside the Englishmen was a preacher's blue serge coat, ringed by riders bearing tall Jedburgh axes with wicked round cutting edges. The Kerrs could not be Ferniehurst Kerrs—Ferniehurst was at feud with Jedburgh. They had to follow Walter Kerr of Cessford, warden of the Scots Middle March, and an ally of Sussex.

The preacher trotted forward, tall and angular, with a stern look and prophet-sized beard. A hush fell over everyone, then he thundered at the crowd, "Where in Scripture does it say yew are ta prance like proud Philistines on this the Laird's Day?"

Anne almost laughed at the question. Her fears had been for nothing. Sussex's men made no move to search the crowd, and must not know she was there. Instead of being dragged off to prison, she was going to be subjected to another lecture on Reformed religion.

Jock stepped forward with the swagger of a wolf who did not fear a hackbutt ball. His only visible protection was a blue-and-white ribbon in his bonnet; Kerrs and Armstrongs shared the same colors. Anne cursed his courage under her breath. Bravado would only draw attention.

"Yer lairdschip's most mistaken," advised Jock. "These people prance like Scotts. Any Kerr can tell yew Scotts are too thick-footed ta learn foreign steps; not from a Frenchman, nor even from a Philistine." The Kerrs laughed at the joke on their Scott neighbors; the English too were enjoying the spectacle. And Alison's eyes shone. Swinging steps and bold words made the curly-haired Armstrong a hero.

Anne hoped that Jock got no one killed impressing serving girls and half-drunk Scots.

The horseman in blue leaned forward, snarling at the Armstrong, "Such Sabbath dancing is pagan witchery. From this Sabbath forward there will be no such mummery—no dancing, no playacting, no gaming, no sacred songs nor playing o' pipes."

"The priest in these parts blesses piping an' dancing." Jock pointed to a small shaven man tending the still-pot. "By act o' Parliament they need no other preacher."

"That man is known ta be a debauched papist, a Highlander, an' a drunkard." The minister growled like a baptized Turk. Anne knew acts of Parliament would not stay this man. He was backed by the Kerrs and Queen Elizabeth, which counted for more on the Borders than a dozen Scots Parliaments.

"The man is a McNab," admitted Jock, "an' all Highlanders drink like royal salmon; but he is our drunkard. He mumbles his mass no worse than most."

Anne could see the Cessford Kerrs, rough-and-ready Border boys themselves, smiling under their pot helms at a market-town preacher baited by an Armstrong. Despite the good humor, Jock leaned dangerously hard on the ancient amity between Kerr and Armstrong. Anne drew Alison back, readying to run.

She saw the minister straighten in his saddle, addressing the crowd. "Any mass is an abomination, banned throughout the land. The Sabbath day was no meant fer work nor song, nor fer drinking heathen brew. On the Laird's Day the herdsman will not shear sheep, the miller not grind corn . . ." The preacher rose higher in his stirrups, face turning red, his fuse burning short. ". . . wife will not work fer sale nor market, but fer husband alone."

Women jeered his sole excuse for Sabbath labor.

"Shut yer shameless mouths." He waved wildly to the Kerrs and English. "Break up this gathering. Send them on their sinful ways."

There was a rush to save the still-pot as the mounted Kerrs began swinging lance butts. Anne hiked up her skirts and ran with the Scotts, holding hard to Alison. Jock could save himself. They fled straight for the village wood

bordering the green; Kerrs knew better than to chase fleeing Scotts into a wood, where dirk or dagger could undo
an armored horseman. Sabbath dancing and Sunday football were at an end.

Anne almost dragged Alison, dodging between timbers,
scrambling up the slope beyond. Crossing a swift burn and
a steep cleugh, the two women emerged on a high moor
thick with thorn and heather. From this treeless top Anne
got a sweeping view of the Teviotdale: woods and shining
water, meadows and plowlands. Below she could see Sussex's soldiers setting to work on the village, throwing
valuables into the street, putting torches to the thatch. The
whole hamlet was going to be burned.

And not just this village. Up and down the river she
could see fires being lit. Farther off there was a dense column of smoke that had to be Hawick. Half the Teviotdale
was already in flames. Horrible, but awesome. Distance
and the beauty of the spring day made it hard to realize
that each wisp of smoke was someone's home and belong-
ings.

As Anne stood stunned, a great bang shook the air. She
looked down and saw the kirk steeple collapse lazily, laying its full length upon the green. They had blown it with
powder—Sussex must want this sweep through the
Teviotdale to be long remembered on the Borders.

"We had best be gone." She took Alison's hand and
clambered over the next ridge, putting more ground between them and the riders below.

They did not rest until they reached the high *sheilings*.
Here no one would ever suspect that farms and villages
were burning in the valley behind. Black-faced sheep
grazed in scattered clumps, and flocks of white-faced
Cheviots cropped the grass together. Spring lambs wobbled about like fluffy clockwork toys with rose-petal ears.
From now until Teltane the shepherds lived in these sunlit
sheilings with their flocks, coming down only for feast
days and Sabbaths.

"He was woonderful, m'lady," sighed the girl between
breaths. Red curls cupped her pretty peasant face.

"Who was *woonderful?*" Anne asked, knowing well the
answer.

"Jock the Armstrang." The name came so ready, so willing. Anne could see Alison was all gone on the man. Spinning on her toes, the girl relived what she had seen on the green. "He stood up ta a score of Kerrs an' a company o' Inglis foot. No ta mention a market-town minister."

"There is more to being a man than bravery," sniffed Anne. She thought of her own foolish-brave husband, Tom, sitting in a dungeon cell waiting for the ax. She wished Jock would add sense to his courage.

"Oh, he be man enough for any woman," the girl laughed.

The young live beyond advice, so Anne said nothing. By now they were deep in the *sheilings;* ridges of sward and rough grass stretched every which way. She was glad to have Alison leading.

"Ye did no dance wi' us?" Alison gave her a timid glance.

"I am more used to French fast galliards than to your wild reels," Anne replied. "Though when I was your age, a low and impudent young man led me through a morris dance on May Day." Anne had seen Alison dancing with Jock. Moving with the pipes, they had made a pleasant couple, but it troubled Anne to see them together. She felt the burden of age and authority. Her handmaid was just gone fifteen, but danced among grown men; bare feet twirling beneath her skirts, hands clasped behind her back, eyes wide, lips parted in pleasure. In Alison's light-footed happiness Anne saw sensual abandon, a girl giving all to the body.

From staying with these shepherd families, Anne knew the Border Scots spent every spring Sabbath in drunken exaltation of the body—if not in dance, then in games. Sabbath dances were followed by Sunday football. Every man and lad in the village made up the sides; tubs of home-brewed heather beer marked the goals, and games ranged back and forth across the common. Alison and her girlfriends hopped and squealed on the sidelines, or lifted their skirts and ran in among the boys.

Alison said Anne had missed much living in such high station, but, "Ye could learn our reels." Raising slim arms overhead, Alison tripped lightly through a step or two.

Anne tried to follow, and tangled her feet on a tuft of grass. Catching her arm, Alison kept Anne from falling. Both women laughed. Not letting go, Alison led Anne through a few steps.

Then Anne put an end to it. "You can dance freely, but I have a husband in prison." Since that hectic Twelfth Night feast in Linlithgow, Anne had not felt much like dancing. The morning after she had learned Tom was in Lochleven Dungeon, and after that came Moray's murder, and then Brampton. There seemed little left to dance about now.

But her serving girl kept hold of her, and Anne continued the walk arm in arm with Alison.

Not until she saw the long loch did Anne get her heading back. By then it was late afternoon, and the water gleamed diverse colors; deep green in the foreground, becoming dark blue, almost burgundy, in the distance. Small stands of trees marked the start of the great Ettrick Wood. Sighting a black wolf trotting through a glen, Anne knew that Jock would be waiting to greet them.

Alison's mother lived on a croft above the loch, in a stone cottage belonging to the Laird of Buccleuch. The Earl of Sussex might mean to burn the entire Teviotdale, but the most diligent arsonist will miss the odd croft and farmstead. The tough stone bothy was beamed with cleft oak; its open windows were shut with boards whenever the wind blew. The four stone walls belonged to the laird, but the roof and thatch of the bothy had been put on by Alison's mother. She had the right to take the roof with her if her laird turned her out.

Anne had come to feel real fondness for this little mess of a house. For two months she had been a guest, with no good prospects of leaving. Jock was tolerated for his talents. When meat got scarce, Alison's mother served a plate of spurs to the Armstrong, a sign that he should slip over the border and return with some stock. Border Scots all subscribed to the belief that "God made the streams full of fish, the woods thick with deer, and the English rich in cattle, so that Scots need never go hungry."

Entering the bothy, Anne found a cottage full of unkept country folk waiting on Sunday dinner. The priest McNab was there, with his wife. So were Crosers and Olivers, bringing news from up the Dale. All the news was bad news. English armies had struck from two directions—Sussex and Hunsdon had marched up the Tweed to the Teviot, and Old John Forster had come over the Cheviots from the English Middle March. Ferniehurst and Hawick were in flames, along with hundreds of towns and villages. Branxholm had been blown up, and the pieces sawed apart. Hume and Fast Castle were besieged. Every keep and tower along the Teviot was being razed.

Jock shook his head. "Anly a single laird managed to save his hold. His granny was a seeress, an' told him the Inglis were comin'. He could not move his tower, so he filled it wi' peat and set the peat afire himself." That was an old trick that even Anne knew. The peat would burn inside the tower for weeks, heating the stone. The English would not be able to bring gunpowder anywhere near it, or touch it with pick and pry bar. When Sussex left, the fire would burn out, and the laird could move back in.

Destruction had not been random. Jedburgh and the Kerrs of Cessford were spared, because they took English silver and helped hunt their fellow Scots. People were appalled, but they were all old enough to have known worse. During the Rough Wooing, Elizabeth's father sought the hand of the infant Queen of Scots by burning out the Lowlands, sparing nothing, saving nothing, and showing no mercy for age or religion. But that inferno had been fueled by Young Harry's violent passion for young females—which also consumed Anne Boleyn and Catherine Howard. Thankfully, Elizabeth was neither as vengeful or as driven as her father.

Anyway, what could simple shepherd do? Nothing but sit down and eat Goodmother Scotts' stewed mutton. McNab offered up a short prayer in painful Latin, then Jock said a Selkirk grace over the meat:

> *"Some hae meat an canna eat,*
> *An some wad eat that want it;*
> *But we hae meat, and we can eat,*
> *An so our Laird be thankit."*

Anne stared at the sheep's flesh and prunes floating in fatty gravy. An awkward silence hung over the mutton. Jock speared a plump sheep's tongue with his dirk, plopping it down on Anne's platter. "Yer ladyschip ates first." He handed her the dirk. Come war or peace, common folk had to fill their bellies.

As delicately as she could, Anne took the dirk and started to carve her tongue. Her guests heaved hungry sighs and tore at the meat. No one bolts flesh better than Scots who have starved through the winter on black pudding—oatmeal mixed with blood bled from live breeding stock. They licked fingers with gusty delight, having no bread to sop the gravy, no table tools but the belt knives everyone wore—used to slice, meat, spear tidbits, and break apart bones. They rapped the broken bones with the pommels to loosen the greasy marrow. Anne still missed her forks and finger bowls, her acres of snow-white linen.

Talk turned from English invasion to the Jedburgh minister, a new manner of devil inflicted on them by the Kerrs. The English were going to leave—they always did when there was nothing left to burn or steal—but the new minister clearly meant to stay and civilize them.

"The man is a weasel," was Goodmother Scott's verdict. "A touch o' swine fever would serve him nicely." A strong woman, Alison's mother spoke her thoughts straight out, dismissing the minister's strange views on the Sabbath as the sort of insanity that infected townspeople, "all crushed tagather in their narrow lanes, breathing naught but soot an unhealthy airs."

Anne said nothing. Her high station did not give her much sway over the Scotts. She was a stranger. Worse than a stranger, she was English. She was no more a part of their day-to-day life than a queen of far Cathay. They came mostly to see Alison's mother, a midwife and herbalist. Calling her "Goodmother," they came for cures, treating her as the lady of the house, and Anne as some rare and fragile object. They fed Anne, and clothed her, expecting nothing in return, neither payment nor opinion. If she had given advice, Anne suspected they would nod, smile, then forget she had spoken. Beltane was all that mattered to them. They

would go to kirk if the minister made them, but celebrate
May Eve in the *sheilings* as they had always done, with
dancing and fornication. Anne saw Alison give the Armstrong another available smile.

She marveled at the priest's part in all this; sitting there
with wife at his side, preparing to say mass at a pagan
May Day—as if Pope and archbishops barely existed. Was
it ignorance, or knowing what his flock wanted?

Once she had asked McNab why he had a wife. He had
seemed shocked, saying priests in his parts had always
married. Anne found it scandalously common for Scots to
figure their descent from sainted bishops and monks; the
very name McNab meant "son of the abbot," inherited
from hereditary Celtic abbots in the Highlands. McNab
limped through his Latin mass, mixing in a language that
Anne guessed was Gaelic. Otherwise he fornicated freely,
always seeming happy.

Later, when dinner guests were gone, Anne sat up with
Jock. Alison hung on their talk as long as Jock was about.
" 'Tis better to bend than break." The Armstrong assumed
a philosophical air. "We will go ta this new minister's kirk
an' see what he is made of. I itch ta hear what a real
Reformed preacher has ta offer."

Anne said in the North of England they had Reformed
religion shoved down their throats. "Northumberland swal-
lowed more than her share."

Jock shook his head in sorrowful fashion. "The man's
views on song an' dance seem hard, but there be a point
ta having anly women at work on the Sabbath." He gave
Anne a sly smile. "It would no be bad ta swig kirk claret,
while being served shortbread by yew lasses."

Anne smiled back. "Yes, but the Kirk will expect a
week's worth of work out of you—no Sabbath's Eve
drinking, no football on the Lord's day, no Holy Monday
to recover from it, no feast days during the week." Half
the Scots calendar seemed to be holy days, and Anne
doubted there was a full week's work in the whole Armstrong clan.

"I admit the man shows no much promise."

Anne felt pensive. "I have an outright fear of him."

Jock took her hands with gentle concern. "I will na fool

you lass, these are fearful times. In Liddesdale the Elliots, an' even Armstrangs, are shining Queen Elizabeth's shillings in their purses."

Anne guessed Sussex would make a clean sweep through Teviotdale, scattering her sometime friends the Kerrs of Ferniehurst, Buccleuch, and Lady Janet. She had no notion what had become of Westmorland or the Darces—nor did she much care. Scotland was locked in its usual civil war, and Anne looked to be on the losing side. She had put her faith in Jock and heathens of his ilk, because there was no one else beneath Heaven to trust.

Jock seemed to realize what a slim reed he was. He squeezed her arm. "Do no take life so seriously, lass, it is purely temporary. An' May Day is a-comin' soon." He grinned at her handmaid, inviting Alison into the conspiracy to comfort Anne.

"Before we ken, 'twill be Beltane," agreed Alison— again the happy anticipation. "Things will be better come summer."

Since autumn and the Rising, Anne had lost her husband, Tom, her titles, her castles, her manors, as well as the cause Northumberland had risen for. Now she shared a straw bed with a Scots serving girl, who longed for a wolfish stock thief. Could another season change luck so stubbornly bad? "What is so special about summer?"

"Do ye na know? The days are lang, an' the air is warm." Jock smiled at her, as if a countess could not know the simplest facts. "Settle doon an' dance, lass. Rome was no burnt in a day."

The shepherds' swains shall dance and sing
For thy delight each May morning:
And If these delights thy mind may move,
Then live with me and be my love.

—CHRISTOPHER MARLOWE, 1564-1593

Sabbath Day an' Night o' May

Six months earlier Anne had sworn a savage oath to die before enduring the torment of another Reformed service. Exile in Scotland had been a revelation, broadening and deepening her religion. By now she knew the all-embracing Church that baptized her, married her, raised her, and restrained her would never rise again. Fleeing into Scotland had forced her to find her faith in strange places, so she was willing to imagine that she might find some shred of faith in the new Scots Kirk. Burying her foreboding, she went to Sabbath services with Jock and the upcountry Scotts, showing they did not resist the Kirk outright.

They gathered down the dale in a new-style kirk, one structure Sussex had left standing. Imperfectly lit and poorly vented, the narrow hall did not bring Anne any closer to God. Women and men were parted to prevent idle fornication in the back rows. Keeping to the rear, Anne could see nothing of the service but the pulpit, since everyone was warned not to kneel or doff their hats, "which were signs o' papist reverence."

The minister of Jedburgh did not preach the sermon, but gave the pulpit over to a skinny, whey-faced graduate of Glasgow University, assuring them that this boy preacher was one of that "new breed of men—the cleanest, most knowledgeable an' closest ta God." Anne admitted the boy cut a cleaner figure than McNab, the hedge priest who ate with his fingers.

The lad began by praising the dim and narrow kirk. In her womanly ignorance Anne had thought the place better fit to be a cattle barn, but she learned it was in no way the role of religion to encourage beauty. Stained glass should be shattered, tapestries torn down, icons and choir stalls chopped to kindling. The old kirk by the green would remain as Sussex's moss-troopers had left it, a ruined reminder of the bad old days. For that old church on the green had been the Synagogue of Satan, Sodom and Gomorrah, the Great Whore of Babylon with the Pope as prime pimp and harlot. The boy assured her, "We shall wage the war o' extermination that God commanded Israel ta execute against the Canaanites, upon them that would make the Roman Whore the immaculate spouse o' Christ." The world, and human hearts, "were polluted wi' all manner o' spiritual indulgences," which the lad listed in shrill tones: "playacting, masques, carnivals, ostentation, drunkenness, an' the wanton conduct inspired by diabolical music that delights an' bewitches the senses."

The congregation listened, neither delighted nor bewitched by the boy. When the preaching was done, they shuffled out to where the laird's table was spread with shortcake and claret. Jock whispered to her, "It were a lang wait fer the wine. That reedy preacher lad would make a better man if he managed himself a bit o' wanton conduct."

Anne trod on his toe to quiet him. She wanted nothing but to leave, to be out in air and sunshine, though she hungered for some shortcake. Since coming to Scotland, she had given up bread for barley porridge. Here the barest sort of pastry was as rare as spice cake in Northumberland.

The claret and cake came with another lesson. The minister of Jedburgh announced that this shortbread and wine were most emphatically *not* the body and blood of Christ. "We deny that sleeveless auld tale o' transubstantiation. As any reasoning man can see, these are plain an' natural substances, unchanged in their nature, *nor ta be adored.*" He took a bite of his unadorable cake, then lifted his glass to wash the shortbread down with a mouthful of claret.

Anne saw Jock's grim smile, and started to say, "No."

Suddenly the minister was spitting and coughing, his face screwed up as though he were poisoned. His mouth opened, and its bright red contents spilled out, dribbling down his chin, staining his blue serge coat. The claret had turned to blood in the minister of Jedburgh's mouth.

Afterward, safe again in the *sheilings,* Anne warned the Armstrong, "Jock, you should not have done that."

He looked shocked. "Is it so bad ta see a man beaten

wi' his own rod? He got down an bended knee, beggin' fer it wi' his arrogance." Jock shook his head. "It were powerful poor claret ta began wi'."

Anne was neither convinced nor amused. She said the trick with the blood and the wine would only bring more trouble.

"An, why blame me?" The Armstrong summoned a look of innocence, though his dark eyes danced. "For all we ken, it may hae been Christ's very own blood in that claret."

So much for introducing Reformed religion to a werewolf.

On May Eve in the *sheilings* Anne might have supposed she was a world away from that Sabbath day. People came over the dark moor, holding pine-pitch torches, chanting to the night.

> *"We cam all so still*
> *War our mother was,*
> *As dew in April*
> *That falleth an the grass."*

Goodmother Scott sang in a voice clear as the night, calling on Mary the Maiden of May Eve:

> *"O' the Maiden sing,*
> *She that is makeless;*
> *King o' all the Spring,*
> *The babe at her breast."*

The chanting line of Scots answered:

> *"We cam all so still*
> *Ta our Mother's bower,*
> *As dew in April*
> *That falleth an the flower."*

By an ancient standing stone Goodmother Scott lit a bonfire with the torch she had carried. Scots filed round the fire. As Alison passed, she offered Anne a deep dipper of Jock Barley's Blood. The Armstrong was with her, playing Lord of the Dance, wearing his jacket trimmed with wolf fur and black cowhide breeches turned hair-side out. Stick antlers were tied to his head. Most of the men were in outlandish costume, and the maids had flowers in their hair.

"None should be sober on Eve o' May," admonished Jock.

Anne thanked Alison for the dipper, but did not drink. The McNab was absent. Had he succumbed to an attack of scruples, or was the priest passed out under a bank? Singing and drinking had begun early in the warm April afternoon.

Never bashful, Jock took the priest's part, casting his torch into the bonfire and leaping into the center of the ring. Playing on his pipes, he danced a jig, joined by Alison and Goodmother Scott. The circle of dancers spiraled in toward the flames, torches turning their reel into a spinning wheel of fire, throwing tall shadows against the standing stone. Goodmother sang to the piping:

> *"Mother an' Maiden,*
> *Was never none but she;*
> *Well may such a lady*
> *God's mother be."*

The Scots roared back as they spiraled around the trio:

> *"We cam all so gay;*
> *War our Mother was,*
> *As the dew in May*
> *That riseth fram the grass."*

Anne held herself back, but the light and movement washed over her, warming and exciting. She smelled the barley juice in the dipper, tempted by its cool intoxication. The Kirk would never drive song and dance from these people. Music was planted in them. They sang at work and danced at play. Shepherds piped lullabies to the sheep. Women sang beautiful waulking songs as they fulled their cloth.

Anne took a drink, telling herself this rite was really neither pagan nor Christian. The spiral dance went deeper, an ancient path of death and rebirth traced by bodies, into the womb and out again. She understood that the Scots danced to real changes in their lives, dancing away winter, dancing away despair, putting black pudding and cold star-

vation behind them. The days *were* getting warmer. From
now until Teltane they could live in the high *sheilings,* and
rebuild the winter homes Sussex had burned.

Sweat gleamed on flushed faces hungry for life. War
and raid were forgotten for a night. Warmed by liquor and
fire, women hiked their skirts up higher. Men tossed off
shirts and cloaks. Anne saw Jock kick off his hairy black
breeches and prance half-naked with Alison, in shameless
excitation. Flustered but unable to look away, Anne
brought the dipper to her mouth, drinking more of the malt
liquor. Floating in her head was the rhyme her French tu-
tor taught her, about the witches' dance under the arches
of the bridge at Avignon: *"Sous le pont d'Avignon, on y
dance tous en rond"*—see them dancing round and round.

The spiral drew tighter, but still Anne resisted. She
would not to be drawn into the dance. Over the heads she
saw Jock's antlers and Alison's red cap of curls. Couples
flashed past her naked. By ancient custom there were no
marriage bonds on May Night. Breasts, thighs, limbs, and
buttocks gleamed in the firelight. Dark groins pulsed to
Jock's piping. The music and madness climbed to a cre-
scendo. With a chorus of screams people threw their
torches to the fire and ran into the night.

Anne stood stunned, gripping her empty dipper. The spiral was gone. So were Jock and Alison, and Goodmother
Scott. Children dashed about before the fire. Crones
crooned in a circle, and old gaffers gathered around the
barrel of barley brew; but the dancers were off in the darkness, save for a few stretched out in a stupor. From that
darkness came overloud laughter and women's squeals.

She set aside her dipper and knelt down to pray. No running off into the night for her. Jock was no doubt busy
with Alison. She assumed he would hardly mind if she
joined them—Jock was more than broad-minded when it
came to women—but how would she ever face her handmaid in the morning? Lying down on the moor, to writhe
naked under the same man, was bound to be rather leveling. She was a married woman, a Christian countess mind
you, not some heathen shepherd lass.

Kneeling by the bonfire, Anne attempted to address
God. It *were no easy,* as the Scots would say. She missed

the mass McNab had promised. Christ's image came to her, but her Lord's bearded face kept grinning. His crown of thorns sprouted antlers. So she spoke to Mary instead, to her Mary, who talked to her and had come to her at Durham and on Christmas Day. Her Mary of the Doves, Mary of the May. She did not pray for herself, but asked first for her husband in his prison cell, praying Tom might be freed. Then she asked what Mary needed of her.

Anne of Northumberland asked, and Mary of the May answered, just as at Durham. The bonfire roared upward, becoming a living blossom reaching for heaven. Anne stared into the burning flower. In the hottest part of the fire rose the Maiden, cloaked in smoke. Mary neither winced nor cried out; her face stayed calm and cool as she beckoned to Anne and sang:

> "Ye cam all so gay
> Ta yer Mother's bower,
> As the dew in May
> That riseth fram the flower."

The Maiden cast off her cloak of smoke, like a witch's smock consumed by burning. Then, like a witch, she twisted naked amid flames that dared not scorch her. *"Come dance, Anne, an' call my name. Ye are the kindling, an' I am the flame."*

Standing up, Anne was struck by searing heat. How could Mary call for her from burning so cruel, from fire so bright? She stepped forward. The heat forced her back to her knees. "Please, I am but flesh, I cannot come to you through fire and pain."

Whirling, twirling, pulling taut, the fire maiden danced and sang, her face both sad and gay. *"Yew are the tinder; I am the flame. Come ta the dance. Come, call my name."*

"Mary." Anne struggled to rise, but the heat pressed her down. Sweat beaded on her body. Sparks singed her hair and dress. The fire maiden flickered, faded, her singing dying on the night wind. *"Do na deny me. Do no fight the fire."*

Fearful screams came out of the blackness, followed by the beat of iron-shod hoofs on the turf. Anne's head snapped hard about. Blinded by firelight, she could see nothing in the night, but the Scots were up and running, the sober seizing the drunk, scattering from the fire. An old woman ran shrieking past Anne, yelling that Kerrs were coming.

It could have been Kerrs coming over the moor, or Sussex, or the Four Horsemen of the Apocalypse arriving late to the dance. Anne did not sit waiting to see. Leaping up, she raced into the night at the heels of the country folk.

Frightened Scots will outrun anyone. Anne could not have caught them on flat ground at full noon. Over black and broken moor she had no hope of keeping up. She blundered on, doing her best to keep her back to the hoofbeats and the fire.

Footing vanished beneath her. Falling straight into a gully, she rolled down a stony slope, scraping her shoulder, hitting hard against the far side. Hoofbeats thundered closer, engulfing her. Chaos filled the night. A horse flashed overhead, showering her with dirt and stones, hiding the stars for a heartbeat. Another mount crashed down the cleugh bank a few yards from her. She heard a Scot's curse. The horse righted itself, mounting the bank in clatter and a cloud of dust—then was gone.

Hoofbeats faded, and the tops grew strangely still. Uncanny calm settled over Eve o' May, eerie in its completeness. Lying nursing her shoulder, staring at cold stars, Anne strained to hear things. Nothing. Afraid to stay where riders had come already, she crawled along the cleugh searching for a hole or high bank to hide her. Searching through the bracken, she heard a stirring close behind her.

Anne froze. She was sure of the sound, not a hoofbeat but softer. A big beast was padding up the gully. Digging her nails into the dirt, she peered over her hurt shoulder. Out of the night came the doglike pant of a wolf. She watched the sinuous dark body separate from deeper shadows. Snout down, the beast came on in silence. Glittering eyes and teeth gleamed in the moonlight.

Big as the devil and black as sin, the wolf trotted right up to her. She could feel his bulk and hot breath. Anne managed to open her mouth and croak softly, "Jock, is that you? God, I hope it is you."

The wolf did not answer. Baring white fangs, he took firm hold of her arm, then started to pull. The animal outweighed her, but his pull was gentle.

"Jock, it is a grown woman you are chewing now. I can crawl on my own."

With a last tug the wolf let go her arm and turned back the way he had come. Anne followed, scraping her knees on stone and earth in her effort to keep up.

Smelling horses ahead, Anne hesitated. She heard them snorting in the damp. There was movement in the blackness. Rising on his hind legs, the wolf grew taller and paler; becoming erect, then human. Jock stood before her, wearing nothing but his fur-trimmed jacket and a whisky-addled grin.

Anne stood up, not desiring to kneel before a man naked from the waist down. Standing upright, she saw two horses and a small, pale mound between them. The white mound was Alison, curled in trusting sleep, heels tucked under bare thighs, one thumb touching her lips. Her free hand clasped her torn shift.

"Has she been harmed?" Anger made her words louder and sharper than Anne had intended. Lifting the limp girl by the shoulders, she let Alison's head loll against her. Closed lashes looked soft as a child's.

"Asleep," Jock explained. "The drink, the dancing, an' the night were much fer her. Lasses will go out like this, an ye can no get them up fer nothing before morning. While the spell lasts, she is wi' the Mother."

"How many young girls have you had this problem with?"

" 'Tis not my first Night o' May." With a low laugh Jock swung into the saddle and bent his arms down for the girl.

Alison had settled deep into her lap, and Anne was loath to hand her over to the man. Struggling to her feet, she found her sturdy handmaid impossible to carry. She could not mount her horse, so she passed her warm burden up to the Armstrong.

As she mounted, Anne whispered, "Where did you get these ponies?" Her horse was a border hobby, small and active. She had to hold tight on the reins, tucking her knees against the beast's belly just to keep her seat and get some control.

"They are in the way o' a loan," replied Jock. "A few of the fools dismounted. It is no easy task ta picket horses in dark o' night on a treeless moor. Not fer Jedburgh men unused ta the *sheilings*, so I took their burden from them. Men that can no care fer horses are safer afoot."

He reminded Anne, "All men's claims ta property are, alas, anly temporary. Beasts were no made by man, nor were the fields that feed them—so I steal stock from my neighbor when I am in need, an' expeckit my neighbor to steal from me." That was as close as the Borders came to the Golden Rule.

Setting out, she saw silver-gray waste and black twisted bracken, and heard the clop of hobby hooves on moss and moor. Every so often they would stop, lean, and listen. Horses' ears twitched in the dark. Anne heard night birds and the eldritch whistle of wind on the moor. When the weight of silence grew too oppressive, they would move on again.

"Things might hae gone farther an' fared worse." Jock rode with his buttocks and hairy legs exposed, not seeming to feel the night.

Fear no longer kept Anne at full tension. Taut limbs turned cold and tired. She drew even with Jock, hoping his talk would help keep her alert. Alison was slumped against Jock's chest, head resting on his shoulder. Bare limbs hung limp, the torn shift hardly covering her. Anne took off her shawl and wrapped it awkwardly around the sleeping girl. Alison stirred, murmured, then went back to sleep.

"In Mother's arms," Jock laughed. "Ye doona need ta worry, Teviotdale lasses are tough."

"That is no reason to treat her roughly," Anne retorted.

"Yew ken I was rough wi' her?"

"I do not know how you were with her, nor do I care to know. No girl needs to be filled with spirit brew and dragged out onto the moors."

"The barley juice was just twice distilled—no the stop-yer-breath whisky that they brew in the Isles. As fer draggin', the girl came runnin'."

After a silence Jock spoke softly. "I ken there is a hard-

ness between us, Anne, that I wouldna have. There are no
marriage vows on May Eve, so I may speak plain, as
though ye were just a maid I fancied. If ye had danced wi'
us and then come runnin', I would have been a happy
man."

"No doubt." She thanked Mary it was so dark. Anne
had long imagined this conversation coming, never expecting it at night upon the moor, over the head of a sleeping girl.

"Yew are no foolish lass. Ye ken that if yew would
whistle, I would come. But yew consider yerself very
much married, an' I respekit that, though I wished yew
were a bit less wed."

"Marriage is not a matter of more or less for me." Tom
was in prison. It shamed her to even speak of adultery
with an antlered satyr so plainly eager for fornication.
"Neither law nor Scripture put loopholes in my marriage
vows."

"There is little law in these dales, as yer ladyschip may
have noted. Since the Kirk refarmed, I have read parts o'
Scripture myself, an' found God's words most fascinating.
From Abraham ta Solomon the Children o' God were
never overmuch confined by marriage. In places Scripture
says plainly what a man should do wi' a pleasin' maid."

"That is the danger of letting every man peruse the Bible, picking and choosing his favorite parts. It lowers
Scripture to a common level." Anne knew there were
whole chapters of the Bible better left in Latin.

"I am no asking yew to lower yer Scripture, nor even ta
raise yer skirt. I am anly saying that fear o' hell an' hanging doono bind Border men much. An Armstrang must
find his own honor, or he will have no honor at all."

"And you have found yours?" It exasperated her to hear
him cloak his romantic escapades in chivalry.

"Enough honor ta no be rough with women, but give
them what they want. Ye have wanted to part o' me. I
have respekited that. Now this lass . . ."

He stopped speaking, shushing Anne when she asked
why. His nostrils flared. She knew his wolf's ears were
keener than hers; perhaps his nose was too. "Thar coming," he growled.

"Who is coming?"

"Do yew wanta wait an' see?"

Anne heard it now, low and far off, the up-and-down drumming of horses' hooves on the tops, the irregular ring of metal on metal. Both grew louder. Only armored men coming on horseback made those sounds.

Kicking their ponies, they plunged into flight. With nowhere to go but away, Anne gave her hobby his head. Broken moor flashed beneath her. Clinging tight to her mane, she let the mount control their careening path. Jock's hobby, carrying double, fell behind. Reining in to let him catch up, Anne caught her first sight of pursuit. A dim, indistinct mass drifted in their wake; small steel slivers winked above it—riders bearing lances in the moonlight.

Off again, Anne's eyes could hardly keep up with their flight—obstacles hurtled past so fast, they were gone before she saw them. Jock and Alison dropped back. Anne started to rein in again, and that small slowing saved her. Her hobby hit a hole, and Anne flew forward over her horse's head, doing wild Catherine Wheels across the dark landscape.

When sense and breath returned, she was lying on her belly, looking back at her horse. Bellowing in pain and fear, the pony kept trying to rise, and kept falling on the same bent foreleg.

Jock came thundering up, leaped from his saddle, and skidded to a stop with Alison slung over one shoulder. His free hand offered Anne the reins. "Go," he yelled, "this pony is fagged. He will no keep ahead carrying double."

"But what about you and her? We need another horse."

"There is no time ta get one. No time ta argue." The Armstrong set Alison down on a grass clump, then lifted Anne into his empty saddle. Alison lay on the ground, half-awake and bewildered.

"Give me the girl," Anne shouted, arms outstretched. Frightened as she was, she would not leave her handmaid to face the riders alone. Jock jerked the knife from her belt and slashed at the hobby's rump.

A burst of terror and the pony was off, carrying her away. Clinging half on the horse, she managed one look back. Her former mount was a struggling mass, still rising and falling in agony. Jock stood over the white form of Alison, the gleaming blade in his hand. Behind them came the armored riders, closer now, hurtling forward.

Plunging down slopes and over gullies at worse than reckless speed, Anne fought for control. She started to turn the hobby's head. Then her mount was off again, a black snarling wolf snapping at his fetlocks. She did not need to ask if this was Jock. He drove the hobby the way he drove sheep, sprinting ahead to check the way, then doubling back to spur the horse on. Anne seized handfuls of mane and hung tight. Pounded by the mad gallop, her body shook with sobs, crying for Alison lying on the cold black moor.

Jock dropped back. Anne took that chance to seize the reins and slow the pony to a sane gait. The wolf came trotting up again, tongue hanging loose, panting in sharp puffs. He made no more moves to encourage the horse. Their pursuers must have fallen behind. Or found something to busy them.

Anne was too filled with anguish to speak. She wanted Jock to take man's form and tell her he had performed some miracle, some magic, to hide Alison, but she dared not ask—afraid of hearing different.

Gnawed by guilt, Anne slipped to the ground and started walking her horse, plodding on tired feet by the first light of May. She saw stars fade and sky lighten. The long lock shimmered molten silver in the gray of morning. The insane gallop had carried her back to her borrowed croft. Jock ran sniffing up the packed earth path to the cottage.

The dry stone stood gray on gray, windows staring like hollow sockets. No smoke climbed from the mud-and-stick chimney. Anne knew no one could be here to greet them. They had come too far too fast for that. Looking down, she saw dark stains on her hands and on her dress hem; blood smeared from her horse's flank. She dreaded what had to come next. Jock would assume his human form, and she would have to ask what had happened to her handmaid. He would have to answer that she had been left for the Jedburgh riders to find.

Growling a warning, the wolf stopped halfway. Anne

froze, wondering what was wrong. Yelling riders bolted
out of the deep gully that ran along the rear of the croft.
Smoke blossomed, and shots rent the air. Anne's pony
squealed in pain and terror, then crumpled. Scared out of
her seven senses, Anne dropped her reins and ran.

Hooves thundered up behind her. Gloved hands seized
her shoulders. Caught between two riders, a mailed arm
about her middle, she felt her feet running in midair.
Hackbutts banged next to her, throwing sparks and smoke
at Jock. Anne knew they had not a chance of hitting a
coal-black wolf that only silver would touch. Looking up
as she struggled, she saw a bearded face grinning beneath
a pot helm.

Then came blackness. Someone had thrown a cloak
over her head and body. Folds closed as a cord tightened
about her waist. Through the thick fabric she could feel
hard armor, and the rough rider who had her. In the muffled darkness she heard Scots accents amused by her
plight.

CHILDREN OF THE MIST

(May Eve to Summer Solstice)

Children of the Mist—Children of the Mist refers to the outlawed Clan MacGregor, but symbolizes the clash between Highland clans and Lowland absolutism. To punish the MacGregors, Lowland governments gave their clan enemies writs of "fire and sword," declaring anyone who killed a MacGregor not only guiltless, but entitled to take the victim's goods. Absolutism's notion of the Rule of Law was to encourage the very worst aspects of clan society—legalizing feud, theft, and murder—while deploring the "lawless" Highlanders. The Children of the Mist survived because the common Highlander was unwilling to murder for profit, even when it was perfectly legal—a tribute to Highland lawlessness and to human nature.

> *I hae brought ye ta the ring,*
> *so hop dance if ye can.*

—WALLACE'S SPEECH TO THE SCOTS
SCHILTRONS BEFORE THE BATTLE OF
FALKIRK ON MARY MAGDALENE'S DAY

One Step, Two Step

Anne's cell had no window, just a tall vertical slit in the
outer wall. There was a stone step beneath the slit and a
small horizontal slot at shoulder height, where a man
could rest a crossbow or hackbutt to fire outward and to
the sides. Barely a hand's breadth wide, this long hollow
cross let in her only air and light. Anne dragged her straw
mattress across the wooden floor, so she could lie looking
out of the keep, over the peaked roofs of Jedburgh to the
green fields beyond.

It was the fields and sky that drew her. She did not care
to look down on crowded houses and crooked streets.
Anne had never lived much in towns, hating London and
York. They were filled with awful smells and worse diseases. She had never liked townsmen either, always trying
to sell her things, and sneering when they thought she
would not see. She far preferred to see peasants; plain-
faced Jacks and Janes who put food on her table, cared for
her horses, sang to her at Christmastime, and came hat in
hand when they were in need.

Anne could imagine what went on in those houses.
Down there sat the burghers of Jedburgh in their russet
doublets, proud of their tableware and glazed windows,
eating corn-fed goose off pewter plates—each a little laird
in his house, lording over women and apprenticed boys.
The whole greedy lot had groveled before the Earl of Sussex, just as they used to grovel for her Tom. The swath of
blackened keeps and burned villages that swept down the
Teviotdale stopped abruptly at Jedburgh. Calculating burghers had bought peace with Sussex by handing over English rebels and turning their coats on fellow Scots. Right
now she guessed they were haggling over her, trying to
squeeze out the odd shilling before giving her over to
royal England.

Anne did not envy their mean comfort and smug security, nor their blood money. She did envy their corn-fed goose and cabbage. The canny burghers were not feeding her goose and cabbage. She got nettle soup with lumps of lard and gristle. Simple English bread and clean water would be welcome when it came. Short rations were a false economy as far as Anne was concerned. If the good burghers kept her on this diet, she should soon be able to slide sideways through the crack in the stone, drop the thirty feet to the dry moat, scale the far wall, and make her escape. Then they would be out her reward.

She passed time reliving banquets and making up meals in her head, imagining meats gilded with egg yolks and saffron; veal, rabbit, partridge, eel, pike, and peacock, all ringed by cheeses and cherries. Her imagination amused her, but did not feed her.

It was far less amusing to think about what was likely to happen. She expected to exchange this cell for an English one; then her fate would be with Elizabeth. Tom was in some other Scots cell, facing the traitor's ax or the felon's rope as soon as Elizabeth and the Douglases agreed on a price. In the one way her cell was liberating. She was free to think about Jock without being disloyal to Tom. Tom and she were on equal terms now. Nor need she worry about committing some indiscretion with the handsome Scot. Walled away from temptation, she could smile at the thought of Jock and his good-hearted thievery. How sorry never to see him again.

Without warning, the oak door swung open. All smiles ceased. The minister of Jedburgh came in, tall and grim in gray broadcloth. Anne found the man's perpetual mean squint almost amusing, but at the moment laughter was neither civil nor safe. The minister was followed by a slight man, with thick spectacles and an educated manner; guards came too, carrying a large leather case that clanked when they set it down.

Anne greeted the guard captain, who had always been polite. One of his thick-headed villains mumbled, "She ar far sure a witch, speakin' soo strange."

The captain reprimanded his man, "If that war so, than Hume an' Fast Castle be garrisoned by witches, because

what she speaks is anly English." Her guard captain
bowed and apologized.

Anne accepted his apology, with forced good humor.
She had heard the word any woman in prison dreaded—
witch. That it had been spoken by an oafish clod with
whey for brains did not make her feel one whit safer. Mo-
rons like him had few original thoughts, speaking mainly
what every man was thinking. Did they dare accuse her?

The minister began by introducing himself and his com-
panion in his straightforward fashion. "Me yew must
know well. This is Dr. Gessler from over the sea. He has
spent some years in yer country."

Doffing his cap, showing thinning hair, Gessler said he
was born in Basel but lived mostly in Geneva and Germany. He spoke English well. "I stayed in London and Es-
sex, but this is my first trip north. Is yours a North
Country accent? Speech is a specialty of mine."

She said no; she was raised in South Wales and at
Court, and became Countess of Northumberland by marriage.

"I passed through Northumberland," Gessler reminisced,
"very pretty, warm and green in this spring weather." Both
Anne and the little man smiled. Neither needed mention
that being dragged through Northumberland by your
tongue was superior to the cold comforts of Scotland.

The minister ended this small pleasantness. "We did na
come ta discuss the climate, but this woman's crimes."

Anne gave him her first bit of attention. "I have committed no crimes in Scotland. You have no right to try or
even accuse an English noblewoman. I rebelled against my
Queen, but that is for Elizabeth to judge." Her station and
nationality were by far her best defenses.

Gessler looked to the minister. "Are you satisfied with
this answer?"

"Most certainly not." The minister glared at both of
them. "I doubt that she is any more a countess than I am,
nor do I care if she rebelled against the Inglis strumpet. As
she said, that is no a crime in Scotland."

Gessler took off his glasses, polished them with a bit of
blue satin, then put them back on and turned to Anne.

"Since the minister is not satisfied with your answers, we must start the first step."

"First step?" Anne looked the little man over, trying to divine his meaning.

"Yes," said Gessler. "I am a Doctor of Truth. Science has devised a method of separating truth from the most stubborn falsehood. We begin by establishing an atmosphere of honesty. Nothing I tell you will ever be a lie. The first step consists of showing the instruments. They may not be used until the third step."

"What instruments?" Anne took a step back, to where her straw pallet was pushed against the wall.

"It is well you ask." Gessler dragged the leather case across the floor to where she stood. Anne watched him undo the latches and release the belts that bound the case.

"These are the instruments." Gessler produced a pair of pincers with a short cord attached, so their pointed tips could be tied down. "Pincers."

Next to the sharp pincers he put out half a dozen thumb-sized vises. *Grésillons.*

"We call tham pennywinkis," the minister explained cheerfully.

Aghast, Anne watched the little man lay out his terrible collection, like a demented tinker displaying his wares. Nails, needles, and ironbeaded cords followed. She scrambled onto her mattress, backing against the hollow cross carved in the stone, jerking her legs up onto the straw, trying to get her limbs as far as possible from those bits of black iron. Each was designed to put cold, unyielding pressure on feeling flesh.

"Lady, you need not worry in the least," Gessler assured her. "I told you this is only the showing. These cannot be used until the third step. Think of it as a ladder. You are safe on the first rung, and never need to climb a step higher."

"Get them away from me." Anne could feel the free air from outside chilling her spine. "You have no right."

"And the *boot.*" Gessler clanked down the largest piece, an iron stock that fitted over the foot and calf, made to be tightened with screws and wedges. Then he knelt beside her. "You stand safe on the first step, as long as you give us the truth."

"I am telling the truth," she yelled, though they were only a pace away. "I am Countess of Northumberland. Alive and whole, I am worth a ransom."

The minister of Jedburgh found this amusing. "In Scotland yew will find that the laws are mar level. High station will no save ye. Last year Lord Lyon, King o' Arms, was burnt fer being a witch. He was a man an' a Scot. Yew are neither."

Gessler nodded. "I have heard all this before. I have heard women swear they were pregnant, possessed, nuns, even queens of the May. None of those are important. None are why you are here."

"Why am I here? What do you want me to say?" The stone cell had seemed merely confining; now it walled off the whole sane cosmos. They did not care that she was a countess, or what Elizabeth would pay for her.

"You will know what you have done, better than we," replied Gessler. "You need only match my honesty. I told you truly that these instruments will not be used at the first step. I tell you just as truly that they will be used, *on you,* at the third step, if you are not honest with us."

"I have done nothing wrong." Anne knew she had done much that was wrong, but not the wrongs they wanted to hear about. She had desired Jock. She had left Alison alone on the moor.

The minister eyed her. "Ta start, yew might admit that ye are a papist."

"I was raised in that religion." Anne tried to control her voice. "I still think that there is Mary in every woman and Christ in every man, in the Pope as well as in you." That last was half defiance, and only half truth. Anne imagined that the minister of Jedburgh and the man at his side would do middling well as devils.

"That statement has a heathen smell," snorted the preacher. "Yer own Pope in Rome has burned people for less."

"Then have my case referred to Rome; save yourself the price of firewood."

The Jedburgh minister called for clerk and parchment.

In the clerk's presence Anne repeated her protestations. The clerk dutifully took them down and left. Anne was not the least reassured.

Gessler looked up at the minister. "Are you satisfied?"

"Na, I am nat."

The torturer got up, packing away his tools. "Then we are at the second step." Both men left.

At first Anne could barely believe they would walk away. She feared they would start using those ugly pieces of iron on her. Time wore on her, and she saw why they were making her wait. Anger and indignation dissolved into gnawing, relentless horror. She did not even know what the second step was, but already she wished she were back at step one.

Gessler had taken firm control of her daydreaming. Racking her mind, she tired to imagine what she could say to satisfy them. They did not care that she was a countess. They were not counting the silver she was worth. That alone was shockingly insane. Driving the dance and devil out of Teviotdale meant more to this minister than toadying up to Sussex and Elizabeth.

What could she say? She knew how these trials went. They did not have a firm accusation or they would have confronted her with it. They must guess she had been out at Eve o' May. They had come to the rites, and to her cottage. Could she claim to be an unwitting observer—nothing like a participant? No, she told herself, *do not dare.* A single admission would set her on a slippery slope above the flames. The least weak word and they would torture her until she confessed to being fully a witch. She could admit absolutely nothing. Better to be tortured than burned. A really ghastly pair of choices.

She watched her door and waited. The bolt slid back. She braced herself. The heavy oak door swung inward, and Alison entered.

Anne felt a flood of relief at seeing the girl she had abandoned. Alison was alive. The girl held her head down, russet hair falling over her eyes, one hand twisting her white shift. Her gaze avoided Anne, but Anne could understand.

She called softly, and her handmaid shuffled awkwardly

forward. Anne felt more guilt, seeing a girl so naturally
graceful stumbling in her presence. "I am sorry, Alison, oh
so sorry," was all she could think to say.

Looking up, confusion on her face, the girl started crying. Sobbing, she threw herself in Anne's lap, saying over
and again that she was sorry too. She clung to Anne with
one hand, still twisting her shift with the other.

Drawing her in, Anne said her handmaid had nothing to
be sorry for.

"Nae," said the girl, her voice falling so low that Anne
could hardly hear. "I have done bad, but I could no name
my mother."

"You have not done bad." Anne felt foolish, correcting
her as though they were still truly maid and mistress.

"I had to give 'em names," sobbed the girl, "an' I could
no name my mother."

"Of course." She stroked her handmaid's hair.

"I named Jock."

"Jock can care for himself." Better by far than we have
done, thought Anne. She wished Gessler would show his
wares to the wolfman. Jock would rip out the little man's
horrid heart and lungs, with no more remorse than a hungry beast.

"I named yew." The girl curled tighter, hiding her head
in Anne's breast.

Anne knew what was coming, and patted the girl.
Among the Border Scots the guest was sacred, but still a
stranger—the pull of blood was stronger. Besides, she and
Jock had left Alison for the riders to find. How horrible it
must have been to fall asleep on Eve o' May and awake
in Jedburgh Gaol. How could someone so young stand up
to the threat of torture? Anne would have to hurt for all of
them. She was the one running from judgment. Her tenants
in England had been beaten and hanged for rising up
alongside her. She would not have more people suffering
for her in Scotland.

"But I named yew as a witch."

"It does not matter," she repeated. Actually it mattered
quite a bit. Alison had brought her a frightful step closer
to the fire. They had a hard accusation. A witness. In law
it was now her word against Alison's—not a countess

against a serving girl, but a suspected witch against her ac-
cuser. Anne's only defense was the strength of her denial.

"Will Jock come fer us?" asked Alison. "The man is a
woonder."

"A knight *sans peur et sans reproche.*" Anne said it
softly, with feeling. It was silly to face pain and death still
mad at Jock. Better to admit her admiration.

"What were that?" French had confused her handmaid.

Anne stroked Alison again. "Without fear and without
blame. He will come for us if he can." The wolfman did
not have a dog's chance of entering a stone keep guarded
by a garrison of Jedburgh axmen, and ringed by a hostile
town; but why tell Alison that?

The heavy door swung open. Gessler entered along with
the minister of Jedburgh and a pair of axmen. Alison
shrank deeper into Anne's arms, hiding her face from the
men.

"The second step," said Gessler, "is for you to see what
the instruments do."

"Get away from us!" yelled Anne.

He signaled to the guards. "Lift up the girl."

Grounding their axes, the guards used their free hands
to tear Alison away from Anne. Gessler walked around to
stand between the two women. He lifted the front of the
girl's shift.

Anne stuck her fist in her mouth, to keep from gagging
or crying out. She saw toes reduced to mangled stubs,
black with blood.

"Show your hand," commanded Gessler. Alison would
not show the hand she had kept hidden in her shift.
Gessler took the girl's wrist, trying to force her. Anne
turned away, clamping her own fists over he eyes. She
could only remember how graceful in the dance the girl's
body had been. She did not need to see the hand.

She heard Gessler stalk around to stand in front of her.
"The second step is totally for your benefit, to show what
the instruments will do. Many will not believe until they
see the work." He sounded astounded by the depths of human folly.

We have piped unto you,
and you have not danced

—MATTHEW 11:17

The Spiral Dance

After midnight Anne was awakened for the third step.
Hands in heavy gauntlets shook her out of sound sleep.
Gray men in quilted jacks dragged her to her feet, guiding
her out of her cell into a waking nightmare. Blinded by
sputtering torches, she stumbled down spiraling stairs.
Blackness danced ahead of her beyond the torchlight. The
guards would not meet her gaze. That alone told where she
was being taken. Exhaustion stripped her defenses, expo-
sing her to the terrors of the night, to fears of what was
coming.

With each step she tried to steel herself. Her life had
come full circle. When she rose up against her Queen, she
had entered into a war. Not a war of armies, but a war of
peoples, fought in prison cells and at the execution block.
She had ridden behind the banners, seen the men into battle, ridden in retreat; now it was her hour for battle, unarmed, not on a fair field but in a tower basement. Say
nothing, or die at the stake.

Down they led her, to the dank bottom of Jedburgh
Keep. Heavy, moldy air let her feel the full weight of the
sweating stones. The tower gain cellar had a wooden trap
set in the flagstone floor. Her guards heaved back the trap,
telling her to descend. Rotted stairs disappeared into a wet
black hole reeking of smoke and earth. The axmen prodded her. A draft of night air blew in her face from stone
vents. By the light of tapers and a glowing bucket of coals
she saw Gessler and the minister waiting below. If these
men were devils, she was entering their private hell.

Halfway down she stopped. Back and forth, half in
shadow, half in light, a body swung from the ceiling. A
man's nude form hung at a sickening angle, hands bound
behind him suspended by straps at the wrists, wrenching
his arms all the way back in their sockets. Between the
twisted shoulders lolled a shining stubbled head. Anne recognized the Highland priest McNab.

Her hands locked on the wood rail, and she tried to back

155

out of the pit. The press of men forced her down. Tearing
her gaze from the obscenely tortured flesh, she felt her
way to the bottom of the stairs.

She stood there shaking, eyes down, seeing nothing but
the packed black earth at her feet. Under her breath she
asked for Mary, over and over again. *Mary, please do not
make me face this alone.*

Someone strode around behind her, grabbed her gown,
and ripped the back open. She clutched at the front, holding it tight to her breasts, terrified they would strip her as
naked as McNab.

"Sit her in the chair," Gessler's voice commanded.

The guards bore her backward, toward a skeletal iron
chair with leather straps, bare and gaunt in the half-light.
The metal seat felt so frigid she feared her naked back and
hips would adhere to it. They buckled straps about her
wrists, waist, and ankles. Then Gessler motioned for the
guards to leave. Anne shut her eyes tight as she could,
feeling only the cold, hard chair and the leather restraints.
*God, this devil plans something so horrible that he does
not want his minions to bear witness.*

"This is the witch's chair," Gessler explained. She heard
him drag the coal bucket across the dirt. With a bang he
opened a metal door beneath her seat. "Coals and tinder
go in there. The fire can be stoked as hot as needed."

*Oh, Mary, help me, for I am alone, and must not an-
swer.*

"You have seen the boot before." She felt them clap the
heavy metal stock about her right foot and calf.

Dear Mary, help me. Keep me from speaking.

Someone kicked a wedge into the boot, locking her leg
in place, scraping her shin and cruelly pinching her calf.
She gasped between her teeth, but did not cry or speak.
Better to endure this than be burned alive.

"We work with the small joints first," Gessler lectured,
taking her foot, forcing a pennywinkis onto her toe. She
felt the screw grate as he twisted it. Metal sank into her
toe. Turning her head, she bit into her bare shoulder to
confuse the pain. In the blackness behind her eyelids Anne
held her breath, trying to force herself to faint. She needed

numbing unconsciousness, but ignorant lungs screamed for breath. Her body fought to breathe and feel.

They moved the pennywinkis to another toe, and tightened it again. The second toe broke. Air shrieked out of her.

"Good girl." Gessler sounded encouraging. "Now we have broken the silence. Honest answers can save you more trouble."

She sat there, held up by the straps, her chest heaving. "I am not a witch. If I were, would I not be cursing you?"

"This is no academic disputation," Gessler reminded her. "Arguments will not help you, only honest truth." He moved to another toe.

"Honest?" Sickened, she felt her hysteria mounting. "You have no notion what the word means."

"See the truth of what is happening to you." Gessler grabbed her hair, trying to force her head forward to make her look at her foot.

She kept her eyes shut, seeing her foot as it had been, not as it felt. *They may maim me, but they may not burn me.*

There was a pause in the darkness. Gessler whispered sympathetically, "Anne, is it the burning that you fear?" There was understanding in his voice.

Who would not fear burning? She felt him kneel at her side. "Is it fear of the witch's fire that keeps you from answering?"

Anne ran her tongue over her lips, then brought her teeth together to keep from talking. Words would only betray her.

There was a clang beneath her. She heard tinder loaded into the firebox. A shovel grated. Her leg felt the heat of coals being put atop the kindling.

She smelled smoke. "Here is your fire." Gessler's voice was flat. "Only the truth will quench it."

Heaving and sweating, she tried to lift her thighs off the hot metal. Straps pulled her back. *Oh, Mary, is this my fire?"*

A bell-like voice inside her answered. *"Anne, do no fight the fire. Yew are the tinder; I am the flame."*

How can I not fight? It hurts so horribly.

Mary danced in the redness of pain. *"Da no deny me."*

"I will admit it," Anne gasped.

"Admit what?" Gessler stepped to her side.

"I am a witch." Searing metal made her scream it.

"Amen. Truth at last." She recognized the minister's voice.

"Good God, I have said it. Please, the fire."

Gessler splashed water over her and into the firebox. "There, is the truth not better? Call the clerk."

She opened her eyes. Steam rose from the metal. She saw McNab as a grotesque crucifix, blurred by her tears. She looked down, staring into the sodden folds of fabric in her lap, waiting for the clerk.

Mary, is it true? Must I be a witch? My body can bear no other answer. She felt a desperate fearlessness. The worst had come. She had condemned herself to burning.

The clerk was a boy looking as shaken as she was. When she lifted her gaze, her parchment rattled. She confessed again for this boy's benefit, so he could put it down on paper.

"As a witch, what crimes have you committed?"

She looked back into her lap. "I said I was a witch, is that not crime enough?"

"Yew must tell everythin'," demanded the minister.

They wanted crimes? At that moment Anne could imagine no crime worse than the law that held her.

"Did you try to poison the minister?" Gessler suggested. "Turning the wine in his mouth into a foul and unnatural substance?"

She looked up. "Blood is not foul nor unnatural."

"It were no blood," the minister insisted. "Do yew dare deny that ye tried to poison me?"

"I dare deny nothing."

"Put down that she poisoned me. Were yew at the Black Mass an Eve o' May?"

"It was not a mass," Anne objected, "there was no priest."

She stared up at McNab, seeing how they must have found the May rite, and her croft. No wonder McNab was so horribly mangled.

"But yew did attend his heathen masses."

Anne said that she had. The boy took down the dates. "What other witches were wi' yew an May Eve?"

"I was drunk on Jock Barley's Blood."

"Note that she drank blood," the minister snapped. The poor scared clerk quickly wrote it down. "Now names."

She looked up at McNab's hanging flesh, thinking what would happen to anyone she named.

So she gave them the name of Harry Percy, her brother-in-law, who had taken the Earldom from Tom. She gave them her lovely cousin Crookback Darce, and the Earl of Sussex, and everyone in England who had ever betrayed her, ending with Queen Elizabeth.

"Queen Elizabeth?"

"Yes, I am an English countess. I did not learn my witchcraft in Scotland. The Queen of England is a witch, and her ladies are her coven."

"This is no surprising. The rule o' women is an abomination before God," the minister concluded primly, "but we need Scots names, Scots witches. Try the boot."

"I admitted. I confessed."

Gessler started to turn the screw. She could hear the scrape of metal on metal and clerk's parchment shaking. First there was pressure, then pain.

"Scots names."

"The priest McNab," she gasped. Much good that name would do them.

"Na more pert answers now," warned the minister.

Calf muscles screamed in the vise, binding, tearing. "Name the girl," suggested Gessler helpfully as he tightened the boot. "We have her confession."

Again she heard Mary speaking in her head, *"Anne, doona give up the dance."*

"Yes, if you must have her," Anne yelled. How could she hold anything back? "Alison was there. She is a witch."

"Good, an' what others?"

"Please, God." The bone seemed about to snap.

"Do no take the Laird's name in vain. Wan more pert answer, witch, an' we break this leg."

Anne needed a name. Only one came to her. "Jock

Armstrong of the Syde. He put the blood in your mouth. Please, I have given you names."

The minister leaned forward, speaking into her sweating face. "The girl Alison Scott admitted to carnal intercarse wi' the devil disguised as Jock Armstrang o' the Syde. Did ye have intercarse wi' him too?"

"No." She shook her head. Then she saw that was the wrong answer. "Yes, yes, my leg."

"What did it feel like?"

"What?" Her leg hurt so.

"Was it hot or cold to have the devil inside yew?"

"Oh, God."

Gessler backed off on the screw. Anne sank down, shaking, wanting to vomit. She could hear the minister and Gessler carrying on a distant debate. "Why did yew back off the boot?"

"The woman has confessed her crimes, and named others. You have enough to burn her a dozen times."

"It were fer sake o' larning. This woman has felt the devil inside her."

"I am here to aid the law. Science must find its own methods. Get a writ that says we must know the shape of Satan's prick, and I will wring the exact dimensions from these women. Until then this step is at an end."

Anne's trial came as anticlimax. Conducted entirely in Scots, it was one of those quick affairs where the only evidence is the word of the condemned. She could follow the language enough to know she had the right to recant her confession. That would mean another round of inquiries in the black hole of Jedburgh Keep. Anne would as well skip that step, and go straight to what was coming. So she held her head high, making a virtue of necessity, and boldly declared she was a witch. She was proud to be something that these mean-spirited men despised. Her judges glared back, damned her devilish arrogance, ordering her to be taken to the market square, bound to a stake, then burned alive.

Their sentence was neither novel nor imaginative; but Anne could not help feeling that these men had got the better of the exchange. Power hath privilege.

Short as the trial was, it distracted Anne from the mo-

notony of lying on her belly in her cell, letting her body
heal. Healing took time, since they would give her no
meat. Her right foot would never be the same. One toe
was missing, another gnarled and crooked. Still, she
trained herself to walk on it. The judges had promised her
one last walk in the open air: the short walk from cart to
stake.

Through her open stone cross she could see the market
square, with its gallows, stocks, and burning stakes. Here
the town fathers offered pious amusements to replace singing and dancing—whipping unruly wives and Sabbath
breakers, or hanging some ham-handed thief.

Her defeat was now complete. She had given in to pain,
accusing herself and those she cared for—and who cared
for her. There was one act left to play. A last penance to
pay. At times she felt completely crazed with fear; at others, uncannily calm—living moment by moment, feeling
the touch of her mattress, the lightness during the day, the
silence of night. She watched spring clouds through the
cross in the stone and made peace with her aching body.
Anne did not fear extinction. Since her childhood the
church had promised and threatened her with the soul's
immortality. But she did fear being burned. She wept for
the life she was leaving, trying to sing the sorrow out of
her soul:

> "We came all so gay
>   To our Mother's bower,
> As the dew in May
>   That riseth from the flower."

The evening before the burning she had another distrac-
tion, a visit from the pimply boy who had preached the
Sabbath sermon in the new kirk. It amazed Anne that the
lad did not seem to have aged at all. That dull Sabbath
was a lifetime ago—so many moments away.

What he would have to say to her Anne could not in the
least imagine. Another lecture on the harlotry of Rome or
refinements in kirk architecture seemed absurdly out of
place. Instead the boy launched into a spirited monologue
on the Reformed religion and the triumph of science over
superstition. Faith was now based on rational reading of

Scripture. For the first time since the prophets, men worshipped a just and reasonable God.

Anne let him run on, barely listening to the words, then she cut him off. "Bring this to an end. My time is more precious than yours. Reasonable men plan to pile fagots around my feet and set them afire at an ungodly hour on the morrow. What is the Kirk prepared to do for me?"

The boy looked flustered.

"I feared the Kirk was not going to be all that reasonable. So what is it? Breakfast at the Lord's Table after the burning—if I bow to your religion? Order me up something better than nettle soup."

The boy brightened. "Well, I hope ta shew yew that such irrational fancies are but papist superstition. No man on earth could promise yew a place in Heaven. God's grace is His ta give, an' nothing we do on earth may sway the Almighty Will. I ken this is a hard doctrine, but the anly reasonable one. Take the thief an the cross, who war never baptized nor heard communion, but Christ gave him . . ."

"You take the thief on the cross. If Christ has His mind all made up, *what are you pestering me for?*"

The boy sawed around his words some more, then said, "If yew would accept the Kirk, we canno see ye inta Heaven, but we can see yew are not burnt an earth."

"Not burnt?" her whole body responded. She leaned forward, nails dug into the mattress, knees tight, heels pressed together. Why had the boy been beating about? Why wait so long to tell her this?

"Yes, yew papists think that burning is some superstitious cleansing. Rational men ken it is anly cruel punishment. If yew fully recanted and accepted the Kirk, thar would be no reason ta burn ye fer witchery."

Her mind reeled through a wild dance. Had they dragged her to the stake just to tell her what they wanted? She would admit it had won her full attention. "What must I say?"

"Oh, there are no fixed words," the boy assured her. "What matters is the heart. Just pray wi' me. Spend yer time left in the bosom o' the Kirk."

"Time left?"

"Well, naturally ye must pay far crimes committed, that were anly reasonable. Ye attempted to poison a preacher, an' fornicated wi' the Devil. That carries a penalty o' hanging, though not o' burning," the preacher concluded brightly.

Anne relapsed into monotonous agony.

"It would be anly intelligent ta take hanging over burning," reasoned the boy. "Burning is so terrible ta endure—an' even ta do."

"Stop," she shrieked, leaping up, stamping with the heel of her hurt foot. "Stop before you make me totally mad. If all the Kirk offers me is to do a rope dance for crimes I did not commit, then leave me to my superstition. I would spend my last night alone, if that *were reasonable?*"

"Yew did no try ta poison the minister?"

"No one did. Otherwise the gibbering fool would be dead."

"That were fer the law ta decide. It would need a judge, not a preacher."

"A judge and a torturer." She jerked back her shift to show the boy her mangled toes. "I have had more Scots law than I ever wanted to know." She twisted her leg, so he could see the burns. "And spare me the lectures on the horrors of burning. I have had my practical lesson."

Taken aback, the boy asked her to please cover her leg. She was not being rational, "but arguing from feelings an' flaunting yer body, the way a woman would."

Anne shouted him out of her cell, free to be the hysterical, benighted female. The insufferable boy had raised her hopes with his dithering, destroying her carefully hoarded resignation. For a terrible long time she stumped about the cell on her hurt foot, trying to recover from his visit. Slowly her anger turned back to sorrow. She knelt before the dark, empty cross.

It was full night outside. The cross hung speckled with stars, letting moonlight into her cell. Hands clasped, she opened her heart to Mary, anguish gushing from its spring deep within. Putting every particle of her fear into prayer, she asked if Mary really meant for her to die so horribly.

No answer. She let her cheek slip down to the cold step, resting her fingers on the stone sill.

From the fields beyond the rooftops came the lonely, wavering call of a wolf. Anne looked up, straining at the darkness. "Jock?" The fields were black, but after a time she saw a dark shape trot through the moonlit market square, between the gallows and the burning stakes. The wolf padded right up to the cleared space around the keep, sat down on his haunches and started scratching.

"Jock, is that you?"

The wolf howled again, lower and deeper, a call to carry through stone.

Flickering wings came out of the night. A dove landed in front of her face, balancing on the narrow sill.

Anne slid back.

The dove cocked her head, studied the woman, hopped down to the stone step, then stepped toward the straw mattress. As she stepped down, the dove grew. Feathers fluttered upward, billowing into a great white cloak, draped over a tall, slim maiden. She had fierce child's eyes and stood naked as a child would, unconcerned by what her feather cloak did not cover. The same sad-gay look was on her face.

Anne summoned her courage and asked, "Mary, do you mean for me to die?" Her heart already feared what the answer was.

"Yes, Anne, all mortals must die, an' return ta the dust an' ashes that made ye."

"Yes, but must I die this sunrise in such a hideous fashion?"

"What does it matter how yew die, if yew have no danced?" She did a swift twirl, becoming Maid Mary of the Greenwood, dancing merry among the homeless and outcast.

"Danced?"

"Anne, we hae piped fer yew, an ye have not danced. Yew have anly struggled against the fire."

"It is so near to morning." She shivered. How could she talk to this immortal Maiden about the fears and horrors that plain people faced? The Scots had finally convinced Countess Anne of Northumberland that she was a very plain person indeed.

The Maiden's face softened. *"Anne, do ye think that I*

*do no suffer when my children suffer? When they nail my
son ta the cross? When they burn my daughters? There is
no time better ta dance than now."*

Anne pulled herself up, steadying her hand against the
cell wall to save her foot. Mary fluttered downward, becoming a dove again. Leaning against the wall, Anne
watched the dove begin to dance atop the cross of moonlight cast upon the stones. Bobbing, weaving, bowing, and
turning, the bird strutted in a spiraling pattern. Anne knew
the pattern. She had seen it on cathedral floors, in pleasure
mazes, and in ancient labyrinths scratched on stone and
bone. She had last seen it on Eve of May. It was the spiral
of death and rebirth, spinning into the dark tomb and out
of the womb.

Anne began to follow. Spiraling in, spiraling out, she
circled her cell behind the bird. As the spiral tightened,
she let go of the wall. Piping sad and gay drifted over the
walls of the keep and through the empty cross, called into
being by the dance. Tones rose and fell, tracing out the
holy spiral in tunes on air.

Favoring her right foot, Anne spun on her left, following the dove across the flags. She clasped her hands behind her back, the way the dove folded her wings, dancing
as Alison had done by the kirk upon the green.

Faster and faster turned the pattern. Anne followed the
labyrinth inward, forgetting her fears, forgetting fire and
death, forgetting all but the dance and the body. Toward
dawn her steps faltered. Sinking down on her tattered mattress, she lay listening, letting the piping lull her to sleep.
The dove hopped up the step, then onto the stone sill.
Spreading wings, she fluttered through the narrow slit,
flying into the fiery light of morning. Anne muttered
good-bye to Mary. The sleep that came was dreamless.

Too soon, too soon, the guards came to wake her, having to shake her hard. Opening her eyes, she saw that they
were annoyed, muttering that they had never seen a criminal sleep so deep on execution morn. Anne made them
wait, brushing the straw out of her hair before they bound
her hands. One said she was "a troublesome lass as well
as bein' a witch."

Then they took her down to a small stone postern where
the cart was waiting, with Alison and the body of McNab.
Hands bound, the women could not embrace, so Anne
greeted her handmaid with a kiss, saying it was so good to
quit of the keep. Shivering in dirty white linen, Alison
gave her a weak, worried look.

"Did Mary come to you?" asked Anne.

The girl shook her head.

"Of course, you already know the dance."

Alison stared at Anne as though she were mad, but
Anne merely turned sideways, so their hands could touch.
"Come close and take my hand while we talk." When their
hands met, Anne felt that two of the girl's fingers were
gone.

The tumbril jerked into motion, rumbling over the cob-
bles of the keep, thundering across the drawbridge planks.
Jolting through the narrow streets, the women stood side
by side, hands clasped, faces turned toward each other.
Anne spoke just loud enough to be heard over the hollow
thump of the wheels, seeing nothing but the girl's wan and
anxious smile. The hands in hers felt feverish-damp despite the morning chill, but Anne did not let go until they
reached the market square.

McNab's body was taken straight from the cart and
bound to a stake. Then the minister of Jedburgh mounted
the wagon, rope in hand. Anne looked away, seeing for the
first time the grim array of bitter faces. She saw interest,
anger, and shame in the eyes of these people who had left
warm beds or morning work to see two women burned
alive.

Morning work was not entirely undone; enough bundles
of fagots were piled round the stakes for swift, hot fires.
The minister of Jedburgh made one last attempt to disappoint the crowd. He offered Alison the rope called the
ringless plum. If she would recant her witchery and beg
forgiveness from the Kirk, she would be hanged before
burning.

Anne heard Alison whisper. She turned, trying to catch
what the girl was saying to the man. Alison looked down,
parting her lips with her tongue and speaking softly. The

minister leaned closer, telling her to speak up, this was her last chance to escape the flames.

She looked up and spit full in his face.

The minister of Jedburgh jerked back, and Anne laughed. He looked to her as if some employer had told him he would "get na more than a groat" for the labor of the parish orphans. Wiping his face, he merely held out the rope.

Still laughing, Anne started to dance. Turning on her good foot, she scattered the straw on the floorboards, spinning about to face Alison. The startled girl stared, then began to dance too, stumbling at first, but finding she could still use her feet. The women laughed and wheeled together as though the cart were a stage, as though it were the world.

Piping sprang up to accompany their dance, coming from the horse lines where spectators had tethered their hobbies.

Anne saw the minister's awful aberration of a face twist into an almost insane grimace. His feet started to twitch. Clinging to his hemp noose, he began to shuffle and trot, dragged into the dance atop the cart.

Dancing mania spread into the crowd. Apprentice boys capered with their masters. Guards threw down their tall, rounded axes and started stomping about with burghers' wives, and with each other.

The piping rose, coming clearer and nearer. Through the excitement a man came riding from the horse lines, piping on the back of a borrowed hobby, towing three led horses behind him. With one hand and a long sword the Armstrong cut the priest's crumpled body from the stake, then slung the McNab over an empty saddle. Leading his hobbies up to the cart, Jock leaned between the rails and cut the women's bonds.

Anne helped her handmaid mount, then took the remaining horse. Puffing his cheeks, Jock played louder, and the people of Jedburgh twirled madly. Anne saw the minister with bonnet askew and coat flapping, sweating with rage and exertion.

Their four horses rode through the capering throng and

across the sleeping fields. Anne looked at Jock with loving eyes, thinking how just this once he "were the anly man not dancing."

Dumbarton's drums, I hear them calling

—REFRAIN FROM CAMP FOLLOWER'S SONG

Dumbarton's Drums

They rode across the cold fields. Jock refused to stop until they reached the edge of Ettrick Forest—not much of a forest in Anne's estimation, really scattered woodland. There the wolfman dismounted by a dark copse of copper beeches and buried the priest, mumbling in Scots over the open grave. "This MacNab was an honest Highlander— rare enuff in our world—whose anly ambitions were ta bring a bit o' hard liquor an' loose religion ta the Lawlands. Small reason ta be tortured ta death."

Not a proper service, but McNab had not been a proper priest. Jock covered him over with dirt and stones. Anne sat dazed, thanking Mary she had been spared, still wondering why, and how, and what she had been spared for. That night they lodged with the owls in Ettrick Wood.

After midnight Anne was wakened by moaning and screeching. Alison was crying out in her sleep, reliving the horrors of Jedburgh Gaol. Putting arms around the shaking girl, Anne managed to pull her out of the nightmare, convincing Alison they were safe. The sobbing girl drifted slowly back to sleep, but would not let go of Anne. At full light Anne found herself curled around her handmaid. It was her first awaking since Night o' May that was not behind stone walls—what a glorious feeling to savor.

Jock was already up, cooking two large hares over an open fire. He greeted her with his usual good humor, as though catching hares for breakfast were a minor specialty with him—like rescuing women from the stake.

Lying there, watching Jock work, listening to Alison's easy breathing, Anne wondered what she was going to do with the two of them. Being nearly burned alive had concentrated her mind wonderfully. She knew now she wanted Jock, wanted him more than any man. Jock was a truly shocking rogue, but he was brave, resourceful, and though not really true, he had saved her life—which ought to count for something.

She still felt married to Tom, but this was totally different. Her marriage had been arranged, a uniting of Worcester and Northumberland. Anne was eternally grateful that Tom was honest and lovable, but she had not chosen him. She had not said, This is the man I want with me and in me. Jock was fast becoming one center of her world. His supple strength and determination had kept her going through the worst of times. She had slept at his side, seen him naked, shared everything with him, excepting only her body.

Two things stood between her and Jock: adultery and Alison. Her husband in Lochleven Dungeon, and her handmaid sleeping beside her, were keeping her from having Jock. Heaven knew Jock had no objections—this Knave of Hearts had made that plain enough. A few months ago she would have banished these feelings with cold fasting and a few bouts of prayer. Not now. Too much had changed. She had given herself to the dance, and there was no going back, no pretending that Mary would disapprove. After all, Mary had been espoused to Joseph when she gave herself to the Holy Ghost—who was also her son—a bit of business priests tended to slide over.

Right now, acting out any pagan desires was impossible. Her tired and broken body would not have stood it. Not if she and Jock were miles from Alison, married by Pope Pius himself and on their honeymoon. Anne was certain no English visitor to Scotland had ever been so thoroughly

ill used—not since Huge de Cressingham, Edward Longshanks's tax collector, had been skinned by the Scots to
make belts and saddle girths.

When she tried to rise, she found her foot so weak and
inflamed she could barely walk. A night of dancing had
taken its toll. Jock had to lift her onto a horse. The three of
them set out through the wood, into upland pastures, then
onto high moors. The trip unfolded in a dreamy haze.
Amazed to be alive, Anne found every view superb. Golden
eagles soared overhead, and rabbits dashed between their
horses' hooves. Heather-covered hills were crowned with
ring forts—everything from faint groundworks and a few
piles of stones to great marvels of ancient engineering, with
concentric walls and ditches, but all decayed and slumping
back into the earth.

They had a spare hobby, now that McNab no longer
needed a mount. So Jock made it his merry task to shift
the women about, hoisting them from one horse to another.
Anne enjoyed his familiarity. Just the feel of his arms was
exciting. She was content to share the ride with Jock and
Alison, not wondering what would happen next. When
they reached Hamilton lands in Lanarkshire, there was no
longer need to hide.

Hamilton itself came next, guarded by the great castle at
Cadzow. There she collapsed again into the warm womb
of Hamilton hospitality. The Hamiltons gave her a large,
airy room in the palace, with a carved oak bed, and tall
French windows opening onto an Italian garden. A few
months before she had fled Hamilton House in Linlithgow,
fearing she would be implicated in Moray's murder. Wanting nothing to do with the Scots civil war, she had tried
living simply in the Teviotdale—for her efforts she had
been imprisoned, tortured, lectured at, and very near
burned alive. With all their faults and feuds the Hamiltons
had to be better than that.

Were it not for her maimed foot, the Hamiltons might
even have convinced her that her weeks in Jedburgh Gaol
were no more real than Alison's nightmares. She propped
herself on feather pillows, watching summer sunlight
stream through the French windows, listening to the Sacred White Cattle lowing on the greensward, sorting

through her feelings. She discovered it was intolerable to think of Jock and Alison being together. The roomy palace and rambling grounds were crammed with nooks and closets, all fraught with indecent possibilities, admirably suited to an accomplished satyr like Jock of the Syde.

When Alison was gone for more than half a minute, Anne would lie abed imagining Jock galloping her in a pantry or under a bush in the rose garden. She knew these were her own guilty desires speaking, but whenever the girl returned, Anne would still search for signs of disarray or unexplained excitement. There was plenty to be suspicious of, because Alison was genuinely happy at Hamilton. Any country girl might be moderately pleased at being plucked from torture cell and burning stake, to live in a palace—but did she have to return from her duties smiling and singing?

As Anne's body recovered, her spirit turned restless. There were only two ways Anne could keep her sanity. She could invite the randy Jock into her big oak bed, or keep a constant eye on Alison. It was easier on her conscience to demand her handmaid's constant attendance. The girl was with her from breakfast through supper, and in her bed at night. Alison put up with Anne's suspicions rather well. She actually seemed to *enjoy* playing shadow to a countess, sharing hot cocoa, dishes of sweetmeats, and great feathered pillows—acting as if it were second nature to eat from the same silver plate, and piss in the same china chamber pot. As for Jock, he could spend his days dallying with them, but it had to be *together.*

It was Anne who found the arrangement annoying. She could not help comparing herself to the bright, cheerful lass who was always about. How old and plain she looked next to Alison. In Hamilton looking glasses she saw prison had added lines to her face and white hairs to her head. But she never once thought of sending Alison away, which was easily within her power. Like Jock, the girl was an important part of her world, though Anne had given up any notion of making this Scots lass into a real lady's maid—most days Anne thought she would be better served by a Borneo savage.

Nights were different. Alison, so strong and gay during

the day, would cringe and cry in her sleep. The girl could no more get over Gessler's torture than she could grow her missing fingers back. Finally Anne found a trick of keeping a lamp by the bed. The light had a soothing and healing effect.

The lamplight also let Anne study Alison in her sleep. There was no denying her beauty. When she was not having nightmares, her face was bright as a child's, with Cupid's bow lips, soft lashes, and hair shining wine red in the lamplight. Enough of this gawdawful foolishness, thought Anne. Tomorrow I must speak to Jock. If this girl is what the man wants, I will not stand in his way.

When Anne awoke next morning, Alison was already at the window, staring into the early morning light. The sky outside was cloudless. "M'lady, I thought I heard thunder."

Anne listened, and heard it too. It was not thunder. She quickly wrapped cloak about her nightdress. "It is cannon. Someone is bombarding Cadzow Castle."

The palace was in an uproar, and Jock was nowhere about. The palace, and in fact the whole town of Hamilton, was evacuating to the north bank of the Clyde. An English army had come up the Nith. Anne assumed it was the Earl of Sussex, but whoever was in command, they were less than an hour's march away.

On the north bank Anne and Alison waited amid a herd of Hamilton dependents, watching smoke billow up from the south. Men began to drift across the river. First came Hamilton cavalry, followed by Lowland pikemen. Then the man she most wanted to see came whistling up the road alone, his doublet torn and singed, his wolfskin jacket slung over his back, filled with clinking bottles. Not caring how it looked, she and Alison both went running up, hugging him, asking how the battle was going.

Jock slung his jacket to the ground with a clank. "Ah, the battle, 'tis gane. An' we're beaten again. The Inglis battered Cadzow inta a pile o' pebbles. All we could do was burn the boats and bridges, tryin' to keep 'em south o' the Clyde."

Anne was stunned.

"Yer would no have some food on yer, lass?" Jock

looked hungrily about. "We fought that battle on nothin' but brandy and raspberry ale."

She was ashamed to admit that she had brought no breakfast with them. "I was raised to be a countess, not a fugitive."

"Many's the poor lass that must learn ta overcome her upbringin'." Jock sat himself down.

The air around her filled with gray smoke. Flecks of white ash fell down onto her dress. Across the Clyde she could see a black cloud billowing up, blocking the morning sun. Hamilton was blazing. The ancient castle of Cadzow, the palace, the barns and byres of the Sacred Cattle, were burning along with the town—thatched huts, chapels, privies, paintings by Titian and Tintoretto, the Archbishop's parchment manuscripts, made one huge summer bonfire. Pyromania was its own punishment. By firing Hamilton, the English blocked their own advance, and lost enough loot to keep Sussex's army in drink for the rest of their lives.

Anne had become a connoisseur of defeats—the pointless siege of Barnard Castle, the botched battle of Brampton, now the vain defense of Hamilton—each defeat more complete than the one before. Now they were trapped in the western tip of the Lowlands, wedged between the wild Highlands and the sea. She was losing her sense of self, feeling her life fraying like old linen. Constant defeat stripped away all shame, as well as worldly goods. She ate what was offered, sleeping under hedges, in hovels, and between silk sheets, as the occasion required.

A great hairy Highlander sat across from them, placidly eating a shoe. He tore off a strip of leather, rubbing it against his bare thigh, then wadded it into his mouth. The Highlander dropped the remainder of the shoe into his pot helm, upturned over a fire, letting it simmer some more. Anne watched with amazement. She was not famished enough to find shoe leather edible—though it looked to be a good shoe of Spanish leather, with Italian stitching and a big brass buckle. She guessed it had come off the foot of an English captain.

Jock shook his head. "I naver saw a MacGregor et a whole Inglisman before, not down ta the shoe."

Anne smiled. Were it not for Jock's insolence and taste-
less good humor, she'd have little left to laugh at.

Jock rummaged through his jacket, producing a pair of
bottles. With a bold flourish he tossed one to the
MacGregor. "Here, wash down yer shoe wi' this."

The Highlander caught the bottle, attacking the lead
stopper with his dirk. He gave the contents a suspicious
sniff, like a dog trying to tell who had pissed there last,
and his grim black-bearded face broke into a grin.

"I bet the man naver tasted bottled beer before." Jock
returned to grin. "But he seems passin' glad ta make its
acquaintance." Digging out his own stopper, he offered
Anne a sip. She found the beer warm and fruity-tasting but
not flat—very sweet. Another beating, and now beer for
breakfast. She saw it would be a smashing day.

" 'Tis the Archbishop's own raspberry ale," volunteered
Jock. "Twice fermented, the second time ower spring rasp-
berries."

The hairy-faced MacGregor lurched to his feet, fished
the remains of the shoe out of his pot helm, straightened
the pleats in his kilt, and came to sit beside them. Anne
greeted him politely.

He replied, *"Cha n'eil Beurl' agam"*—meaning "I have
no English," the Highlander's all-purpose reply to
Lowlanders—then he rattled happily on in his own language.

Anne knew no Gaelic—Scots was hard and barbarous
enough—so Jock translated. "Yon Rob MacGregor, Child
o' the Mist, is offerin' ta share his shoe. He says if ye rub
the boiled leather an yer thigh, or some other sweaty
place, it gives a salty taste. Forgive his familiarity. I wager
the man has naver talked ta a countess, or even ta a plain
Ingliswoman." Anne admired the way the Armstrong's
clever tongue slid from English to Scots to Gaelic.

The Child of the Mist saluted Anne with his bottle, saying something similarly incomprehensible. Jock smiled.
"He's thankin' yew for the bottled beer, saying 'tis the
second-best thing ta come out o' Ingland."

Anne could not take credit for the beer. "The Dean of
Saint Paul's invented beer bottling. But what is the first

best thing to come out of England?" She wanted to know
what civilized thing this wild man would value above beer.

Jock did not bother to translate. "Why he means yew,
yer ladyschip. What would yew expeckit a Scotsman ta
say?"

From somewhere behind came the dull boom of mus-
ketoons, punctuated by the thump of cannon. The rear of
the retreating army straggled into view. Trudging pikemen wore crown-and-acorn Hamilton badges, and behind
them came mixed Border horse wearing the black crosses
of Maxwell's moss-troopers. These were Lord Herries's
reivers, driven out of Nithsdale by the English invasion.
Following the horsemen came the horde of camp followers—wives, mistresses, nurses, whores, and children—without which no Scots army could properly
function.

Jock rounded up their horses—the hobbies he had stolen
from Jedburgh. Anne had ridden them so long that she
thought of them as theirs; a sign of how Scots she was becoming. Jock helped the women mount, then slung the
jacket full of bottles over his saddle. The Child of the Mist
dumped the boiling water from his pot helm, putting out
the fire, and set off shoe in hand after the beer.

Anne saw Alison take up a child to ride in front of
her—a very natural gesture for the girl to make. Half a
child herself, Alison had a caring way with everyone. Such
easy generosity made Anne feel even worse for being jealous of her and Jock. Anne stopped an overburdened
mother, asking if she wanted her boy to ride as well. The
surprised and grateful woman gave her child up to Anne.

From the top of her hobby Anne could see the end of
the little army coming up the road. Italian musketeers,
under a Spanish corporal, ceased firing back at the English, and helped the women along—showing their fine
blend of Latin chivalry and Dago cunning. Last of all
came a ragged schiltron armed with partizans, spiked hal-
berds, and bearing the red-and-white Hamilton banner. Behind them, she could see the great burning pyre where
Hamilton had been.

They swung wide to the north and west, headed for
Dumbarton Castle, the last Hamilton stronghold in the

Lowlands, pressed between the Stewart earldom of Lennox and the Firth of Clyde. Since Moray's murder, Earl Lennox had led the King's lords, allied with Elizabeth and England. Jock outlined the trek ahead. "We must move quickly, an' pass a line of hostile castles—Dunglass, Mugdock, an' Duntreath—ta get to Dumbarton. An' avoid Glasgow as well, which is a Lennox town, an' a Kirk stronghold ta boot."

Anne could barely believe how miserable her luck was running. Dumbarton, the last castle in the west Lowlands still holding for Mary, was a very small mousehole watched by several big cats.

Throughout the grueling, weary ride Jock continued to pass around warm beer. After the first dozen miles Anne saw the worst-burdened following behind. Bundles were dropped by the roadside as footsore women staggered to keep up. Corporal Mendoza's mercenaries and Hamilton pikemen picked up children to carry them on their shoulders.

Mendoza himself, marching beside Anne, opened his cartridge box, giving something to the boy in her lap. With a sly little bow he handed Anne a bit of stale bread wrapped around a dark tablet. She put it in her mouth and bit down, enjoying the bittersweet explosion on her tongue. She thanked Mendoza, asking where he had got sugared chocolate.

The man had campaigned in France and Flanders, and spoke a wretched sort of French. *"M'dama,* old soldiers always carry sweets or dried apples in their cartridge boxes. Bread and chocolate will save you more often than powder and ball." Damned smart for a Dago, and far better than chewing shoe leather; she only wished he had more.

Dusk found them deep in Lennox country, past the line of castles but still short of Dumbarton. As the night grew blacker, Anne closed her eyes, clutching her reins and the sleeping boy in her lap, trusting to her hobby to keep up with the others—any signal from his blind rider would be pointless. At last the column shuffled to a confused halt in pitch-darkness. Anne heard firing ahead. She dismounted, giving the sleeping child to his mother, who had been hanging at her stirrup. Sitting down, Anne held the reins of her hobby so she would not lose him.

She asked Mendoza, "How can there be shooting ahead of us?"

"Fools burning off powder, *m'dama*. You do not see my *esquada* doing that."

"I *see* nothing at all," replied Anne.

Mendoza brought out a glowing slow match and lit a stump of candle. Anne made out the Spaniard's grinning face. Women cheered the light. Hackbutteers always carried fire for their guns, so Mendoza's men lit more candles. Anne could see the women settling down on either side of the roadway, preparing to camp right there rather than blunder into the firing ahead. Spanish and Italian mercenaries played with wee Scots babies, and tried to converse with their mothers. Like most mercenaries, they knew basic idioms for "friend," "food," and "fornication."

The firing tapered off. Hamiltons and Maxwells drifted back, reclaiming their women by firelight—much to the dismay of the dons who had been doing their darndest to make the foreign women forget their husbands and lovers.

The Scots said someone had got across their path.

Everyone complained. It was not fair. How could Sussex have got ahead of them? "No after such a terrible lang day o' marchin'." Alison lay her head in Anne's lap.

She stroked the girl and said nothing. By now Anne assumed she was a horrible Jonah. Nearly every place she had laid her head in Scotland was burned to the ground. The line of blackened homes and razed holds stretched from Hamilton through the Teviotdale to the Borders. She wanted desperately not to bring disaster to these people as well.

From far off she heard the low, heavy beat of kettledrums. "It's Dumbarton," a Hamilton whispered. "They're beatin' the castle drums ta call us in. They must not know that the Inglis have gotten between us an' them."

" 'Tis no the Inglis ahead o' us," announced a voice in the night. Jock Armstrong came sliding out of the dark, a half-bottle of beer in his hand. The hulking Child of the Mist loomed behind him. " 'Tis anly Gordon Highlanders. Come ta help the Hamiltons, an' as lost as we are."

Mendoza asked what the Scot was saying. Anne translated.

"How does he know?" Mendoza was wary of the wild-looking pair.

Anne shrugged. "I suppose he trotted through their lines, sniffing out their camp and stealing a meal."

"¿Cómo?"

"The man is a *loup-garou.*"

Mendoza still looked puzzled. Either he could not follow her French, or did not believe in beast-men.

Jock was soon proven right. Hundreds of Gordon horsemen came trotting into the firelight wearing dark green tartan trews, the plaid pants of Highland cavalry. Round targes and basket-hilted broadswords hung from their saddles. They had come south into the Lowlands to uphold Queen Mary's claim to the throne—and see what they could steal.

As the Gordons settled down alongside the Lowlanders, Anne found both groups were grateful to Jock. The allies had been exchanging shots in the dark, until the Armstrong slipped through the Gordon *piquets* and found out who was firing. Were it not for Jock, there might have been a pretty little fight between friends—a Scots civil war being very much an armed free-for-all.

Anne heard bawling cattle. Dinner marched up the road out of the darkness. A Hamilton complained, " 'Tis so like Highlanders ta come jes as the food arrives. First ta feast, last ta fight."

The castle drums were drowned out by a great bellowing, as Gordons and Hamiltons began to slaughter the cattle. Anne could see the beasts were white aurochs, with graceful horns. These Sacred Cattle of the Hamiltons had been bred through generations for sacrifice, which did not make them a whit happier about their fate. The Gordons butchered by leaping torchlight as though it were a pagan rite. Men in dark plaids held the half-wild oxen with ropes. An executioner, stripped to the waist, dispatched the struggling victims with a poleax.

Seeing the cattle crumple, spitting great gouts of blood, Anne closed her eyes. With eyelids shut she could still hear their pleading bellows—sounding like crying children. The slaughter went on and on. Then, with the death of the last frightened animal, an eerie silence echoed over the crowd.

Anne smelled the steaming blood, mixed with urine and dung. Dumbarton's drums boomed hollow in the distance, sounding softer now. Opening her eyes, she saw a tall woman with dark hair and chalk-white skin step out from among the Gordons. She wore a black ankle-length gown, with a dark mantle, and a crown of purple blossoms, so dark they too seemed black. Her face was long, with large, staring eyes and a strong nose. Gown and features fairly screamed, "Witch."

Jock whispered, "The Gordon Witch, a familiar o' Lady Huntly."

Where her skin showed, the witch was as white as the waning moon. She announced in a clear voice, "I need a woman an' man of royal blood."

From fear or modesty not a soul stepped forward. The Gordon Witch walked around the circle of onlookers, stopping when she came to Anne. "Yew have the blood royal."

Startled, she shook her head. "Only on the wrong side of the blanket." Her ancestor, Edward Longshanks, had ruled both England and Scotland. But two of Anne's forebears had been bastards.

"Do yew think that matters ta me?" The witch motioned. "Come, I must have a royal couple if any here are ta win through ta Dumbarton."

The fears and expectations of the crowd pushed her forward. Were she to back down now, it would be the worst possible omen for this pathetic little army. She stood where the witch indicated, at the edge of the sacrifice area. The castle drums seemed to beat louder.

Staring at the slaughtered cattle, she wondered which man the witch would pick. Jock was more likely to have spilled royal blood than to have been born with it. Perhaps the courtly Mendoza? More likely it would be a Hamilton captain, kin to the Archbishop, descended from the Angus Kings of Moray.

A hairy-chested Scot stepped up next to her. Out of the corner of her eye she saw it was Rob MacGregor, the

Child of the Mist. My God, what kind of king did he come from?

Moving slowly in the hush, the Gordon Witch knelt by the gashed throat of a bull, collecting a bowl of hot blood. Straightening, she brought the bowl over to them. Anne wanted to slink into the crowd, but did not dare move. *Do not make me drink that.* With nothing but beer and chocolate in her belly, she would have puked the blood right back.

Low and grave, the witch intoned, "This will bring yew ta Dumbarton." Drums pounding, she lifted the bowl overhead, her long white arms forming a graceful crescent, like bull's horns, or the limbs of the moon. Blood held high, she wailed in Gaelic. Not understanding a word, Anne snuck a look at the Child of the Mist. The rugged MacGregor tensed, turning almost white and looking stone sober. Whatever prayer or spell the witch chanted was powerful enough to drive the beer out of a Highlander.

Bringing the bowl down, the witch spoke slowly to Anne. "I am going ta mark ye. Wear this blood an' it will bring us safely inta Dumbarton."

Anne stood rigid. *I will submit to this. I will not fail these people too.*

Reaching out, the witch opened the front of Anne's dress. Her back was to the crowd, but she was shamefully aware of the big Scot beside her. The witch dipped a finger in the bull's blood and traced a smooth, cool crescent above Anne's breasts, starting and ending at the collarbones. "Do no wash off the mark till yew are safe in Dumbarton."

The witch stepped sideways and made the same mark on the MacGregor, saying something in Gaelic. Then she turned back to Anne. "We will meet again, when the hurly-burly's done." Turning a third time, she disappeared into the darkness between the trees.

Anne watched the Gordons gut and cook the cattle, feeling the blood drying under her dress. She could see the same curving line of black blood under the MacGregor's loose tartan. It was a slim bit of superstition on which to pin her hopes of reaching Dumbarton, but the witch had promised.

Leaning over to Jock, she asked, "What king's line could he have come from?"

"*S' rioghal mo dhream,*" Jock replied. "Means *My blood is royal,* a MacGregor motto. They descend from King Alpin o' Argyll. Alpin also claimed kingscip o' the Picts, through his mother, but there are those that dispute it. 'Twas all a lang time ago."

The hollow between her breasts itched intolerably. Anne had Alison take hold of her hands, to keep from scratching off the sign. Alison held tight, using even her maimed hand. The girl was so helpful and trusting, better by far than Jock deserved. Anne felt half-jealous and half-maternal.

When the meat came, they ate like starved bears.

Mendoza sat beside them, using knife and ivory fork—not tearing at greasy meat with greasy fingers, the way Scots preferred. Between polite bites he asked, "Is it true *m'donna* is a *bruja* too?"

Anne was startled. "A *bruja?* Do you mean a witch?"

"*Sí.*" The Spaniard went calmly back to his meat.

"I suppose that depends on your faith in Scots law. I was convicted of witchcraft in Jedburgh, and very nearly burned at the stake. But I am not the sort of witch that casts spells, just the sort that gets jailed and tortured." Anne discounted the dance in the market square, which must have been Mary's work, and was very much a one-time thing.

"*Madre de Dios.*" Mendoza shook his head. "In Galicia we do not like to burn women as witches. The stake is saved for heretic preachers, and lapsed Catholics."

"The sign of a civilized country." She said it sarcastically, humoring Mendoza, who was trying to cheer her. Actually she wished people would not roast each other. Religious burnings had been almost unknown in the North Country—like bottled beer, they were a southern innovation.

Mendoza sighed over his meat. "Well, I do wish we had an honest *bruja.* One that could cast a little fog. I would have asked this dark Scotswoman, but I do not speak her tongue."

"A fog?"

Mendoza nodded, "Normally I like to see what I shoot, but tomorrow morning I would not mind a thick, dense fog."

"What on earth for?" Anne was looking forward to seeing where they were going.

"So our enemies will not see how few we are."

"What enemies have we ahead?" asked Anne.

Mendoza looked to Jock, who was bound to know better than anyone. The wolfman answered in French. "A great mob is coming up from Glasgow to meet us. Lennox Stewarts, Glasgow militia, even students from the university." Anne remembered the boy who had preached in the new kirk—"that new breed o' men; the cleanest, most knowledgeable, an' closest ta God." He had been a Glasgow graduate.

"Well, I will work on a fog." There had been a time when gallant Latin gentlemen made a pretense of wanting her affection. Now all they were after was a change in the weather. Fires burned low, and a quiet commotion came from the Gordons' camp—hard, fast breathing, male grunts, women moaning.

Stretched out next to her, Jock whispered, " 'Tis an auld Highland custom to give yer wife a lively thumping afore a battle. It has been the salvation o' many a clan. At the Battle o' the Shirts, the Frasers an' MacDonalds shed their armor an' hewed away at each other until anly eight MacDonalds an' five Frasers were left standing. Clan Fraser might have been extinguished, but for the lucky fact that every one o' them had left his wife in foal."

From the admiration in his voice, Jock clearly favored the Highland custom. But with Alison lying on her other side, and stirring in her sleep, Anne contented herself with a few evening prayers; passing on Mendoza's request for morning mist, to cover their run into Dumbarton. As the heaving and sighing subsided, Alison needed to be held, and Anne drifted into a black, dreamless sleep.

Loud voices jerked her instantly awake. Her eyes opened so suddenly it was like a light going on. It was day—and she was totally surrounded by a bright white wall of fog that spread the light without letting her see more than a dozen yards in any direction.

Hamiltons shouted, "The Gordons are gone! The Gordons are gone!"

As far as she could tell, the Highlanders had vanished along with the landscape. The shouts were all in Lowland accents. The Gordon camp was deathly quiet. Anne could see a wet pile of embers where the nearest Gordon fire had been. Even the big MacGregor, who had been lying beside their fire, was gone. Behind her some Hamilton woman was babbling the Ninety-first Psalm:

". . . thou shalt not be afraid for the terror by night . . .
nor for the arrow that flieth by day . . ."

The words were less than comforting in the misty half-light.

Alison was awake next to her. Jock and Mendoza were crouched side by side, staring at the wall of fog. The woman's voice rose:

". . . a thousand shall fall at thy side,
and ten thousand at thy right hand,
but it shall not come nigh thee . . ."

It was a survivor's prayer, not the words of someone who expected to win.

Anne congratulated Mendoza on getting his mist. The man nodded. "But I smell a slow match burning."

"Where?" Jock sniffed the air, crouching in his wolfskin coat and tattered hose, a rapier in his fist.

"There." The Spaniard pointed.

"Where?" Jock stared.

"Over there."

Anne listened to the absurd dialogue, straining to see into the mist herself. For once the wolfman's keen nose had failed him. The gunner smelled burning powder better than Jock.

The white wall erupted in their faces, shattered by a wild Scots yell and a ragged fusillade. The volley flew over their heads, splintering branches and bringing down twigs.

"Ta the horses." Jock gave her a shove, and hauled Alison upright. Anne scrambled aboard her hobby, seeing Mendoza take the spare mount.

A gleaming hedge of pikes appeared. Behind them a mass of shadowy men stormed out of the mist, screaming, "A Stewart, a Stewart," the Lennox battle cry. The wave of flesh and steel swept over the ground where the Gordons had been. Startled Hamiltons turned and scattered.

Anne urged her horse into a mad sprint, following Jock. The Armstrong had been over the ground before, in pitchblackness. Crashing breakneck through the fog, Anne heard yells and shots from all sides. Friend or foe might be firing at her, but fortunately neither had a hope of hitting. Gunsmoke just added to the mist.

The frantic clamor fell behind her. Jock eased up. Alison and Mendoza came galloping into them. High above, Anne heard the booming of kettledrums. Dumbarton still called to them through the fog. Taking his bearings from the drums, Jock set off again, urging her along. Anne had no idea how close they were to the castle—fog thickened as they approached the Clyde Estuary, and the low drums gave little hint of distance in the wet, heavy air.

Without warning, the ground opened in front of them, becoming a deep ditch. As they leaped the trench, someone's *piquets* banged away at them—point-blank. Her horse squealed beneath her. She felt a hack-butt ball flap through her dress, another thumped into her boot, a third flicked her finger without drawing blood. Hamilton or Lennox, who could say?

Beyond the dry ditch was a cleared space, then a towering stone wall—gray squared boulders seemed to materialize directly from the fog. "Dumbarton," Jock announced, proud as if he had piled the stones himself.

Following the wall, they found a small wooden postern, protected by an angle of stone. Dismounting, Jock began beating on the gate, yelling at the Hamiltons inside to "Get off yer sleepy arses an' open this damned postern."

Shots spattered against the wall. Their hobbies reared and plunged. Slipping from the saddle, Anne lost hold of her mount. More shots slammed into the stonework. Chips and splinters flew about. Alison's good hand closed round Anne's wrist, jerking her into the shelter of the angle covering the postern.

Jock pounded on the wood with the pommel of his rapier. Mendoza knelt by the gap between the angle and the main wall, priming his hackbutt. Anne saw dim figures rise from the ditches behind them, preparing to rush the postern.

"Open yer bluddy gate," bellowed Jock.

"Excuse me, *m'dama.*" Mendoza elbowed her behind him, poking his hackbutt out the gap. The gun banged, filling the gap with smoke. Anne's ears rang, and she stumbled against Alison.

"Fer the love o' Gawd, open yer kunt-fukin' door." Jock mixed prayer and curses—the man was a font of words when it came to enticement and persuasion.

Mendoza reloaded furiously. "Here they come."

Smoke thinned. Anne saw dim figures sprint toward them with leveled pikes. She backed away until the postern blocked retreat.

Jock ceased his banging and spun about, preparing to meet the rush.

The first man at the gap got a double load of ball from Mendoza's hackbutt. As the fellow screamed and fell, Jock grabbed the man's pike. "That's fer bein' an eager villain." He reversed the point, jabbing at the next man.

A dozen pikes stabbed back at them. Anne cringed as the points advanced, preparing to pin her to the door.

Then there was no door behind her. The gate swung inward, and she tumbled back, landing in a heap beneath the legs of Hamilton pikemen who thrust through the postern at the advancing Stewarts. Alison, Jock, and Mendoza scrambled in over her.

A falconette sited just inside the gate went off with a roar, spewing a muzzle load of buckshot through the postern. Pike- and partizan-wielding Hamiltons ran cheering over Anne in a furious countercharge.

Blinded and deafened, she lay at the threshold, caught between defenders trampling over her, and attackers trying to puncture her. Such was the fate of a noncombatant in Scotland. Then the Hamiltons recoiled, fired a parting blast from the falconette, and slammed the postern in the Stewarts' faces.

A handsome young Hamilton captain with a curly brown mustache pushed through the press of men. Leaning down, he took Anne's hand, helping her to her feet. "Wel-come ta Dumbarton, m'lady. Will yew be stayin' fer din-ner?"

MACBETH *Though castles topple on their warders'*
heads;
Though palaces and pyramids do . . .
tumble all together,
Even till destruction sicken, answer me
To what I ask you.

1. WITCH   Speak.
2. WITCH   Demand.
3. WITCH   We'll answer.

SHAKESPEARE, *Macbeth*

Witches' Sabbath

"If all the sea were anly beer, instead o' salty water, our problems would be gane." Jock leaned against Dumbarton's seaward battlement, watching gray storm clouds cover the broad entrance to the Clyde Estuary. Anne was too discouraged to speculate on the chance of drinking their way to safety. Dusk was coming, and the fog had long lifted. She stood beside silent kettledrums, looking down onto the flowing Clyde and the Stewart lines. A web of trenches sealed off the entire landward side of the cas-tle; Glasgow militia and Lennox pikemen had settled down to a siege.

As far as Anne knew, only she, Alison, Jock, and Men-doza had made it into Dumbarton, out of all the refugees

who had fled Hamilton. Now this last safe hold in the
Lowlands was tightly encircled, leaving her as much a
prisoner as Tom at Lochleven. An English twenty-gun galleon swung at anchor in the lee of the castle, just out of
cannon shot. Even if she could somehow escape
Dumbarton, she had nowhere to go. First England, and
now the Lowlands, were barred to her.

"Come"—Jock took her arm—"wishin' fer beer will no
cool yer throat. An' there is a feast below."

They walked back along the wall toward the gatehouse,
where stone steps descended into the bailey. It was their
welcoming feast. Being in a castle under siege was so utterly boring, the Hamiltons seized any chance to dress up
idleness as a holiday. Feasting off castle stores was easy
enough in Scotland, where beer and salt beef could make
a meal, and hard bread was a treat. Jock acted as eager as
if the fare were roast peacock. "Eat when ye can, worry
when yew must," was the wolfman's motto.

The high roof of the Archbishop's hall was supported by
smoke-blackened timbers, but no fire burned in the
hearth—it was near midsummer, and Dumbarton needed
fuel for winter. At the high table, false pomp and forced
gaiety were presided over by the kindly and dottering clan
patriarch, Archbishop Hamilton himself. Old John Hamilton had been so good to Anne that she could not imagine
him plotting with Bothwellhaugh to have Moray murdered. Yet anything was possible in Scotland. The saintly
Archbishop's half brother had been the terrible "Bastard of
Arran," who marked Lennox prisoners with a slash across
the face, murdered one cousin, and saw another burned at
the stake. Archbishop Hamilton was no such ogre. But
good or bad, he was plainly ineffective—better fit to be an
abbot in his garden than a fighting archbishop. Since Moray's murder his keeps and strongholds had fallen one by
one—even Hamilton was no longer his, leaving Old John
a prisoner in his last castle.

At dinner the Hamiltons succeeded in ignoring every
one of these harsh truths. Instead of facing their own troubles, they talked of fanciful plots for freeing Mary of
Scotland. Mary had been moved again, this time to Chats-
worth, where she was apparently allowed rides on the

moors. So the current scheme was to whisk her away to the Isle of Man with the aid of the Stanleys. What Mary would do on Man was left unsaid—the first parts of the scheme were hopeless enough.

But hunting was by far their fondest subject of conversation (aside from abusing English when they assumed Anne was not listening). Anne was told over and again how hard it was to keep hounds and horses in trim when you could not spend the summer slaughtering red deer and rabbit. Eventually they must exhaust the castle's salt beef and barley, and have to eat the horses and hounds. What would the Hamiltons have to talk about then?

Dull food and dull talk did not prepare her for the evening's entertainment—which turned out to be fairly hairraising. All she saw was a high, empty seat facing the dining tables, with a cloth-of-silver canopy. A staff shaped like a hollow reed lay across the seat, resting on a hen's-feather cushion. Alison nodded toward the seat and staff. "M'lady, there will be magic here tonight."

First, however, the Hamiltons put on a tableau more bombastic and less comical than the Twelfth Night masque at Linlithgow. Men marched in wearing broad felt hats and crude white surcoats, with the red cross of Saint George—pretending to be English. With them came Scots traitors—wearing pig's ears and snouts, and the badges of the King's lords—Lennox, Douglas, Stewart, and Campbell. On their shoulders they carried a wood-and-canvas tower. Sitting atop the tower was a woman in crown and veil, made to look like Queen Mary.

Everyone jeered the Queen's jailors. A band of lads wearing oak-leaf badges and wielding oak staves burst into the hall—Hamiltons determined to rescue the Queen. They battled back and forth before the diners, making no headway, though the English were armed with nothing worse than pig bladders and firecracker cannon.

Finally the young bravos seated at the benches could take it no longer. Crying "Cadzow" and "Hamilton," they hurled cracknels, and leaped over the tables into the fray, armed with carving knives and ale tankards. The bladder-armed villains gave a great shriek, scampering off in the direction of the scullery.

Cheers rang through the dining hall as the victors led their queen to her high seat; exultant boys and grown men flourished pig bladders taken in battle. The display would have been entirely childish, if the Hamilton's had not been so deadly serious—earnest enthusiasm gave the farce an air of real tragedy. Queen Mary mounted her throne, holding her reed staff like a scepter. More cheers: Hamilton was victorious; Queen Mary restored. They reminded Anne of mad inmates in a lunatic dungeon, holding parades, crowning their own royalty. Mary sat rigid on her throne. Applause died, and a hush fell over the hall.

Anne sensed this was the real test of the show. If things ended here, there would only be a relapse into deeper depression. The drama had to be taken higher. Otherwise the saner inmates would realize they had no more hope of freeing Queen Mary than they had of escaping their own doom.

Holding tight to her reed-wand, the woman in the high chair reached up with her left hand, loosening her cloak, letting it drop, then lifting her veil. She was the Gordon Witch.

Hamiltons gasped. If Queen Mary herself had been under the veil, Anne could hardly have been more surprised. She had not known the witch was in the castle, expecting her to be halfway to the Highlands along with the rest of the Gordons.

Beneath her queen's cloak she was all witch, wearing a long gown of black lambswool, lined with white catskin. Her neck and shoulders were bare, down to the cleft above her breasts. Startling white skin looked all the more naked next to the black wool. Anne had seldom seen a woman project such raw, sensual authority, making Elizabeth at her best look like a milkmaid. The gown ended in a skirt of Gordon plaid, cunningly embroidered. Bracelets decorated her arms, and she wore a belt of glass beads; her hartskin boots had boars' tusks tied to the lace ends.

The woman's witchy gaze ran over the throng, "Let the women come form a ring an' attend me."

There was no rush to be first. Women looked up to see if the Archbishop approved such pagan rites. After all,

the man had seen his own cousin burned for heresy. Old
John nodded, half in a trance, but apparently enjoying his
coma.

Female diners filed between the tables into the space
around the throne. Anne found herself standing hand in
hand with Alison and a small, grave-faced girl.

"Bring me my knife, my salt, an' my meat." The
witch's words came forth like a chant.

Anne could see the ritual had been planned well ahead;
serving girls entered carrying a copper kettle and an ancient knife, its handle carved from walrus ivory and its
point broken off. They placed the kettle at the witch's feet,
then joined the ring. The cauldron was filled with cooked
animal hearts of all sizes, some as big as a horse's, others
as small as a bird's or rat's. Repulsive, yet fascinating. The
witch sprinkled salt on the hearts, then ate with her knife
and fingers while everyone looked on.

After sampling one of every kind of heart, swallowing
the small ones whole, cutting bites off the larger ones, the
witch began to sing in a high, keening voice. Half chant
and half lay, the song was lovely and otherworldly. The
hearts in the kettle, the silent crowd, and the singing Gordon Witch made a scene that was not even near canny.

As the Highland Witch sang, she rose in her seat, her
arms beckoning. Each refrain ended with:

> "Join in, join in,
> Bring the singing tagither,
> Move the spirits wi' song."

Women joined in. An echo of women's voices filled the
hall, right to the smoky rafters. Alison sang on one side of
Anne, and the small girl sang on the other. All around the
circle women sang—not all of them, but here an old ma-
tron, there a scullery maid. Women from every station
knew the tune. Others stayed silent, either from ignorance
or prudence. Taking part in such a ritual was easily a burning offense—simply knowing the words could send a
woman to prison or the gallows pole.

The witch let her arms fall, and the singing died away.
She surveyed the hall. "No spirit can resist the voices o'
women. Ask what you would know."

The old Archbishop broke from his trance. His voice quavered. "I would know some o' the future, so I need not grope forward in guessin' an' fear." Anne wondered what in the world the man could hope for, shaken and infirm, locked in his last castle, awash with enemies. It was too much like Tom, begging hope from Lady Janet the night before he was taken away.

"Put names to yer fears." The witch's voice sounded hollow, as though she indeed dwelt half in Faerie. "Ask three questions. Three Norns will answer."

The haggard clan leader leaned forward. "I fear the Inglis will blow down these walls, doin' here what they have done ta Branxholm, Ferniehurst, Cadzow, an' Hamilton."

"Elizabeth's men will never take Dumbarton from yew."

The old man was wary. "But I have other enemies, Scots enemies, who have sworn to try me for treason, an' the murder o' Earl Moray."

"No enemy, Scots or English, will ever try or convict you o' treason, nor any other crime."

Anne saw encouragement spread among the Hamiltons. What Scot would not dance to hear he was pardoned beforehand? The old man was getting free license to scoff at the law, plot murder, fish on the Sabbath, fornicate if he felt up to it—knowing he would never be brought to court.

Old John Hamilton's watery eyes gleamed. "Then I need fear nothing from my enemies, no matter how fierce an' powerful they seem?"

The Gordon Witch wore a trace of a smile. "All men must fear their enemies, an' fear death, which comes as an end. But no foe shall shed yer blood. You shall ken your end comin', an' have time ta make yer peace."

"No man can ask fer more." The Archbishop sighed, leaning back as though sentence of death had been lifted.

Anne was not impressed. She would not give a lead shilling for the Archbishop's chances. She had seen the Gordon Witch go through an even more pagan rite, streaking a blood sign on Anne's breast—but not a single Hamilton who had taken part in that cattle sacrifice had made it into Dumbarton. Even the huge MacGregor who had stood beside Anne with the witch's crescent finger-painted across his hairy tits; even he had not made it through the surrounding army of Lennox Stewarts and Glasgow schoolboys.

As far as Anne could estimate, the Archbishop would do as well looking for lucky clovers as listening to the Gordon Witch. She said as much to Jock as she sat down.

"Lass, we are in no fit state ta mock the Norns." Jock licked a bit of meat from the corner of his mouth, eyeing the Gordon woman intently—as did most of the men.

Anne took a drink of fortified wine. Jock was surely in no fit state to judge—licking his lips, as enthralled as if the witch were bare-assed. The woman's face was cunning rather than pretty, but her huge, intense eyes fairly projected erotic power, promising a man wild abandon—if she were of the mind. "Do not let your desire run away with your good sense."

The Armstrong looked at her and laughed. "Oh, I do desire her. What man would no? But I will no end up like the auld Laird Gordon, lyin' in Aberdeen Tolbooth."

"What was that?" Highland history was mostly new to Anne. All she knew was that the Gordon lairds were hereditary Earls of Huntly.

"Auld Laird Gordon took inta his head ta rebel against Queen Mary; seein' she was a ripe young widow, an' a ready target for forced matrimony. Afore marchin' on Aberdeen, Laird Gordon consulted his wife's witches, who swore they saw him in Aberdeen that very night, lyin' in the Tolbooth without a wound on his body. But when Gordon met the Stewart at Corriche, the laird an' his sons were roundly beaten."

"Then the witches lied?"

"Not at all. Laird Gordon was brought before Earl Moray. Seein' his enemies triumphant was too much fer the Gordon chief. He swelled up an' burst, topplin' stone dead off his horse. The Stewarts slung him inta a pair of fish baskets—Earl Gordon o' Huntly being a hugely big man an' hard ta carry—an' dumped him in the Tolbooth. There he lay, just as the Norns said he would, safe in Aberdeen without a mark an him. There's usually more ta prophecy than meets the ear." Jock ogled the witch again. "With this wicked lass there is bound to be much more."

Anne and Alison were lodged in a tower room, spare and fortresslike, but not a cupboard either. The bed was big and sound, and stone walls were covered with rich cloth to keep out the cold. Having gone from hovel to prison cell, to palace, to sleeping in the open, Anne had to rate this lofty chamber as one of the better holes she'd been put in of late.

As she stripped Anne for bed, Alison rattled on about the Hamiltons and their bleak history. She told how the Earl of Arran—not the Bastard, but the true laird of the clan—had been party of yet another attempt to commit matrimony on the unwilling Queen Mary of Scotland. (Half the Scots nobility seemed provoked to violence by the notion of an unwed queen. If only Elizabeth had been born Scots, she would not have to constantly complain about finding a suitable husband. The Virgin Queen would have been dragged to some castle and properly wed by now.)

"Arran meant ta bring Mary right here, ta Dumbarton." Alison's eyes glowed with excitement. "But the spirits were lookin' over Queen Mary. They drove the Earl o' Arran stark blinkin' insane. Had him wanderin' about in plain daylight, conversin' with demons an' ghosts. For a time they locked him in Edinburgh Castle, but servants here say he is now kept by his mother—one o' the great Earls o' Scotland, mad as a March Hare."

Cheery news to hear about your hosts. From what Anne had seen of the Scots nobility, not one in twenty were safe strolling loose, but the Hamiltons seemed especially fey. Bothwellhaugh, the Bastard of Arran, the Mad Earl, and this Archbishop with his Gordon Witch; the Hamilton family oak had more than a few bent limbs. Such thoughts made for a splendid evening. Alison had her normal nightmares. Anne slept and fretted until near to dawn, fearing she would have to sit in Dumbarton until Lennox took the place, or she herself went as mad as the Hamiltons. What alternative was there?

A sturdy knock rattled the wooden door. Anne threw on a nightdress and drew back the bolt. There was Jock, filling her threshold, looking as easy and as confident as ever. "I ken it is time we should be goin'." As though passing through stone walls and a small army were but slight problems.

"Going where?" At least he was not with the witch, which seemed a small miracle.

"Ta the Highlands." Jock cocked his head to indicate the hills beyond the stone walls. Had he said they must seek lodging in hell, the prospect could hardly have been more daunting. The Highlands were the oldest, least civilized, most utterly barbarous corner of Scotland. Hardly Scots at all—the rugged hills and isles were really an extension of Ireland. The inhabitants spoke not Scots, but Gaelic. Their lairds claimed descent from the High Kings of Dublin, and from the primordial mating of Mother Earth and the Faerie King. For her, heading north was like stepping off the edge of the earth. "Where in the Highlands?"

"Does it matter?" He sat himself on a stool, perfectly at ease invading her bedroom with bizarre notions. "One bit o' the Highlands is about as untamed an' treacherous as another. We could make fer Cameron country. 'Tis anly a few days north of here. The Camerons are *Na Cambeulich,* a terrible lot, ferocious even fer Highlanders. But they are allied wi' the Gordons, an' will not likely eat us on the spot."

She gave him a dubious look.

"Come, lass, I admit the Highlands will be no golfing holiday."

"Then why go at all?" It was unsettling to be in love with a man who would take nothing seriously. Easygoing rogues were more appealing in troubadours' tales than in real life.

"Because it is better than waiting here ta take prime parts in a kirk hangin' bee."

Why were the choices given her always the worst she could imagine? Over her shoulder she could see Alison was up, bustling about, getting dressed and packed—prepared to go wherever Jock went. There was nothing to do but give in to him.

Jock helped them gather their few possessions, then he led them, taper in hand, down the circular stairs that wound toward the base of the tower. Assuming Jock meant to slip out some postern or sally-port, Anne was alarmed to see him pass the guardroom and the door that opened onto the bailey. The steps wound deeper round the newel, like a corkscrew boring into the earth. Dark, damp smells brought back the musty torture pit beneath Jedburgh Keep. Alison's nails dug into her arm. This time they would face the dank underworld together.

The first floor of the tower was a windowless storeroom, lit by flickering candles. Anne expected there would be a trap or tunnel leading to the outside, but instead she saw the Gordon Witch standing in the gloom—a faerie godmother fit for the Borgias—flanked by the Corporal Mendoza and the MacGregor. It was disconcerting to have the witch waiting for them, but even more astonishing to see the big MacGregor, who had disappeared the night before along with the Gordons. Clearly there were ways in and out of this castle that would take even Archbishop Hamilton by surprise.

The Highlander greeted Jock in Gaelic. Jock translated for Anne: "He says he was sorry ta leave, but when he heard the Gordons goin', he went wi' the witch. MacGregors have another motto: *A battle lost wi'out a MacGregor will likely be lost wi' one.* Comes from havin' royal blood, an' hatin' ta see it spilled."

"Countess Anne, we meet again, as I said we would." The witch laid immediate claim to another piece of dubious prophecy. Anne could not see what the Gordon woman had to be proud of; not a single Hamilton refugee had made it into the castle. None of the Gordons were here, other than the witch herself.

"I said *some* would make it. Others did not." The raven-haired woman read her unvoiced objections.

"Foolish me," Anne retorted, "for thinking *some* meant more than six."

"Six is a sacred number, and enough for our purpose."

"What purpose?"

"To take you out of here, and to the Ends of the Earth."

Anne hesitated. The Ends of the Earth was where Mad Anne said she was bound, so many months ago, but she had no real reason to trust this Gordon woman.

"M'lady." Jock took her shoulders in his hands, turning

her to face him. "She is offerin' the anly chance we have. Yew cannot blame her fer what happened. The Gordons are safe in the Highlands by now. True, Hamiltons are scattered hither and yon; but you must admit they would be no help here, eatin' up this keep's meager stores." The storeroom around them bulged to the rafters with sacks of salt, bales of forage, and a great mound of coal—all very handy no doubt, but not much to make a meal out of. "They would anly make the place fall all the sooner."

"And fall it will." Anne turned her eyes toward the witch. "What makes this woman's promises to us any better than those she gave the Archbishop?" Bad as things were, it was good to have Jock holding her shoulders in this chill, inky chamber, even though his was pleading the case of yet another woman he would like to bed.

The witch reached up and removed a copper pin from her hair, letting the black locks fall free about her white shoulders. "My promises are true. Dumbarton will no fall ta the Inglis—it will fall ta the Scots."

"And the Archbishop?"

"He will no be tried, nor will his blood be shed. Lennox will take him ta Stirling an' hang him wi'out trial." She looked Anne square in the eye. "I told a doomed old man what he wanted to hear. He will see his end comin' while waiting ta be hanged. It will be a sad, terrible time fer him. Would yew have me extend it? Should I tell him now, so he may have months instead of hours ta chew it over? Prophecy is maddening because we must see the bad mixed with the good. We cannot separate them—except by tellin' half-truths ta others."

That too was what Mad Anne had said, when they turned back from Yorkshire, and Anne had to admit it was true—real prophecy was very much like a curse. She had no impulse to run upstairs and wake the Archbishop with the happy news that he would end his days stretching his neck to amuse the Stewarts. Nor did she feel like sitting in Dumbarton waiting to see it happen. "So it's off to the Highlands."

"An' the Ends o' the Earth," the witch added.

Anne turned to Jock. "Will you go with me? Even to the Ends of the Earth."

He gave her a broad smile, squeezing her shoulders. "Lass, yew make me so happy—but it will no be easy. I warn yew now, I canno be wi' ye always. That is no half-truth, or witch's promise. It is as much honesty as ye'll ever get from a rogue an' thief like me."

She reached up and took hold of the man's wrists. As his arms dropped, she slid her hands into his. They stood for a moment hand in hand. "I have no reason to hope the Highlands will be any better than here. But I want you beside me, Jock of the Syde."

"I'll do my best, woman, but do no put too much trust in me—yew have enough trust in ye to bust a weak vessel like me."

Anne let her hands drop and looked about. There was still no door or exit except the stairs they had come down. "How are we to get to the Highlands and beyond—fly?"

Jock cocked his head toward the witch. "She will let us inta Faerie."

Anne did not know what to say. Alison squealed with delight, putting her arm around Anne's waist. "Did yew hear m'lady? We are goin' ta Faerie." The witch girl made the Land Beyond sound like Edinburgh or Linlithgow, only better.

"Aye"—Jock nodded—"ta Faerie. As you'll see, Faerie is no yer normal country. The Earl o' Sussex an' this mob o' Glasgow militia will no be followin' us there. Happily the Highlands an' Faerie blend together, an' we'll have the MacGregor here ta guide us through ta Cameron country."

It sounded like a totally mad business, but desperate situations required desperate remedies. Anne glanced at the Child of the Mist, looming in the shadows alongside the black-gowned witch. "Can we trust him?" The huge MacGregor had deserted them once already.

Jock's gaze followed hers. "The man's an outlawed MacGregor, a Child o' the Mist—like every man, woman, an' babe among 'em, he was born wi' a price on his head. How could we fail ta trust him?" Anne did not share Jock's cousinly affection for felons, but there were no other options.

The witch ordered the men to clear a space, and construct a crude altar, piling up sacks of salt. She extracted a promise of absolute silence from everyone. "Faerie is not easily entered. This is Friday, the Mother's Day, the Witches' Sabbath. If anyone breaks the spell, we will have to wait a week to find a day as good."

Anne swore a quiet oath to Mary that she would not say a word until she was in Faerie. This witch would have no excuse to blame her if the magic failed.

Scrambling about on her knees, the witch inscribed a rough pentacle on the dirt floor, going over the lines with trails of salt. In the center she lit a small fire using a bag of fine tinder. Then she stood up, waving her reed-wand like a marshal's truncheon, directing each of them to stand at a different apex of the five-pointed star. She poured dried hemp buds on the fire, exhorting them to breathe deep. Half-smothered by the pungent hemp smoke, Anne's mind began to drift. Shadows swam around her; the small chamber shrank.

"Now disrobe."

Anne blinked. The witch let her gown drop, and was wearing nothing in the way of underclothes. Like Lady Janet, the Gordon woman was older than Anne had imagined, with pointed breasts and bony hips. Her black pubic tangle showed a rib of gray hairs.

Anne looked about, finding the men and Alison already obeying. Alison had a peasant's savage immodesty. She made no attempt to hide her breasts or the red thatch between her thighs, covering only her three-fingered hand. The men, of course, were shameless. This was an outrageous test of silent obedience, having to strip naked in front of three men—two near-strangers and a happy satyr who had fairly hooted after her.

She heard a laugh in the blackness, and Mary's voice, *"Anne, did yew think it would be easy ta find Faerie?"* Reluctantly she let her dress slip. All her modesty won her was an attentive audience. The others had finished and were waiting on her.

Anne had seen Jock in the buff before. He had a sinewy body, a flat stomach, and tight rear. The tool between his legs was adequate, but not nearly as long and handsome as Tom's. Now she saw Mendoza had sleek, courtly lines, but his little, pointed cock was smaller even the Jock's. The

MacGregor was a big man in every way, with a thick, blunt instrument. Despite her shame, Anne took a certain vain pride in knowing none of them could match her husband. She had often had a penis inside her as good as any two of these.

While they stood there in various states of discomfiture and arousal, the witch stoked the fire. Warm, dreamy smoke billowed all about them. Through the intoxicating fog Anne heard an ancient and grisly invocation of Hecate, the Death Crone, the All-Mother in her most fearsome guise. The witch cried out in Latin:

> *"Come infernal Queen of Night,*
> *Goddess of the crossroads,*
> *Guiding light,*
> *Grandmother of Darkness,*
> *Terror to men,*
> *And Dog's delight.*
> *Black Hecate, hear me,*
> *Mother of the Midnight Moon,*
> *Accept my sacrifice."*

Chilled by the chant, and the clammy air, Anne hugged herself.

The Gordon woman raised her reed-wand over her head, then bent her body back until she was lying on the sacks of salt. Spreading her legs upon the salt altar, she began to moan, first baying like a bitch at the moon, then writhing like a woman making violent love. Her hips heaved up and down. Chalk-white thighs and dark crotch glistened with sweat.

This heaving and thrusting was having its effect on the men, who were sweating and panting along with the witch—almighty eager to climax the ritual.

She beat her rear against the salt, harder and harder, in tempo to her crooning. The men stood, jaws agape—Jock just as bad as the other two, worse even, hunching his back, arching his neck, and yelping with lust, as though he meant to turn into a wolf right there.

"Now," gasped the witch, twisting in ecstasy atop the altar, motioning to the men. "Mount me," she screamed. "Make your offering to the Mother o' Life an' Death."

Enough foreplay. The men were frantic to oblige, with
Jock and Mendoza quickest off the mark. Anne thought
they might try to enter her both at once, but on reaching
her splayed legs, the Spaniard stepped aside with a little
courtly bow, letting the Scot go first. Mendoza was a guest
in Scotland, too much a gentleman to be greedy.

With a grunt of thanks Jock lunged at the woman, lapping her like a dog, then plunging into her. He matched
the witch howl for howl as they thrashed atop the salt.
Through the murk Anne could make out heaving buttocks,
and white legs locked about Jock's waist, pulling him tight
into her. Their moaning must have raised dogs' hackles in
Glasgow.

Shivering and naked, Anne was not the least bit jealous,
or inclined to join in—laboring away in a bare-assed
crowd, with a line of men waiting, was not her notion of
true love.

Mendoza mounted the witch next, murmuring a few
French endearments for form's sake. The sentiment was
wasted. His partner made no reply except to grab him by
the head, burying his face in her breasts.

Once the novelty wore off, Anne began to worry about
the noise. Half of Dumbarton had to be awake and wondering what the hell was happening in their cellar. She
heard a pounding on the door that was not her imagination. To the Hamiltons outside it must have sounded like
the Stewarts were digging their way up through the floor.

And there was still the MacGregor to go. When Mendoza was spent, the Child of the Mist shambled up and
seized the witch. Pushing his knees into the altar, he grap-
pled her about the waist, half lifting her. The witch's white
arms twined about his shoulders. Ivory fingers sank into
his curly hair. Hamiltons beat louder on the door behind
him, but the MacGregor just banged away, like a mariner
in port, showing no sign of tiring.

The knocking grew more insistent. Anne could hear stri-
dent voices, demanding entrance.

"Do no answer, do nothin' ta break the spell," shouted
the witch over the MacGregor's heaving shoulder.

At last even the mighty MacGregor had to cry quit. The
men staggered back to their places on the pentacle. Ignor-

ing the knocking, the witch rose up, eyes hollow, chest
heaving, still in a supremely exalted trance. She slipped
off the salt altar and knelt before the fire. Anne gasped as
the nude woman reached down into the embers and picked
out a glowing coal with her bare hand.

The witch broke open the hollow reed-wand and placed
the coal inside, nestled on a small bed of tinder. The wand
was made in two sections—like the hollowed reeds used
by peasants to carry fire when they did not have flint and
steel.

The banging on the door grew rhythmic. Anne guessed
the Hamiltons had brought down a bench or log to use as
a battering ram. The door would be down in a matter of
minutes. There was no time even to dress before more
men came pouring in.

Closing up the reed-wand with the living coal inside it,
the witch held it out to the two women. "Here," she commanded, "grab hold."

Trying to ignore the splintering door, Anne took a ten-
tative hold on the reed-wand. She could feel warmth from
the coal in its nest.

"Harder," admonished the witch, eyes blazing.

Anne put both hands on the wand, as did Alison. The
three women faced each other, clutching the long wand between them. The witch reeked of sweat and sex. Alison's
body smelled like a spring blossom. Behind them the door
rattled angrily on its hinges.

The Gordon woman raised the reed-wand, pulling the
women's bodies into contact—breast to breast, thigh to
thigh. Alison felt smooth and cool, the witch hot and
sticky.

"You may stay in Faerie for as long as this fire burns,"
the witch declared. "Make your campfires from this fire.
Carry the fire by day in this reed. If you let the fire go out,
you will be brought instantly back ta earth. Yew ken that?"

Anne nodded, as did Alison, both clinging to the reed as
if it were their lifeline.

"Good," breathed the witch. "Keep faith wi' Mary an'
the charm will last until the wand returns to me, its maker.
Keep faith, carry it wi' yew, an' we will meet at the Ends
o' the Earth."

The door gave a last groan; wood splintered and metal screamed horribly. A hinge came flying off. My God, thought Anne, here come the Hamiltons.

The witch let out a high-pitched keening that came near to splitting Anne's skull.

Men burst shouting into the chamber, waving swords and dirks. Giving a Highland yell, the MacGregor leaped at the Hamiltons, swinging his huge two-edged claymore like the berserk ghost of some naked Gallic warrior.

The air around them shimmered and winked. Witch, walls, and castle were gone.

> O ye'll tak' the high road,
> An' I'll tak' the low road,
> An' I'll be in Scotland before ye.
> But trouble it is there,
> An' there's mony hearts are sair,
> On the bonnie, bonnie banks o' Loch Lomond.

—ANONYMOUS

The Devil's Stair

Without moving, Anne was suddenly in the open—under pale blue skies, surrounded by the slumped and grassy ramparts of a decayed ring fort. Morning sun streamed through a notch in the eastern ramparts. Through an opposing gap, Anne saw the broad Clyde Estuary sparkling in the dawn light. The Gordon Witch had vanished, as had the incoming Hamiltons, taking Dumbarton with them.

She was still naked, clutching the reed-wand alongside Alison. The MacGregor was flailing at empty air with his

Claymore. Mendoza looked madly about. In the place of Jock sat a big black wolf, indolently scratching himself.

Clothes and possessions were strewn on dewy grass. Despite the two naked men and the leering wolf, Anne felt no rush to dress. She was in a place for nudity; air felt vibrant on her skin, almost alive. The day was not yet warm, but the morning chill was a bracing caress. Her body had been carried beyond cold and care.

" 'Tis Faerie, m'lady," was Alison's blissful whisper. Anne had no name for it; this was surely a place she had never been or expected to be.

"We are here as lang as the fire burns." Reverently Alison let go the reed-wand, giving it into Anne's care. "Or so the witch said."

Anne examined the wand. Whatever she thought of the witch's lusty technique, the ritual lovemaking had produced a miracle of no mean proportions. Using the staff for support, she climbed to the top of the nearest embankment. Her maimed foot did not complain. The ground seemed to spring back at each step, filling her with strength. The ring fort must have been unused for generations—great oaks grew right up out of the ditches and ramparts.

At the top of the grassy battlement she stood, wand in hand, letting the dawn wind whip through her hair, lashing it against her bare shoulders and hips. She could see with incredible clarity—the Clyde, the clouds, the distant peaks, were no farther off than her fingers. Purple heather and red blooms turned green hills into a wanton tapestry. The only sign of the Hamiltons were clumps of their sacred white cattle, grazing in the dry moat.

Farther off, she saw a huge herd of white horses between her and the hills. The great white herd extended in either direction, filling gaps in the forest like new-fallen snow.

She glanced at the group behind her. Mendoza was pulling on his hose. The two Scots luxuriated in the summer sunlight like healthy young animals awaking from winter. Rob MacGregor leaned on his sword, grinning as Alison festooned him with blossoms, twining flowers in his beard and hair. God what a wrong moment for Jock to turn totally wolf.

By the time Mendoza was fully dressed—in hose, boots, jerkin, and cap—Anne felt compelled to at least cover herself with a shift; somehow Mendoza's putting on his pants had set a different tone. Minutes before the man had been bent over bare-assed, plugging away at a witch-woman in heat, but Anne knew good manners required a bit of polite hypocrisy. The Spaniard asked in halting French if she had any idea where in God's great world they were.

"I am fairly sure we are not in the world. This girl"—she indicated Alison—"calls it Faerie. Wherever we are, we seem safe for the moment." There was no sign of peril. The colorful landscape held nothing more frightening than lowing cattle, a herd of white horses, and the cries of seabirds.

"But how did we get here?"

Anne cocked an eye. "You had as much a part as I did, maybe more."

Mendoza acted shocked, *"M'donna,* my role was merely supporting. I cannot help that I have led almost a monk's life since coming to this country—few Scots ladies are as friendly and forward as that *bruja."* Having seen the Spaniard play court to nearly every woman in sight, Anne decided Spanish monasteries must be lively indeed.

Alison came up, still artlessly nude, and Saint Mendoza could not keep his gaze off her. The girl got up on her tiptoes, stretching her lithe body, pointing to where the River Leven looped over the floodplain. "The MacGregor says Cameron country is ta the north. We follow the river an' the loch beyond for three, four days. After that it is all high moor and mountain."

"He has been in Faerie before?" Anne looked back at the Child of the Mist, standing with his claymore slung over his shoulder, wearing nothing but summer blossoms and an engaging grin.

"Mayhap he has." Alison shrugged bare shoulders. "The Highlands are where Earth and Faerie run tagether. See how the land is the same, except where the work o' man has touched it. In the Highlands the very trees an' rocks are the same. Yew would not know from one step ta the next if yew were in Earth or Faerie."

Anne could see what Alison meant. Faerie country was greener, more fervently in bloom, but land was not much different. Forests that had hugged the hilltops now spilled down to fill the river valley. The castle and town of Dumbarton were gone, along with the fields and the English galleon—but this was still the plain where the River Leven flowed into the Clyde. Yet if people had not re-shaped Faerie, who had built the ring fort?

She showed the Spaniard the reed with its smoldering ember inside. "We are safe in Faerie as long as this fire burns."

Mendoza understood at once. "Nothing could be simpler, *m'dama.*" He got his shooting bag and produced a long coil of slow match. "A musketeer must know how to keep fire burning." Cutting a length of match, he threaded it into the hollow reed. "I have powder as well, and if need be, I can braid more match out of linen." He glanced at the undergarments lying about.

With the fire secured, they collected their things. Mendoza scooped up Alison's gown, using signs to indicate he would carry her clothes if the girl did not want to be encumbered. He got a kiss on the cheek, and a chance to walk beside the gaily-chattering girl, finding her conversation fascinating although he knew nothing of the language.

As soon as they walked out from the shelter of the oaks, Anne got her first lesson in the beasts of Faerie. The herd of white horses came thundering toward them. She saw the horses had goats' beards and single curling horns growing from their foreheads. They were unicorns.

Angry unicorns at that. There must have been a thousand—flashing their horns and stamping their cloven hoofs. The white herd would not let the party proceed up the valley.

Anne was more awestruck than alarmed. The hundreds of slim, powerful beasts were not attempting to harm them, merely to keep them hemmed in, confined to the trees and the ring fort. Damned odd behavior, and disconcerting. But who knew what was normal for unicorns?

Anne had no ambition to settle in the ring fort, living off acorns and Hamilton cattle.

Then it struck her that the unicorn was a Stewart badge, just as Hamiltons used the oak. Hamilton cattle and Hamilton oaks were penned in by Stewart unicorns—the earthly siege of Dumbarton reflected in Faerie. Anne had assumed Faerie would be an open road, and she damned the witch for not even hinting this would happen. Having enjoyed three good men, the Gordon woman had gone off who-knew-where, leaving them no better than they had been in Dumbarton.

Anne gave Jock an exasperated glance. Having him playing wolf was silly. She hated asking an overgrown dog what to do next. Meeting her look with a toothy grin, he trotted around behind her to bring up Alison, nudging her slim legs as though she were a young ewe.

As soon as Alison stepped forward, the unicorns lowered their horns and parted for her.

Everyone else followed in her wake. Mendoza marched directly behind her, carrying the reed-wand. Anne and the MacGregor walked on either side of the wolf. The unicorns closed in behind, jostling them along. The beasts simply could not get enough of the girl, and trotted as close as they could to Alison, nuzzling her breasts and hips with their lips. The girl enjoyed their attention, patting them on the forelock, tugging at their wispy beards.

The king-stallion came up, with more than his horn erect. Alison just laughed, looping her arms around the whimpering beast's neck. Grabbing a handful of mane, the girl slung her leg over the unicorn's shoulder. In a moment she was riding the king-stallion barebacked.

With the unicorns for an escort, they made excellent time. Anne learned the beasts were not as ethereal as people thought; their behavior toward Alison was grossly indecent—like randy old goats with a young girl, and their shit did stink (and stick to the feet). They were also immensely vain, fighting fiercely among themselves—mostly to be close to Alison. But the herd was exceedingly useful; their great bodies broke down the brush and made wide trails through the trees.

That evening they camped around a blazing fire by the

southern shore of Loch Lomond, eating acorns gathered from beneath the Hamilton oaks. Despite hiking all day, Anne was hardly hungry—Faerie seemed so invigorating that she could almost live on air and water. Alison sat braiding the king-stallion's beard, and Anne had one question she was burning to ask.

"Alison, are you a virgin?"

"Why, m'lady?" She sounded flustered.

"Because I had heard that only a virgin maid could charm unicorns." On Night o' May Alison had gone off with Jock—later the man had certainly implied that he had made love to her. Yet the unicorns had lavished attention on Alison, paying no heed to Anne.

The girl blushed. "M'lady, strictly speakin', I am."

Later that night, sharing a bed of pine boughs beside the loch, Anne pressed the full story from Alison.

"I have been wi' no man exceptin' Jock on the Night o' May. An' . . ."

"And what? Come tell." It was unladylike to prod her handmaid, but Anne was consumed with curiosity.

Alison wriggled closer. "Jock did not make the type o' love that makes babies." The girl had a peasant's practicality—no right-headed Scots lass wanted to bear a fatherless child. Anne gave an approving murmur. She could feel the girl's warm body beneath their shared cloak. "So, what kind of love did he make?"

"Yew are a married lady. Yew must know." Alison squirmed and whispered, half-embarrassed, half-excited to share what had happened. "Well, he rubbed me an' caressed me, gentle, wi' his mouth in mine. His hands went everywhere, pressin' harder. An' wherever his hands went, his lips followed." Anne lay listening to the girl's voice, seeing the huge sheet of Loch Lomond reflecting back the stars. The white coats of the unicorns sparkled in the firelight.

"I thought I would about burst wi' pleasure. Then he put his head between my knees an . . . Gawd, m'lady, that was the best. He kissed me wi' lips an' tongue, suckin' an' lickin' like a hungry animal. Yew know where. I mean, ye can no make babies wi' spittle. An' I twisted about, holdin' hard to his cock, until there was this great rushin',

a terrific burstin'. But he would no stop, an' I swooned."
All this and still a virgin—very artful, these Scots.

A high-pitched yip and howl shattered the silence. The
quavering call of a wolf baying at the silver moon of
Faerie echoed over the loch. Jock had keen ears.

For the first night since Jedburgh, Alison had no nightmares, sleeping safe in the womb of Faerie.

Loch Lomond on a misty summer morning was as beautiful as Highlanders said—a glistening expanse of water,
the largest of all lochs, stretching between bonnie green
banks and braes. The morning air had a million hues, and
unicorns came down by the hundreds for a drink and bath.
From the lochside Anne saw the Highlands rising tier upon
tier into the purple sky. A dense green tangle of mossy
pines, cankered old oaks, and hip-deep bracken turned the
hills a dozen shades of green.

Anne wished horribly Jock were not a wolf. He made a
good-enough guide dog, bustling ahead to help scout the
way, keeping watch at night, but he was not much at conversation. Anne found it difficult to glean information on
the trackless way ahead. Mendoza was happy and talk-
ative, but he knew less about Scotland than she did, and
could go on for hours about guns and powder. (All Anne
cared to know about a hackbutt was which end to avoid.)
The MacGregor was on first-name terms with every burn
and crannie, but Anne could not understand a word of his
Gaelic. She was forced to depend on Alison, with her
smattering of Gaelic and vast stock of stories about the
Highlands and Faerie.

At the Highland line the unicorns turned back. The land
rose almost straight up, running in a wall from southwest
to northeast, following the line of the glens. This Highland
boundary fault had been formed ages ago by a tremendous
folding and splitting deep in the earth. The same process
had formed the Great Glen that divided the Highlands, and
the line of Outer Isles that held back the open Atlantic.
Once the Highlands had been high as the Alps, but time
had worn them down, leaving only the exposed roots of
this ancient mountain system, half-sunk in seas and lochs.

The Child of the Mist led them along the east bank of
Loch Lomond. Water lapping the rocks teemed with trout

and char, which the MacGregor caught by wading bear-fashion into the stream and grabbing them with his hands. He did not turn away from the loch until they had to skirt the huge mass of Ben Lomond, rising half a mile straight from the water's edge. There they plunged into the somber green Loch Ard Wood. A hundred steps and Anne asked Alison, "Are you as lost as I am?"

Her handmaid nodded vigorously, but said not to worry, this was MacGregor country. The Child o' the Mist did stroll like a man passing through his parlor, his tartan wrapped loosely about him, clearing brush with his claymore. He seemed to fear nothing, not even the Highland lions that abounded in Faerie—the black lions of Buchanan turned out to be clawless and toothless, and the vicious brown lion was a MacGregor beast. But beyond Glen Falloch at the northern head of the loch, the MacGregor showed more caution. Here Jock trotted ahead to check the turnings.

"Campbell country," Alison explained. "There is an ancient and deadly feud between the Campbells and the Children of the Mist. Fifty years ago a MacGregor laird raped the Campbell of Glenorchy's daughter."

"And the Campbells are still punishing the man's family?" Highland feuds could last forever.

"Oh no, thet MacGregor agreed ta marry the girl. An' the Campbells made their new son-in-law chief o' all MacGregors. The Children o' the Mist are descended from the MacGregors that refused to follow this Campbell-in-law usurper. They are loyal to the old line o' disinherited chiefs—an' are totally outlawed. To kill a Child o' the Mist is no a crime, but a form o' public service, fer which the Earl o' Argyll will pay in minted silver."

All the walking did not weary them, and when they did need to eat, there was always game about. In Campbell country the land produced big black pigs, immense herds of them, unhunted and unmolested, except by prides of brown Highland lions. One day a terrific sow with a litter of piglets walked right up to them. The black giantess had white curving tusks, and enough meat for a week of meals. Mendoza handed Anne the reed-wand, and raised his hackbutt.

The MacGregor leaped over and knocked the hackbutt aside, spoiling the Spaniard's aim. A useful little debate ensued, half in Gaelic and half in Spanish—with neither man understanding the other—to Anne the argument sounded like one of those Italian improvisational comedies where none of the actors know the others' lines. Finally Alison was able to translate the MacGregor's objections. "The boar is the Campbells' clan badge, an' sacred ta Mother Earth ta boot. The MacGregor wants ta give no notice ta the Campbells that we are here. It is Campbell country from here ta Glen Coe, an' we must step softly ower the ground."

Mendoza impatiently asked if the Highlander was "some northern species of Muslim or Jew, passing up pork roast on the hoof?"

Anne explained the danger. "We want no excuse for the feud following us into Faerie." Remembering how the Stewart unicorns had threatened to block their path, Mendoza confined his hunting to ducks and grouse. With game so abundant there was no need to anger the Campbells.

Mendoza was not the only huntsman in Campbell country. At night they heard the wild baying of hounds—which Jock was prudent enough not to answer—accompanied by the weird, mournful tones of a horn. Sometimes they even heard the clatter of hoofs from a ghostly cavalcade galloping through the glens.

" 'Tis the Wild Hunt," whispered Alison. "The horn is the Campbell's hunting horn. They are most likely after MacGregor lions—pray we never become their quarry."

If Faerie could be terrifying by night, by day it was incredibly pleasant, lush and cool, shaded by huge gnarled oaks, carpeted with herbs. Pearl fritillaries and checkered skippers fluttered among wood sorrel and red campions. Forest gave way to moor and uplands as they crossed over Mam Carraigh, and skirted Black Mountain. Anne still found the walking easy; in Faerie she need not limp, or favor her toes.

Then, climbing a shoulder of ground, they saw the deep, rugged slopes of Glen Coe, tremendous rounded hills rising right out of the valley, funneling the Coe Water toward a steep canyon.

Near to dusk they stopped to cook supper. Alison and the MacGregor had a long, agitated conversation in Gaelic and hand signs. The girl listened with set expression as the Highlander jabbered and pointed, tracing the route ahead up the high wall of the glen. Thanking the MacGregor, she sat down to dine on berries and pheasant with Anne, saying, "What would yew hear first, the good or the bad?"

"Give me the good, it will fortify me for the bad."

"We are at the end of Campbell country. Yonder glen belongs to the MacIans o' Clan Donald, blood enemies ta the Campbells. A trail ahead, called the Devil's Stair, runs straight up inta Cameron country."

"Will we be safe there?"

"As safe as can be expekited in the Highlands. Camerons are at feud wi' the Campbells. They'll gladly give us sanctuary, an' spite their enemies at the same time." Hospitality was one of the Highland's great virtues, along with an easy attitude about law and religion. Even a clan enemy with blood on his hands could claim sanctuary from sundown to sunrise—and a two-hour start at dawn. The Camerons could do the right thing, while thumbing their noses at the Campbells and Argyll.

"Now give me the bad."

"Ahead is Glen Etive, home of the Fachan, a flesh-eatin' beast wi' one foot, one hand, and one eye."

"Sounds passing lovely." Anne shook her head. Just the thing to hear as the sun sank behind gloomy forested hills.

"Goin' or stayin', we chance meetin' the Fachan in the dark."

Anne told Mendoza. The man was all for going on. "Why wait in sight of our goal? Things may be worse by morning." Anne agreed. The Fachan was a one-armed, one-legged Cyclops, who might be mostly myth. Two men and a wolf made four solid arms, as well as jaws and claws, and if they failed, she could always show the Fachan how fast two legs could carry a woman. There was no consulting Jock, who was lying by the fire biting at fleas.

Mendoza made sure there was plenty of slow match inside the reed-wand. He had shown meticulous devotion to that tiny fire, lighting the campfire from it each night, placing a fresh ember in the wand each morning. Perhaps the tedious task was making him anxious to leave Faerie behind.

He moved the MacGregor's pot helm onto the fire. Opening his purse, he dropped several silver reales into the pot. Anne watched as the silver melted, wondering why he was wasting perfectly good pieces-of-eight. Next the man got out his bullet mold and began to cast the gleaming metal into shot, saying, "Silver bullets are a useful antidote for devils, and maybe even northern bogey monsters."

Jock stooped scratching and watched keenly as Mendoza smoothed the castings into half-inch balls, using a small iron file. One ball went into the Spaniard's hackbutt, the other three into his shot bag. Anne knew that silver bullets were one of the wolfman's few fears.

In the broad bottom where the Etive forked off from the Coe, they came on a tall stand of pines. Jock loped forward, scouting out the grove. The MacGregor pointed to something shining in the trees, half-visible in the gloaming. To Anne it looked like a silver body, a headless torso hanging from a pine bough.

Approaching closer, she saw it was not a body. It was an old-style mail shirt with three-quarter sleeves, the type that could cover a tall man from neck to heels. It glittered in the dying light, perfectly polished without a speck of rust. The gleaming metal could hardly have been hanging long in the green and damp of Faerie.

The MacGregor cut the mail coat down and tried it on. The iron suit fit like a stocking. He smiled, saying a few happy words in his heathen tongue.

"He calls it a *lurich*," Alison translated. The Latin was *lorica*. Anne supposed the Romans must have first seen such armor worn by ferocious titans much like the MacGregor. "He says 'tis a sign we'll soon be in a fight. An' that someone is watchin' out fer our side." Anne began to see how things worked in Faerie. Armor came hanging like apples on a tree, just when it was needed. What could be more natural, or unnatural?

From within the grove came a tremendous growling and yelping, followed by the snap of breaking boughs. With a crash Jock came flying out, baying over his shoulder. Behind him the pines bent aside. A dense black shadow bounded forward.

Anne had supposed the Fachan would be no more than an oversized man, and a badly lamed one at that. But the ogre that burst on them was a behemoth. The Fachan's one leg was as large around as her waist, and stout as an oak. Far from being slow, the Fachan moved with an unpredictable hopping motion. In a couple of crazed leaps the towering fiend was among them.

Everyone bolted. The creature selected his target, hopping after Alison, trying to catch the girl in his huge, clutching fist.

Anne screamed, and saw Jock wheel about. The wolf ran straight up the Fachan's huge thigh, burying his jaws in the monster's crotch. The Fachan let out a bellow of pain, hopping sideways. The wolf was clamped onto the ogre's privates, which were as large in proportion as the rest of him.

The wounded monster batted at the wolf. Anne saw Mendoza turn and raise his hackbutt. Jock was still clinging to the Fachan's essentials, being flung about in the Spaniard's line of fire. Anne yelled a warning in Mendoza's ear.

The hackbutt's hammer came down, burying the hot match in the powder pan. There was a wild sputter of sparks. Warned by Anne's outburst, Jock opened his jaws. He was tossed aside as the hack butt went off with a smoky bang.

Anne heard the whack of the silver bullet burying itself in the Fachan's thick chest. This blow set the monster spinning on his one leg, a giant whirligig gone mad. With a blood-chilling Highland howl, the MacGregor flung himself at the Fachan, his claymore whirling round his head. The beast moaned and bounded backward, terrified by three different forms of attack.

Mendoza loaded and fired a parting shot. The Fachan cleared both banks of the Coe in a single leap. He fled back up Glen Etive, making a terrific racket, each hop punctuated by squeals of pain.

The four fugitives and a wolf smiled at one another,

happy to have disposed of the bogey so neatly. The
MacGregor juggled his claymore like a baton. Mendoza
leaned down and patted Jock between the ears, asking in
coarse French how Fachan's prick had tasted. Anne could
not say she had contributed much, aside from scampering
about in terror and screaming at appropriate moments.

Above their head floated a long, sorrowful note. It was
the Campbell's hunting call.

Anne stood rooted, horrified by the chilling wail. She
heard Alison say, "Campbells are comin'. We've maimed
an' gelded their monster."

The MacGregor cursed a stream of Gaelic a mile wide
and five fathoms deep. The horn sounded again, closer,
more ominous. The Wild Hunt was racing their way.

"Run," Anne yelled, "up the Devil's Stair." She lifted
her skirts and set an example, sprinting through the grove
of trees. On the far side rose a high, frowning cliff. A mile
of goat path wound through the rocks and gullies, clinging
to the near-vertical slope. Above was Cameron country,
crowned by a mass of dark clouds. Scrambling up the
slope like a startled hare, Anne felt her feet slip on the
slick grass and loose rock. A patter of rain splashed in her
face.

Level with the pine tops, she heard the horn again, and
looked back. Moonlight slanted through a rent in the
clouds. The ghostly hunt was pouring out of Glen Etive,
splashing across the swift-running Coe Water. First came
the hunting pack, huge, smooth-skinned mastiffs, with big
black muzzles and misshappen heads. Behind the dogs
rode specters on horseback, gaunt, vengeful wraiths in
Campbell hunting tartans, waving their boar spears.

In their foreranks ran a giant boar, big as a Black Angus
bull. Anne saw gleaming saber tusks, and burning red
eyes. The bristles on the boar's back flashed a hundred
different hues—violet, crimson, gold, and orange—as
though the beast were dragging a burning rainbow behind
him.

Seeing the demon pig put renewed urgency in every
step. Anne was halfway to the top before the Wild Hunt
burst through the pines, hitting the slope, mounting the
Devil's Stair. But the hunt had a horrible implacability—as

though once they fixed their quarry, the prey was doomed. The hunting horn moaned again, blown by a skeletal bugler.

Anne fairly flew up a long gully leading to the top. The rocks were wet with rain, hellishly slippery. Feet and fingers were raw from climbing.

An angry yell echoed behind her. Over her shoulder she saw the MacGregor turn to face the hunt. Planting his feet on the Devil's Stair, he unslung his claymore, gripping the great sword with two hands.

Alison caught hold of Anne's gown, dragging her to the top of the gully. The two women were in Cameron country, for what little good that did—the Wild Hunt had galloped straight through Glen Coe, though that was Clan Donald land. They showed no sign of stopping for the Camerons.

The dogs swarmed over the MacGregor first. Anne saw the beasts had vivid red ears, and terrible fangs. Roaring in Gaelic, the Child of the Mist laid into them, his claymore cutting a silver circle about him. Hounds flew every which way, thrown as though they had been slashed by a mill saw. Jock was there, guarding the MacGregor's back, snapping at red-eared mastiffs that had run up the gully walls to get behind the Highlander.

The first horsemen, with the troll-boar in their midst, came a heartbeat behind the dogs. Mendoza handed Anne the reed-wand, leveling his hackbutt at the lead riders. Flicking the cover off the firing pan, he brought the hammer down. There was a sputter, but no explosion. Rain had spoiled his powder. Screaming *"Madre de Dios,"* Mendoza flung aside the hackbutt, drawing dirk and rapier.

Mother of God indeed, thought Anne. Where was Mary now? Busy with good deeds no doubt. Anne could hardly believe Mary would abandon her on the brink of safety. She felt the warmth of the reed-wand in her hand—the fire that kept them in Faerie still burning within it.

With a shriek she pulled the two halves of the wand apart.

The wave of riders parted. The huge boar slammed into the MacGregor, bristles flashing, bearing him down, slash-

ing at the Highlander with curved tusks. Jock leaped onto
the beast's forehead, clawing at the red pig eyes.

Anne rammed the hollow wand fire-end first into the
wet mud at her feet, smothering the embers. Faerie winked
out around them.

> *Love me not for comely grace,*
> *For my pleasing eye or face,*
> *Nor for any outward part,*
> *No, not for a constant heart.*

> —TRADITIONAL MADRIGAL

Ends of the Earth

What was a patter of rain in Faerie was a gale of incredible violence on Earth. Black rain lashed around Anne,
blinding her, drenching her gown, welcoming her back to
the world. Warm, gentle Faerie was gone. She could see
nothing of the Highlands but its venomous weather. Huddled in the gully next to Alison, clutching the cold reed-
wand, she heard the MacGregor still hurling insults at the
ghostly hunt. Only wind and storm replied.

A hand lifted the plaid sheltering her. Long, wet legs
slid between her and Alison, followed by a shivering body.
Jock was back, nude but for his jacket, in a thoroughly
wretched state and selecting the most comfortable spot
about—with a tartan covering his head and a woman on
either side.

Anne made room. The wolfman had earned it—he had
been more than heroic in Faerie, facing down the Wild
Hunt, turning the Fachan into a hopping eunuch. And

Anne had missed him. A thousand times during the trek through Faerie she had wanted to hear Jock's advice, his chidings, his sly humor.

"Jock, it's priceless to have you back. Why did you stay a wolf so long?"

He struggled into the shirt and hose they had been keeping for him since Dumbarton—now completely soaked. "I had no choice, lass. In Faerie we all revert to our true natures. You are a woman, Mary is a goddess, an' I am a wolf. Anly on earth can I bend the rules, an' take on human form. 'Tis one reason I am found o' this sorry world."

That was disconcerting. Anne had always thought of Jock as a man with animal powers. Now it was the other way round—he was a Faerie animal free to romp on Earth. Could she be in love with a canine? The thigh rubbing against her felt warm and human.

"So you will always be a wolf in Faerie?" She was starting to think of Faerie as a place she might like to see again.

"I can only assume human form in Faerie on high holy days: Midsummer, All Hallow's Eve, an' the like." Human on holidays, a dog during the week. He sat back as though he did not mind the wet, one arm around her shoulder, the other about Alison's waist.

Dog or man, he had been damned brave with silver bullets flying about, and Anne said so. The arm around her tightened. "Aye, lass, faint hearts naver yet won fair ladies."

They sat waiting for dawn. The storm blew past, leaving behind an industrious drizzle. Out of the damp and dark came the slosh of footsteps, and muffled conversation.

"Is it MacGregor and Mendoza?" Anne had not heard or seen the Spaniard since leaving Faerie.

"No, those two can no carry a conversation further than hello an' good-bye. These are Highlanders. Half a score at least."

Jock's ear was tuned perfectly to the night. Man-sized shadows loomed up. Anne saw the gleam of drawn blades and heard hard questions in Gaelic. Jock answered in his usual careless tone, then pulled on her. "Come, m'lady. I

have got us a roof an' floor fer the night. It'll be a wee
lang walk."

She unbent her frozen limbs and floundered off through
the mud and downpour. By the end he was half carrying
her, over rocks and slides, through shin-deep patches of
bog. They fairly blundered into their destination, a thatch-
and-stone bothy that seemed a natural part of the dark, wet
hillside.

Within was another world: warm and dry, packed with
people, smelling of sheep dip. The oblong hut was cen-
tered about an open hearth, where someone's granny
tended a peat fire. In one corner stood a massive wooden
foot plow for breaking the flinty earth. Children and goats
lurked in the shadows. The clansmen who brought them
bore broadswords and round targes—little shields of
leatherbound oak, with sharp-pointed spikes in the center
and intricate trefoil designs embossed about the rim. The
MacGregor was there, along with Mendoza—as wet and
bedraggled as badgers washed out by the flood.

The wizened granny escorted Anne and Alison into the
spence, where they stripped, changing behind worn blankets and swinging beef carcasses. The clothes Anne got
were tolerably clean, and above all dry—an embroidered
coat and a long plaid dress.

When they emerged from the pantry, Jock did introduc-
tions. "These are MacKails, a subclan o' the Camerons. I
told 'em yew are Queen o' Northumbria, come ta pay
them a visit—by way o' Campbell country an' Faerie.
They were much impressed, so please act the part."

"Thank them for rescuing us from the rain" was all she
could think to say, smiling at her hosts. Every pair of eyes
was turned toward her, and she hoped Jock's inventive
tongue did not get them tossed back out in the storm. But
the man was in his element, spinning a tale full of off-
handed boasting, doing his best to entertain the MacKails.
Anne only understood the bits Jock or Alison translated.

"They would no have found us if it were not for yon
MacGregor." Jock nodded toward the Child of the Mist.
"A shepherd lad bringin' in sheep heard him yellin', an'
ran to alert the clan. Seems the MacGregor cried out,
'Chlanna nan con thigibh a so's gheib feoil—son's o'

bitches come an' eat flesh.' Which happens ta be a Cameron war cry. These MacKails thought their laird had lit the fiery cross, an' came charging out in defense o' Clan Cameron."

Once the cross was bathed in goat's blood and set afire, the MacKails were bound to support *Na Camshroinaich* against Campbells, MacIntoshes, or even the King of Scotland. But having proven their determination, the MacKails were happy to sit back and hear a strange tale from guests they half believed. Anne discovered that the parts they doubted were not those that a civilized person would have questioned. Faerie was closer and more real than Edinburgh. The MacKails thrilled to Jock's description of the fight with the Fachan, but found it harder to credit that Anne had been to Italy.

She was happy to stay half a week. They fed her beef-tripe soup from a horn spoon, and she found their company enjoyable once she was used to the lice. The old lady of the croft was a widow who sat up late nights, spinning by the hearth and muttering in Gaelic to faeries only she could see. She, and dozens like her, were clan dependents, maintained by the chief. Highlanders were poor, but they spread their poverty about. Clan lands were held in common, and Anne saw no one begging by the roads—but then she saw nothing remotely resembling a road.

Her hosts introduced her to handsome young Cameron lairds who figured their descent from Aonghas, the sister of Banquo. The lairds and fighting men were mostly fresh-faced and charming, because the Camerons too had been at the Battle of the Shirts, where these dashing young fellows had lost their fathers and older brothers. As Jock said, Camerons were "ferocious fighters, an' proud ta a fault."

During that half-week the Child of the Mist took his leave. Having brought them safely through Campbell country, he was only a couple of days' walk from home. He thanked them for their company, and for the bottled beer, adding that if they found any more randy witches needing help with their spells, Rob MacGregor was ready. Then he disappeared down into Glen Coe.

Mendoza elected to stay with them, having no clan

nearer than the Bay of Biscay. Totally adrift in Scotland, he found the Highlands to his liking, reminding him of his home in Galicia where the hill Celts wore kilts and played bagpipes. He claimed he could recognize a dozen Gaelic words already.

Anne was fairly adrift herself. Hospitable as *Na Camshroinaich* was, she did not mean to settle among the Camerons and spend her days spinning with the faeries. The Gordons, who might keep her in semicivilized style, were a long way off, at the far end of the Great Glen. She was left with that dubious destination "The Ends of the Earth," pressed on her by the Gordon Witch and Mad Anne.

Jock saw no difficulty. "After being hunted through the length o' the Lawlands, from the Borders ta Faerie, we can now do as we pleeze."

"Well, what do we *pleeze?*"

"The Ends o' the Earth would be a bonnie direction."

"Fine, but which way is that?"

"Why, that is the pleezing part—we do na know. All we can do is pick the easiest path. We have the word o' two good witches that yew at least will get there."

So on a sunny summer day they left, along with Alison, Mendoza, and a-lad driving horses down to the head of Loch Leven. The horses were wild Highland geldings for sale in the south, never mounted but tough as the mountains, accustomed to foul weather and worse forage. Much in demand as hobbies.

Walking along, Anne could see the differences between the Highlands and Faerie. The land was rougher and more barren, not as thickly wooded. Oats and barley grew in unfenced fields. People had wrought changes even in this remote country. The walk itself was a delight, steadily downhill, with firm footing, following rivulets and waterfalls toward the sea. Faerie had done her limp good, and her foot was growing used to travel.

Beached at the head of the loch was a MacLean ship, ready to take on the horses and sail with the tide. The craft was a clinker-built cog, with round lines, a high stern and a straight prow; bound for the Isle of Mull.

Jock's notion of an easy and enjoyable trip was to make

themselves guests of one laird, then another. "I was no made ta be a tinker, or plowman, workin' my furlong o' field an' robbin' my neighbor's dung heap at night."

"You were made to be a wolf," Anne reminded him.

"An' what is a wolf but a noble-lookin' beggar?"

He found the ship's master—a rough-cut felon with a graying beard and a too-ready grin. Informing him they had important news for the MacLean of Duart, Jock secured free passage to Mull. It went so easy, Anne wondered if the master could be trusted. "We are paying him nothing. He might decide to turn businessman, and sell us as slaves in Ireland."

Jock dismissed her hesitation. "True, MacLean ships have had a bad name—ever since auld Lachlan MacLean tried ta discard his Campbell wife by stranding her on a tiny island, now called Lady Rock. But really MacLeans are as honest as Highlanders can hope to be."

"Unless you are married to one."

"Exactly."

With a long stride and a fair wind the day's sail to Mull was not like a sea voyage at all. The cog passed out of Loch Leven into Loch Linnhe, a huge fjord connecting the Great Glen to the sea. The ship hugged the northern shore—MacLean country—then crossed the narrow Sound of Mull, anchoring in Duart Bay, beneath the bleak, frowning seawall of Duart Castle.

Duart, home of the MacLean on Mull, was a massive black keep, perched on a rocky headland, unapproachable from the sea and shielded on the landward side by a thirty-foot windowless curtain wall. Seeing the evil-looking hold, with its high-peaked roofs and stained chimneys, Anne remembered Jock's story of a previous MacLean leaving his Campbell wife on a rock to be washed away by the tide— that the poor woman had been rescued did not make Anne feel a whit safer.

Alongside their cog was a splendid forty-oared war galley, flying a four-quarter flag showing the Lion of Scotland, a rock and tower, the Galley of the Isles, and a red hand surrounded by nine red fetters.

"A MacNeil galley," was Jock's verdict. "That's the Red Hand o' the MacNeils, an the Rock an' Tower o'

Barra. It may be the MacNeil of Barra himself is here."
Anne had never heard of Barra except as a pirate's nest
that preyed on English shipping.

This MacLean of Duart did not act the monster. As soon
as they landed, he invited them all to share his evening
meal, seating them at a tremendous oaken table that ran
the full length of his hall. They ate from hoop-and-stave
vessels that resembled small boats, and conversed in
French, telling the MacLean most everything that had happened, from the Rising against Elizabeth to the trip
through Faerie. The worst the MacLean did was to gloat
over their news from the South. "Ah, Lowlander kills
Lowlander, and the MacLean may do as he pleases."

He turned to his wife. "Perhaps it is time MacDonalds
and MacLeans hired out to opposing sides—and were
properly paid for carrying on our own feud. I must make
a truce, and speak to the MacDonald about this."

Lady MacLean thought the notion sound enough, but
sourly warned her lord not to trust the MacDonalds too far.
"Truce talks can be thrice as fatal as battle, where Clan
Donald is concerned."

Seated near to Anne and Jock were the couple who had
come up from the war galley docked in the bay—Ruari
MacNeil of Barra and his sister, Brigid MacNeil. Brother
and sister made a handsome couple. Both were tall, with
reddish-blond hair; Ruari had a sharp, triangular face, a
neat spade beard, and a devilish smile. Brigid was erect
and slender, with long, thin hands. They had piercing blue
eyes and spoke excellent French.

Ruari advised the MacLean to forget his interminable
feud with Clan Donald. "Sail to Ireland with me instead."
Ruari MacNeil had numerous relations in Ireland—the
Red Hand and Nine Fetters on his flag showed he was descended from Niall of the Nine Hostages, pagan High
King of Ireland when the Romans ruled England. "I plan
to make an offering at the Shrine of Knockpatrick in
County Mayo, then harry my cousins, the O'Neills of Ty-
rone. If it is revenge you want, never forget it was Shane
O'Neill who captured your old aunt Catherine of Duart—
making her his concubine, and keeping her chained by day

to a small boy, so she would not run away. What MacDonald has done worse?"

While the MacLean and the MacNeil concluded their business, Brigid MacNeil asked Anne, "Where will you fare next?"

"To the Ends of the Earth, I suppose." It was the only destination she had to give.

Brigid gave her brother a knowing look. "Then it is the Norns that brought us together, for we are just the people to take you there." Talk passed on to other things, but the MacNeils of Barra were serious. On the morrow Ruari invited them to cruise with him. "I can take you to Skye, the Outer Isles, and the Ends of the Earth." Brigid added warmly that they were welcome to guest with them, "Through summer, winter, and beyond."

To Anne the offer seemed to go beyond Highland hospitality. "We could never hope to repay you."

Brigid's lips curled into a slight smile. "Only a Lowlander would worry about pay. We MacNeil women are blessed—some would say cursed—with *taishatr*—the second sight. I am sure you will earn your way."

Jock had no qualms about accepting undue generosity. He and Mendoza were already climbing over the galley with Ruari MacNeil, inspecting the beautiful ship. She was trim and single-masted, with low fighting castles, a ram at one end and a rudder at the other. There was a culverin in the bow and saker on the stern castle. Mendoza was ecstatic to be able to talk guns in a civilized tongue.

"See"—Brigid nudged Anne—"you are repaying us already. There is a sore shortage of good gunners in the Highlands. My brother would be most pleased to have that Spaniard at Barra, to help him work his toys."

They sailed up the Sound of Mull, a slim corridor of the sea separating Mull from the mainland. The galley was manned by brawny clansmen, who took turns at the oars—galley slaves were an extravagance the MacNeils could not afford. Every rower had to be equally handy with targe and broadsword. The ship had a small awning and day couch on the stern castle, but no room for sleeping or eating on board. They beached the craft each evening and for midday meals.

North of Mull they entered the strait between the mainland and the Isle of Skye. Standing by the starboard rail, Anne saw gray Highland cliffs and emerald braes falling straight into the sea. Jock spoke above the salt wind: "We are sailing along the auld boundary o' Albany. For four hundred years this sea line divided Scotland an' Norway. Mull, Skye, an' all the great isles were ruled by Viking sea kings."

"Some isles still are." Anne tilted her head to where Ruari MacNeil was lounging on the day couch, teaching Alison a French rhyme.

Jock laughed. "The MacNeils are no kings. They just think they are."

"But he is certainly a Viking." It was transparent that, like the Vikings, the MacNeils of Barra spent their summers cruising about, calling on friends and enemies, generally making mischief.

They sailed up the Sound of Sleat, and halfway around the great Isle of Skye, past the wide mouth of Loch Snizort and into the tighter Loch of Dunvegan. In the narrow gut of the loch was another towering sea keep, Dunvegan Castle, home of the *Siol Tormond,* MacLeod of MacLeod, chief of the Clan Leoid. The high, angular fortress covered the entire summit of a rocky headland overlooking the loch. At the base of the curtain, cliffs fell thirty feet straight down to the beach. The single landward side was protected by a fosse sixty feet wide. Anne saw no drawbridge or gatehouse. The only entrance to the castle was through a sea gate and up steep stone steps cut into the rock.

The deeper Anne went into the Isles, the more formidable and inaccessible each new keep appeared. No wonder these clan leaders did as they pleased—no mainland prince had defenses so secure. On land a castle could always be breached, the way Tom's batteries had smashed the walls of Barnard. But to take Dunvegan would require a fleet, as well as an army. And pitting wooden ships against stone walls was at best a chancy business, particularly on the unknown waters of a narrow loch.

Opposite Dunvegan Anne saw two flat-topped hills. "The MacLeod's tables," Brigid MacNeil anticipated

Anne's question. She had taken a place between Anne and
Alison on the stern castle. During the voyage the
MacNeil's sister had played hostess, speaking mostly
French in deference to Anne's station. There was no reason for her to take Anne's nominal title seriously, but the
MacNeils liked having a Lowland countess as a guest.
Brother and sister were both accustomed to indulging their
likes and dislikes. Since Anne's French was better than Alison's Gaelic, she found herself in the novel position of
translating between two Scots. Nothing showed the division between Highlander and Lowlander more sharply
than that they understood foreigners more readily than the
other.

"Do you know the story behind these twin tables of
rock?" asked Brigid. "Of course you would not. Well,
some thirty years ago the Old MacLeod of MacLeod, Alasdair Crouchback, visited the court of James the Fifth. A
Lowland laird sneered at him, saying a Highlander had to
be impressed by dining in a real hall. The MacLeod said
a king's hall was impressive, but at home he had 'a finer
hall, a greater table, and taller candlesticks,' A wager was
made, and a year later King James's court visited Skye.
Alasdair MacLeod invited them to the higher of these two
flat-topped hills, serving them a banquet by the light of
torches held by his clansmen.

Anne admitted that it must have been a spectacle.

"It won the wager. And I think we shall see it repeated."
Brigid gave her a sly smile.

"In this mist and drizzle?" The day was far too wet for
dining out; gray clouds hung over the loch like a wet blanket. Anne thought the MacNeil woman was stretching her
second sight.

Dusk descended as they disembarked. They were met at
the water stairs by the MacLeod, a grandson of old
Alasdair Crouchback. With him was his heiress, Mary
MacLeod, a fine-featured young woman with a great shock
of brown hair, high cheekbones, and intent blue eyes.

Ruari MacNeil had come to pay court to Mary. He let
his sister—and his guests—entertain the MacLeod, while
he spent every free moment with the girl. Brigid slipped
artfully into her role. The MacLeod was a widower, and

allowed himself to be thoroughly distracted by the MacNeil's sister—so long as Ruari did not actually run off with young Mary. A not-uncommon danger in Scotland.

Brigid flirted shamelessly, asking for the MacLeod to feast her on his "best table." Damp twilight shrouded the castle, and the MacLeod said the wet would hardly do for dining on the hilltop. "We women will see to the weather." The MacNeil's sister spoke very matter-of-factly. Anne realized Brigid was looking right at her and Alison.

The MacLeod was delighted by the promised magic, saying another miracle always added luster to a hall. "Our females are not noted for having the second sight, the way the women of Barra are. Yet we MacLeods are a lucky clan, and magical as well." He ordered his retainers and kin to get food and fire, and find boats to cross the loch.

The chief himself fetched the faerie flag of the MacLeods. When he brought in the banner, Anne could see nothing of the flag except that it was furled and made from some colorful silken fabric. While the boats were being readied, the MacLeod told the story of the faerie banner. The flag has first been given to Harald Hardraade of Norway, during his great wanderings east of Byzantium. "As long as his luck lasted and he carried this flag, Harald Hardraade was unstoppable. He unfurled the faerie flag three times, then his luck changed. Harald left it with his ships when he went to fight at Stamford Bridge."

Anne knew the rest of that story. At Stamford Bridge on the Derwent in Yorkshire, Harald of Norway demanded Danegeld from her Saxon ancestors. The Saxons made a counteroffer. "Seven feet of English earth, seeing that the King of Norway is bigger than most men." So Saxon and Dane hewed at each other across the shield ring until the Danes were near annihilated.

"Of Harald's whole army," intoned the MacLeod, "only a single ship, Godred Crovan's galley, returned to Norway. Godred Crovan was our royal ancestor, King of Dublin and the Isles. The faeries passed the banner to him, founding the luck of the MacLeods."

As they descended the steps to the sea gate, he prattled on about how the flag gave victory in battle, and cured diseases in cattle. "But it can only be unfurled three times, and Alasdair Crouchback used it twice to defeat Clan Ranald." So the flag was kept furled, but brought along to lend its magic to the proceedings. Boats were waiting by the lochside to carry them into the long summer twilight.

They were piped across the loch by bagpipers standing erect in the prows, blasting a MacLeod pipe march into the sodden air. Clansmen beat at the oars, splashing in cadence to the pipes, and one boat contained a big black bull, bellowing along with the pipers. The whole way across Anne wondered what would be expected of her in this savage show.

Even on the far shore the clamoring music did not let up. Despite falling rain the pipers continued to beat out a lively tune, leading them up the "table" closest to the loch.

She arrived thoroughly drenched. "What now?"

"Why, ye'll relight the fire in the reed-wand," Jock replied. "An' get us ta Faerie before we die o' the freezin' pneumonia."

"I'm not sure I can do it."

"If yew don't do it, we will look the complete fools. This is where we pay fer the pipin' an' supper. Com'on the MacNeil woman thinks it will happen." Brigid MacNeil was standing solemn as an icon, letting the rain run off her, waiting for Anne to begin. Anne could see how the MacNeils' hospitality had made her fair sport for this sort of torture. From Glen Coe to Loch Dunvegan they had been eating out on a wild story only a Highlander was required to believe.

"But I could not repeat that ritual, even if I wanted." Anne was not about to lift her skirts for a line of clansmen, while moaning heathen lyrics.

Alison came close to encourage her. "We can do it, m'lady. An' we don't need ta repeat that ritual. Every witch must find her own words an' ways—ones that match her heart."

"Aye," agreed Jock. "Fun as it was, all that fukin' were not strictly needed. Different things move different women—that Gordon lass just wanted it done her way, an' who were we ta say no?"

Alison pleaded with Anne to attempt it. "She said the wand would remain charmed until it returned to her."

There was naught to do but hope and pray. Asking Mendoza to help her with the fire, Anne opened the reed-wand, taking care not to let the inside contact the rain. Alison knelt behind her, covering her with a cloak and crooning in Gaelic. It might have been another magic chant, or one of Goodmother Scott's lullabies—most likely it was both.

Anne said a silent, fervent prayer. "Mary, Mother of Us All, please don't leave me looking silly in this cold rain."

Painstakingly, she transferred an ember from Mendoza's fire pot to the match inside the reed-wand.

Rain put it out.

Suppressing a curse, she prayed again, then tried a second time.

Again the ember went out.

On the third try the rain vanished. It did not just stop—clouds completely evaporated, the ground dried. Droplets disappeared on the way down. A warm wind sprang to life, igniting the dazzling stars of Faerie.

With a loud hurrah the Highlanders shouted heathen slogans and skimmed bonnets into the air. The MacLeods were impressed beyond measure, and perhaps a bit terrified to see the lights of Dunvegan disappear as the moon and stars came out. Mary MacLeod was holding tight to Ruari MacNeil, and Anne heard him reassure the lass that the witch could take them back anytime. That was what she was now, the witch. So strange.

Heaping a mound of earth in the center of the small plateau, the MacLeods sacrificed the great black bull atop it. Then they made a crackling bonfire from Faerie wood, and cooked the animal while pipers wailed around the pyre. Anne felt a thrill build inside her. For the first time she had made magic not in fear and desperation, but coldly and logically, and mostly under her own control. Alison hugged her. She would have loved to share the moment with Jock, but he was, of course, a wolf, salivating over the roasting bull. Faerie seemed to bring out the worst and best in everyone.

Clansmen took turns holding torches for the feast. By the time the MacLeods were done, they had eaten the black bull, hide and all—right down to the bones, hooves, and horns. It was splendidly barbaric—a feast worthy of

Faerie, washed down with the watered blood of Jock Barley Corn.

Brigid MacNeil made the usual glowing predictions, proclaiming there would always be MacLeods at Dunvegan. "And your clan shall rule here even after the Kings of Scots are driven overseas and passed away."

A clanswoman brought Brigid a year-old daughter, named Mary, asking what the seeress saw for her. The mother had carried her child into the damp and across the loch in hopes the infant would find a blessing in Faerie. Brigid did not disappoint her. "Your Mary, *nighean* Alasdair, will live more than a hundred years. She shall be a great poetess, inventing modes of verse even Islanders never heard before." The mother poured out thanks, but to Anne it was just another witch's double blessing—she wondered what the dark side was.

In the dawn light by the loch Anne got to do her own deliberate magic again. This second time was even more exciting, knowing it would work. Still she was careful to pray, thanking Mary for all the help God's Mother had given her. Then she plunged the reed-wand into the waters of the loch. Dunvegan Castle appeared before them, massive towers and curtain rising right up out of the rock. And Anne had made it happen.

Climbing the slippery black steps up from the sea gate, she did not mind the rain, hardly felt the cold and exhaustion. Best of all, Jock was no longer a wolf. He was there to share her success.

When the galley threaded its way through Dunvegan Loch, making for the open sea, the MacNeils could not do enough for their guests. Laird Ruari was especially pleased with Anne's performance, and the visit to Faerie. Though he had not got the chief's consent to court Mary MacLeod, it was whispered about the ship that Ruari had "gotten the nod that means most to a man." During the stay in Faerie, Ruari and Mary had slipped away from the piping and dancing, presumably to rest. But what lass with a head full of whisky could resist giving her maidenhead to a handsome sea king on a warm summer night in Faerie?

As Dunvegan Castle sank into the hills behind the galley, Anne even dared to question Brigid about how much truth lay in her prophecies. "Absolute truth," Brigid answered. "No sane witch wants to risk lying in Faerie. Not with the Norns looking over your shoulder."

"And what about what you did not tell?"

The seeress turned at the rail, to look right at Anne. "If truth is telling everything, then all speech is a lie. Tell me truthfully, when I said that baby would live out a century, was it a blessing, or a curse?"

"Her mother certainly thought it a blessing."

"But it is also a curse. She will live to see family and friends die before her, even her own children. She will endure the aches and heartaches of age for longer than most people live. Did I need to tell her mother that?"

"And what about other, unknown tragedies?"

"Oh, the MacLeods are a lucky clan. They will outlast the monarchs of Scotland, but they will suffer too, sometimes grievously. Do you know the worst tragedy the MacLeods will suffer in that babe's lifetime? It concerns your birthplace in England."

"Worcester?" Anne was startled, having never mentioned her birthplace to Brigid.

The MacNeil woman nodded. "When Mary is old and gray, a Lowland king will convince the MacLeods to march with him, deep into England. At Worcester he will lose a desperate battle, leaving the MacLeods to make it home if they can—more than half the clansmen will perish, nor will women and children with them be spared by the English."

"A Lowland king? Of Scotland or England?"

"Both. So now you know the worst. If you wish to inform the MacLeods, my brother will be pleased to put about; he's been completely taken with your powers, ever since Faerie. Go tell the clan that they are doomed to be slaughtered on the place where you were born. I warn you, they will not think it friendly advice. There will be MacLeods who'll say you cursed them, after taking their hospitality."

"You are not being fair."

"Prophecy never is."

Mad Anne and the Gordon Witch had said as much, but from Brigid the message did not sound so devious. Anne

had suffered enough lessons in how helpless people were
in the hands of the Norns—she no longer leaped to judge.

Brigid placed an arm on hers. "We witches and seer-
esses tell people what they want to hear, because it is our
best defense. It makes men want to have us around. If we
told the plain truth, men would burn us all and be done
with it."

The sea between Skye and Barra was dark, almost
black. Thoroughly untamed too—not penned and limited
by land, like the locks and sounds they had sailed through.
The slim galley pitched alarmingly from one wave trough
to the next, and Anne lost sight of land. Engulfed by water, they ran before a bitter north wind.

Gray sky and gray waves were broken only by a pod of
huge sea unicorns. Anne saw the great beasts almost brush
the ship, flashing their gleaming white horns and blowing
little puffs of spray from a single nostril at the tops of their
huge heads. She called Alison to the rail, and they watched
the broad backs go by, finding them more fantastic than
the horned horses of Faerie.

The sun sank, becoming a red line beneath the western
clouds. Anne was relieved to sight land in the sunset, seeing for the first time the great curving buckler of the Outer
Isles, the archipelago that shielded the Highlands from the
open sea.

"Here are the Ends of the Earth," Brigid pointed to the
line of black hilltops rising from the sea. "Beyond lies the
world-circling ocean."

The galley slipped through the Sound of Barra, going
past the crashing reef into Castlebay. Here Ruari anchored,
at the southernmost end of the island chain. Surrounded by
the green hills of Barra, Anne saw the most protected of
all the Highland keeps, Kisimul Castle, stronghold of the
MacNeils of Barra—"The Castle on an Island in the Sea,
on an Island in the Sea."

Castlebay was really an open lagoon, with Kisimul Castle completely filling a tiny inlet. No heavy-gunned ship
could sail up to the castle walls. No land army could cross
the lagoon. Galleys and small boats could approach, only
to face sheer stone battlements rising straight out of the
water. Anne saw hardly enough room beneath the walls to

rest a siege ladder—just a berth for the galley, a small guardhouse, and a catchment for trapping fish when the tide fell. The entrance to the keep was through the upper floor of the gatehouse, by means of an interior drawbridge. When the bridge was lifted, unwanted guests were faced with blank walls, and a single thick door eighteen feet above ground level. Crossing the drawbridge, Anne noticed "murder holes," cut so stones or less pleasant articles could be dumped on anyone approaching the door.

In Castle Kisimul's splendid isolation brother and sister MacNeil were accustomed to being judged only by themselves and by Clan Nail. Clan law was the only law, and Kisimul had its own pit and gallows.

That night they feasted Anne and their guests in the Great Hall. Harpers played in the galley, accompanied by gale winds howling about the towers. The hall was ancient, with no chimney or fireplace, just an open hearth. A peat fire burned day and night, the smoke finding its way out through gaps beneath the eaves.

When the meal was done, the head druid went to the highest battlement, blew a great blast on an immense horn, and faced westward, toward the angry Atlantic. The leather-lunged old man announced to the roaring waves: "Hear ye, oh ye peoples; listen, oh ye nations. The MacNeil has finished his meat. All princes, monarchs, emperors, and potentates of the world may now dine."

While clansmen and clanswomen continued to drink and carouse in the Great Hall, Brigid led Anne and Alison up to her bedroom. "The morrow is Friday, the Friday before Midsummer, a holy day among the women of Barra. You must be ready at dawn for one last short trip. Then you will truly be at the Ends of the Earth. No men may come, and you will be gone as long or as short as Mary wills it, so a strong good-bye would be the best."

She showed them her canopied bed, table, chests, hearth, and polished-steel mirror. "You may use this room for the night. I will sleep in the laird's room; since childhood my brother and I have often shared a bed. Though I expect he means to drink himself silly tonight, and pass out in the main hall among his men. Will you be comfortable here?"

Anne looked about. "Oh, very." She felt already at home. Brigid might be half-Irish, and speak French, but she had all the best qualities Anne had seen in Scotswomen: She was generous, bold, strong, and courteous, mistress of her own life. A woman to admire, and to emulate.

"Very well. And in the morning," Brigid reminded them, "one final journey, to the real Ends of the Earth. Will you be ready?"

"It appears I must be," replied Anne. Alison nodded eagerly.

Brigid went out. For a moment Anne could hear the merriment downstairs, then the heavy door closed, leaving her alone with her handmaid.

Brimming with excitement, Alison helped Anne undress, her flying young fingers undoing the laces. "Yew feel at home here, don't ye, m'lady?"

"Yes, I do feel safe." Finally, Anne stood staring at the steel mirror, which was full length, painstakingly polished, watching her body emerge from the clothes.

"We are in the hands o' the MacNeils. An' we can anly trust 'em. Not even the King o' Scots could get us oot." Or the Queen of England, thought Anne. Here she could stop fleeing, and think about having a life not dictated by fear and circumstances. She realized she had been running from her fears ever since Tom received Elizabeth's summons at Topcliffe. Even when she was advancing, she had merely been fleeing in reverse.

The polished steel showed her hair had lost half its luster to brittle strands of white. She could thank Jedburgh Gaol for that. And for her bent foot. Wind, rain, and salt spray had drawn tight little wrinkles around her eyes. She imagined for a moment that Mad Anne looked back at her from the steel surface. *Am I her now?*

Alison held out a wool robe. "Brigid means we will return to Faerie. Not ta escape, or ta impress the MacLeods. We will return fer the sacred third time, fer ourselves, ta become witches—real witches."

Anne faced the happy lass, flushed with pleasure, red hair shining. "You want that terribly much, don't you?"

"Lord yes, m'lady. I suckled wicca with my mother's

milk. I know it is all new to yew. An' yew do no have ta go. . . ." The girl's voice trailed off, showing she hadn't the least desire to go alone.

"I will go with you," Anne reassured her. "It seems I have been preparing too, without knowing until now."

Alison brightened, slipping the robe about Anne's shoulders, drawing it tight but not letting go, fingers under the fabric resting on Anne's breasts. After a quiet moment the girl's lips moved. "An' Jock will no be with us. He is a man, an' a wolf in Faerie. Doubly barred."

Anne nodded. Reaching out, she put her hands on the girl's hips, still thinking, how could she have Jock without hurting Alison?

"Are yew no gonna bid him good-bye?" the girl asked. "We can no just leave him hangin'."

"Of course." Anne squeezed the girl's firm waist. "Of course. Go run and get him."

Alison leaned forward, kissed her on the lips, then raced out of the room to fetch Jock. When she returned, Anne had the robe tied securely around her and was feeding the fire. Jock looked thrice as serious as usual, deeply concerned, though his face was flushed from drink. Hands behind him, he made a little bow. "I'm told we must say good-bye."

Seeing his dog-eyed look, and hearing real regret in the man's voice, Anne felt a hollow anticipation. Alison was bustling about, pulling extra bedding from a chest—blankets and a feather pillow. Clutching the bundle of bedclothes, she backed to the door, reaching behind herself, fumbling with the latch. "M'lady, I will sleep oot in the hall, ta see yew are not disturbed"—as though an oak door and stone walls were not protection enough.

Anne caught her before she could slip out, taking the girl's good hand in hers, letting her keep the maimed one tucked beneath a pillow. "You won't mind that?"

"Oh, no." Alison shook her head hard. She leaned forward and kissed Anne again, whispering in her ear, "I will have yew to myself afterward." Under the circumstances it was a damned strange thing to say.

Then she was gone, closing the door behind her. Jock was already seated on the bed, a bemused smile on his face. "Delightful girl, an' most thoughtful. Could charm the pants off the Pope." His hands came out from behind his back. As if by magic, he was holding a bottle of fortified wine and two cups.

"And still a virgin," Anne added. "You Scots are a thrifty lot."

Jock started to pour. "Yew know she loves ye dearly. Nor is she the anly one that does."

Anne accepted a cup. "I very much fear it is you she loves." She looked back at the ironbound oak door, thinking of the girl lying down on the stones outside.

Jock took a thoughtful sip. "M'lady, yew are more loveable than ye may imagine. Did she tell ye what happened on the Night o' May?"

"Some." Anne felt the muscles tighten over her stomach, along with a twinge lower down.

"Did she tell how we talked first, about ourselves and about yew?"

Anne shook her head. She was very aware of the man's body, seeing lean strength in his legs, noting how his weight dented the bed. Jock drained his glass, setting it down on a cedar chest. "We agreed that she and I were never likely ta be wed. Meaning we had ta be careful. We also agreed we did no want ta hurt you. In our own ways we both love yew."

How much of this need she believe? The man was as full of tales as a trip to Saint Thomas at Canterbury, especially when he had eyed something he wanted.

He took hold of her robe between her knees and her waist, bunching the fabric, drawing her toward the bed. "It is true, Anne. Ye have not known witches as I have. She loves yew the way a witch girl loves a woman she admires, an' aspires ta be. With them it is women who have power—men are fer makin' babies, an' havin' fun."

He was gripping her hips. "But I love an' admire ye too—since the day I first saw yew in the Dale—anly not the way a witch girl does." His wolf's eyes looked hungrily up at her. "Anne, yew cannot ken how lovable yew are, strong and gallant, resourceful and tender. . . ."

Jock stood up, kissing her on the lips. She kissed back. (Oh, Tom, forgive me.)

By some wizard's trick he had the knots in her robe undone, and his hands were on her flesh, kneading, stroking. . . . "I thought yew'd never forget yer dumb-as-a-dick husband." Deftly his jacket was off, and his hose was down around his knees.

Swaying on her feet, she leaned forward, overbalanced, and they were together on the bed, laughing, shedding what was left in the way of clothes. She had been so precious proud, but the time for that had passed. She reminded herself she was not falling for his flimflam, not entirely; she was getting what she wanted.

Their whole bodies touched. His tongue explored every crevice of her mouth, then moved on. Lips brushed her chin, throat, shoulders, breasts. Then he was between her legs, just as Alison had described, slow and exciting, teasing, firmer as her body demanded more.

Waves of pleasure rippled through her thighs, up her spine. She felt whole again, happy, no longer old or hurt. "Do it," she yelped. "Don't stop, do it all." She felt his weight, heavy and fervent. But he was still holding back.

"Yes, yes. But fuk me all the way, you fool." She used low Scots because no English word said it so hard and well—she knew she would not conceive, but had no time to tell him how she knew.

Jock was not a man to keep a lady waiting. In a moment he was plunging away, her whole body shuddering under the impact. It had been a long time since she'd felt this, and there was nothing in the world like it.

For some time afterward they lay together talking, holding each other close. Her release was complete. And she was not in the least worried about having Jock's child— not yet anyway—since in a roundabout way Mad Anne told her she would not be pregnant.

The wind outside died. There was a soft scratching at the door. Anne sat up, calling, "Come in."

Alison came shivering in, wrapped in a blanket and trailing her pillow. "It's cold sleepin' on the stones, an' I dreamed . . ."

"Of course." Anne lifted the blanket, letting her handmaid burrow in beside her, feeling ashamed for forgetting the girl in the midst of her own pleasure.

Jock propped himself on one elbow, saying, "I am gonna sorely miss the two o' yew."

"I am certain you will." She gave the rogue a smug look.

"Nah, 'tis true. I have never had better travelin' companions. It is hard ta see ye go where I may not follow."

A moment later he was showing her just how hard he felt. But she was not ready for another bout, not with Alison there. Disappointed, Jock drifted into sleep, having more drink aboard than she did.

Anne lay back. Alison's chaste body felt comforting after the fierce sin Anne had committed. The girl had done all her bad dreaming in the hallway, and did not cry out again—her soft, easy presence, as powerful as the fragrance of poppies, lulled Anne to sleep.

She woke before first light, to tend the fire and choose a strong velvet dress, well mended, looking as though it could take some traveling.

A rustling on the bed told her Jock and Alison were up. She turned and saw them kissing good-bye, not paying the least attention to her. She watched with conflicting feelings: love, envy, compassion. Alison knelt naked on the bed, hiding her maimed hand but totally shameless in other ways, bending right down, and giving Jock a kiss between the legs that near knocked him backward off the bed.

Anne turned her back. When they were completely finished, she gave Jock a more formal and restrained good-bye. "I will miss you very much."

He smiled. "Anly think of me in Faerie when yew are sportin' nude among the witches, an' I will be a happy man."

Brigid MacNeil was waiting outside, her smile saying she was glad to see her bed getting serious use. Without speaking, she led the women through the silent castle, across the inner bridge, down to a small skiff tied alongside her brother's war galley. Brigid rowed—in addition to having the Sight, she had been born amid boats. As they splashed across the lagoon, Anne found the bare, rolling landscape and the half-lit sky eerie. Last night's gale had blown by. On the main island she saw points of light, sparks moving in a line, leaving the fisher village, curving to meet them on the shore.

Brigid beached the skiff amid sea wrack left by the storm.

Drawing even closer, the points of light resolved into torches held by Barra woman wearing crow-black dresses and chanting. Their singing rose up, growing louder, greeting the dawn light. The women filed in around them, torches whipped by the morning wind. Singing ceased.

Brigid spoke to the women in Gaelic, leading a prayer and invocation. Then she said to Anne in French, "We should enter Faerie at sunrise, taking with us the luck of the dawn."

Anne knelt in the beach sand, surrounded by the storm debris, opening the reed-wand, readying the fire, praying to Mary. "Make this third entry into Faerie holy. After today I want nothing to be the same."

Sun swept over the lagoon, as Anne lit the tinder in the reed-wand. Kisimul Castle vanished, taking with it the boats in the harbor, the fishing village, the sheep on the hillsides.

Gone too were all traces of the storm. Summer weather was a chancy thing on the Outer Isles. To windward seethed the North Atlantic, the world's most tumultuous ocean. Storm, sleet, and rain could come roaring down in any season with appalling violence. But in Faerie the summer was real and warm, almost tropical in its intensity. The lagoon sparkled under a rising sun, surrounded by tree-clad hills, forming a temperate island paradise. Ancient oaks and pines came almost to the water's edge, spreading a black canopy full of strange birdcalls.

Brigid spoke again in Gaelic. The women shed their black garments, showing their full bodies to the sunlight—a rare pleasure made better by the radiant air of Faerie. Anne and Alison did the same. Despite Jock's leering gibe, nudity was an essential ritual. Cast aside with their clothes were the laws of men—they were no longer countess and handmaid, laird's sister and fishwife. They were women, small girls, and aged crones, slim bodies, big bodies, smooth and wrinkled, white and brown. Hair was blond and red and black, hanging in thick coils or thin strands.

Brigid drew them into a circle on the sand, and began a calling chant that flowed round the ring of women. Anne chanted with them, becoming just one link in the circle. She imagined the circle extending out into the world, reaching out for other women; the women who danced away winter on Eve o' May, or danced to defy the Kirk on Twelfth Night, or dared to form the Faerie Ring locked inside Dumbarton. She pictured women who sat in prison, and women who ruled nations. And the women on Maiden Hill who had held their babies out to her—who nurtured life even in the face of death. From Orkney to Lands End women sat in the cold, sleepless dawn, rocking hungry, restless children, while they carded, combed, and spun, to clothe their family, to pay their fines. No wonder Alison's mother had given her daughter to the Goddess, no matter what the risk.

The singing merged with dance, a long, glorious spiral that celebrated the beauty of Faerie, the coming of Midsummer. Dancing among so many women, Anne still remembered Jock, thinking how he always claimed life was incurably contagious, and invariably fatal. Well, now he too had what he wanted; she was thinking of him while dancing with the witches of Faerie.

Dancing ceased, fading like a tone on the wind. From out of the forest came a coven of women, walking with animals—red deer, a wolf bitch, a huge elk with monumental antlers twice as wide as the women were tall. Anne recognized the Gordon Witch, and with her Lady Janet, as aged as when Anne first saw her at the door to Jock's hovel. Faerie showed her as she was, not beautified by magic. Between them was a coven leader older than both witches combined, who could have been Lady Janet's mother's mother.

"We meet again." The Gordon Witch held out her hand to take the reed-wand. Anne gave it up, giving with it all control over how long she stayed in Faerie. The pit of her belly tightened.

The little wrinkled crone standing between them said, *"There is na need for fear in yew."*

Anne knew Mary's voice. "No, Mother, when you are here, I have no fear." It was true.

"*Good.*" Ageless light shown in the ancient eyes. "*Dress and bid these women good-bye. Yew have a ways ta go wi' me.*"

With Alison's help Anne slipped on her velvet gown, feeling the girl's reluctance to let her go. One by one, she kissed the women; when she came to Brigid, the MacNeil woman gave her a tartan wrap. "You are going into the cold. Wear this. It is not the faerie flag of the MacLeods, but it will keep you warm, and bring you back to Barra."

Her last kiss and embrace were for Alison. The girl could say nothing; Anne tried to speak for both of them. "Some mysteries we must face alone. I love you and will return to you if I can."

She told Mary she was ready. They entered the wood, walking at an old woman's pace, across a neck of land to the seaward side. The Ends of the Earth for sure. An end to fighting her fate, to putting off Jock, to thinking she knew best, but also a beginning. . . .

Mary did not speak until they reached the rocky beach, where the encircling Ocean of Faerie beat against the shore. Lying on a wide stone was a crown of dried summer flowers: heather, with thistle and forget-me-nots. Mary took the wreath, placing it on Anne's head, coiling the blossoms in her fair hair. "*Are yew really ready to do my work?*"

Anne nodded gravely. As ready as could be hoped.

"*Ta say prayers in kirk on Sunday is no enough for me, not if ye whore an' kill throughout the week—I will have the whole person or not at all. I called to yew, Anne, and ye did not turn back, not even when yew saw the road was strange an' rocky.*"

"I think I understand."

The old woman seated herself on the stone, where the wreath had been, looking up at Anne. "*I am yer mother. A mother gives life, an' freedom, but I bore yew in my image, free to choose. All I can do is point the way.*" The crone spread her small hands to include the sea and sky, the sunlight and the forest. "*Any fool kens what is good in life—what is warm, nurturin', lovin', an' kind. Yet many*

*will still seek power, pain, an' death. You have turned yer
back on that. Given yer upbringin', that was no easy. Now
it is your turn to point the way for another, to lay the same
choices before her. Do that, an' when the time is right, I
will bring ye back here ta Barra."*

"Who is she? How will I know her?"

The crone smiled wider. *"You will know her when you
see her, as sure as you know me."* She rested a tiny hand
in Anne's. *"Close yer eyes when yew are ready."*

Anne stood for a moment looking at Mary, old and wizened now, no longer strong and wild as she had seen her
before. Behind her was the beach, and the slow Atlantic
rollers that come in the wake of a storm. Worn as she was,
Mary radiated all that was good and growing in life. Anne
closed her eyes. Mary raised up and kissed her.

When Anne opened her eyes, it was winter, the Fool's
Season. She was standing in her shawl and velvet gown,
wearing her crown of flowers. Sea and isles were gone.
Homeless beggars huddled around her, and before her was
the frozen, rutted Brancepeth Road.

Riding toward her at the head of armed retainers was an
overfamiliar figure, the proud and obstinate Countess of
Northumberland—the noblewoman who would not bow,
not even for her Queen. She sat straight in her saddle, her
stern gaze searching the beggars' faces. Countess Anne
was on the road to Durham, expecting a madwoman, about
to meet herself.

Afterword

The Spiral Dance is fantasy and fiction, but the people and settings are real. The sixteenth-century Border Country between England, Scotland, and Ireland was a rich landscape of feuding clans and poetic rogues that could hardly be invented. Anne of Northumberland, her husband, Tom, Jock of the Syde, Lady Janet, the Darces, the Hamiltons, and a host of minor characters are all historical. Many of the events and lines are taken from life. The quotes that begin each chapter are only slightly altered. However, other characters, events, and conversations have been cheerfully invented with the intent of telling a good tale.

The Rising in the North (1569-1570) was the last stand of the old northern aristocracy against Tudor absolutism. In typical feudal fashion it mixed dynastic, religious, and social grievances. Led by the Percys and Nevilles, a huge section of northern society rose up against Queen Elizabeth—lords, ladies, priests, peasants, constables, bandits, and beggars all marched southward together. They were defeated for the reasons depicted in the story. Their leaders, including Countess Anne of Northumberland, fled into Scotland, where there they were taken in, and robbed, by Border bandits—principally Black Ormiston and the Armstrongs.

Here in Scotland is where fact ebbs and fiction flows. Countess Anne did lose her husband, and spend Christmas in the hovel of Jock of the Syde, but the rest of Anne's story is fantasy. The various clans, feuds, and customs are as real as I can make them. Descriptions of the Borders, Edinburgh, the Highlands, and the Isles are taken from first-hand accounts and modern maps. Many events are real. Earl Moray was shot down in a Linlithgow street from behind a line of washing. The Battle of Brampton and the subsequent English invasions happened more or less as described.

Historical hindsight makes prophecy easy. The predictions in the story all came true. Dumbarton fell, and Archbishop Hamilton was hung at Stirling. The MacLeods and MacNeils survived all attempts by the central government to destroy their culture, dictate their religion, ban their customs, and otherwise civilize them. Despite such churlish treatment, the MacLeods bled for the British monarchy at Worcester, and the MacNeils came out to support the last Stewart King at Killiecrankie, under Bonnie Dundee. They have remained lucky clans, and respected members of Britain's warrior aristocracy; last I heard, there was still a MacNeil at Kisimul and a MacLeod at Dunvegan, though the Kings of Scots have been gone lo these many years now.

Not everyone fared so well. The Children of the Mist felt the full brunt of government attempts to expunge the clans. Of the chiefs' immediate family, twenty-two MacGregors were hanged, four beheaded, three murdered, and only five killed in honest fights. The last of the Stewart Kings, the "tyrannical" James II of England, lifted the ban on the MacGregors. But the Children of the Mist were again outlawed after the Glorious Revolution of 1688, showing that one person's toleration can be another's tyranny. The ban was not lifted again until the eve of the American Revolution.

Nor was Mary Queen of Scots ever rescued. She was moved from place to place in the Midlands, and never allowed to be too close to Scotland or London, where she might influence events. Mary's charm, intelligence, and fairness had won over one set of jailors at Lochleven, and Elizabeth always feared the same thing might happen even in England. When Mary was finally brought to the block after nineteen years in captivity, she told her retainers not to weep, pardoned the headsman, prayed for Elizabeth's forgiveness, and generally made a poor case for capital punishment. By then many of our principals were gone from the stage. Westmorland died in exile on the Continent. Black Ormiston was either pardoned or hanged—I've heard both stories. Anne, Tom, and Jock are all in the sequel, so I will say no more about their fates.

The novel makes no attempt to accurately reproduce sixteenth-century dialogue—which would be incomprehensible to modern readers. Accents are used only to indicate how things sound to the main character. Anne speaks Court French and Court English, and knows Church Latin, so these all sound "normal" to her and are represented in the novel by modern English. Scots and broad Northumberland sound strange to her ear, and I have invented accents to indicate this. Spanish and Gaelic are foreign tongues to her, and are presented untranslated.

One thing I did not invent is the savagery of sixteenth-century government. Most Western European states, including Elizabethan England, were totalitarian theocracies. Governments assumed the right to legislate religion, morality, economics, and thought, backing their commands with torture and execution. The descriptions of witch-hunting and the suppression of the Rising are taken directly from the writings of the men who committed these crimes—they were proud of what they did, seeing no reason to hide their work.

Women were especially at risk. English common law placed them under the control of fathers and husbands, who had the right to beat or imprison them—rebelling against this control was a form of "domestic treason" punishable in extreme cases by burning at the stake. In Scotland it was roughly as common for a sixteenth- and seventeenth-century woman to be executed for witchcraft as it is for a twentieth-century American woman to die in a traffic accident. Yet in every age there were people how stood up for toleration, the rights of women, and the right to think and speak as a person pleases. These are the people who inspired this story.